CRIMEUCOPIA

What the Butler Didn't See

A Murderous Ink Press Anthology

****

Murderous Ink Press

CRIMEUCOPIA
What the Butler Didn't See

First published by Murderous Ink Press
Crowland, LINCOLNSHIRE, England
www.murderousinkpress.co.uk

Paperback Edition ISBN: 9781909498709
eBook Edition ISBN: 9781909498716

Acknowledgements

To those writers and artists who helped make this anthology what it is, I can only say a heartfelt Thank You!

And to Den, as always.

Contents

Crikey, Mellors, It's The Filth!
(An Editorial of Sorts)

Up on the third floor of the stately MIP Towers, Mellors checked his attire in the Long Gallery mirror, then deftly sidestepped as the Tweenie skateboarded past—completing a perfect Suzie-Q without dislodging her Ladyship's toasted kipper-and-marmalade breakfast sandwich.

Now, if only she'd stop doing a 5-0 grind down the main stairway bannister... he thought.

As he reached the ground floor, from the kitchen at the back of the ancestral home came the sound of a 12-bore shotgun discharging—which meant that Cook was starting to prepare her famous Fish in a Barrel Pie. Famous, sadly, for all the wrong reasons, as the local constabulary would readily testify. Especially on a Saturday evening after closing time....

The aged valet de chambre shook his head. Now wasn't the time for dallying around, there were things to be done before the 18 guests arrived for the evening's dinner soiree.

Mrs Handshandy, the MIP Towers housekeeper, had shown him a list of names during their breakfast earlier that morning.

"And believe you-me, Mr Mellors, they sound a very unsavoury collection, and no mistake!"

He had dabbed at the corners of his mouth with a napkin. "How so, if you don't mind me asking?"

"For one thing, they openly claim to be..." she paused to take in a long breath, before exhaling the word: *"Writers!"*

"Hmmm. In that case I think it would be prudent to lock the silver away—including all the teaspoons."

"My thoughts exactly! And I've already instructed the Parlour maids to put mouse traps in the silver drawers and to throw covers over the display cabinets!"

The butler had taken another look at the list.

Richard Zaric, Daniel Marshall Wood, S. B. Watson, Ron Bruguiere, Aimee Kluck, Alexander Frew, Roly Andrews, Marian McMahon

Stanley, Gerald Elias, Gregory Meece, Neil K. Henderson, AP Warren, Michele Bazan Reed, Bonnar Spring, Carol Goodman Kaufman, Kathleen Marple Kalb, John M. Floyd, & Dave Dempster

He pursed his lips for a moment. "I think it would also be best practice to lock away the good brandy. Also the good whiskey, the good gin, the good rum, the cooking sherry…" Another glance at the list, "And I'll tell Chisholm, the head gardener, to make sure that the methylated spirits bottles are out of sight as well…"

His reverie at the foot of the main staircase was abruptly broken by one of the Scullery maids appearing at the doorway to the Morning Room, with a very worried expression on her face.

"Begging your pardon, Mr Mellors, but several of the guests have arrived early. Cook says, if they don't stop hanging around her back door, then it'll be both barrels, and pork pie salad for most of next week's lunches."

Although not a religious man, Mellors crossed himself, muttering "Spectacles, testicles, 'baccy and pipe! Do none of these buggers understand proper etiquette?" Turning to the young maid, he said, "Tell Cook to direct them to the main entrance. And remind her that such directions do not require the use of any expletives, colloquial or otherwise, no matter how descriptive she feels the use of such might be. I shall receive them in the main foyer."

The maid said, "Very good, sir," then hurried back to the kitchen.

Unconsciously adjusting his already impeccable attire one more time, Mellors strode purposefully into the foyer, and opened the large Main Entrance door, so as to be ready to greet the guests in a more-than-they-deserved civilized manner. Looking up at the doorway lintel, he silently read the MIP Towers family motto carved into the stone:

Numquam scis quid tibi placeat donec id legeris.

The butler nodded his head. *Indeed, you certainly don't*, he thought…

Croutons and Sweet Wine
Richard Zaric

I reach for the box of croutons perched on the top shelf when I bump into a middle-aged woman. Our eyes lock and she smiles. The thin lines around her mouth reveal that it is something she does frequently. She brushes a stray auburn lock away from her eye. "That's okay, you can have it." I'd seen her in the store before, but only recently, in the past few months. Her nose has a slight bend to the right.

My eyes look back up to the crouton box I had grabbed. It's the last one. My chivalrous side kicks in. "No, it's yours. I think I still have some at home."

She forms a wry smile. "Then why are you getting another box?"

I stammer. "I, uh, you know, for when I run out."

"You must eat a lot of Caesar salad."

I don't know how to respond to that. It's true I like Caesar, but not that much. I give her a quick smile and hand her the box. "Thank you," she says and places the box of croutons in her cart amid fruit, a few veggies, some frozen food and a tub of ice cream. She's a little pudgy on the sides, but who isn't? There's no way can I get even one leg into the pants I wore for my high school graduation.

She gives me a little wink before continuing down the aisle. Not a ravishing beauty, but she seems to have a certain style to her. Maybe it's the way she walks. Sally Fields with flair.

*****

Rosalyn did all our grocery shopping. We had a deal: she handled everything on the inside of the house while I took care of everything outside, including the garage. Rosy did most of the cooking and cleaning and I made sure the yard remained weed-free in the spring and summer and shovelled snow in the winter. Okay, that's not entirely true, she did most of the work in the garden, but I did the heavy lifting including rototilling each year, spreading the soil when it arrived in the spring, and keeping the hedge and other trees at bay with my clippers. If a dead squirrel or bird ended up in a flower bed, I got rid of it. If it was anything smelly or gave off fumes, it was my job. A pretty simple arrangement that worked.

Until Rosy lost her fight to cancer.

That was tough. After the initial shock, life went on but it forced me to learn new things, like washing clothes, cleaning toilets and cooking.

I went through learning pains. White socks turning pink. Shrinking my favourite shirt. Burning the heck out of my bacon and eggs. Cleaning the toilet too vigorously and scratching the porcelain. Stuff I was able to figure out by trial and error. My cooking wasn't the best (it could never be as good and Rosy's, ever) but I didn't go hungry.

Shopping for groceries was a pain in the neck. I winged it the first time and ended up spending two hundred bucks. When I got home I realized I'd forgotten half of what I needed. Instead, I bought junk and convenience food like frozen pizzas and TV dinners.

After a few months, I got better. I figured out which stores had the best prices and watched for coupons. At the end of each week, I scanned flyers to find deals. Sometimes I visited two or three different stores depending on what items were on sale.

The hardest part is the loneliness. These days, every time that I come home after work to a dark house it reminds me of Rosy. She would have come home from work before me and already had supper going. Sometimes from the garage I'd be able to tell if we were having roast or fish or chili. But now there is no welcoming aroma. A lump forms in my throat. Sometimes I feel so bad that I have to sit in the blue chair in the living room and stare at Rosy's framed picture perched on the bureau on the other side of the room. Sometimes I cry.

Life is all about decisions. When we were a young couple, we decided that we wouldn't have children. Given the cost of raising kids, we planned to have that money go towards our retirement. We talked about traveling. But Rosy never made it to retirement, so now I have to go the rest of the way on my own. It's during those sensitive moments that I wonder if we made the right decision.

There are a couple buddies I can hang out with, but they drink a little too much for my liking. Always hard stuff like scotch. Bitter, vile crap. And the booze is killing them. You can see it in their big bellies and the red veins that poke through their cheeks and the tips of their noses. It annoys me that they are still kicking while Rosy, who always watched what she ate and drank, got cut down.

I like my job as a civil engineer at EWP Consulting and work on earth retention, erosion, seepage and slope stability projects. Most people don't find it the most exciting, but it pays the bills and then some. What's sad is that I was only about five years from retirement when Rosy died. She was going to work a few more years and join me. We even talked about maybe getting a place in Arizona. After Rosy passed, they let me take as much time off as I wanted, but to be honest, the work helped me cope with the loss.

As the months wore on, I had gotten bored. I found myself watching more TV and being listless. I missed Rosy's companionship something horrible. Mark, my buddy, suggested I should join a group or something. But what could I do? I don't golf. I'm not outdoorsy, so no hunting or fishing or camping.

Just to get out of the house, I started walking. I figured I had to stay active. Truth is, I discovered that I felt good after my walks. I didn't venture out for that long, maybe a half hour, shorter if it was cold out. There is a park a couple blocks away with all kinds of paths. You have to keep your head up, though. Sometimes kids rip down the paths on their bikes. If you don't pay attention, you can get mowed down.

✴✴✴✴✴

"Fancy meeting you here," she says.

I don't recognize her at first. "Hi," I reply, a tentative squeak.

"Did you use up your box of croutons?" That's when it clicks: the woman from the grocery store. She's sitting on a bench facing a small stream in the park on a secluded path. It's early June with the temperature in the mid-20s and lazy clouds hanging in the brilliant blue sky.

My heart quickens. "Uh, yeah, I have to get a new box."

"See, you should've taken the box at the store instead of letting me have it. It's still in my pantry, unopened."

I walk over to the bench. She shuffles over and pats the bench seat beside her.

"You live in the area?"

"A few blocks away." She gestures with a slight wave of her hand. I notice her pretty blue fingernails. She's got the same aging spots on the back of her hand that Rosy had. "I moved to the neighbourhood a few years ago. You?"

"I live a short way from here."

"I love this park. I find myself here almost every day." She smiles, a little crooked and I can see her bright, shiny crowns in the back of her mouth when she talks. She keeps a straight posture while she sits on the bench.

"To be honest, I never used to come here that often. We were pretty much home bodies. It's only recently that I've started taking advantage of the park."

"After Grant died, I wanted a fresh start. I sold the house and cabin and moved into a condo. The kids yelled and screamed about the cabin, but I was the one doing all the clean-up after they left. I never got any peace and quiet. Besides, who needs a cabin when you have this?" She motions, Vanna White-style, to the bubbling creek in front of us.

*****

We bump into each other in the park every few days after that initial meeting. I'd see her on the same bench and would stop to chat. The visits get longer each time. We talk about our lives, past and present. Then we start setting a time so we could walk while we chat. At first it was a few times a week. Daily, by the middle of July.

In early August she invites me to her place for lunch. Of course, she makes a Caesar salad using the box of croutons from the store that she still hadn't opened. Big place, her condo. Must have cost a pretty penny. Pictures of her adult kids and their young families are on the wall. While she shows me the beautiful view of the park from her balcony, our eyes lock. It's our first kiss. My first with another woman since Rosy. I feel like a teenager again.

A few days later at my place she marvels at my yard. "You maintain this yourself? It looks like you have a professional gardener." But I can tell she's not the gardening type. More of a city girl. Funny, seeing as she used to have a cabin at the lake. Rosy didn't mind getting her hands dirty.

Sometimes while lying in bed in the gloom of an early morning I close my eyes and think of Rosy. A tremor of guilt rumbles in my gut, like I'm cheating or doing something naughty. But then I remind myself that Rosy has been gone for over two years.

After each meeting with Samantha Bellows, those guilty feelings melt away like butter on a piping hot cob of corn.

*****

"Mmmm, this wine tastes nice," I say at the kitchen table. "So much flavour."

"I thought you might like it," Sam says, swirling the remnants of her glass in her right hand.

I motion with my empty glass for Sam to refill it. "I hope I don't have a hangover tomorrow for work."

Sam smiles as she drains the bottle into my glass. She's always smiling. It's so radiant!

"Thanks for coming to Rosy's grave with me today. It meant a lot to me."

Sam clutches my hand. "I'm honoured. By the sounds of it, she was a very fine woman and I can see why you miss her an awful lot."

"Do you visit Grant's grave?"

Sam drops her smile and looks down. "The last time I visited his grave was a few years ago. After each visit I end up a wreck, down in the dumps for a week."

"What about the kids…?"

She shakes her head and looks away for a moment. "Remember when I told you that Joanne and Brent are from Grant's previous marriage?"

I nod.

Sam's eyes begin to glisten. "Grant's ex suffered from mental issues. Bi-polar or something. The kids were well in their twenties when their marriage broke off. The kids didn't take it well. Eventually, Grant met me. His ex ended up committing suicide a year after the divorce. Joanne and Brent somehow blamed me for it. They became resentful. Called me a gold digger." Sam grabs a tissue and dabs her eyes. "It disappointed Grant to no end. He ended up writing them out of his will. After his death, the kids tried to get the court to tear up Grant's will. Through it all, I tried to remain civil, but it didn't matter. We haven't talked much since the shouting match on the courthouse steps. Sometimes I wonder why I have their pictures on my wall."

✻✻✻✻✻

Just after Labour Day, Sam moves into my house. It's a big step for us, but everything about it seems right. She's able to quickly get rid of her condo. We share the chores, although thankfully she doesn't want anything to do with the garage. But I insist that I do the grocery shopping. Sam puts up a fight at first, but relents. Each Friday Sam starts a shopping list and I fill in the cracks. Then the next day I hit the stores.

Sam teaches me an appreciation for wine. She giggles when she asks what kind of wine I prefer and I say, "Red." It isn't long before she demonstrates the difference between a deep, full-bodied cabernet sauvignon and a fruity zinfandel. She shows how you have to let a bottle air out and then swirl it around in a glass to release flavours before tasting it. At the time I thought she was full of it, but it's really true. Rosy never much cared for booze. Sure, I had a few beers now and then, but it always felt awkward because Rosy didn't drink much. The funny thing is that wine seems to taste better when I have some with Sam at our place instead of in a restaurant.

We continue to go for our walks in the park. We watch the shadows grow longer in late September. Soon after, the red and golden leaves drift into the creek while large Vs of geese fly overhead, looking for a place to congregate before their trip down south. It doesn't bother us when the snow comes, leaving a thin blanket overtop the wilted long grass. We stand back to back and spin in a slow circle marveling at the beauty on those rare winter mornings when sparkling hoarfrost clings to every bare branch and limb. We play Spot the Bunny in the early spring when the furry critters awake from their sleep. When shorts replace long pants and we feel our first mosquito bites, we knew we have something special that no one can take away.

We cap off the evenings with a glass of wine.

That summer, on a humid August day, we marry at the court house, a little over a year from when we first met.

By the end of September I can't believe how dark my arms and legs have become. I don't think I worked outside that much more the past summer than any other year. And I usually always put on sunscreen. (I made a promise to Rosy that I would). I attribute it to all the walks with Sam.

Around Thanksgiving I start to notice a tingling in my hands. I don't think much of it at first, but it seems to get worse. Sam wants me to get checked, but I can't be bothered. Besides, after seeing what Rosy went through, I'd learned that doctors bring bad news. Why curse myself?

In January we fly south to get away from the cold weather for a few weeks. When we get back I start to feel really crappy. I must have caught a bug while in Fort Myers. My gut bothers me and sometimes I have the runs. My hands and feet are still tingly. I even miss a few days of work. After I get a little bit better, wouldn't you know it, I get sick all over again. This time worse. Maybe my body hadn't completely recovered the first time around. It feels like someone is punching me in the gut.

Damn near soil my pants a few times.

The problem is that Dr. Hoffman, my family doctor, retired a couple years ago. At the time he encouraged me to see another doc from the clinic, but I never felt comfortable with any of them. Sam suggests I see Dr. Stone, her general practitioner.

*****

I feel lousy one night, nursing a small glass of merlot. Sam says that while the wine might not help, it shouldn't hurt. That's what I love about her. She's always thinking the angles. And with that sexy, slightly bent nose, how can I refuse? Why should I suffer just because I feel crummy?

She has to go to the mall so I plop in front of the TV. Nothing but garbage on. It's hard to believe that I used to watch TV for hours and hours. That was before Sam. I'm glad I don't do that anymore. I take a sip of wine and think about Rosy. She would be happy for me and how things have turned out with Sam.

I flick up and down through the channels, eventually settling on something on the golden oldies movie channel. I recognize Cary Grant. Rosy liked those old movies. I always thought they were a little dated, but I didn't mind watching them with her. I miss those days.

I'm pretty sure I'd seen the movie before. A comedy. Cary Grant is a writer who'd just gotten married. He discovers a dead body in the front landing and finds out that his kind, old aunts had bumped him off. Then I remember the name of the movie. *Arsenic and Old Lace*. The aunts had used arsenic and other poisons.

The wine tastes a little too sweet. I thought merlot is supposed to be deeper. Maybe it has to do with the region it's from. I raise the wine glass to take another sip, but before I do, I stick my nose into the glass. It smells okay. I lift the glass back up, but before the red liquid can touch my lips, I put it back down on the table.

*****

"You don't like my cooking anymore?" Sam asks from across the kitchen table. "You used to gobble it up."

I twirl my fork around in the mashed potatoes. "I don't know … I feel … off …."

A pout forms on Sam's lips. "Mmmm. That's too bad. Maybe you should get some rest. I can make you some tea with a little bit of honey."

I smile and nod. "That would be great. Sorry, I'm just not that hungry these days." I put down the cutlery and push my chair away from the kitchen table.

Sam keeps eating. I walk over and gave her a kiss on the top of her head. "You know I love your cooking. I'm just not one hundred percent yet." Sam takes my hand and gives a reassuring squeeze.

I got back to work a few weeks ago after being off for two weeks and haven't had any wine in three weeks. I reason that the booze can't be helping. Whenever Sam gives me a cup of coffee or tea, I only take a sip or two. When she isn't looking I spill the rest down the sink. Then I start getting nervous about food. I don't eat much. Sam makes sure to pack my lunch for work with whatever I didn't finish at dinner the night before, but I chuck it out and eat something else.

I start feeling better. Is it just a coincidence? Is Sam actually trying to poison me? I must be crazy to think that. During the worst stretch Dr. Stone couldn't figure out the problem. He said I just needed a bit of rest.

I lay on the bed with the reading light on. My stomach growls but something inside me tells me to hold off. After ten minutes Sam comes into the room with a steaming cup of tea. She places it on the night stand and sits down on the bed beside me.

"I wonder if you should go see Dr. Stone again," she says, her lips pressed together with concern. She runs her hand gently through my hair.

"I was just there a few weeks ago. He couldn't find anything. Maybe I should see someone else?"

Sam flashes her uneven smile. "Nonsense. Dr. Stone is a one of the top-ranked doctors in the city. He treated Grant."

I sigh. "Well, I'll have to do something."

After a short pause, Sam gets up. She takes the tea and hands it to me. "Here you go. Drink up before it gets cold."

I accept the cup and put it to my lips but immediately recoil. "This is like molten lava! I don't think it's going to cool off for a few days."

Sam laughs. I love it when she laughs and I can see those crowns in the back of her mouth. And there is always a sparkle in her eye. She kisses me and leaves the bed room. She can't be poisoning me. I must have picked something up in Florida. The sub tropics are a breeding ground for all kinds of exotic bugs. But that doesn't explain why I started feeling tingly before we went on our trip.

*****

I look up arsenic on my phone. It was the preferred poison from days gone by. If administered in the correct dosages, the victim's sickness would appear to be natural, looking like a type of flu or food poisoning. Stomach cramps, headaches, a tingling sensation in the extremities. I experience all of those. It also makes skin become darker. That would explain why I look like I'd been lying on a Mexican beach for a whole month. It even says that it enhances the flavor of wine. No wonder the vino tastes so good when Sam's around.

Okay, so now what? Go to the cops? File for divorce? What would be the grounds? *My wife is trying to kill me.* Who would believe that? I have no evidence other than I feel crappy. Still, I have to do *something*. The trick is that I can't act too paranoid. I have to keep things on an even keel. I need more proof. On top of all that, we changed our wills soon after we married. She gets everything if I kick the bucket.

Starting the next day, when I can, I make sure that I stay in the kitchen when Sam makes meals. That way she doesn't have a chance to slip me something. I stuck to water that I pour myself from the sink. No booze. Each day when Sam gives me my travel mug for the drive to work, I don't touch it. I chuck out the contents in the parking lot of the coffee shop near work and pick up my own cup. If I get up first on the weekends, I make the coffee.

But after a few weeks I can't help it and lower my guard. We share the occasional glass of wine. I do a sniff check on the coffee or tea she gives me but it always smells fine so I drink it. But then I start to feel lousy again. That convinces me that I'm playing with fire. My wife is trying to kill me to take everything. With no kids that means there aren't any heirs. No nosy adult kids to poke around.

As the weeks wear on, I can tell that Sam is on to me. Fewer cuddles and kisses. She starts to get after me about little things like not wiping the bottom of the shower or forgetting to buy something at the store. She especially gets after me for not eating enough. In the evenings she teases me for not having a glass of wine. I try to get around this by opening and pouring new bottles myself. I make sure to not leave the room until I finish the glass. That way she can't say I wasn't having a glass with her.

*****

"Okay, so her name used to be Rebecca Logan."

I pause for a moment before replying. "Was Logan her maiden name?"

"Probably not and she also obviously changed her first name," Raj says. He's from a private detective agency I hired to do a check up on Sam and look into her background.

Raj continues in his thick Indian accent. "Apparently there was a Michael Logan that died ten years ago. That was her husband."

The news hits me like a two-by-four. "She never talked about a Michael." I give Gina a little smile and mouth a *Thank you* as she hands me a report. She turns around and leaves my office to go back to her desk. I lower my voice and turn my back. "Her husband was Grant and he died about five years ago."

"Grant Bellows was *also* her husband and you are correct, he died about five years ago."

"She's been a widow *twice*?"

"Here's something else you might find interesting," Raj continues. I press the phone closer my ear. "Neither husband had any relatives. Bellows and Logan had no children, no siblings."

"That can't be right. I saw pictures of her kids in her condo."

"Probably fake. Who knows where she got the photos. Also both men were well off from what I was able to gather. Bellows was a retired accountant. Logan was a dentist, also near retirement."

"So the family cabin…."

"There wasn't one. Grant Bellows lived in a house in Autumn Hills. Once he died, she sold everything and moved into that condo. She didn't even own it; she just rented it."

"How did he die?" I'm almost too afraid to ask.

"Not sure. Medical records are difficult to obtain. All I know is he got sick and died within months. It was right in the obituary."

"What about the previous husband?"

"Rebecca–or Samantha–started seeing Logan just the year before he died. They had a whirlwind relationship and married. Then he suddenly got sick and died within a year. According to a neighbour, Logan was super fit. He went to the gym every day. Ran marathons. And here's something else: both Logan and Bellows happened to have the same family doctor, Julius Stone."

Stone. The doctor Sam is having me see. Could he be in on it?

"Anything else?" I am almost too afraid to ask.

Raj breaths heavy into the phone. "There could be others. It's hard to say. She's probably changed her identity several times and lived in different places. She is very good at covering her tracks. So good that she's never had a problem and may now be getting sloppy."

I put my hands behind my head and stare straight up at the white ceiling tiles in my office. This is crazy! Did I get duped by a cold-blooded con-artist? One that kills her prey?

Sam isn't home when I get home from work. It feels suspicious at first, but then I remember that she was going to get something for Valentine's Day.

I make myself a peanut butter sandwich to fill me up. This way I'll have some food in my gut and can get away with not eating much dinner.

I wipe my mouth with a paper serviette and throw it on my plate. I lean over and cup my head in my hands. What am I thinking? That Sam is some kind of *black widow* or something? My mind races. What can I do? What should I look for? Proof that she isn't Samantha Bellows? I open her side of the bedroom closet and begin to poke around. I pull a pink box down from her closet. It holds her personal papers and things. I feel dirty flipping through it. She doesn't have much. No income tax records, no medical records. A few credit card bills and receipts, but everything is recent, over the last few years. Nothing from the past. Everything features her present name.

I stop and stare at myself in the mirror. What the hell am I doing? Do I *honestly* think she is trying to bump me off? That kind of stuff only happens in the movies. Right?

After I put back the pink box, I go on my hands and knees to examine the closet floor. She has about a dozen shoeboxes. The woman definitely likes her shoes. A pair of blue pumps are in one box. Another contains dressy black flats. Some don't look like they've been worn. She even has a pair of new winter boots. She must have found them on sale, waiting for her current pair to wear out. Faux fur lines the inside. They sure look comfortable. I stick my hand in one of the boots and hit something hard.

A small bottle of arsenic.

A chill runs down my spine: it's true.

I hear a squeaky door open, the one than leads from the garage. "Hello!" Sam yells from the landing. She's back!

My heart thumps hard against my ribs. What do I do? Confront her now? She'll wonder what I'm doing poking around her things. She'll say that she doesn't know where the bottle came from. Somehow twist things around and blame me.

"I got you something special! Where are you? " She sounds closer. She might even be in the hallway!

"Hi, dear!" I yell back as I quickly place the small bottle back in the shoe, put all lids back on the boxes and scramble to put everything away just as I found it.

I slide the closet door shut and turn around just moments before she enters the bedroom.

"Is everything okay?"

"Uh, yeah, I was just getting up." I move away from the closet door.

"You sure? Your face is all red. Do you have a fever?" She places her hand on my forehead.

"N-no, I'm okay." I brush away Sam's hand.

"Hmm. You feel a little warm. Maybe you're coming down with something. You should take some Tylenol."

I shrug. "I don't feel that bad."

Sam smiles and gives me a hug. "I'll change into something more comfy, those pajamas you gave me this morning for Valentine's Day. Go into the kitchen. I picked up a couple subs. I got you the cold cut combo you like. It's not the fanciest dinner, but you have to eat *something*. And have a couple Tylenol."

I see the two tightly wrapped subs on the kitchen table, a 6-inch and a foot-long. The long one must be mine. There's also a small red gift bag with white tissue sticking out from the top. I take Tylenol even though I know I don't need it. My discovery has me so worked up that my flushed look must give the appearance of being sick. It's best to play along.

I'm working on the second half of my sub when Sam brightens the room with her broad smile. She looks great in the new deep blue cotton pajamas I got her.

"See, you're famished," Sam says as she unwraps her sub. "Sometimes a little treat goes a long way."

I nod. My mouth is stuffed. That peanut butter sandwich wasn't enough.

"I love these pajamas." She runs her hand on a sleeve then nudges her gift to me. "Open it up."

"You didn't have to…"

"Nonsense!"

I pull out the small bundle from the bag and unwrap a book. *Crouton: A Love Story and Other Tales* by T. Alex Miller. I flip the book over. It's an anthology of short stories. The blurb says that the title story is about a guy who finds a stray crouton in his clean apartment which sparks a love story.

I can't help but chuckle. "This is perfect."

"I figured you'd like it. Remember we met fighting over a box of croutons."

"How can I ever forget?"

Sam works at her sandwich. I stare at her while she's looking sideways out the sliding glass door that leads to the deck. What's she thinking? What's going to be her next move? Tomorrow morning I'll pretend I'm going to work, like normal. Instead, I'll go to a doctor. Get tested. Get the bottle of arsenic and take it to a lawyer and the police. To take her down, I have to do it right. Until then, I have to act like I don't suspect a thing. I'll let the black widow get caught in a spider web of my own.

That evening I settle down in front of the TV in the basement like we normally do each evening. While I'm checking the list of shows we've recorded on the PVR, I can hear Sam coming down the stairs. She takes ginger steps, careful not to spill any of the two glasses of red wine she's carrying.

"Here, this one is yours." She places it on a coaster on the coffee table. I look at it with a mix of fear and anxiety. Should I drink it even though it's likely poisoned? If she's been poisoning me slowly, will just one more glass really matter?

I rub my belly. "You know dear, I don't know if I'm up for wine tonight."

"One glass shouldn't hurt. You know what they say: one glass a day is good for you. That Mediterranean diet."

Nodding, I put on a faint smile. No, I can't have it. My mind races while I try to think of how to get out of drinking the wine. "It would be great if we had a few slices of cheese to go with this. Is it pinot noir?"

Sam narrows her eyes. "Are you sure you want to eat something if your tummy is bothering you so much? Cheese is really hard to digest."

She's right. I've had the runs for a couple days now. "Cut up a few pieces. It certainly can't hurt me any more than the booze."

She winks. "I'll be right back."

After she goes back upstairs I quickly exchange the glasses. Now she'll get a dose of her own medicine. I can drink her glass of wine and then act sleepy. Maybe over emphasize some of my ailments and then retire for the evening. In the morning I can fake it, say I feel great and pretend to head off to work.

I lean back on the sectional. My mind swirls. Mixed emotions are popping in my head like fireworks. I'm crazy for her, but this doesn't feel right, especially now that we've redone our wills. All the pieces of the puzzle are beginning to click together.

She's upstairs for about five minutes when I notice that I've made a mistake. I didn't move the charms! She always uses charms attached to the bottom of the wine glass stems to tell them apart. Hers is a lavender butterfly while mine is any of the other colours. Today it's a red butterfly. She picked them up at a little shop in the mall because it reminded her of the butterflies we'd seen on our walks in the park. Smart girl. That way she can never confuse the glasses and drink from the wrong one.

I finish exchanging the charms just as she's coming down the stairs with a little plate of cheese and crackers. So now the one with the lavender butterfly contains the poison.

"Here you go," Sam says, placing the plate with small slices of gouda on the coffee table.

She doesn't bat an eye when she picks up her glass and takes a sip. I wait for some sort of reaction from her, but get nothing. I get up to fetch the remote. "What do you want to watch?"

"Whatever you like, my dear. You can even put it on the news."

She takes another sip. "Mmmm, this pinot noir tastes wonderful. Have you tried it yet?"

"No, not yet, but I'm sure it does." I grab my glass, the one with the red butterfly charm, and take a sip. Sure enough, a cascade of flavours fill my mouth. Raspberry. Or is it black berry? In any case, the wonderful wine delights my taste buds. I wink at Sam. "Another lovely bottle you've selected."

We watch *The National* during which Sam and I finish our wine. My gut is churning and boiling. I definitely don't need the wine. Then my head starts to ache like someone hit it with a hammer. Despite the pain, I feel I could fall asleep in a second.

"Are you okay?" Sam asks.

"I don't know. I think I have to turn in for the night." I motion to get up, stumble against the coffee table and almost fall over. I correct myself, but in the process realized that I've crapped myself. Dark diarrhea explodes out and gushes down my legs, coming out at the bottom of my jeans. What's going on? I try to run to the washroom, but my lags cramp and I tumble in a smelly heap on the blue carpet. My gut feels like it's on fire.

I try to get up, but can't move.

"Call 911," I sputter. It takes all my strength to move my head to see Sam still seated on the sectional, calmly refilling her wine glass.

"Sam?" I plead.

She slowly walks over and crouches down. "That's alright, dear. It won't be much longer."

"But the glass…?"

"Yes, I know you switched it. I made sure to put the poison in my glass, thinking you might do something like that. It would have worked but I noticed my wine charm was positioned differently. In your haste you put it on upside down. The original plan was to switch them around if you got up to go to the washroom. Otherwise I would have *accidently* spilled my glass. But it all worked out. I also slipped a little something in your sub and rewrapped it. By the way, I noticed that you were going through my things in the closet."

"…but I put it back…"

"In one of my black flats. It was supposed to be in the winter boot. When I saw you standing in front of my closet I knew the jig was up. I also took the time to have every call recorded. I heard some of the initial conversations you've had with the investigator. Unfortunately, this didn't go as smoothly as it usually does. I've been getting sloppy in my old age."

I vomit, almost choking on it.

"But now I have to leave," she continues. "I've cleaned out our bank account and I'll take anything that's of value. Can't really stick around if I'm a murder suspect. Normally I take things slower, but you forced my hand to give you a killing dose."

Sam finishes her wine and leaves me in my vomit and filth. I feel weak and close my eyes.

Farfetch
Daniel Marshall Wood

Farfetch is the stone cottage I purchased sight unseen in the English village of Farwythe, Shropshire, a place I had never visited, where I knew no one. I sought an existence far from where I had spent some forty-odd years, but never felt at home. Was I crazy? I hoped this was the new life I had dreamt of for early retirement.

I kept the name Farfetch as it was rather whimsical and nonsensical. The rooms of the house were well placed. A small vestibule with a cloakroom led into a large stair hall. Beyond, in the back, was the dining room. To the left of the stair hall, a drawing room with a fireplace and four windows on three sides. To the right of the stair hall lay a small library in the front, with a kitchen and scullery in the back. Upstairs were two bedrooms of ample size and sunny aspects, an old-fashioned dressing room, a bathroom, and a box room. All in all, quite satisfying.

I immediately felt a sense of place among the clutter left behind in an apparently hasty removal, the air redolent with musty old books arranged haphazardly on sagging shelves, boxes and bins awaiting investigation.

Though I had been in place only a fortnight, speculation about who I was and where I came from passed between the lips of gossipers, as in any small village. I had paid cash for Farfetch, so the estate agent may well have inferred evasion of a shady past. Internet searches would reveal little about me, as I shunned social media. I carried as much baggage as anyone – perhaps more – so I cared little about extra weight in that category. Let them talk!

Farfetch apparently had its own baggage. A lengthy rainy afternoon chit-chat with the longtime postmistress, Indeera Ramnath, revealed the cottage's storied past, replete with séances, hippies and LSD, a flock of dead chickens, and a family with seven children.

The last resident, Fenella Crutchlow, had owned the cottage for 35 years. She had evolved from a proper church lady of apparent modest means into a paranoid recluse, dying alone in the cottage at age 84, about three years ago. Rumour had it that Mrs. Crutchlow's only child, a daughter, had died childless in the past two years. The daughter seemingly had little communication during her mother's latter days.

Mrs. Ramnath further informed me that Mrs. Crutchlow's will had been filed with a local solicitor. In it, she left a small sum to her daughter, Elizabeth. The remainder of the estate was to be divided among St. Anselm's Anglican Church, the Farwythe Museum, and heirs. The will also contained allusions to an unspecified valuable item hidden in the cottage. Searches by the solicitor had uncovered no bounty other than a landscape painting that surprisingly sold at auction in excess of £10,000 – which explained the brighter rectangle of green damask wallpaper above the fireplace. With no known remaining heirs, proceeds from any further "find" in Farfetch would thus benefit Elizabeth, the church, and the museum.

The furnishings I brought from my flat included a well-worn burgundy leather Chesterfield sofa, two mismatched antique wing chairs, several threadbare Oriental rugs, plus bedroom and kitchen items. An odd lot of small tables and chests, window hangings, and several lamps remained in Farfetch, all duly appropriated. I especially liked a well-worn pine table in the kitchen, pondering the many families and pets it had served for more than a century.

Once I had Farfetch in a semblance of order, my daily routine of solving crossword puzzles and catching up on five-plus years of *Country Life* magazines wasn't as fulfilling as anticipated. I was drawn to Fenella Crutchlow and her mystery enshrined at Farfetch.

A shelf in the oak-panelled library held gilded leather-bound classics so pristine I knew they had never been opened. Dog-eared, tattered whodunnits, suspense novels, and romance stories attested to Fenella's bent. No literary pretensions for her.

Tucked into those shelves were several of Fenella's journals. The latter ones were all but incomprehensible prose and poetry with references to ghosts of her late husband, werewolves in the night garden, and a plot by the vicar to send her to "the loony bin."

Early volumes told of a seemingly happy wife and mother, active in church altar and flower guilds and the Women's Institute wherever she lived. Fenella had been an excellent baker, winning prizes at local fêtes for Victoria sponges and lavender-infused shortbread. She was also a great seamstress, fashioning dresses for her daughter, costumes for various pageants, and running up draperies and curtains for every window, plus portières for doorways.

In the mid-1960s, Fenella suspected her husband, Henry, of having affairs with any number of "tarts and trollops." Henry had become less attentive and spent more evenings at the pub. "A bastard! The worst possible outcome a wife could endure," Mrs. Crutchlow wrote. Her journal held references to Henry's belligerence and extreme thrift. He finally abandoned the family. "A blessing in disguise," she penned, "but I fear he might return and endanger Elizabeth. Perhaps she'll come home from her aunt's, where I sent her for safety. I trust one day Elizabeth will realize I truly love her." Mrs. Crutchlow's torment was readily apparent.

A sharp rap on a front door windowpane returned me to the present. I opened it to a distinguished man in priestly attire. "Please come in."

"Vicar George Marston, from St. Anselm's. Welcome to the village."

I indicated a wing chair by the fireplace. "Would you like tea? It's at the ready."

"Brilliant. Very welcome, indeed."

I brought forth a tray including a large hot water jug and a plate of chocolate biscuits. Pouring for the vicar, I added a big glug of hot water to the Darjeeling tea, which I had brewed before delving into Fenella's journals.

"Ah, perfect," said the Vicar. "Again, welcome to Farwythe."

"Thanks. How long have you served at St. Anselm's?"

"All of 15 years now. It's a small parish, of course. With the faithful few, we've barely managed to keep it afloat. Mrs. Crutchlow was quite active until she experienced, uh, a decline, in her later years."

"So you knew her well?"

"Certainly. Mrs. Crutchlow was on the flower rota for many years. Her garden flowers graced the altar beautifully and bountifully and were envied by many."

"I'm afraid the garden here has rather gone to seed. That's not my forte, but perhaps you can recommend someone who might put it in order."

"Oh, yes. Someone who might appreciate such a challenge comes to mind. I'll inquire for you. Please do join us on Sunday if you can. This week it's Morning Prayer with choir at the ten o'clock service."

"I'm quite lapsed, but I may well take you up on your offer," I said. "The Jacobean style is unexpected."

"Quite so. A rarity for late Victorian, but with all that slate, beams with dry rot, drafty leaded windows, and bats in the belfry, it's rather expensive to maintain. I'll introduce you 'round so you should soon feel at home in our fair village."

The Vicar and I chatted easily over tea, touching primarily on the village and its inhabitants. His inquiries as to my past were answered as vaguely as possible.

"I see you kept some of Mrs. Crutchlow's furnishings," Vicar Marston noted, glancing about the drawing room.

"I didn't bring much, so the additional items were quite welcome. Farfetch is larger than I anticipated for my retirement."

"You've done it up splendidly. I'm sure you've gone through some of the boxes left behind. Find anything of interest?" Vicar Marston eyed me intently over the rim of a blue-and-white ironstone teacup.

"Oh, this and that, bits of Mrs. Crutchlow's history. I've begun reading her journals. You were mentioned."

"Was I? Since we knew each other so many years, that's not surprising."

The vicar rose from his chair. He picked up a small silver frame I had placed on a side table. "That's Mrs. Crutchlow and her daughter. Twenty years or more ago, I'd say. The daughter was long gone by the time I arrived."

"That's who I assumed they were. Found it in a bedroom. I was surprised it was still here."

"The legatees were reluctant to disperse the rest of the furnishings for fear of losing the hidden treasure hinted at in the will," the Vicar explained. "Well, I mustn't keep you. I have another fundraising meeting. I look forward to seeing you on Sunday."

"I appreciate your visit. I'll see you soon."

I wasn't quite sure what to make of Vicar Marston. Friendly and engaging, but the not-quite-as-subtle-as-he-had-hoped references to the church's need to replenish its coffers left me somewhat unsettled.

*****

Late the next morning, still in my dressing gown, I answered the sharp rap of the door knocker. Before me stood a sturdy middle-aged woman in an ivory blouse and mustard tweed skirt, her mousy brown hair pulled into a bun. Her countenance seemed vaguely familiar, but many women of her vintage held similar appearances.

"Looks like you need someone in the garden. Bettina Farrand, I am."

Assuming the Vicar had sent her, I opened the door farther. "Please come in, Mrs. Farrand."

"Miss Farrand." She entered the stair hall. "I peeked around back. That garden is a mess, all but a jungle it is now, but I can show it who's boss and bring it back to its former glory."

I was intrigued. "When can you start?"

"Right away." Bettina ran a finger atop the back of a stiff walnut hall chair. "Looks like you could use a daily woman, as well. I can give you three days a week — mornings in the garden so as not to disturb your highness in his slumber and afternoons inside. But today I'll start with the kitchen, as I'm sure it needs a good scrubbing. I brought an apron." She bustled off.

Well, that had been quickly settled. In an instant, I had "staff" – housekeeper and gardener. Nowhere in my wildest imaginings had I visualized myself as lord of the manor, so to speak, overseeing household help.

I sensed one mustn't question Bettina Farrand and her strong will. The vicar could fill me in on her background.

On my amble around the village following afternoon tea, I noticed the Vicar in the rectory garden. "Good afternoon."

Vicar Marston ceased cutting white dahlias. "Oh, hullo. Nice to see you on this fine spring day." He gestured to a basket filled with a colorful mixture of blooms. "Mrs. Ransom is on the flower rota this week, but she's ill, so it's me by default, though I enjoy the duty now and then."

"They'll make a lovely altar arrangement. How did the meeting go?"

"The fundraising committee? Many ideas were forthcoming, but more bake sales and raffles aren't the answer. I don't know how long we can hold on. The Bishop is threatening to close the parish. It's rather grim unless we come into substantial funds soon."

"I'm sorry to hear that, Vicar. I wish there was some way I could help."

"Let's discuss that another time. By the way, Gareth Langley isn't available to tackle your garden. He broke an arm yesterday, falling off a thatched roof he was repairing. They can get rather slick with moss. He should know better, as old as he is and as many rooves as he's been up on."

I was stunned. "Then who is Bettina Farrand? She came by earlier — had all sorts of plans for the garden, so I thought you sent her."

"I only know Bettina in passing. She's not a parishioner. Came to the village about two years ago. Keeps to herself most of the time. Seems a bit odd, but I suppose most of us would fit that bill. This morning when I was on my way to visit Mrs. Keeling, who's ailing with lumbago, I saw her poking around Farfetch's garden. Seen her several other times, as well."

"Since I assumed Miss Farrand came with your recommendation, I hired her. She'll also take care of the house. I've got her three days a week. Hadn't planned on that, but it just came about somehow."

"A force to be reckoned with, it seems," the Vicar said, carrying flowers into the church and shutting the door.

*****

Since I wasn't sure which three days Bettina had deigned to give me, I was pleased to hear her puttering about the garden when I turned over around ten the following morning. I was also pleased to find a Brown Betty pot of Earl Grey tea covered with a cosy of off-putting orange and green knitted acrylic on the kitchen table.

I opened the door leading to the garden and raised my cup toward Bettina. "Thanks for the tea," I called. "Just what I needed."

"You're welcome, sir. Took a cuppa for myself, I did. Hope you don't mind."

"Not at all."

"Found the cosy in a drawer. Mrs. Crutchlow had unusual taste. It'll do for now, but you might find a better one at the church fair." She paused, gesturing toward the garden. "Once I get this under control, it'll be quite nice. When I was little, I'd help my mother weed and plant. In the middle was a great elm with a V-shaped trunk I could climb up into and hide. Such carefree days then."

"Must have been. I grew up in a city with only a small plot in the rear, just me and mum. She wasn't much of a gardener."

"Surveying this space, I'm thinking of a sea garden. My mother had one in a plot rather like this."

"What's that?" Perhaps I wasn't fully awake. "We're nowhere near an ocean."

"Sorry. I mean a garden with flowers and plants all starting with the letter C. Camellia, crocus, calendula, carnations. All in a crescent shape. If I run out of Cs, I could add a straight row across the side and put in D flowers there, since that would make it D-shaped, at least from one direction. Dahlias, daisies, daffodils."

"Whatever you decide is fine." Only the result of her gardening was of interest.

"Better set up an account with the garden centre so I can get what I need."

"Will do. Thanks again for the tea."

Following breakfast and a bath, I brought out another box from Mrs. Crutchlow's stash. This one held photo albums. I leafed through them, learning more about the woman who had once owned Farfetch. Her garden was once quite resplendent in summer bloom. It would have taken a lot of work, as Bettina realized. I smiled at old cars, bathing costumes at the beach, and picnics in meadows. Black-and-white photos of three smiling Crutchlows were bittersweet, since I never knew my father. Only on her deathbed had my mother divulged a few details about an older man who took advantage of an innocent barmaid.

"What's that?"

I hadn't heard Bettina come in. "Photo albums Mrs. Crutchlow left behind. Somehow, all old family photos look alike, don't they?"

"Perhaps," Bettina said, taking a small album from the box. "From the looks of them, could have been my childhood. I grew up in that era."

Bettina headed to the kitchen, and I soon heard her washing up the breakfast dishes.

I opened another album and pictured myself as a member of the family.

*****

I slipped into St. Anselm's just as the first hymn began, sitting near the back. Surprisingly, I remembered the tune from the times my mother took me to church. The Vicar's homily, based on the parable of the woman who lost a coin, swept the house until she found it, and then partied with her friends, lasted less than ten minutes. Short and to the point — good chap.

Vicar Marston greeted me heartily after the service. I commented on the flowers, and then he quickly shunted me to a smiling young woman.

"How nice to meet you. I'm Leigh Marston."

"The Vicar's daughter?"

"Yes, and unnamed head of the welcome committee. I'll introduce you 'round."

"That would be lovely. I haven't met your mother yet. Is she here?"

"No. Mum's been in Leeds for six months, looking after dear granny."

True to Leigh's word, I met many parishioners over coffee. They ranged from proper blue-haired church ladies, as expected, to a handsome young man who obviously held Leigh in high esteem, to those peculiar shy types one finds hanging about the fringes in any church or village gathering.

In his rounds at coffee hour, the Vicar steered me to a woman named Gwendolyn, whom he termed a most important part of his life. I learned she was the Senior Warden, likely an arduous and thankless position, given the parish's uncertain future. Gwendolyn had grown up in the village, sought a life in London, returned a decade ago after a failed marriage, and now ran the museum, which I promised to visit soon. We chatted about the village and its residents. I mentioned taking on Bettina for the house and garden.

"Bettina has done occasional cleaning for me. Nice enough woman. For a somewhat recent arrival, she's quite familiar with the area. Please let me know how she works out, especially in the garden. Mine's rather a tangle."

I shook hands with a somewhat formal couple who approached me. "We're the lesser Wassermans," the woman said in introduction.

"There's no need to denigrate yourselves," I responded.

"Oh, no," she laughed. "L-O-E-S-S-E-R Wasserman, with a hyphen."

Mercifully, a saviour in the form of an elderly man with huge white caterpillar eyebrows prevented further embarrassment. "Alistair Connaught," he said, extending his hand. "You bought Farfetch. I was Fenella Crutchlow's solicitor."

"Yes, I've just recently settled in."

"Taking to our village? Beginning to feel at home?"

"Indeed. It's been an eventful few weeks, I must say."

"Stop by my office on the High Street tomorrow afternoon and I'll fill you in on the will. Since there are no known heirs, I won't be breaking confidence. Everyone in the village knows about it, anyway. No secrets here."

*****

Alistair Connaught's offices were exactly as imagined. A prim woman, efficient and not unfriendly, sat at reception amidst wood panelling, dark green patterned wool carpeting, red leather chairs, and white shutters at the windows. She rapped on a mahogany door, opened it, and directed me to pass through.

"I'm glad you could stop in." Mr. Connaught took a file folder from atop a neat stack.

"You've likely heard the terms of Fenella Crutchlow's will, but I'll recap. Apart from the house and the painting, the remainder of the estate wasn't substantial. Her daughter, Elizabeth, was bequeathed £5,000 outright, but we couldn't trace her. The remainder is to be divided between St. Anselm's Church, the Farwythe Museum, and Elizabeth. After 10 years, Elizabeth's share would then revert to the estate for dispersal if she's not located. No other heirs are known."

"What if a distant relative was to be found?"

"That seems unlikely after so many years, but the court would probably then divide the estate four ways," Mr. Connaught explained. "The sale of the house has enriched the assets substantially."

"Wasn't there something about a reference to hidden treasure at Farfetch?"

"Oh, that. Mrs. Crutchlow included a few cryptic lines – I'm not sure I'd call it a poem – which no one, including me, understands."

I remained silent.

"Shall I read it to you?"

"Please."

Mr. Connaught cleared his throat, donned spectacles, and began reading, "Once so shiny and bright/So highly valued long ago/Now so carefully hidden/Yet so keen to shine again."

"That's it?" I, too, didn't know what to make of her words. "Perhaps Mrs. Crutchlow was insane."

"Not at all. Mrs. Crutchlow was of sound mind when she had me draw up her will. You can ask the doctor. She didn't go barmy for several more years."

"May I have a copy? I'd like to ponder her message."

"I anticipated that. Miss Notting at reception has it for you. Good luck deciphering it. Cheerio."

*****

As I turned the corner near Farfetch, my sightline blocked by an overgrown rhododendron hedge, the Vicar and I all but met head-on.

"Oh, my," he said, running hands through salt-and-pepper hair and straightening his collar. "Are you all right?"

"Collision averted," I said. "You seem to be in a hurry."

"A vicar's duties take me everywhere. I'll see you Sunday, then."

The afternoon post had been placed on a side table in Farfetch's vestibule. This wasn't Bettina's day to be in, though. I heard a thud in the drawing room and sighed with relief when I recognized Gwendolyn. "What are you doing here?"

She replaced a book on a side table. "Oh, hello. The door was unlocked, so I let myself in. Took in the post, too. I brought a banana loaf to welcome you. It's in the kitchen. You have a lovely home. I see you kept some of Mrs. Crutchlow's things."

"Yes, they rather seemed to want to stay in the house."

"You've certainly made a cosy nest for yourself. Must dash." Gwendolyn paused at the vestibule mirror to dab a tissue at her lips and cheeks. "Perfect. Perhaps I'll see you Sunday."

I sensed Gwendolyn had been up to something not quite right. Had she been searching for the treasure that would benefit the museum?

*****

A week later, as soon as I opened the door, the scent of furniture polish told me Bettina had been in. I made a pot of Earl Grey, plopped into a wing chair, and pondered elements of the mystery of Farfetch.

Mrs. Crutchlow's enigmatic lines in her will made little sense. What valuable item could it refer to? I contemplated the riddle for clues. The words 'so, so, so' from Mrs. Crutchlow's riddle kept repeating. Like 'sea garden,' could those words have another meaning?

When enlightenment eluded me, I pulled out another of Mrs. Crutchlow's photo albums and was startled by a shot depicting a young girl perched in the V-shaped notch of a tree trunk.

A girl in a tree. Typical childhood snapshot. And yet... Hadn't Bettina mentioned something similar?

I picked up the photo of Mrs. Crutchlow and her daughter. The innocent face of a child was unknown to me, yet familiar, particularly the eyes.

Was it possible that Elizabeth Crutchlow, presumed dead, was alive as Bettina Farrand?

Lost in another of Mrs. Crutchlow's journals, I barely heard the "brngg-brngg" of the telephone. In my haste to answer, I tripped over a needlepoint-covered footstool. I grasped at the draperies as I fell, bringing a wooden rod down on my head.

I awoke befuddled, not sure of my surroundings, sunlight fading. How long had I been out? My head throbbed. I tried to wipe away blood from a cut on my forehead, breathed deeply, and struggled to collect my wits. Fumbling with the drapery fabric, I felt something in the corner of the hem.

Amid my jumbled thoughts, the words 'so, so, so' from Mrs. Crutchlow's riddle again came forth. What could they mean? Sew!

Mrs. Crutchlow might have sewn items of real value into the draperies, virtually hiding them in plain sight. I ripped the drapery hem open, finding a plain shiny silver-tone metal disc like a coin in each corner. They were used as weights so the panel would hang straight. The other panel for that window held the same discs at the corners.

What about others? Exhilarated about what I might find, I hastily removed draperies from those three windows and sat in a sea of fabric in the middle of the room to examine them.

The front door opened. When she saw me on the drawing room floor, all but shrouded in linen, Bettina rushed over.

"What in heaven's name?"

"I think your mother sewed something valuable into the draperies. Help me look."

"You know?"

"Yes, but I just realized it."

We lapsed into silence. Bettina followed my lead in ripping open the hems of the other panels.

"Eureka!" Bettina shouted.

"I've got something, too!"

In all, we found four old gold Sovereigns from 1843 and 1863. I am not a coin collector, but they must have been of great value for Mrs. Crutchlow to have concealed them so carefully.

"Your mother took great care to hide these. They should be worth quite a handsome sum, which will benefit you and the estate."

Bettina failed to hold back tears. "So Mother truly loved me."

Amongst all the turmoil, Bettina only now commented on the blood from the cut on my head. I assured her I was fine.

Bettina was quiet for a moment and then asked, "How did you know I'm Mrs. Crutchlow's daughter?"

"Even though the family photos are old, you still have the same expressive eyes. The photo of a girl in the tree left no doubt."

Like my own, Bettina's eyes glistened with joyful tears.

"There's more to this story, Bettina. I'm really Henry Crutchlow Parfitt, your half-brother."

✳✳✳✳✳

The Vicar had all but invited himself for afternoon tea when we chatted after Sunday's service. He said it was important to speak with me privately and immediately accepted my proposed Tuesday.

"Good afternoon, Vicar. Please come in."

In the stair hall, the Vicar hurriedly glanced into other rooms.

"It's just us. Bettina prepared tea but left a short time ago."

The Vicar's hand trembled as he accepted the cup of apricot-infused Darjeeling. "I must come straight to the point. The parish situation is dire, most dire. Unless we come into substantial funds very soon, the Bishop will close the parish. I've tried to no avail to extend the deadline, but he's adamant."

"I see. And how is it that I can help in this matter?"

"The will! Mrs. Crutchlow's will! The valuable hidden item that will benefit St. Anselm's." The Vicar sat back in his chair, dark eyes nervously observing me.

I said nothing.

"I'm desperate, as you can see. I don't want the parish to close and have to move away from someone special. Did you decipher Mrs. Crutchlow's riddle? Have you found anything? Can't you help me?"

I remained silent, savouring the Vicar's awkward situation and watching him beg.

"Perhaps I can."

Tears followed the Vicar's sigh of relief, which changed to alarm as I outlined my conditions.

*****

I had always wondered about the source of my middle name, Crutchlow. After Mother told me about my father, I sought clues, finding none in birth, marriage, or death records. Internet searches for the name Crutchlow eventually led to the sales listing for Farfetch. I bought it immediately, a means of retribution for those who hadn't accepted me, shunning my existence, banishing me as a bastard child. Farfetch was now my family home, as it should be.

The conditions I laid out to the Vicar? I confronted him about his affair with Gwendolyn, the "someone special" he didn't want to leave. Since Mrs. Crutchlow's will would benefit both of them via the church and the museum, I arranged a "finder's fee" of one-third of their proceeds. The greedy priest had no choice but to acquiesce to my demands, but he would still have enough to prevent the immediate closure of St. Anselm's.

In solving the mystery of Farfetch, my retirement will thus be far more comfortable. Greed? I call it restitution, a repayment of my lost birthright.

I had come to like Bettina more and more. We are very much alike, the heritage of our wayward father profoundly apparent in both of us. She will never know of my arrangement with the Vicar, which superseded my original plan to keep the proceeds of any "find" all for myself. I will introduce Bettina to Mr. Connaught so she can receive the rightful share of her mother's bequest and I will defer my share to her.

Now I had a sister, a proper garden on the way, and a lovely cottage which no longer held a mystery.

The Locked Igloo
S. B. Watson

As Sir Thomas finished his tale, all sound in the smoking room at Blackwell's was drowned beneath an apocalypse of sudden thunder. The windows rattled in their mahogany panes. The great fire in the lounge hearth flattened against the logs, spewing ash and embers across the frothy Persian rug. The lights flickered, and went out. Solemnly, the rolling drums of the heavens receded, leaving only the cold clatter of the midnight rain against the windows and the snapping of the fire.

Mumbling excuses, the bartender, shocked awake from his trance behind the bar by the roar and the darkness, stumbled to the door and disappeared into the hallway in search of candles. A few of the gentlemen in the room moved closer to the fire, shifting their suits down into the warm leather chairs, careful not to spill their half-emptied drinks.

"An excellent tale, Sir Thomas," said a voice in the darkness, creaking like the bones of an old ship against a dying wind. "But I think I can do you one better."

The lounge hushed; this man rarely spoke, but when he did, remarkable things were said. He sat in the shadows beside the fire, his face sculpted in the gloom to its skeletal foundations, diamond eyes glinting in sallow pits, the scruff around his cheeks and neck unshaven like mold on a corpse. A hoary mustache drooped across the bone-line of his jaw.

He reached for his brandy, sitting in the light on the fireside table. The hand that broke the light was gaunt; three stumps wiggled where fingers used to be. Carefully, he encircled the glass between his thumb and ring-finger, the stumps gripping on for good measure, and pulled it back into the shadows.

"Must have been thirty years ago," he said. "Right after the Great War. I think it was my first expedition to the Frozen North with the Geological Survey of Canada. Yes, it *must* have been the first, because I still had all my fingers then…"

*****

We made basecamp on the western coast of Ellesmere Island, on the banks of Nansen Sound. Ellesmere was a frozen rock, covered in sporadic drifts of deep snow, the tundra marred and sliced by the flows of the huge glaciers that crawled endlessly down to the frozen seas.

The ice shelf was vast that year, stretching endlessly across the Arctic Ocean, its flatness broken only by jagged pressure ridges where the depths below had forced the ice up into jumbled heaps. From Ellesmere, the shelf ran as far northward as the eye could see, unforgiving and harsh, swept by frozen spindrift that glittered in the never-setting sun. The same shelf filled Nansen Sound. Where Ellesmere's barren tundra dropped to the waters of the sound, the ice started and ran westward to the horizon.

I remember looking out onto the cold ice of the sound, from our shelters on Ellesmere. It was a twenty-mile journey across the ice to Axel Heiberg. I hoped the mapping of Axel Heiberg didn't fall to me. Of course, it did… To me, and a grizzled old Finn, named Jorgen.

We set out early onto the ice by dogsled. We planned for three days, so the sled was well provisioned. Equipment, food, charts and drafting supplies, a sextant and a small brass chronometer, some basic tools, a rifle, and a tent, were all strapped tightly to the sled beneath a cover of caribou skins.

We took turns, Jorgen and I, guiding the sled and jogging alongside it. Hour after hour we beat across the ice. Ellesmere fell away behind us and we were surrounded by the maze of pressure ridges. There were no sounds on the shelf, other than the cold whistle of the wind, the snarling of the dogs, and the slithering of the sled runners. Jorgen and I talked at first, but the air was too cold, and it parched our throats. When we reached Axel Heiberg, my gloves were frozen to the handle of the sled and the snot from Jorgen's nose had formed icicles in his mustache like the tusks of a walrus.

For two days we worked along the coast, charting as we went. We sledded beneath the shadows of great, white icebergs that broke the shelf and loomed up into the naked sky. We skirted sharp breaks in the ice that allowed the black waters of the Arctic Ocean up to form frigid, bottomless pools.

After two days, we returned to Nansen Sound and started the numbing trek back to Ellesmere. We didn't see the storm coming until it was too late, and we were already well into the sound, and at that point there was no turning back. We had to reach Ellesmere before it caught us.

Behind us the horizon grew murky and grey. The wind picked up in sudden, unexpected gusts, scattering the loose snow from the pressure ridges and swirling it across us. By dead reckoning, Jorgen and I guessed we had ten miles as the crow flies left to travel. But we had to thread the maze of those damn ridges—we couldn't sled straight across the sound.

The unending daylight dimmed. The horizon before us, our lodestar of salvation, softened, and became vague between the coarseness of the ice and the cream-colored sky. The wild winds scoured snow from the icy shelf and whipped it across our path, tearing at our fur jackets and leggings. Through it all the dogs plodded on, looking back occasionally, as if to see if they'd lost us yet.

Then the horizon disappeared. The sky dissolved into the whirling flurries. The pressure ridges became dark shadows, rising above us. When I realized I couldn't see farther than the length of the sled in from of us, I had a sudden bout of honesty with myself: we were dead. We hadn't reached land, and we hadn't prepared shelter. The only escape was death.

But just as the cold fingers of dread took hold, a shape loomed in the swirling ice. I almost missed it, stumbling along beside the sled. I grasped Jorgen's jacket and jerked at his elbow, pointing to the structure on the ice.

It was an igloo.

Jorgen stopped the sled next to the ghostly mound. I ran to unhook the dogs. Visibility had dropped even lower, but in the white mists I saw them prance out into the blizzard and begin to dig their beds into the snow.

Jorgen and I pulled our provisions from the sled, and began to walk the structure's periphery, looking for the door block. It only took moments to walk around the half-dome. When we reached the sled again, Jorgen turned to me and shrugged. No door.

That was a little strange, but we didn't have time to wonder at a doorless igloo. Jorgen pulled the army shovel from the sled and dug into the side of the structure, cutting a small squarish block with the bit. I kicked it into the igloo when he finished and slid into the black opening feet first.

The sounds of the blizzard dulled to a muted rumble; the tearing winds dropped to a dry, icy stillness. Jorgen stuffed our packs through the opening and slid inside. Together, we struggled to lift the ice block back to the opening. It fit roughly, shutting out the last of what dim light there was. We smoothed the rough fit with our gloved hands, rubbing powdered snow into the cracks. Then we fell back, panting like dogs in the darkness.

Outside, the blizzard whipped and rumbled against the dome of ice. The winds screamed against the rounded edges, but inside the air was still and calm. It must have been ten minutes before I had the strength to sit up in the darkness. It was so black I couldn't see my hand in front of my face.

"What's that smell," said Jorgen. It was the first time I'd heard his voice in hours. "Smells like meat," he said.

Slowly, faculties and reason began to return. We were in a stranger's igloo, it was pitch black, and silent, and the faintest odor of roast beef filled the air. The hairs on my head stood rigid. A different kind of panic rose inside me. I think Jorgen sensed it too; we both scrambled immediately for the packs, searching for a light.

Jorgen found it first—a box of matches. The stick scratched and flared in the darkness, pinpoint light flickering between us. Jorgen turned, and put it into the room, and then we saw him.

The man lay on a bed of ice, wrapped thickly in caribou skins. He didn't move. His head was hooded in the skins.

Jorgen and I rose to our feet. The match went out, putting us in utter darkness again. Jorgen fumbled with the box, swearing good English oaths under his breath. Finally, he lit another one, and we approached the figure.

I put a hand out, and gently tapped the shoulder. It was stiff under the skins. The smell of meat grew stronger. I patted him. I gently shook him. Jorgen lit another match. I gripped the man's shoulders, and pulled him over onto his back. The blankets fell from his head as he rolled, revealing charred flesh, drawn taught across his skull like the skin of a mummy, blackened and crusted with ash, his eyes roasted to jellied beads. The light went out.

Jorgen lit another match. I half expected, with the return of the light, to see the horrid body moving towards us in the darkness. But the corpse still lay, just as it had, on the bed of ice.

"What do we do now?" I asked.

Jorgen frowned at the body, slowly grinding his teeth. Finally, he shrugged, and turned back to our packs. "We sleep," he said.

Someone had the forethought to bring a candle. Jorgen scrounged it from a pack and lit it, propping it in the ice next to the dead man's feet. The igloo flickered in the sallow light.

Now, the igloo was constructed in the usual fashion. Blocks of ice had been cut from the ground and raised to form the walls, spiraling around at a gentle incline, until they curved to meet at the top. The quarry formed from mining the ice blocks lowered the floor below the 'ground level' outside, giving easy room to stand. Customarily, a few 'beds' of ice would be left, to sleep upon; the only bed in our igloo was occupied, and neither Jorgen nor I cared to move the eternal sleeper.

We lay our bedrolls out on the low floor and sat. Jorgen brought out the slab of cold meat we'd packed. We both looked at it, smelling the aroma still lingering in the room, and put it away again.

Then Jorgen asked a question. "How does a man burn," he said, "without burning his robes?"

I looked at the body, wrapped in skins as though he'd been freezing when he lay down. The thick skins were completely uncharred, yet the body within them was blackened.

"And how does a man burn without a fire?" Jorgen asked further.

Indeed, there was no fuel for fire anywhere in the igloo. Just the body, and the skins, and the ice, and us.

"And what about the door," I asked.

An igloo is built from the inside. When it's complete, you cut your way out, either by an angled tunnel, so the wind can't blow straight in, or by removing a small block that could be replaced. At this point, Jorgen and I were too curious to sleep, so we took the candle, and inspected the perimeter of the igloo.

No tunnel had been dug below the ground level of the ice. Opposite our entry, on the other side of the corpse, we found a square crease in the wall. It was the door we'd missed from the outside. But here was another problem: just as we'd sealed our crude door by rubbing ice into the cracks, so had this door been sealed. Jorgen carried the candle up the wall from the door. Our eyes followed the vague seams between the igloo's ice blocks. They had *all* been sealed, meticulously smoothed over, *from the inside.*

"There has to be another opening," I said. But there wasn't. No marks of tunnels in the floor, not a scratch or blemish in the smooth curve of the walls. The only opening was a small, two-inch circle at the very top, that had been left as a draft hole.

Jorgen said it was impossible, and I suppose it was. A dead man, burned without fire, lying alone in a cairn of ice that had been sealed from the inside. And yet, impossible as it may have been, there it was.

And there we were.

Outside, the winds howled and beat against the igloo, but that clever structure had been built too well—it never so much as quivered in the storm. I'm told temperatures dropped as low as sixty below, but in the igloo we were warm. That night, the candle burned all the way down. It was a waste of fuel, but neither Jorgen nor I could bring ourselves to sleep in the dark with that cursed body. We sat, huddled in the furs we'd brought from the sled, the steam from our breath rising in the still air, gently sucked towards the draft hole above us. Neither of us spoke. We just watched the little candle flame flicker, and tried to stop thinking about the man wrapped in the caribou skins on the bed of ice beside us.

At some point I fell asleep. I dreamt no dreams. I didn't rouse. It was a sleep of exhaustion.

And then, as suddenly as I fell asleep, I awoke in a panic.

The storm had passed. The ice walls glowed soft blue; a shaft of clear light struck down through the draft hole. The igloo sat in icy stillness, and yet, *something* had awakened me— a rasping noise, like metal against ice.

I scrambled to my feet, stumbling against the corpse's icy bed. Jorgen was up too, standing stock still, listening.

Then I heard it again—a sharp grating sound. I turned in time to see a blade hack through the wall. The ice block burst into the igloo, shattering into crumbled pieces on the floor as a swarthy Inuit slid in behind it. For a moment, we just looked at each other, but then he pointed an old pistol at us, and motioned to the fresh door.

I looked at Jorgen. The Finn raised his hands, marched to the door, and crawled out. The Inuit turned his pistol to me, and said something I couldn't understand, so I put my hands up and followed Jorgen.

Outside, the sky was clear. The jagged pressure ridges around us were smoothed by the coating of fresh ice and snow. It was bitter cold. Colder than the day before. Everything was soft and white.

I stumbled up into the frozen snow, and stood next to Jorgen. Four Inuit hunters stood next to their sleds, rifles unslung and ready. Their faces were grim. They didn't look pleased to see us.

*****

With a crash, the door to the smoking room swung open. The old explorer paused his tale. All eyes turned to the darkness at the far edges of the flickering firelight. After a pregnant silence, the bartender staggered triumphantly back into the room, holding a crate of kerosene lamps and supplies.

The fire popped and fizzled against the hearth as a stout wind beat against the club windows. The old explorer leaned forwards and put his brandy glass back on the fireside table. The bartender put the box down, and began unpacking the lamps and trimming the old wicks.

"Well, they turned out to be quite friendly chaps," the explorer said, as the wind died down. "They were just as surprised to find us in that igloo as we were to see them. And there you have it, Sir Thomas. What do you say? Does my tale beat your disappearing race horse?"

A deep voice grumbled from the back of the room. "A good story it may be," said Sir Thomas, "but you haven't explained anything, yet. How was the igloo sealed from the inside? Who sealed it? How had the man been burned? And why?"

"The dead man sealed it," the explorer said. "Does that give you information enough?"

"Hardly," muttered Sir Thomas.

The bartender pulled an old can of spirits from the crate and began to fill the lamps.

The explorer laughed. His voice cackled above the rattling of the rain against the windows. "It's really very simple," he said, "and not a little tragic. Those Inuit hunters built the igloo, days before. The igloo was *their* basecamp. On the last day of their hunt, they had planned on having a bonfire, with a few good spirits, on the ice. To that end they had packed wood and whiskey in one of their sleds."

The bartender lit a match, and carefully brushed it against the wick of the lamp before him.

"The day of the storm," the explorer continued, "one man stayed behind while the others hunted. Unfortunately, this chap was a bit of a drunk, and he got into the spirits. When he was good and sloshed, he started the bonfire early, and built it up high. He kept drinking, and kept stoking, going so far as to burn his sled in the blaze. He drank himself into a stupor, fell into the fire, and burned with it.

"That day his friends returned early—they had seen the storm on the horizon. At the igloo, they found the man's body, still smoldering in the fire. They found the bottles. They had to make a choice. They didn't have enough sleds for the body *and* the seals. They had a perfectly good igloo, but, just like us, they didn't fancy the idea of spending a night with a charred corpse. So, they wrapped him in skins, out of respect I believe, and laid him to rest inside. They fit a block in the door, and left well ahead of the storm."

The kerosene lamp glared to life in the darkness of the room just as the club's overhead lights surged and hummed back to full brightness. The bartender looked up sourly and blew out the match.

"That's all well and good," said Sir Thomas, a plump little man in a bulging three-piece suit, sitting in the corner of a feathery couch by the windows. "But you said the dead man sealed the igloo himself... *How?*"

"Inuits have their own lamps, you know," said the explorer, his haunting figure now reduced in the light to that of a simple old man, frail and forgettable. "Kudliks, they call them. Fueled by whale oil. They're often used to seal the inside of an igloo, by raising the temperature enough to melt the inner layer of ice. It melts, and refreezes, forming smooth, air-tight walls. The hunters put that poor fellow into the igloo still hot. He acted like a human kudlik. His heat melted the walls, enough to form a smooth seal across everything, including the door."

Somewhere in the distance a long, peeling crash echoed through the streets, cutting through the incessant pitch of the storm. This time there was no flicker—the lights went abruptly off, plunging the club back into darkness.

With grim cheerfulness, the bartender struck another match and moved to the next kerosene lamp.

"Another excellent story," said a new voice. This voice was younger, brighter, with more energy and force to the shaping of its words. The speaker moved slowly from the shadows into the light of the fire. He was a tall man in a thin suit. He gripped a smoldering cigar between his fingers, gentle smoke curling up from the glowing cherry at the end. "But I can do *both* your stories one better."

The explorer shifted in his chair, the leather creaking beneath his weight, and crossed his legs. He dropped his arm across the table, stretching the gnarled stump-fingers towards the warmth of the fire.

"Can you, Doctor?" he challenged.

The young man took a draw on his cigar, fanning the dull ember, and smiled. "This happened only two years ago," he said, "on the estate of one of my wealthier patients, near Braintree. I wrote it up, back then, but never did anything with it. So, friends, you will be the first to hear about my involvement in the unusual case of the crippled sleepwalker…"

And as the bartender trimmed the next lamp, the doctor told his tale.

The Insidious Chameleon
Ron Bruguiere

Family events were rare, but for my sixteenth birthday, four uncles, five aunts, and ten older cousins met for the first time since my father passed when I was seven years old. I felt the occasion warranted their acknowledgment of my existence, as I would join the family business after I graduated college. To celebrate my turning from boy to man, I shaved the fuzz from my chin.

Mom had filled our New York City apartment's spacious living room with more long-stemmed yellow, red, pink, and white roses than I'd ever seen. As it was springtime, and lilacs bloomed, three bunches with their heady scent permeated our apartment's foyer. Our fifteenth-floor apartment overlooked the west side of Central Park. With the view, your eyes took in the wide expanse of greening treetops.

At the door, I greeted every arrival, but they ignored me except for the initial greeting. My aunts and uncles were first-generation Americans whose parents had emigrated from France. Some relatives circulated; others formed groups. Their conversations veered between French and English. Mom insisted we do the same, so I wouldn't forget my heritage.

At an early age, I learned children didn't speak unless spoken to. But it was my party. I stood up, and out of respect, addressed the family in French. *"Je voudrais poser quelques questions."*

The room quieted.

Aware some cousins didn't understand French; I smiled and said, "I'd like to ask some questions," and continued in English.

"Since my youth, I've heard rumblings that my great-grandfather was murdered. How was he killed?"

Ignoring the shocked expressions, I pressed on. "What was his occupation?"

No one said a word.

"How old was he?"

Mom rose from her chair. "It's time for Thierry's birthday cake."

Chitchat resumed, and I couldn't fathom why no one answered my simple questions about my great-grandfather, René Rochemon.

Later, an aunt took me aside and told me of a biography written in 1880, *Le Caméléon Insidieux,* but stopped short of offering any further information. I thanked her, then slipped into my room, opened my French-English dictionary, and translated the title. It became *The Insidious Chameleon*. I thought the title was ridiculous. Maybe that's why my family remained silent.

When the family departed, they smiled at me and either shook my hand or gave me *le bise* on both cheeks. Except for Aunt Lillian, no one addressed or acknowledged my questions.

In the morning, as Mom and I ate breakfast, I said, "Aunt Lillian told me someone wrote a biography about Great-grandfather and gave me the title."

Mom raised her eyes to the heavens. "When your father and I met, we were the age you became yesterday. Being around his family, I overheard conversations about the book and about a murder. Neither your father nor I ever saw the book. Questions were impermissible."

"Mom, you puzzle me. I laid awake all night, wondering about the murder. Is it possible the biography isn't about Great-grandfather but about someone else?"

She shrugged her shoulders. "I'm needed at the store," and left for her three-day-a-week position at the family business, Rochemon's Fine French Antiques.

We had no further conversations on the subject.

My family's silence aroused my curiosity, and I searched French newspapers and ancestry websites until I found my great-grandfather's obituary in the Paris newspaper *Le Figaro*:

"René Rochemon, born 6 May 1850, died 6 August 1879 in Saumur, Maine-et-Loire when attacked by wild dogs while hunting wild boar. He leaves his wife Marie, their son Thierry, three brothers and two sisters."

That was the extent. Not only did his death at twenty-nine stun me, but his manner of death confused me. I couldn't comprehend where my family got the notion someone had murdered him. I needed to find *Le Caméléon Insidieux*. New York City had many used bookstores, but old French books were a scarce commodity, and in my search, failed.

The only facts I knew were after he died, the entire clan immigrated to New York City. With them, they brought enough fine French antiques to establish a successful Manhattan business. My great-grandmother died before my birth, and my great-grandfather's brothers and sisters, too. At age two, my grandfather and grandmother passed away three weeks apart. My father was only thirty when he died.

*****

While in high school, I worked Saturdays and summers at the family business selling furniture. I concluded it wasn't an occupation I wanted but enjoyed the persuasion aspect and its power. When I graduated, I attended Columbia University, majoring in rhetoric.

After I received my BA, Harvard Law accepted me, and during the summer breaks, I interned with the CIA in Washington, D.C. When I graduated, I took and passed the New York State Bar Exam and at twenty-five became a full-time CIA analyst. I'm sure the reason I chose the bureau was my youthful efforts to discover what happened to my great-grandfather.

My first year was at the bureau's headquarters in D.C., and the next twenty-four in Southeast Asia. I returned to the States only once when Mother passed. At her funeral, only one cousin appeared. So much for family unity. I turned the lock on our apartment and returned to my job. When I'd served twenty-five years, I retired and returned to Manhattan with my wife.

Now I was sixty-nine-years-old, my wife dead from breast cancer, no children, the family business closed, and any relative a distant memory. I was beside myself to find a project.

While rummaging through papers from my youth, I discovered my great-grandfather's obituary, and my French-English dictionary contained a piece of paper with a fading penciled *Le Caméléon Insidieux*. It was an eureka moment. I'd found the tool. Perhaps I could solve the family mystery.

On a French website, I inserted *Le Caméléon Insidieux*, and up popped a 1955 edition of *Le Figaro*. It was an obituary and contained the book's title. I shouted so loud my ears rang. After I printed the obituary, I translated it into English.

"Gilbert de le Proulx, the last living descendant of the de le Proulx dynasty, born 10 June 1862, died on 16 July 1955. His late father, Françoise de le Proulx, gained notoriety because of similar deaths that occurred on his estate. In 1880 Pierre du Valle, rumored to have written and privately printed Françoise de le Proulx's biography, *Le Caméléon Insidieux*, died when attacked by wild dogs while hunting wild boar on Françoise de le Proulx's estate. Two years earlier, René Rochemon died there in the exact manner. Gilbert de le Proulx spent his life tracking down copies of the book and destroyed them. When asked for an explanation, he refused to reply. *Le Figaro* has never seen the book. As there are no heirs, his Loire Valley home, Chateau de le Proulx at Saumur in Maine-et-Loire, become the property of the French Government."

I felt rewarded. The du Valle article provided me with names and quizzical situations, signaling me to probe deeper with my investigation.

In my search for Françoise de le Proulx, *Le Figaro* offered only his obituary with basic facts. No mention of the book, or clues about his life other than his birthplace and death in Saumur, Maine-et-Loire. Born 2 January 1838, died 25 March 1898.

While I sat at my desk, I pondered what connection my great-grandfather had with de le Proulx or du Valle. So many questions needed answers. One of the deeper and more sinister ones I chewed over was whether Great-grandfather was someone's lover he shouldn't have been. Discovered and killed.

My unfounded assumption about du Valle's biography was vengeance. He spilled the horrendous deeds Françoise de le Proulx committed, and he'd witnessed.

Next, I searched for du Valle. After I translated the details from the 1881 article, it became:

"Pierre du Valle, born 3 November 1836 in Saumur, Maine-et-Loire, died on 2 December 1881 when attacked by wild dogs while hunting wild boar on the estate of Françoise de le Proulx. He was a poet, rumored to have written, and privately printed, a biography of Françoise de le Proulx whose land bordered his. He left no heirs. The house and land become the property of the French Government."

His obituary gave me further hope. With their land adjoining, things became clearer.

I considered the word insidious. Crafty, sinister, deceitful, Machiavellian. In addition, someone who over time causes harm.

My first thought on a chameleon was a lizard that changed colors. Did Françoise de le Proulx have multiple personalities?

When I combined the title's keywords, I concluded de le Proulx had an irrational persona. That made sense to me. But was I fantasizing?

I prayed Pierre du Valle's poems survived, tucked away in Saumur's library if one existed, and his home hadn't crumbled into dust, although that was over a century ago. And what of the Chateau de le Proulx?

I wouldn't accomplish any more in New York, and as I had no obligations, I decided my targets lay in France.

*****

My only visit to France was as a six-year-old when my father took my mom and me on a store buying trip. The total memory of that outing was inky-colored water with white tops and our boat—Mom corrected me often, "Thierry, it's a ship, not a boat."—bobbing up and down as water pounded our tiny round window, as she held me tight, and my father held her hand.

Because the Paris Bibliothèque nationale de France might yield further information, Paris was necessary before I traveled to the Loire Valley. I booked a hotel room for three nights with a Friday arrival, giving me time to get acclimated. After I fulfilled some tourist interests on Saturday, I'd visit the Bibliothèque on Sunday. Then on Monday, embark on my search in Saumur.

With all I'd been through in my CIA career and its inherent dangers, only my first assignment put my nerves on edge. But that was short-lived. Now, I felt jumpy about the impending trip. None more so than when I boarded the Air France flight at JFK. My rationale was the possibility of failure. Doom had cast its shadow over me before I set foot on French soil.

The cabin attendant provided a glass of champagne, a decent meal, and coffee. After a snifter of brandy, I fell asleep. I woke in a groggy state, still apprehensive about my future. As the taxi took me to the hotel, I acted like a wide-eyed kid. My head swiveled, looking every which way. I giggled as I reflected on my age of sixty-nine. The pins and needles vibe was extraordinary.

After I arrived at the hotel, I strolled through the neighborhood. Exhausted, I returned and woke Saturday morning.

Warm weather and a bright sun welcomed me when I left the hotel. The top of Notre-Dame caught my eye, and I walked toward the cathedral. When I arrived, a long line made me decide against a visit. I continued my walk, and as I crossed over a bridge, I stood for a moment to gaze down at the River Seine. When I lifted my head, the first thing I saw was the Eiffel Tower and proceeded toward it.

The second thing I noticed was a bookstall. Looking farther, there seemed to be more. As I strolled, I stopped at many. Besides Used Books, they sold postcards and cheap prints of Paris sights. Excitement registered when I stopped at the *Livre Anciens* stall. But as I examined some, they weren't ancient, just dusty, dog-eared junk. I laughed. Had I expected du Valle's poems, and *Le Caméléon Insidieux* awaited my materialization?

Hunger hit me when I spotted a crepe stand, and then I continued to the Eiffel Tower. Again, a line too long to wait. An empty chair at an outdoor café caught my eye, and I ordered a beer. As I sipped, I realized boredom had set in. Visits to tourist sites weren't one of my life's pleasures. I needed to get on with the reason I'd come to France.

*****

Early Sunday morning, a taxi dropped me at the Bibliothèque nationale de France, proclaimed one of the world's largest libraries. When I exited the cab and viewed the complex, I believed it was. Positioned to resemble open books, four towering glass and steel structures, two on either side, overlooked the Seine.

When I entered the Reference Library, I found a computer and entered *Le Caméléon Insidieux* into their catalog. My inquiry drew a blank. Frustrated, I headed to the Research Library. There, I needed to register. After I filled out the form, I requested all materials for Françoise and Gilbert de le Proulx, Pierre du Valle, and my great-grandfather, René Rochemon. About an hour later, the documents arrived. I'd already seen those about my great-grandfather and du Valle. But the quantity of the de le Proulx papers overwhelmed me. The family's lineage dated back to the Crusades. I spent hours leafing through their history. Most of the information was irrelevant to my needs, but I wrote all the pertinent dates leading up to Gilbert de le Proulx's death.

That was enough for day one. When I returned to the hotel, I spoke with the manager about Saumur. He discouraged me from driving, suggesting a train would be quicker and cheaper, and rent a car there.

*****

The following morning, an express train got me there in two and one-half hours. At the car rental agency, I asked for directions to the hotel I'd pre-booked. The drive was uncomplicated, and after I found the hotel, I continued touring the region. Dense, wooded areas on Saumur's outskirts gave me a clearer picture of the wild boar and wild dogs of many years ago.

When I checked in, I inquired if anyone knew where I might locate the Chateau de la Proulx. Of the four middle-aged people I asked, all gave me negative headshakes. I realized it was too late in the day to visit City Hall for information and sat by the hotel's pool, basked in the sun, and conversed with tourists. I felt proud that my French was on par with French citizens.

In the morning, I visited the Land Registry office in City Hall. A youngish male served me.

"Where will I find the Chateau de le Proulx?" I asked.

"I've never heard of it," he said.

"Do you have a list of property owners?"

"We only have the current owners, nothing from the past. For more information, you must complete this form."

As I looked at it, he said, "Most often, nothing happens. I suggest you contact a lawyer." Filled with disappointment, I left the office.

My next stop was Saumur's library. At the desk, I asked, "Do you have a copy of *Le Caméléon Insidieux* or the poems of Pierre du Valle?"

The woman, maybe in her sixties, stared at me. Her look gave me the chills.

"Those names aren't familiar. Are the books old?" she asked.

"I believe they're from the late eighteen hundreds."

"We only have new books."

I viewed her answer as another defeat.

"What is your name?"

My mind wasn't able to figure out her request, but said, "Thierry Rochemon."

She smiled. "Monsieur Rochemon, I'm new to this position. Perhaps our head librarian might help you. She'll be here tomorrow. Can you return?"

Her remark gave me hope, but also apprehension. "Yes, what time shall I come?" "We open at ten o'clock."

"Another question, if I may?"

"But of course,"

"Do you know where the Chateau de le Proulx is?"

"I've never heard of it."

As I shut the library door, failure rumbled through my brain.

*****

I couldn't recall the last time I had butterflies as I opened the library door at ten o'clock. The same woman was at the desk. She looked at me. "You've come back. One moment."

She went into an office behind her. When she reappeared, accompanying her was an older woman.

The woman, clutching a cane, gazed at me as she hobbled to the desk. "Do you have identification?" she asked.

I considered it a strange request, but removed my passport from my pocket and handed it to her.

After she looked at it, she scrutinized me so hard I felt uncomfortable.

Her frown turned to a smile, and she said, "Please come with me."

I imagined she didn't think of me as threatening and followed her into the office. "Please sit," she said.

"May I ask a question?"

"Please. But first, may I ask why you are here in Saumur?"

"I'm seeking two books written by Pierre du Valle, who lived in Saumur in the late 1800s. I thought this library might have them. Also, I'm looking for the Chateau de la Proulx. No one I've spoken to in Saumur has ever heard of the Chateau. Have you?"

"Are you related to René Rochemon?" she asked.

"He was my great-grandfather. I've come to Saumur to solve a family mystery."

"What mystery is that?"

"How he died."

"I am Madame Laval; my great-grandmother founded this library. My grandmother continued running it, and then my mother, and now I. We have been its only librarians. Treasures of Saumur's history are hidden. Both books you seek are here."

Seated in a slouched posture, I bolted upright.

"They are fragile. You must read them here."

"How did the library get them?"

"Pierre du Valle was a friend of my great-grandmother. The start of our library was because of him. His travels were extensive. On each return, he brought books he gave to her."

As she spoke, she handed me a pair of white cotton gloves and put another pair over her hands. Then turned her back, bent down, opened a safe, reached in, removed two thin books in clear glassine envelopes, and placed them on the desk. Again, she reached into the safe. When she sat erect, a clear glassine envelope with a letter was in her hand.

She handed me the letter envelope. "It's dated 1880, and the ink is fading. No need to remove it. You can read it through its cover."

At first glance, I saw long flowery sentences with archaic French words I didn't understand. But the signature was clear: Pierre du Valle. As I reread the letter several times, its content became clear. Pierre du Valle requested his books find a secure place away from prying eyes.

Satisfied I'd located the books, I asked, "Where is de le Proulx's chateau and du Valle's home?"

"After Pierre du Valle died, Françoise de le Proulx purchased the property from the government and demolished it. The Chateau de le Proulx is gone."

"I'm eager to find answers in the books."

"After you read, you will have questions. I hope I can answer them. Your chair may prove uncomfortable. Please use the couch."

She left the room; I picked up the envelopes and moved to the couch. Both books seemed less than fifty pages and removed *Le Caméléon Insidieux* first.

The title, debossed on the front and spine of the black leather binding, appeared to be gold-leaf that had dulled.

After opening the book, I turned pages but didn't read, only scanned. More archaic words. I deciphered some, sighed in exasperation, closed the book, and shut my eyes. After taking deep breaths, I reopened it and took a pad and pen from my case.

As I read, I translated Pierre du Valle's words. With this documentation, I could pass along the story to the family. I laughed. Where were they?

Reading further, I realized this wasn't de le Proulx's biography but a brief history of Great-grandfather and the aftermath. Yet, the ultimate subject was de le Proulx.

It surprised me to learn the entire Rochemon family worked at the Chateau, including Great-grandfather's wife Marie, who was Françoise de le Proulx's wife's maid. Great-grandfather's first position was stableboy, but when de le Proulx bought six Russian wolfhounds, he tended to their needs, which generated great affection between the hounds and him. Two of his sisters served as chambermaids, two brothers, footmen, and the other brother a gardener.

With my edits, Pierre du Valle wrote:

"I became acquainted with René Rochemon when he walked Françoise de le Proulx dogs through my property. He was twenty-five, and we had many conversations. René had expert knowledge about the hounds, who were obedient and well-groomed.

"I learned a show of dogs would take place in Paris as part of L'Exposition Universelle de 1878 and proposed to de le Proulx he enter his hounds with René as the handler. He agreed on the condition I accompany him. He would travel in a separate coach and have a four-horse-drawn coach constructed to accommodate the six hounds, René, and myself.

"All turned out well at the dog show with one wolfhound winning a ribbon that de le Proulx accepted to polite applause, and he remained in Paris for a day to celebrate. I took René to the Louvre, and we visited Bois de Boulogne with the hounds.

"Two days later, we departed. Outside Paris, torrential rains fell, making visibility unclear and the dirt roads hazardous. On one road's downhill slope, our coach's front axle cracked, and its right wheel broke away. The coach veered to the right and plummeted downhill into an already overflowing river. The driver jumped off as the coach descended. We, enclosed in the carriage, struggled to open the doors, but the descent's speed was too fast, and our attempts failed. After the movement stopped, the coach was mostly underwater. Our driver arrived at the sinking coach and helped open a door. We got out, but all six dogs drowned. We could not save them. In the rushing water, we struggled to unhitch the horses. After we did, we rode them back to Saumur.

"That we had allowed his prize-winning dog to die outraged Françoise de le Proulx. He fumed at the sight of us, ordered us out of the Chateau, and dismissed René from service. René came to live with me, but the rest of the family stayed at the Chateau, including his wife."

Now, I had a general concept of the apparent hatred leveled at Great-grandfather. I needed to rest my eyes and brain, as translating du Valle's words had taken its toll. I returned the book to its envelope, placed both on the desk, and left.

At the front desk, I said, "I've read all I can today. May I return tomorrow?"

"You are welcome anytime. We open at ten."

Once dinner was done, I relaxed in the lounge with brandy and contemplated the book's title. I'd yet to encounter evidence of insidiousness, only anger. Was the book's title du Valle's way of retaliation to inflame and agitate de le Proulx?

*****

In the morning, when I arrived at the library, Madame Laval gave me a pair of gloves and both books.

"Questions?" she asked.

"No, I haven't reached an area of doubt yet."

I sat on the couch, took out my pad and pen, opened the book to where I'd left off, and translated.

"René was grateful for my invitation to live with me until another position became available. However, de le Proulx conveyed detrimental comments of René to his associates and recruited his son Gilbert to spread malicious gossip among his friends. I believed those actions would hinder employment for René in Saumur."

His story laid out de le Proulx's insidiousness. Everything applied to my 'why' quest, but I realized the investigation was for my satisfaction alone and jotted down only its most essential content.

"Unable to secure a position, René took to hunting and selling his kill to the Saumur butcher. Money that René earned, he shared with me, which, unknowing to him, I saved. René's hunts were on de le Proulx's vast estate. He ignored the posted signs that prohibited hunting, as he knew the gamekeeper overlooked poachers. However, de le Proulx learned of his lenience and dismissed him. The new man enforced the rules.

"Fearful for René's safety, I joined in the hunt. We hunted where the woods were thickest, and wild boar plentiful in an area bordering the estate. The butcher bought. The townspeople delighted. However, de le Proulx pressed the butcher and discovered René killed the boar. He inquired about the location. The butcher replied the woods.

"On our hunts, we always kept fifty feet apart, so if one missed his shot, the other might still make a kill. The day René met his death, we followed that premise. It was late in the day when I heard René scream.

"I ran toward him and witnessed six wild dogs attacking him. One was at his throat. Another his head. One dog had bitten off René's right foot and chewed it. Two dogs gripped their teeth on his left leg and attempted to drag him away. Another dog chewed on René's hand. I fired two shots, killing the dogs at his throat and head. The others ran away."

I stopped reading and put the book aside. I needed to catch my breath. My stomach churned, and I rushed to the restroom and vomited. When I recovered, I took both books to the desk.

"Are you all right?" the librarian asked. "You look unwell."

"The story is brutal. I'll return tomorrow."

*****

I had a restless night. Bad dreams with howling dogs kept waking me. Instead of going to the library, I sat by the pool. After lunch, I returned to the library.

Madame Laval greeted me. "I understand the book revealed your great-grandfather's death. The event was violent. I'm sorry your discovery was unpleasant."

"Thank you. I'll look at the book of poems this afternoon."

She handed me gloves and the book. I took a seat on the couch, and she remained at her desk.

I was careful as I opened the book; it was older than the other. Its black leather was dry and had thin cracks on both its front and back. Debossed in fading gold-leaf on the cover and spine was *POÉMES*. When I opened it, I turned pages without reading and counted twenty-four poems. I returned to the beginning, and as I read, translated as best I could, but didn't consider it necessary to transcribe them. The poems were expressions of reverence, character, compassion, and cooperation. Overall, Pierre du Valle's verses represented principles.

When I finished, I looked at Madame Laval. "Madame Laval, after reading these poems, and how Pierre du Valle treated my great-grandfather, I've concluded not only was he enlightened but also a man of integrity and humility."

"My belief is he gained those attributes from his broad-ranging travels and reading. Would you like the other book?"

"Tomorrow. Thank you."

*****

The following morning, as I translated and transcribed the few remaining pages, I realized this might be my last day.

"The police concluded René's death a tragic accident, but added he should not have trespassed on de le Proulx's property.

"On the day of René's burial, I walked through the woods with my gun, avoiding de le Proulx's land. In a small area, about half a mile from the estate's fencing, I found a conspicuous amount of dried animal feces and a sleeve from a shirt similar to the type René wore. I picked it up.

"At the same location, under trampled brush, were three strips of wood with nails. I wondered if there had been a pen to hold the dogs, and if the shirt's scent led them to René. When I lifted the largest piece of wood, beneath it was the rest of the shirt. I left it and returned home.

"During the service at Saumur's cemetery, I stood next to René's wife Marie and his family. As we departed, I invited her to come to my home and collect René's belongings. One of René's brothers came with us. As they departed, I asked Marie to stay and presented her with the money I had kept for René. The gift surprised her.

"I showed her the shirtsleeve and told her where I had found it. She acknowledged it belonged to René and wept, and then said that more of his garments remained at the Chateau.

"Marie reported de le Proulx expressed sorrow over René's death but told her if she remained in Saumur, she would have dreadful memories. Then she astonished me. He had offered Marie, her son, and the entire family passage to America, along with some Chateau furniture so they could establish a business, forget the tragedy and enjoy a new life.

"To me, it sounded like bribery and guilt. His settlement would never compensate for their heartbreak. However, I advised her to accept the offer.

"After the family sailed to America, I went to the police with the shirtsleeve. They asked where I had found it. I took them to the site. The wood and shirt were still there.

"I believe Françoise de le Proulx furthered the death of René Rochemon.

"The End."

Finished, I breathed a sigh of relief, but I had struggled with his last line. He didn't use the word killed but the archaic verb *fainct* that means make, act, create. I assumed du Valle meant killed without using the word.

My examination of the books completed, now questions about the aftermath. I closed the book and inserted it into its glassine envelope, looked up and observed Madame Laval watching me.

"You've accomplished your task?" she asked.

"With the books, yes. Now the questions."

"Before you ask, I will tell you what knowledge I have."

"I'd appreciate that."

"The book scandalized Saumur and shocked those who read it. No one knows how many copies Pierre du Valle printed."

"I read Gilbert de le Proulx searched for copies and destroyed them," I said.

"Friends of Marie corresponded telling her of the book. No one knows if anyone sent a copy to America, but correspondence continued as events occurred."

"When I asked my family about Great-grandfather at my sixteenth birthday party, I got silence. Later, an aunt took me aside and offered the book's title."

"What generation were they?" Madame Laval asked.

"Children of siblings who went to America. Their secrecy confounds me."

"Opinions were different in those years."

"Did de le Proulx sue for slander or defamation?" I asked.

"When the book appeared, the Napoleonic Code of 1804 was in effect. They treated defamation of private citizens less severely than they did public officials. Pierre du Valle received the maximum sentence of 18 francs.

"The judgment enraged Françoise de le Proulx, and gossip persisted. The book made him unbalanced. Servants remained until they died, but not replaced. His son attended his father, but they allowed no Saumur resident into the Chateau. Both became recluses.

"As Gilbert aged, his need for money forced him to sell pieces of the estate. The Chateau crumbled, and when he died, it was in shambles, and the French government tore it down."

"Pierre du Valle's last line is a powerful statement," I said.

"Yes, accusing him of setting the dogs on your great-grandfather."

"When du Valle died the same way, most in Saumur believed the story was true."

"I appreciate your help in aiding me in solving this mystery."

"You're welcome."

"I will visit Great-grandfather's grave before I return to America."

"An unsolved mystery still exists," she said.

"What is that?"

"As reported in the press, they found Pierre du Valle's body on the de le Proulx estate. Not disclosed was a quarter-mile trail of dried blood led back to du Valle's property. If it was du Valle's blood, no one established how the body moved there. Investigators doubted the dogs' ability for such a maneuver.

"Who discovered the body?"

"The gamekeeper."

"Do you know his name?"

"Gaston Benoit. His family stills live in Saumur."

I grinned. "I'm a man without responsibilities. Maybe I'll remain in Saumur."

Teardrop Murphys
Aimee Kluck

Five boisterous young women, bures dressed in green plaid Catholic school uniforms, hustled through my office door, just as I poured myself a cuppa' and laid out the biscuits.

"Well, what have we here?"

"Are you Bertha McGoey, the private investigator?" the lass with the braid down her back asked.

"Aye. How can I help you?"

They all spoke at once, each voice louder than the other, words tumbling out like a creek over stones, none of it making any sense.

I pressed my fingers to my lips and let out a loud whistle. "Quiet yourselves. Now take a seat and one of youse tell me what's the deal."

With only two client chairs in my brand new office, the quickest two sat and two others gathered behind them as if posing for a group shot. The tall, demure redhead stood in the corner.

"Someone stole our instruments."

"As if we don't know who."

I held up my hand. "What instruments?"

They looked at me as if I were an idiot. "Our musical instruments."

"And tonight is the Battle of the Bands at Dargan's Pub," the girl with the braid said.

I took out my pad and pen. "Okay, let's start at the top. What are your names? One at a time."

A sparkly youngster with a ponytail pulled tight and tied up in a green shiny ribbon like a birthday present, pointed to two other dark haired, blue eyed beauties. "We three are sisters. I'm Siobahn, and I'm the lead singer. I play violin." The bossy one.

"We all sing, Siobahn." A retort from the redhead.

Siobahn snarled at her, then turned back to me. "They didn't get my violin because I always take it home with me."

"She sleeps with it, 'cuz she hasn't got a boo." Three girls giggled.

"Feck off." Siobahn poked her insulter. "That's Shanae, the rude one, on guitar and fiddle." Long, brunette locks with a green streak in front, heavy eye makeup like Cleopatra.

"Shannon plays accordion and flute." The braid who wore an annoyed scowl.

Siobahn pointed to the pixie with the rainbow bob and impish smile. "Our cousin, Bridget, drummer, and in the corner," the demure coppery redhead, "our other cousin, the bass player, Fiona. And the name of our band is the Teardrop Murphys—that's all of us last names."

"Shall I make a cup of tea, then, whilst you tell me what happened?" Mine was getting cold. I turned on the kettle, brought out the cups and teapot.

Siobahn moaned. "We loaded our equipment in the van last night after rehearsal and parked it where we always do, in the lot of our uncle's gas station. And this morning when we got up, the side window was broken, the doors were thrown open, and all the instruments were gone."

A collective female wail erupted. The teapot whistled. A plane landing at Logan soared overhead. The cacophony troubled my ears.

"Hush, now." I poured the water into the pot with tea leaves and spoke in a soothing voice, to keep a wrap on these aggrieved angels. "Who might you think is responsible?"

Harmonizing again, they yelled, "The Brat Boys." More rasping and bawling.

Siobahn perched forward in her chair. "We've been competing this month against bands from all over Boston and it's down to just two, us and them. The final is tonight."

Bridget cried out. "Without equipment, we can't go on. They'll win by default."

"It has to have been them, the snakes. Scared they couldn't win on their own merits, they cheated," Fiona said. They all nodded like bobbleheads.

"Have you reported the theft to the police?" I didn't mind a spot of work but having been a copper myself in my younger days, it seemed more like their responsibility.

Her voice high and squeaky, Shannon said, "They're too busy with the parade today, either marching in the darn thing or walking up and down acting important."

"Or popping in the pub for a nip," said Shanea, her face wrinkled with disgust.

"And they didn't seem like it was a priority," said Bridget.

"What is it exactly you want me to do? So I can get it down in me notes." I liked to be clear about my assignment.

All five shouted at once. "Help us find our gear."

"All right then. Here are my terms." I explained my daily fee plus expenses. I felt guilty taking money from the wee lasses, but I couldn't go and get all sentimental. I had bills to pay.

They pulled out their phones. "You take Venmo?"

This being just my third assignment since I opened my PI business, I wasn't fully set up. The first client, a man who thought his wife was cheating on him, only to find she snuck out at night to attend school against his wishes, "to better herself" as she insisted, paid me in cash. My second client, a swanky woman from one of them fancy houses up on the hill, whose husband was cheating on her, left me a substantial check along with a pile of soggy tissues.

"Have you got cash or check?"

They simultaneously burst out laughing. "So last century, Miss McGoey." Shanea rushed to my assistance. "Let me show you how to set up an account."

With a few clicks and me entering my bank password while she looked away, I now had a 21st century payment process. Each of them tapped away on their phones and sent me one-fifth of the first days' fee. Very organized, these young people.

I grabbed my pocketbook and coat. "Let's go have a look at your van."

We left the tea cooling and hustled out the door. The six of us squeezed into my aging Ford Fiesta, pushing aside the empty candy wrappers and used coffee cups, and made our way to their uncle's gas station. Their offended, beat-up van sat sadly exposed in the corner of the lot.

The sisters and cousins guided me around the side of the vehicle, cooing and grumbling, to a shattered side window. Broken glass was scattered on the ground and a rock lay inside on the floor. I noticed a spot of blood on the edge of the glass shards.

"They banjaxed the window, opened the door, and unlatched the back."

We walked around the rear. The doors were swung open, and inside, among walls lined with posters of the girls at various gigs, stood a few battered amplifiers and a tambourine.

"What time does your uncle close the station?"

"Eleven. He has a light over the front of the main building but not here in the corner. And before you ask, there are no CCTV's." Siobahn shook her head in displeasure. So last century.

"We asked the neighbors already. Nobody saw or heard anything, but that's Southie for you." Shannon, apparently unsatisfied with the details, folded her arms.

"You've done half my job." Would they be asking for a discount? "Where can I find these Brat Boys?"

"That bully Billy works at the lumberyard." Shanea scrunched her face at his name. "Steven, the sleeven, is a bike messenger downtown." She scowled and pointed east. "And Devin, the dosser, works at Dunkin, over on D Street."

"Who's the weakest link?" I asked.

They chimed together. "Devin."

"Have you taken yourselves to talk to him?" They didn't seem the type to shy away from confrontation.

"He ran in the back when we went there. And his manager told us to leave, or he'd call the cops. That's when we came to get you."

Fiona spoke up. "My mum told me about you. That's Maeve Greene.

Said she knew you from school. Said you could help us."

I remembered Maeve, who took me under her guidance when I first arrived here from Ireland. When I felt so alone and alienated. A fire-spitter of a girl, always getting into a bit of trouble. Funny her daughter turned out quiet.

"Speaking of school and seeing this is Sunday, why are you all in uniform?"

"We already graduated." Lots of eye rolling and huffing. Next time, I'll check ID's. "And no one at the school wears uniforms anymore." Bridget snapped the elastic on her braces.

Shanea pouted. "We were planning a dress rehearsal today. This is what we wear when we perform."

"Ya' know, railing against the establishment." Shannon flipped her thumb against her nose. "We're a punk band."

"With a Celtic twist." Bridget danced a few Irish steps and curtsied.

In my day, the school was run by nuns, and cross my heart, they'd be dropping to their knees and praying to the Almighty if they could see a gaggle of punk girls performing all sorts of gyrations dressed in their beloved uniforms.

I bid the lasses goodbye and told them I'd be in touch soon. Not much of a lead, but a little fire that warms is better than a big fire that burns.

I had to cross Broadway to get to D street, which was no easy feat since thousands of revelers adorned in gawdy, green outfits on their way to being drunk were already lined up for the St. Patrick's parade. A bossy policewoman, so young she must have been right out of the academy, tried to stop me from crossing, explaining as if I were daft that the parade was about to start.

"I'm just popping round to the Dunkin. And, love, I used to be on the force, just a few years back. Right here in District C-6. So, give a pal a break." I flashed her my sincerest smile while her face stiffened, as if she heard that before. If she insisted I walk the ten blocks around, I'd make a run for it. But with a dithering wave of her hand, she let me go.

At the counter in the shop, I debated whether to break my diet and order the Leprechaun special, a green frosted donut with green jimmies and coffee with milky green foam.

A pimply youth barked at me. "Whaddaya want?"

Not exactly happiness in a cup. I checked his name tag. "Are you Devin O'Connor? From the Brat Boys? In the competition tonight?" I tried to act as excited as an aging groupie could behave, batting my eyes and grinning like a fool. Ridiculous.

He glared at me as if about to gag. He clearly couldn't figure out if this knob was yanking his chain or if I came serious like. "That's me."

"I'm Bertie McGoey, an investigator, and I'd like to know where you were last night and what you were up to because it's all over town you were out thieving." For effect, I pounded my fist on the counter.

Poor lad went white as the icing on a frosted donut. "I don't know what yer talking about."

"And what happened there, son?" I pointed to the sloppy bandage on his wrist. "Cut it on broken glass, by any chance?"

"None of your business." He hid his arm behind his back. "Do you want a darn order or not?"

"I want the truth." I stared at him, hard and serious.

He licked his lips and called, "Next."

"I'll find your hidey-hole and your fingerprints will be all over those missing musical instruments and we'll get you. We'll put you away for a long time. Write a song about that." I stepped aside for the burly construction worker behind me.

I returned to my car. Changed to my sneakers, took ahold of my flashlight, and waited, sorry I hadn't ordered the Leprechaun special. The roar of the crowd and the beat of the band drifted from the parade.

I didn't have to wait long. About twenty minutes later, Devin the donut boy, came running out, and raced down D Street. I exited my car and followed him. When we hit Broadway, the police league marching band strode by. Devin hesitated, then wove through the rows of men in full Highland dress, plaid kilts and feather bonnets playing bagpipes. Their melancholy sound drew me in, and I had to stop for a moment in deep respect, flashing a memory of my dear dead da. The family bagpiper, who played at all the relatives' weddings, celebrations, and funerals, and even taught me to play. His pipes lay soundless in the back of my closet now. Aye, me da was a true musician, performing straight from his Celtic heart. How I missed the sound of his bagpipes and the smell of his smoking pipe…

Daydreaming? I had no time for that feckless nostalgia.

I saw Devin slip around the backs of the color guards and dodge the blaring trumpets. I stuck to him, best I could, weaving and wobbling, the drum beat rumbling in my ear, deafening me, the sliding trombone extending treacherously close to my face, and almost tripping over the toes of a clarinet player. All the time, keeping an eye open for that unfriendly copper who might try to nab me and whisk me away.

Having made it to the other side of the street, I kept my gaze fixated on my wee man. He ran fast down the side street, empty now compared to the parade route. He rushed along one block, then another, until we ran five blocks, me keeping my distance but never losing sight of him. It was a good thing I'd kept up my gym membership.

Finally, we hit the storage warehouses. Devin darted between buildings until he came to a garage door with a padlock. He fiddled with the lock combination, occasionally glancing over his shoulder, but I hid behind another structure, and he didn't spot me. After multiple attempts, he opened the lock, rolled up the door and stepped inside. Didn't even think to close it behind him. I stalked over and peered at him. The eejit was wiping down the musical instruments with a raggedy towel, as if to rid them of his fingerprints.

Mustering my former policewomen's bold voice, I hollered, "Put your hands in the air. Now." I held my flashlight out in front with two hands like a pistol. With any luck, the light would blind him, and he wouldn't see I wasn't armed.

Devin raised his hands and began sniveling. "Don't shoot."

"Back up and don't turn around. Come outside."

He followed the instructions and I kept myself positioned behind him. "Get down on your knees."

I beamed the flashlight into the storage area. On one side were a set of drums with the name Brat Boys emblazed on them and a few guitars and speakers. On the other side were another set of drums with Teardrop Murphys's logo, a guitar, a fiddle, and an accordion.

"Look what we have here. Yer not in a girl's band, are you mate?"

"It wasn't my idea. They made me do it." He might have been crying, poor gob.

"Aye, they say, lie down with dogs and you'll rise up with fleas." I pulled out my phone and pretended to call in to the station. "This is McGoey reporting. I've got a 10-74 out here at the storage warehouse." Those familiar words almost made me want to go back to service. Almost, but not really. I retired at fifty, the youngest age possible to still receive my pension. And never regretted it. My career life had been lonely, with not many friends outside the force and not many inside either. The policemen wanted something I wasn't willing to give, the policewomen suspicious of any competition. Not to mention, the citizens in this part of town didn't totally trust the cops, even though one in every family seemed to be on the force. I kept to myself, rarely went out.

I called Siobahn and gave her directions to the building. I figured the worst punishment for my boy Devin would come from the wrath and retribution of the five screeching songstresses.

While we waited for the girl band to arrive, I gave Devin one of my famous 'do-the-right-thing' lectures. How following others blindly made him a plonker and winning only counted if you played fair. He interrupted my words of wisdom complaining that his knees hurt, and he had to pee. I told him to get up, but under no circumstances should he relieve himself in public. He hopped from foot to foot.

The van roared around the corner and came to a halt inches from Devin. The Teardrops jumped from the vehicle. Fiona and Shannon ran to the garage to inspect the instruments while the other three circled Devin and, with raised fists, screamed bloody epithets at him. I let them go on as long as they didn't assault him. They seemed to know better, letting their words bruise him more than their hands.

"I can't even believe you and your fuckface friends stole our gear. How lame is that?"

"You're a friggin' hosah. And you smell worse than the hahbah at low tide."

"Have you even looked in the mirror lately, you gobshite?"

"Was this Billy's and Stephen's idea? 'Cuz I know you're too stoopit to think up anything like this." Siobahn stood, hands on hips till he nodded.

She stomped her feet and twisted her hands. "I'm going to wring their necks."

"Winning tonight will be your best revenge." I winked at her. Didn't want to incite any violence, confident the girl could do anything she proposed.

The rich tone of the accordion's bellows resonated from the garage, followed by the distinct tinkling of the melodious keys. Then, the boom of the drum.

"Don't touch my set." Bridget ran toward the storage unit.

"Are my guitar and fiddle there? Are they not damaged?" Shanae took off after her.

Leaving only Siobahn, who had no loss of words to insult the poor robber, stopping only long enough to call the pub and tell them the battle was on.

The Teardrops pulled their equipment from the unit and set up on the pavement. Bridget banged out a harsh rhythm. The guitar players strummed acoustically. Siobahn, without her violin, played the fiddle. The accordion hummed out loud.

I pushed Devin to a place in front of them.

"Listen and learn, loser," Bridget shouted as she smacked a riff on her set.

The music, with its Gaelic undertones supplied by the fiddle and the accordion and its punk overtones courtesy of the heavy bass beat and screaming, cranky lyrics, amused and delighted me. I clapped when they finished the song. "Grand. Awful good."

"Wait till you hear my violin," Siobahn said. "All we need is a bagpipe player to complete our ensemble."

"I play the pipes," I blurted out.

Shanea ran over and took my hands. "You must come to our show tonight. You saved our reputation. And bring your pipes, you can join in."

I blushed with embarrassment. "I haven't played in years, love. I'm rustier than a broken water line."

*****

That night, heading down the streets of Southie still overflowing with drunkards and troublemakers, I made my way to Dargan's. Inside the beer scented, dark walled, packed pub, I ordered a Jameson, neat, and looked around for anyone I might know. It wasn't my habit to hang out in bars, so that would be doubtful. Up on stage I spotted the Brat Boys, squawking like furious crows, banging the beat like a butcher tenderizing meat. Devin, on drums, had the look of misery on his sourpuss and the lead singer swaggered, clearly fluthered. They sounded awful. They would have been eliminated from the contest if the organizers had learned of their robbery, but the Teardrops chose not to inform them. They wanted to win on their own terms, their music. And I was certain my girls would succeed.

A sudden tap on my shoulder and I twisted around to see the still recognizable Maeve Greene. She held her arms out for a hug.

"It's been too long, Bertie." In her embrace, the years of our friendship rekindled, and I felt a wisp of a tear forming in the corner of my eye. She held me at arm's length. "Me and the other girls' mothers want to thank you for the grand job you did finding their missing instruments in such a short time. It would have been a monumental disaster if they hadn't played tonight. They've been working so hard and looking forward to the contest. You're a charm, for sure."

"Aye, they deserve it then."

She dragged me to a large round table where she introduced me to all the Murphys, the Greenes, the Durrigans, and a host of other relatives. The families alone must have taken up half the tables. Everyone, in that old Irish way, hugged and thanked me. I felt at home again.

The Teardrops took the stage and began their first song, the one I heard earlier in the parking lot. Only now ear-splitting louder. They played on, their snappy rhythm with that Celtic whine and catchy lyrics.

After the end of one particularly energetic song, Siobahn approached the mike. "We had quite a day today, a wee bit of trouble with our instruments, you might say." She scowled at the Brat Boys, downtrodden and lackluster, ordering more beers at the bar.

"We want to thank our guardian angel, Miss Bertie McGoey." A round of applause made me feel as foolish as a feather on the wind, as all heads turned to me. "And if you ever need a good private investigator, she's your woman." Aye, free publicity. Can't shirk that off. I tipped my glass to her and beamed a satisfied smile.

"Now we want to ask her to come up and play a tune with us on her bagpipes." Siobahn held out her hand and Maeve pushed me from behind. "Your mum got them out of your closet."

Mum would have some answering to do, but then I spotted her coming towards us, carrying the bagpipes, a sly grin on her face. "Here you go, love. Have at it."

I stumbled to the stage, hoping I wouldn't embarrass myself and make a giddy fool of the girls. I tucked the uillean pipes under my right arm, placed my fingers on the keys and pressed out a few notes.

"You mum said "O'Sullivan's March" was yer da's favorite. Should we spark that up?" Fiona asked.

My heart opened and soared, as the notes flowed through me like my da was sitting there beside me. A few old timers danced a jig with young punks. Others in the crowd clapped along. One or two from over across the ocean wiped a tear from their crusty eyes. Just like home.

At the end of their set, the Teardrop Murphys were awarded the title of the "Best Boston Band." The band members, their families and I hugged, and we celebrated with Guinness all around.

My mum came up beside me. "May your home always be too small to hold all your friends."

A craic good night.

The Forger
Alexander Frew

You get some curious cases in the business. Not enough, in my opinion, but then again what do I know?

'Sonny,' my mother said to me when I was a young lad—well not that young, I was bout thirty at the time. 'You have two ears and two eyes and one mouth. Look, listen, and speak as little as possible.' She was right.

I was in my office that morning when the blonde arrived with the brunette. The blonde was a big man in a silvery suit. He looked a bit fishy like a herring but with a less intelligent face. Yet it was a face I vaguely recognised. The brunette was younger, in her early twenties and not bad looking at all, piquing my interest. She was almost dressed in a short skirt and tight top, and knew that she had the figure to show them off. I suppose the fishy blonde was good looking in a kind of sleek way, but the girl did all the talking.

'I'm Annette, this is De Bourbon, before you think wrong thoughts about us, he is my employer.' That takes the biscuit I thought. The name, though stirred some thoughts in my mind.

'You own an art gallery here in Glasgow,' I said. 'Yet your forebears are French and English. Your father is the head of a corporation dealing in industrial diamonds. He is also a patron of the arts.'

'Hence the reason for my gallery,' said De Bourbon inclining his head a little in my direction. You seem to know a great deal about my business Mr George.'

'You can call me Henry or Harry if you want,' I said.

'We need your professional help,' said Annette.

'That's what I'm here for.' I said, glad that there was a desk between us so something else that was growing besides my curiosity was not showing. 'What is your problem?'

'Our problem,' said the brunette, 'is that someone is marketing fakes of our paintings,' Once more my mum's adage came to me and I favoured her with a tight smile. 'Jim Hoyt is having his work devalued by an art forger,' she said.

'Who the hell is Jim Hoyt?' I asked. The girl and her boss glanced at each other.

'I think we should show you something before you accept the case,' she said, which is why in less than ten minutes we were walking down Argyll Street to the relatively new gallery. I didn't tell either of them that I had only known about De Bourbon as the gallery was self-titled because I had a feed on my computer that told me when any new businesses were opening in the local area. Sometimes, and I can't stress this enough, some of these new enterprises were a short-lived cover for certain other enterprise, and the local authorities needed my services to help them if they were under stress and wanted information to uncover what was really going on. It saved bringing in the police enough for them to give me a retainer, my only regular income. It wasn't a great deal of money, but it paid the rent.

The gallery was on par with many of those private ones I had seen in Glasgow in that it was housed in a building that had not been designed for that purpose, made of red sandstone, built in the 19th century, originally offices for an insurance company. The doors, though, were made of silvered glass and evidently a new addition. Given that this was Glasgow they were protected by steel roller shutters at night. The sign above the doors proclaimed the words 'De Bourbon Gallery,' in a colour so crimson it made blood look pale in comparison. This was obviously a man who believed in putting his name where his mouth was.

Once through the doors there was a reception area manned by a young lady who was only marginally less attractive that Annette, and a curving passage inlaid in a honey-coloured wood that looked as if it was terribly expensive, it was obvious that no money was being spared here.

I know we're not supposed to judge by appearances, but it seemed to me that the current De Bourbon was not the kind of person who could conceptualise the processes needed for it to be built. He appeared, if I can be so cheeky; to be as dim as a three watt bulb, one of the old-fashioned bayonet ones, not even a modern LED.

Mind you, as Annette strode on and we entered the gallery proper, I expected the walls to be festooned with the kind of twattery, if I can coin a phrase that seems to pass for art these days. I can't claim the be an expert, but when I see a pile of bricks artfully piled up on the floor, or a section of New York paving, square, cut up and hung on steel cables against the wall, I begin to feel slightly defrauded.

But what do I know?

It just seems to me that literally anything can pass for art as long as the so-called artist is confident enough. Therefore as we rounded the corner that led to the main gallery I expected to see more of the kind of rubbish that a fond parent would refuse to put on their fridge even if it had been painted by their favourite child. Instead, the first thing I came across was a composition by Picasso from his blue period. It was a work that showed a mother holding a child in such a way that it was a blatant parody of 'Madonna and Child,' but of course Picasso was Spanish and Catholic in upbringing. The gallery was fairly dimly lit, but each painting had one of those little, filtered strip lights above to show their facets clearly.

I moved on reluctantly and looked at the next painting, another Picasso, this time a female nude, but Cubist. The next painting was far bigger, taking up a huge space, all dribbles, squiggles in various colours, but with something at the core, clearly recognisable as a Jackson Pollock. I managed to close my mouth at this point, realising that I was giving a better fish impression than young Mr De Bourbon. To cut the story short, I saw paintings by Picasso, Pollock, Modigliani, Andy Warhol, Van Gogh and Renoir amongst others. They were of a variety that you don't normally see with each other, a strikingly eclectic bunch.

'Come into my office,' said De Bourbon. They say comparisons are odious, but as he led me inside his inner sanctum I had to compare and contrast his office with mine. My box, on the third floor of a business unit in Wellington Street was about the size of the atrium beside his reception desk, when three people were inside it was crowded. I had room for a desk, a mini fridge and a kettle. His 'office' on the other had could have housed a fairly large Scottish Pipe Band with room enough for them to march around in a circle. I imagined it was a place where he would do his business deals with those purchasing the incredible art displayed just a short distance from where we were standing. The price of the carpet on which we stood would have paid my rent for more than a year. He had his own bar, for God's sake!

'Drink?' asked De Bourbon, moving imperceptibly towards the bar. Annette flashed him a warning look and I had a feeling that if she let him he would indulge in this particular activity all day. Once more I began to ponder on their relationship.

'Scotch please, malt if possible,' I said. He drifted off to pour the drinks — plural of course because he clearly asked because he wanted one. While he did so, Annette brought me up to date.

'You've seen our collection,' she said, 'what do you think?'

'Marvellous,' I answered, 'first time I've seen an exhibition that impressed me for quite a while.'

'What are your thoughts?'

'You must be displaying them only; they can't possibly be for sale.'

'Why would you say that?'

'Well, they're clearly forgeries.'

'You remember we mentioned James Hoyt earlier, Harry?'

'Aye, that I do.'

'Well they're his creations.'

'First of all, for one man to do this kind of work, he must have been some kind of genius, and secondly the same point applies.'

'You're wrong,' said Annette just as De Bourbon, ironically named considering what was in his hand, returning with a soft drink for his assistant and two glasses of whisky. I thanked him and took a sip of my drink. It was one of the finest malts I had ever tasted, I doubt if it was less than thirty years old. Opulent like his gallery, office, and Annette.

'I knew Jim,' said De Bourbon, who was in his late thirties, I gauged. 'He was quite a man. Took on the entire art establishment.'

'How did you get to know him?' I asked.

'He sold my father a painting,' said De Bourbon, 'essentially a Whistler, actually a Jim Hoyt original.'

'You gave me a hint of what's going on,' I said. 'This Jim Hoyt is a forger and he, or someone connected with him has done something that's worried the hell out of you, but that can't be it, given what I've seen.'

'I'll explain,' said De Bourbon coldly — just like a fish — 'Jim Hoyt started out in this very city over forty years ago. He was a graduate of the Glasgow School of Art, a building designed by the venerated Charles Rennie Mackintosh which is sadly in a ruinous state due to the major fire a few years ago. You can explain in greater detail Annette.' He did not really unbend a great deal towards me. I sensed he really was a cold man, but perhaps that had a great deal to do with his father. It was a good guess, as I was to find out.

'Hoyt — Jim — couldn't catch a cold in this city,' said Annette. 'He tried to get exhibited as an artist and found that very few doors were open to him, so he got a job as an art researcher for the Glasgow branch of one of the big auction houses.'

'An art researcher?'

'It was his job,' said De Bourbon, 'to look into the background of paintings — his speciality — that came into the purview of such houses. That was where he met my father, who has a huge amount of property in Scotland, and who collects art.'

'I see the connection,' I said, 'so he offered to paint in the style of — whoever — and your dear old dad gave him the patronage he so sorely needed.'

'I'm afraid not,' said De Bourbon, 'what he did was more than a little heinous.'

'I'll take over,' said Amanda. 'No, in fact Hoyt sold De Bourbon senior an original Whistler, Girl by a Pond, unsigned, that had been overlooked in the stock of a Glasgow art clearing house.'

'I'm getting this,' I said.

'It was a steal, Jim said he couldn't authenticate it, but if it was real it was worth a great deal more than he was asking for — in this case ten thousand pounds.'

'Which my father paid,' interrupted junior. 'And which painting he authenticated with one or two so-called 'experts'.'

'The trouble was,' said Annette, 'after a short while Jim sold a few more paintings to other collectors, a couple of Whistlers, a small Picasso, and a Vermeer. It all began to seem a little unlikely. He used the money to become a full-time artist, but again nobody wanted his work — so he kept his job as a researcher.'

'He slipped up,' said De Bourbon flatly, 'as most unsophisticated people do, and ended up with a three year jail sentence for forgery.'

'When he came out he approached Mr De Bourbon senior with a proposition.'

'My father, he's a genius at spotting opportunities. By then though, he had serious heart problem, treated with digitalis, so he asked me to run the new business.' By the law of averages there had to be at least one person in the family capable of such things because Junior sure as hell didn't have the brainpower to do much more than float around looking high and mighty and supercilious. I had the feeling the senior member of the family was still holding the reins while looking after his health.

'Jim was many years into his career by then,' pointed out the girl, 'and he also pointed out that his first sale was not the bargain the buyer thought it was. Mr De Bourbon could have had him hauled back to jail, but business is business.'

'I don't see how it can be,' I said, 'Hoyt is obviously a genius, but selling forgeries is illegal.'

'That,' said Annette gently, 'is where you're wrong. Passing off forgeries as genuine is illegal, but you can copy as many pictures as styles as you want and nobody can do a thing.'

'I still don't see why a person who had been duped would take up with a forger.'

'By then — it was about twenty years ago, my father spotted that Hoyt was prolific.' Said De Bourbon. 'Hoyt could knock one of his paintings out in five days. An average of one a week. Also, at the time he was notorious, he became known as the 'forger's forger,' giving tips to others who wanted to paint in the same style as various old master. Father is a business genius. He killed two birds with one stone. Instead of sending Hoyt back to prison he offered a chance to sell his paintings from his own website, and make connections with some very rich men.'

'I know rich people are not sentimental,' I said, 'so it wasn't respect for the artist that kept him from the arms of the law.'

'No,' said Annette, 'it was economics. It was the old Capitalist paradigm of supply and demand. You see there are a lot of boardrooms around the world, and tons of space on the walls of said boardrooms. With an original Jim Hoyt you could have a Picasso or Vermeer or a Van Gogh lookalike on your walls and no-one would be any wiser, for a fraction of the cost, yet each individual painting making the seller a profit of ten thousand pounds and more. A Jim Hoyt version of such artists became a very desirable item indeed.'

'The trouble is, someone, somewhere is now ripping off Jim Hoyt,' said De Bourbon. 'We need you to find the source and get them to stop. You don't need to stop them; we'll bring the law to bear on that once you find out who it is.'

This was a supreme irony; the work of a forger was being forged.

'Sounds like the job for me,' I said, finishing my whisky and casually turning the glass over in my hand, angling, visually as it were, for another. 'So when do I get to meet the artist?' I realised that they were both staring at me with sober expressions.

'You can't,' said Annette, 'you see Jim Hoyt died shortly after the opening of this gallery.'

*****

I was out on the street away from the strange couple, my mind filled with thoughts. In the office, my host deftly hooked the whisky glass out of my hand, it was plain that the job interview (surprise, that's what it really was!) had ended. I was hoping to meet them both again, De Bourbon for my wages, and Annette because — well she was young, attractive and intelligent. I felt uncommonly drawn to her. She exuded a powerful force that young women have in droves; with the added factor that she was obviously a strong woman. I like that.

They were not the least interested in looking at the death of their artist. From what they had said already I guessed that they already had hundreds if not thousands of paintings by their star forger. They wouldn't be running out of revenue for a long time.

I immediately went back to my office and switched on my somewhat battered computer and searched for all the information I could find about Jim Hoyt. Then I discovered a documentary on YouTube call 'See you Jimmy — the man who fooled the experts,' in which I finally got to see the man of the moment. Jim turned out to be a wiry little Glaswegian whom you wouldn't have looked at twice in the street, except with his scruffy grey clothing you might suspect he had a drink problem.

When I saw him in his studio it was a revelation. He would prop up a poster, postcard or photo of some famous painting, and then he would compose a piece in the style of that painter, but not an exact copy. I know that time can be telescoped in these documentaries, but it was clear that in real time, with previous preparation, he could produce a superb piece of art. I liked him, he had the whiskery look of a peppery little terrier, laughed and talked incessantly while painting and had a cheerful outlook on life despite the obvious rejections he had suffered. He would pause now and then, and take a hearty swig from a bottle of tonic wine created by monks in Devon.

He was a real character.

It made me sad to think I would never get to meet him in the flesh. That kind of homework was over.

I didn't have time to think any more about Jim, at least not right now. Instead I concentrated on sales from various art auctions here in Scotland and elsewhere in the country with the sole intention of finding out when and where Jim Hoyt 'originals' were being sold. It wasn't a hard thing to do, just a little soul-destroying and tedious.

I searched for about a week. Not surprisingly the person who had bought a 'Jim Hoyt,' 'Picasso,' was not exactly forthcoming with me, but I soldiered on and was able to find where it had been purchased.

A pattern soon emerged — that is what humans beings are by the way, we're pattern recognising machines, designed that way by nature. Given this, it wasn't too long before I was waiting in Central Station for a train down to London. Again, time consuming and tedious, but luckily I had been given a couple of thousand pounds upfront by Annette. She hadn't actually handed me the money, but simply used my name, sort code and account number to pay the cash into my account. Along with rent and other expenses the money wouldn't last long, but to me that wasn't a real issue as I hoped to get the whole thing cleared up in a couple of days.

You may think everything could have been conducted via the internet and Zoom or Teams, and it is quite possible to do that kind of thing these days because most auctions are conducted online as well as in person these days, but for most of my work there is nothing that beats being there in person. On the odd occasion this has led me to being beat up, person, but these are the chances we take in life.

On the journey down I read up on the lives of the famous art forgers such as Ketteridge. It seemed to me that these were people who were not so much greedy as bitter that their talents had not been recognised. Most of them ended up in jail at one time or another. One American forger, Mark Landis, got round this by creating non-attributed works of art in the style of American Gothic and others, dressing up as a priest and going around donating the works to museums. He never claimed the works were from this painter or that, he simply presented them as something he wanted to hand on for posterity, but the scary thing was that nine times out of ten the museums accepted the 'originals' at face value.

When I got to London this was not my final stopping off point. I changed trains at one of the large stations and travelled to sunny Wiltshire and an exclusive auction house in Salisbury. I am deliberately not giving names of particular firms here. The owners of such places are notoriously tetchy and I don't want to give them a chance to sue. Suffice it to say that once I settled down in my hotel room, I sallied out to watch the auction and see the bidding wars in action. I had always pictured these places as being dusty, musty and a little bit sad. Instead what I got was a modern, well-lit room with large windows looking out to a manicured lawn comfortable seating, and a stage that could have been designed for a theatrical performance, which in a sense I suppose it was.

I deliberately came in early because I wanted to get a sense of the place. I noted that many of those around me were well-dressed but not opulent. The place stank of invisible money. These people did not wear their prosperity on their collective sleeve; it was just in their whole attitude and their sense of entitlement.

The auctioneer was a tall, sleek lady who introduced herself as Portia, of course. There wouldn't be many people around here called Senga or Lisa. She started and performed the ritual with practised ease, giving the reserve price for each item concerned, and withdrawing those that didn't meet the reserve. Then the item I had been looking for was carried on stage, it was an almost identical copy of the 'Blue Lady' that I had seen in the De Bourbon gallery just a couple of days before. 'We have,' said Portia, 'an original Jim Hoyt in the style of Pablo Picasso. May we start the bidding at ten thousand pounds?'

Eventually the painting fetched just over one hundred thousand pounds, sold to a tweedy gentleman who looked as if shooting game might be one of his hobbies. To say I was astonished would be an understatement, but if this was the kind of money a Jim Hoyt 'original,' could fetch, no wonder the gallery were so protective of their dead protégé.

Then came the tricky bit.

At the social gathering afterwards, I approached Portia. I was wearing my best suit but her whole demeanour made me feel as if I was something that had been scraped off a pavement.

'I need to ask about the 'style of' painting I said, in my most polite Glasgow accent, which to a Southerner probably sounds like a dog barking in their face.

'Yes, how can I help you?' she asked, looking as if she would rather be anywhere else than speaking to me.

'Well you see, I'm here on behalf of the estate of the late Mr Hoyt, I'm his nephew, because as you know he never married, and I'm writing a book about him, I'd just like to speak to anyone who might have known him, and this seemed like an interesting lead. I will, of course mention you and the auction house in the book.' She perked up at this, very few people, I have discovered, are immune to flattery.

'I'd just like to know who sold the painting and a few details about them,' I said. 'It won't take long to get an interview for my book.' She took me into her inner sanctum and looked up a few details, the ones on public record. She had no real reason to refuse because it was a public sale. The only thing she didn't give me was the full address and phone number, but I was able to get these easily enough through social media. The seller was a Ms Elizabeth Adams, a local lady, who lived in her own cottage in the wilds of Wiltshire, which truth to tell are not exactly wild. I decided I had to stay for another day or so and prepare for my visit.

I was not foolish enough to speak to Ms Adams directly, at least not at first; instead I went to the area. Being used to the mean streets of Glasgow, (only joking my fellow Weegies, Glasgow is beautiful and stunning) I was not used to how wonderfully rural Wiltshire is and was. I had to travel out in my hire car past cottages with thatched roofs (you don't get many of those in Scotland,) and detached mansions of all sorts. It was a rural environment where, as far as I was concerned, ordinary people could not afford to live.

At last I found a lane that led, or so my navigation system informed me, led to the Old Gamekeeper's Cottage, which was where Ms Adams lived. I parked the car, wishing that I had invested in a pair of wellies, and went for a little walk. It wasn't long before I found the cottage tucked nicely out of site amid some woodlands.

This was a foreign, isolated atmosphere to me. I was used to bustling streets and the comings and goings of a large city. Out here I would have freaked out at the slightest noise, but at least the isolation both helped and hampered me in one of the principle tasks of a private investigator.

I walked straight past the building on the other side where I was shaded by the woodland and slipped into the woods on her side further on. England has a different law of trespass from Scotland, I imagined I was breaking all sorts of law as I found the back of the cottage. Every footstep felt like a thump, I could hear my own clothes rustle as I walked, and the crack of twigs under my feet. I was sure any resident of the cottage would be alerted instantly to my presence.

In the garden I found a garden room made of some robust wood-textured material that was not actual timber.

Still on constant alert, with the hair on the back of my neck standing up, I walked around the building, finding what I was looking for at last, a large picture window facing the south. I cursed, then, letting out an involuntary 'fuck' before restraining my Celtic temper. The curtains were closed. Luckily, though, people are less diligent than they think they are and the curtains had a chink in them. (No, I am not going to come out with that old racist joke.) I pressed my face up against the glass and managed to look into the shadowy interior, seeing enough to confirm my suspicions.

That was when I heard the car arriving.

A few hours later I turned up at the red front door of the cottage. Earlier I had fled the scene as the sound of the dying engine cut through the woods. Breathing heavily, and suppressing panic, I had hidden in the woodland along from the cottage, waiting until I heard the person slamming the very door in front of which I was standing before making my escape. Now I was here, I knocked and a middle-aged, fair haired woman appeared. I showed her my press badge. This wasn't a fake, I'm a stringer for The Glasgow Times.

'Ms Adams? Henry George. I'm here to follow up a story about our own Jim Hoyt.'

'Come in,' she said, 'but be warned, I have CCTV inside and out.' She didn't, I'd already checked.

Once we got settled with the obligatory cup of tea and a biscuit, I asked her some fairly direct questions.

'How come a lady living in rural Wiltshire happens to be selling paintings by a glorified street peddler from Govan in Glasgow?'

'Don't let the accent fool you,' she said, 'I'm ethnically Scottish, my parents moved about a lot when I was young, so I picked up this accent, but I lived in Glasgow for ten years. Jim was my tutor at the Glasgow School of Art when I was eighteen. We fell in love with each other. He made me presents of some of his paintings. Now that he's passed on I'm selling the ones I have.'

'When was the last time you saw him?'

'It was quite a few years ago, we lost touch when I moved back down south with my family. I know I'm making money from his death, but in a way I see it as a way of perpetuating his memory.'

'Where do you keep his paintings? And can I see them? Being a Glasgow boy I'm a bit of a fan.'

'I have a garden room, but it's up to date and air conditioned, I have storage racks. As for seeing them, it's not a good time, I would have to unlock and open up the sliding racks and I have other things to do.'

We chatted a little bit more about Jim, and then I closed my notebook.

'Well, I think I have enough to go on, thanks for the interview Ms Adams, this is big news up North.' She narrowed her eyes as she looked at me.

'You came all the way for this interview? That seems a bit strange.'

'Oh no, far from it,' I said, 'I'm on holiday, visiting relatives, and when my editor found out I was down here he asked me to cover the story.' She was appeased by this and we parted on good terms, I was quite happy to lie to Ms Adams, because she lied through her pearly teeth to me. Tit for tat.

Luckily I had brought my Canon Coolpix with me, a discreet little camera that had backed me up many times. It was the work of a few minutes for me to get online back at the hotel and send the story to my contacts along with a few photos. It hadn't taken long to write, or to extract and send the peek-a-boo photos of the studio interior I had taken through the slight gap in the curtain. Just to complete the process

I sent the same details to Portia at the auction house. The whole thing would be a lesson for cheats and liars everywhere.

After that I made a hasty retreat. The woman I'd been interviewing could possibly make enquiries on her own behalf and I didn't want to receive a visit from her agents on her behalf, because it was clear that she was not working alone.

As I went back up on the train I thought about what I had seen. The picture I'd managed to get showed a proper artist's studio complete with several large easels, stacks of blank canvases, paints, but most telling of all, a half-completed painting on one of said easels. The image was the second one I had seen when entering the gallery, which argued that she had been there a few times over the last few weeks taking her own digital records. Truth to tell, that was where she was slipping up. Jim Hoyt was quite brilliant, he never did the same painting twice, and every painting was suggested by and composed from multiple images, rather than being a forgery of a particular image.

I was triumphant, this one job alone would make me enough money to live on for the next year or so even including rent and other expenses. I might even be able to get a couple of weeks off and get to Spain on a package tour.

However, arriving back in Glasgow, I did not immediately go and visit my temporary employers; instead I visited the South Side of Glasgow and went to where Jim Hoyt had made his final trip to meet his maker. It turned out he lived in an old-style terraced house in Strathbungo, which in today's market would be worth quite a lot of money. No-one was around so I made my way to the back of the building, the back door and inside the house. From what I had learned it was only a few weeks after he had died so the house wouldn't even be on the market. You see I have a ridiculous theory that you can learn a lot about a person by their surroundings. It was easy enough to get into the building since picking locks is one of my skills. I had a good look round, made a few observations and went home.

*****

Sometimes you need time to process facts and figures you have learned, so it wasn't until midday that I found myself outside the gallery. Annette and De Hoyt were waiting for me in the office. I was not slow to notice the unopened bottle of champagne and the three glasses on his desk. Celebration time I thought. Ironic really.

'Congratulations Harry,' said Annette warmly. She still looked as beautiful as before but I was unaffected. A snake can be beautiful. De Bourbon was more reserved but he still managed to contort his face into something resembling a smile, and the pair of them shook my hand in turn. De Bourbon had a limp grip as I expected, carrying the fish resemblance to his actions, but Annette's handshake was as firm and strong as my own. She really was a stunner in every way; it was a pity, really.

'We've already paid the money into your account,' said the girl. 'You're self-employed I presume? So you can sort out your own taxes.'

'How was the artist going about her business?' asked De Bourbon.

'In much the same way as Hoyt,' I said. 'A consortium of interested buyers set her up with the cottage and the facilities and she promised to work with them. Very methodical she was too, she had a pile of prepared canvases, and she was working on the next copy, the image she was working on pinned to a board. If her work had gone unchallenged then she would, I presume have made a good living, while those benefiting from her gifts would have made a great deal more. Have you alerted the police yet?'

'That's not going to happen,' said Annette quickly.

'What?' I was somewhat staggered by this. People who aid and abet the commission of crimes that gain a hundred thousand pounds at a time are usually reported and punished.

'My people have had a word with those concerned. The lady in question folded quite quickly when she learned that a prison sentence was quite possible given the circumstances, she gave the businessmen away.'

'It turns out that they were associates of Mr De Bourbon senior,' said Annette. 'They have been informed that the sale of original Jim Hoyt creations will be tightly controlled in future, even the ones that are out back on the market. In addition they have paid back the money to the auction house, who has accepted the return with no questions asked. Thankfully the new owner had not yet taken possession of their property. It was a large, local landowner, and when they found out the circumstances they too were quite happy to take back their cash.'

'All tied up in a neat little bow,' I said. 'So word never gets out to the newspapers and there's no hint of a scandal anywhere, and the art world looks as if it's pristine. The whole thing stinks worse than a dead kipper that's been lying around for weeks.'

'That's all very well,' said De Bourbon, 'but before we part, we've arranged a little celebration, to raise a glass to your efforts. With the Hoyt market sealed we stand to make a lot of money.'

'You may want to take a slight pause your celebrations,' I said even as Annette was going over to open the bottle of Brut. She stopped and they both stared at me.

'You might like to know that I have been looking into the circumstances around the death of Jim Hoyt. He'd had rheumatic fever while under the tender care of Her Majesty's Penal Authority — as it was at the time — and the one thing this does is to weaken the heart.'

'Yes, that's what led to his death.'

'Oh I've read the coroner's report, it was all settled very quickly, wasn't it Annette?'

'It was an open and shut case, he hadn't been seen for a few days, I went around and checked on him, and he was dead in his studio. It was a shock,' said the girl soberly.

'Yes, and of course his estate was settled quite quickly. He had a couple of siblings, and they got his fairly substantial savings, but he left all his paintings to the De Bourbon corporation, hadn't he, Annette?' Her employer looked at her tellingly but gave a slight nod of the head. He wasn't as daft as he looked, mind you that would have been difficult.

'Jim didn't really own his paintings, we funded him, paid for all his materials, bought his house, and in return he willed his paintings to the gallery.'

'This is why you killed him Annette, with instructions from Mr De Bourbon to do so.' They both drew back from me as if I had threatened them with a gun, which I suppose I had done so, the metaphorical smoking gun.

'Get out of here,' said De Bourbon tightly.

'Don't you want to know what I've found out?' I said casually. I had them there; the implied threat of ejecting me from the premises was suddenly withdrawn merely by my continued presence. They say you should know your enemy, and all at once I was theirs.

'It doesn't make sense,' said the fish man, 'why would we kill the goose that lays the golden eggs?'

'Hoyt made money for us,' said Annette tightly, pointing out the obvious.

'I thought about that as I was searching his house for evidence,' I said, 'then the answer occurred to me. Sunflowers.'

'You are mad,' said De Bourbon.

'When Vincent Van Gogh was alive he was practically giving his paintings away for food and materials. When he was dead his work increased in value exponentially. Despite being a copyist — which he wasn't, quite, and a forger, which he wasn't either, not really because all his work was original but based on particular styles — Jim Hoyt is famous in the art world. A Jim Hoyt original is worth money and worth even more money now that he's dead. A Jim Hoyt 'Picasso,' has already jumped to four times the original price.'

'Even if this murder accusation was true,' said Annette, now smiling and extremely calm, 'which of course it isn't, you can't prove a thing.'

'That's where you're wrong,' I said, 'you see Jim had a habit of leaving his old tonic wine bottles around the studio, you came in and disposed of them when he died, didn't you? The problem was, you don't know the habits of drinkers, and I do. I suspected that when you made Jim a 'present' of four bottles of tonic wine, he would have stashed them away and finished the ones he already had in the studio. Upon his death you came in and cleared away half a dozen bottles.'

'I deny that,' said Annette.

'Of course you do,' I said absently, 'but you see his tonic wine was an integral part of his life. I searched the house and found his stash under a loose floorboard — and three intact full bottles of tonic wine were there. You see, with his weakened heart it only took one bottle of the doctored wine to kill him. He suffered a seizure and fell down, striking his head on a bench on the way down, an added bonus from your point of view, meaning he was unconscious and could not call for help.'

'This is speculative nonsense,' said De Bourbon.'

'Is it?'

'We can prosecute you for breaking and entering,' said Annette.

'No you can't, I was able to get a contract from you when all this started, giving me full permission to investigate Jim's case, including powers to investigate premises. I have printed out our agreement.'

'Get out,' said De Bourbon.'

'The remaining wine is being analysed as I speak. I think we'll find the presence of digitalis,' I said. 'Your mistake, Annette, was in thinking you had found all the bottles you had given him, when really some were purchased on his own. You were smug and a little careless, thinking you had committed the perfect crime. I've no doubt your fingerprints will be found on the bottles concerned. The prosecution will make a great deal of that particular fact.'

'Get out,' roared De Bourbon, losing all patience.'

'It was his idea,' said Annette, dropping all pretence.

'Shut up,' said her employer.

'No, you were the one who worked out that Jim was a step above being a wino. It was you who got the medicine from your father's cabinet, and it was you who put it into the wine — because that's what your father does, isn't it, only in the small does that help him. You made me do it.'

'Goodbye,' I said at that point, leaving the building just as the police were arriving to investigate the murder of a talented and unique man with whom I had formed a bond despite never meeting him in real life.

The List
Roly Andrews

Steve's twin was an arse; always was, always would be. Born first, and first in everything ever since. He was the most competitive and selfish man alive. Steve hated him.

"There's sibling rivalry in every family," his wife Donna once told him, "You need to get over yourself. Grow up and move on. Brothers are evil; you should know that. And, as for twins, well…."

That might be true, but it didn't change the fact that Steve's brother was an arse, working a job reserved especially for the biggest arses. No, he wasn't a bus or train driver. He wasn't a weather forecaster or cladding salesman: he was a detective. A friggin homicide detective to boot. Arsehole job for an arsehole man!

Steve hated his job, but it was all he'd ever known. He was a ketchup salesman. He had other lines, of course, but his bread and butter was ketchup. He worked for The Great Kiwi Ketchup Kompany, famous for *"putting the joy on saveloys."* How he hated that expression! It was even emblazoned all over his sales rep Station Wagon. Painted white panels with a giant pink saveloy lazing on top, liberally drizzled with thick red ketchup. Whenever he drove anywhere, especially in small-town New Zealand, people would point and stare, kids would wave enthusiastically, and vegetarians would turn their heads in disgust.

Travelling the length and breadth of New Zealand was the only decent thing about his job. He would be away weeks at a time, which suited him well. Since Donna's tragic death five years ago, he was a free agent, had no responsibilities. He could come and go as he pleased, where and whenever he wanted.

While Steve was peddling ketchup, his brother James built an impressive career and reputation in homicide. Arguably, he was the most famous detective in the country. *What an arse,* Steve thought.

Steve had just got back from three weeks on the road. As usual, the air in the house was stale and foul; he opened the windows to let some fresh air in. He put a load of washing on and made a coffee. Sales were good this month; he'd blitzed his target, so decided to take the afternoon off. After his coffee, he decided to ring his mate Inky.

"Hey Inky, it's Steve-O; you got any free slots this arvy?"

"You want your usual?"

"Yeah, if you can fit me in, that'd be brilliant!"

"Come round at about six; bring some cold ones with you. I'll be thirsty by then. You might have to wait while I finish a job, but I'll fit you in, no worries."

Steve smiled. It'd been a while since he'd seen Inky. It'd be good to catch up.

At 6 pm, Steve walked into Inky's. A blonde with beautiful long hair was lying face down on the table, denim shorts, nice legs. She wore a half-corset bra, and Steve hoped she'd roll over.

Inky was a professional. He didn't look up when the door opened: one hand remained on the tattoo gun, the other gripped the woman's right butt cheek. A rolly fag dangled perilously low, clenched between thin tobacco-stained lips.

"Grab a seat, mate," he called through his pursed mouth. "Nearly done here."

Inky's tattoo gun hammered away at the woman's silky skin. The noise was intoxicating, *clack, clack, clack,* a million times a minute; how he loved that sound. The woman's fingers were blood free white, scrunched into tight fists. Steve could see muscles twitching in her forearms and biceps. She was in pain—he liked that too. Steve pondered, *Tramp stamps; why do women do it?*

These days most tattoo parlours are sterile clinics full of light and green plants. The walls covered in Rothko prints or Warhol-inspired soup tins. Steve couldn't stand soup, and he hated modern art. He also hated the hell out of accent lighting. Thank God Inky was old school.

Inky's Squid Pistol was not a clinic; it was not a parlour or studio. Fuck no! It was a dive, pure and simple. Calling it a grotto would insult grottos, so as Steve sat down in the waiting room on a wobbly and sticky school chair, he decided 'den' was the most appropriate word. It inferred danger, something sinister. After all, if there wasn't the risk of sepsis or hepatitis, then you couldn't call it a tattoo.

The black skulls, snakes and dragons adorning the walls were fierce, yet they were somehow softened by rich ruby roses and arrow-pierced hearts pumping thick spurts of red blood. Macabre tributes to mum never looked so right. It was good to be back. Inky's rum-infused tobacco smoke choked the air and diluted the light. Steve smiled: not the slightest whiff of bleach or disinfectant. He cracked a beer, leant back and closed his eyes. The beer tasted good, and the gun sounded alluring; the only thing missing were squeals of pain. He wanted to tell Inky to dig a little deeper. That would make things perfect.

"So, you want your usual?" Inky called out, disturbing Steve's thoughts.

"Yeah."

"Name?"

"Gina."

Inky went silent as his gun roared into attack mode again. *Clack, clack, clack.*

Inky's was hidden out the back of a dishevelled warehouse in the oldest part of the port. You could never stumble on the den; it was strictly invite-only or word of mouth. Advertising and social media were foreign languages to Inky. It was his reputation that brought the punters in.

His clientele were thugs, crims, sailors and bikers. To see a woman here was unusual. To see an attractive young one, a rarity. It was rumoured that Inky was a dealer, that he fenced electronics for the gangs. *A man's gotta make a living somehow.* Perhaps the woman was tied in with that side of the business.

The gun suddenly stopped. Inky wiped away plasma, blood and excess dye with a giant swipe. He slapped the woman's butt.

"All done, it'll give your boyfriend an even nicer view now. Wanna have a look?" He pointed to the smudged and dusty mirror standing out the back.

As she stood, she saw Steve checking things out.

"Nah," she said emphatically.

She quickly pulled on a black tee shirt and was out of the door in an instant.

"Nice," Steve said to Inky.

He smiled. "The tattoo or the girl?"

Steve raised his eyes, smiled back.

"Gina, it is, then; take your shirt off, jump up on the table. Oh, and bring a can over for me."

Inky liked inflicting pain; he believed that by inflicting pain on people, he could absolve their sins. He preferred the term '**pain**ting' rather than tattooing, and he loved **pain**ting Steve, for he knew he needed more absolution than most.

"So, how was Gina, Steve?"

"A damp squib, mate, all bluster, no blow. Promised way more than she delivered."

"Disappointing for you."

"Yep, complete and utter disappointment."

"So, where've you been lately, ketchup man?"

"Piss off, Inky. You know I hate that name!"

"Okay then, Steve-O, where've you been recently?"

"Everywhere, I was up north, mate, Waikato. Huntly, Cambridge, Hamilton. Sales were good, always are up there."

"And how's that arsehole brother of yours?"

Steve's body stiffened. "What do you think?"

Inky just smiled, ploughing on with the job.

Ten minutes later, the den's door burst open.

"Sorry," a woman's voice called. "I forgot my handbag."

The door slammed closed a moment later. Inky didn't look up; he just dug a little deeper with his gun.

Six Months Later

Detective Superintendent James O'Sullivan stared at the file. Another homicide. He flicked through its pages: no murder weapon, no witnesses, no forensic evidence. What the hell was he supposed to do with this?

The deceased, Miss Gina Brunning, was strangled—no sign of a struggle, no evidence of sexual assault. Found fully clothed in her flat, there was no forced entry, no evidence of a burglary gone wrong. James shook his head; the woman was a nobody—although he meant that in the nicest way. No one could possibly want to harm this model citizen— it was another murder mystery.

The file had been sent up from the Hamilton Bureau. Their investigation had gone cold. They'd worked it solidly for six months without developing a single lead. They sent it to him in the hope he might be able to crack it open. *Fat chance*, James thought, throwing the file on top of a growing list of cold cases.

Over the last five years, there'd been a statistical spike in the murder rate. This coincided with increased gang activities and the repatriation of 501s from Australia; but murders from these catchments were predictable and easy to solve. Paint by numbers detective work: gather forensics, interview witnesses, press associates, force a confession, and *bim, bash, bom!* Before you knew it, you had a conviction and a perp put away.

No, the growing list of cold cases and unsolved murders was alarming. The victims were all random, good folk—people who should not have been murdered. Now he was tasked to solve these crimes.

This afternoon James compiled a list. Since 2017, seventeen murders remained unsolved, and their files were now collecting dust on his desk. He gulped down his cold coffee and grimaced; there was nothing as unsatisfying and bitter as cold coffee and cold cases. Then, he stared at the list again.

Ella Bromley, aged 28, Auckland
Iris Marshall, aged 59, Whakatane
Josie Butcher, aged 17, Dunedin
Keni Sharp, aged 63, Bulls
Mona Cotton, aged 40, Greymouth
Neil Frisk, aged 71, Taupo
Rita Keene, aged 82, Waikanae
Tino Rodriguez, aged 22, Whanganui
Vicky Dukes, aged 36, Blenheim
Gretel Saville, aged 17, Tauranga
Howard Heke, aged 39, Twizel
Ana Packer, aged 46, Kaikoura
Lucas Ngwaka, aged 78, Hastings
Ruby Stent, aged 29, Manukau City
Cody McCain, aged 62, Invercargill
Eva Adams, aged 31, Palmerston North
Gina Brunning, aged 20, Hamilton

Was there a connection, or were they random? James was in two minds. One part of his mind wanted to believe they were random, a statistical aberration, but that would mean seventeen unknown murderers were now walking the streets of New Zealand's towns and cities. If they were connected, or at least some were, it would mean a serial killer was running amuck, stalking the streets. What was worse? What was more likely?

He sat. He thought. After an hour, he deduced he should be looking for a serial killer. If the murders were a statistical aberration, why were they continuing? What was the chance of that? No, it was most likely that one person was responsible for some, if not all, of the murders. Even if a serial killer murdered only half of these people, James had to get the killer off the street as soon as possible before they killed again. So, what was the connection? Clearly, it was somebody free to travel around New Zealand—that's all he had.

The phone rang, disturbing his concentration.

He picked it up in frustration.

"O'Sullivan."

"Jim, it's Mack from OCU."

James smiled. He and Mack went way back; they'd worked together years ago, cracking the Morris Brothers' gang in Christchurch. The Morris Brothers were a couple of nasty right-wing skinheads bent on building a drug and crime empire in the garden city. Now, Mack headed up the Organised Crime Unit.

"Hey, Mack, nice to hear from you. How's Joyce and the kids?"

"Jeeze, Jim, for a clever guy, you don't keep up with the news, do you?"

"What do you mean?"

"Joyce has moved on, mate, left me."

"Oh shit, sorry, I had no idea… When did that happen?"

"Two years ago."

"Fuck me, sorry Mack, that long, oh God… We have to catch up more often."

"It's okay, Jim; she had good reason to leave."

"Oh, why's that, then?"

"I was knocking off Jenny from Traffic."

"Bloody hell, mate, I hope she was worth it; Joyce was a bloody good woman. Anyway, I'm sure you didn't ring for a social. What's up?"

"It's probably nothing, nothing at all, but have you started working the murder cold cases?"

"Yep, and 'probably nothing' is so much more than what I've got now. What is it?

"Well, The Black Daggers moved into Christchurch a year ago. The local gangs made them feel welcomed, as you can imagine, but despite this welcome, they've managed to carve out a decent-sized corner of the local drug market. There's been a glut of meth hitting the streets. Prices are low, and sales are high. Not good. My team and I have been working hard to identify the key players, put them away, put a dent in the trade."

"Okay," James said, "Yep, I heard about the turf wars. It doesn't surprise me about The Daggers, I've had the misfortune of crossing swords with them on a number of occasions."

"Yep, nice people. Anyway, my team arrested a low-level street dealer. She wouldn't talk, scared to death. She may have been working the streets, but she was a dead end when it came to signposting those above her. You know how it goes. We confiscated her phone as evidence, wanting to gain access to her contacts. And this is why I'm ringing you."

"You got me interested, Mack; go on."

"She'd taken a photo of a guy in a tattoo parlour. She didn't know him but thought he was a bit of a douche. She took the photo when she saw the guy had a whole bunch of names tattooed on his back."

"Sounds weird, but so what?"

"Yeah, yeah, nothing to see there, except…."

"Except what, Mack?"

"It's the names themselves: Lucas, Ruby, Cody, Eva. That was just on the right side of the guy's back. There are about another dozen names on the guy's left side. The woman won't talk, but it looks as though the tattoo on the guy's back was like a chronicle, a book of sorts. The names were listed like chapters, like a tablet from the Old Testament. I had the forensics lab look at the photo to see if they could blow it up and make it clearer. The photo was taken on a cheap phone, it was dark, and the phone didn't have a flash, but after jigging around, they could decipher two more names, Donna and Ella. It got me thinking, were the names some kind of trophy or remembrance?"

James sucked in air.

"I had no idea who belonged to these names, so I ran them through the police computer. That's led me to you. What do you think?"

"I think I'll jump on the first flight to Christchurch in the morning. Are you going to be around?"

The stewardess was far too young and pretty. Impossibly nice and impeccably dressed, she was precisely why most middle-aged businessmen preferred to fly. James O'Sullivan wasn't one of them. He'd been up all night trying to memorise every detail of the cold cases he was working on.

"Good morning, sir: 14b, halfway down the cabin on the right. Mind your head."

She smiled as she spoke. *Brown eyes like Josie Butcher*, James thought. She looked about 20 years old, the same age as Gina Brunning. Taking into account her half heels, she stood about 5.9, the same height as Vicky Dukes. He would play this game all the way down to Christchurch, picking out different passengers and mapping their characteristics against the files of the deceased. By the time he reached Christchurch in just over an hour, he would have cemented every detail he needed to know.

It was already blistering hot when Damien Macalester – Mack – picked James up from the airport. It was going to be a nor-west stinker—a day for ice-cold beer, swimming pools and air conditioning units.

Mack handed him a coffee as he arrived.

"It's strong and cold."

"Just the way I like it. Cheers, Mack. How's Jenny?"

"Who?"

"Jenny from Traffic."

"Oh, her… Ah, we're not together. It was just a short-term thing – kinda."

"You mean you trashed thirty years of marriage to a great woman for a fumble with a glorified parking maid?"

"Jeeze, give it a rest, Jim; who do you think you are, the police or something?"

Both men laughed.

"So, who's the guy with the tattoo?"

"Don't know, Jim?"

"Where was the photo taken?"

"The informant wouldn't say, but it's Inky's. I'd recognise that shithole anywhere. Do you remember him?"

"Far out, is that bastard still going? I thought the council or Ministry of Health would have closed him down years ago. Is he still walking both sides of the law?"

"Hah! Walking? I'd call it skipping or dancing. He's as crooked as a pug's tail."

"Wow, he's lucky he's still alive. You and I should have invested our Kiwi Saver into pharmaceuticals with all the drugs he's indulged in over the years."

They laughed again.

"Who's he running with these days?"

"Just the same… no one in particular, anyone who's gotta dollar. He's not too fussy."

"Is he still playing with the big dogs?"

"Nah! Since you put him away, Jim, he's a bit of a has-been. Eight years in Rimutaka shortened his curly tail, made him a bit cynophobic."

"Is that where we're going now?"

"There's nothing like the smell of grease and diesel first thing in the morning."

Jim smiled then grimaced after taking a plug of coffee.

"So, will you catch up with your brother while you're down here?"

"Not sure, Mack. Since Steve's wife died, he's been pretty cold to me. He doesn't want to know me. Something inside him snapped when she died. He's never been the same since."

"It's not easy losing your wife in any circumstance; hell knows, I know that better than anyone. She can't have been too old, how did she die?"

"It was the weirdest thing. Donna was always a bit different. Not my type, but each to their own, I suppose. She was a weather spotter!"

"A what?"

"In America, they call them storm-chasers. She was one of them!"

"Didn't even know they had them in New Zealand?"

"Oh yeah, they're a special breed. Donna was constantly glued to National Geographic and the Discovery Channel. Anyway, she drowned in a sea surge after chasing a massive storm. They never found her body, and Steve's never been the same. I feel sorry for him. Perhaps I will go and see him."

It was 8.45 am when the unmarked car pulled into the lane leading to Inky's. The lane was full of parked vehicles and skips chocka-block full of industrial waste. Driving down the narrow lane would be like playing dodgem cars, and finding a park almost impossible.

"Just park here, Mack; we can walk the rest of the way."

Inky lived in a small flat above his tattoo business. James remembered it well: a bedsit with a dilapidated kitchen and bathroom. The floors were rotten, the pipes leaky. It smelt bad. It smelt really bad! James expected Inky to be still comatose this early, and it would be a bugger rousing him from his slumber. He was wrong.

"What do you want? I'm closed," Inky yelled down the stairs when he heard the knock on the shop door.

James knocked again.

"Fuck off, ya wanker; I told you, I'm closed."

James and Mack smiled at each other before James called up. "Inky, how are you? It's your old mate James O'Sullivan; do you remember me?"

They expected silence or a volley of abuse, but the two detectives heard Inky frantically moving about upstairs.

"Making the place nice for us, doing some last-minute housework, putting things away," Mack said.

James replied, "Do you think he's getting the best china and biscuits for us?"

After a minute, Inky called down: "If you want a tattoo, come back after lunch. If you want anything else, you can fuck off."

"Charming," James yelled back. "Look, I know we have history, but I've got no interest in you. Not in the slightest. And I know you're not a narc, but I want to have a friendly chat about one of your clients. That's all. I can be gone in five minutes. Promise."

"Fuck off, cop."

"Oh, come on now, Inky, we both know how this works. We can have a quick, quiet chat now, or I can come back later with search and arrest warrants, then drag your sorry arse down to the station. I'm sure there are a thousand and one charges we could bring. But no one wants that. You might have drugs up there now – I'm not interested! You might have some stolen gear up there; not interested. Just let me in, have a chat, give me what I need, and you'll never see me again."

Three minutes later, the door opened.

"What do you want, arsehole?"

"A name."

"I'm not a narc."

"There was a man who came in here about six months ago. He had names tattooed on his back. Who is he?"

"You're the detective, you tell me; why don't you go and ask your mother?"

"Please help me out here, Inky; you don't have to give me a name, I understand. Just let me look at your appointment book."

"Don't have one; people walk in."

"Who is he, Inky? I'm asking nicely."

"Don't know anyone with names on their back."

"We've got a photo; you wanna have a look? It might jog your memory."

"Not particularly."

"Humour me… Mack, show him the photo."

Mack pulled the photo out of his internal breast pocket.

Inky looked, squinted.

"You see, that's you, that's your shop, and a guy is lying on your bench with names tattooed all over his back. Who the fuck is he, Inky?"

Inky scratched his head, then smiled. Staring Jim in the eyes, he spat, "No idea, you fucking arse."

Back in the car, Mack chuckled. "That went well."

"Didn't it! You got anything on him? Could you get some warrants?"

"Oh yeah. Low-level stuff, but enough to drag him in, piss him off."

"Great, could you do that today and then tomorrow ring the council? He's sure to have broken some bylaws. Get him inspected and shut down. Also, ring the Ministry of Health; once again, get him inspected and shut down. Let's put some pressure on the prick. Can we meet back at Inky's at 4 pm, so we can tell him what we've planned for him tomorrow? Hopefully, he'll change his mind and attitude."

"Got it, Jim. Where to now?"

"Can you please drop me off at Bromley? I think I might go see my brother."

Steve's house was the nicest dwelling on the worst street. Located in an old state housing area, the neighbourhood accommodated the unfortunates, the unemployed and the unlucky. Steve was unlucky but equally had always been unmotivated and ungrateful. Steve's house was brick; those around him were wood, and all except Steve's were in various states of disrepair. James smiled as the nursery rhyme *Three Little Pigs* came to mind. The front garden was concreted and painted green. Practical, if not imaginative.

James smiled again as he walked up the driveway: Steve's saveloy car was parked by the front door. It always amused him, although he would rather be dead than be seen driving it. Steve was in; he was pleased. The front door was open, so James didn't knock; he called out instead.

"Steve, it's James. Are you in?"

"What… who is it?"

"It's James, your brother."

"Oh, hang on, be with you in a minute, just having a wash."

Steve stood shirtless at the door a moment later.

An awkward silence filled the space between the two brothers.

"You should work out more, Steve," James said, noticing Steve's paunch. "Join a gym, get fit like me."

Steve scowled but stood in silence.

"I'm in town for the day, so thought I'd call in and say gidday. It's been a while. Too long."

"Aw yeah. It's lucky you caught me; usually, I'm away, but I got home last night. Been up north."

"Okay, well, it's good to see you, brother. How's business?"

"Sales are good; I've already met target for the month. That's why I'm taking a day off today."

James nodded in silence, looking for the right words to bridge the yawning gap between them.

"So how are you, Steve, really? I feel we've drifted apart since Donna died. I've probably not been in contact with you as often as I should have."

"So, what's new, James? You always put yourself first."

"What do you mean by that?"

Steve rolled his eyes, scoffed.

"Oh, come on, you've never given a shit about me; you were always the favourite. I had to go to work while you got to go to university. Have you ever thought about that? When the old man got crook, when mum got old, I was left here looking after them. Taking care of them, running around, all the while listening to them tell me how the sun shone out of your arse. You used to swan into town, treat them to a Sunday roast at the club, and then swan out again. Then, for the next six months, all I'd hear was how well you were doing and how proud they were of you."

"Shit, Steve, I never knew you felt that way. I just didn't think."

"It's always been that way—you only think of yourself and your precious career. You didn't give a rat's about mum and dad. You certainly didn't give a rat's about me. When Donna disappeared, the best support you could manage was to leave a voice mail message, telling me she was sure to turn up; most missing persons did! Thanks, mate!"

"I know I've made some mistakes, Steve, and I'm sorry. But my career...."

"Your career. It's always about your career, or your future, or your… whatever. You just don't give a shit, do you? You can shove your career right up your arse."

"That's a bit harsh. I'm here now, aren't I?"

"Not for much longer, James. You've said gidday, so now you can fuck off back to your glorious career."

With that, Steve turned and walked back up the hallway.

That was when James saw something that made him feel sick, sicker than he had ever felt before in his entire life.

He walked outside; he needed air. The stifling wind tried to steal his remaining breath. He stumbled to the low brick fence between the property and the footpath. He sat down, trying to hijack shade from a lonely bay tree.

Did he really see what he just saw?

He shook his head, trying to think. He knew he had to arrest his brother. He knew he should ring for backup and remove himself from the case. This was a conflict, if there ever was. He pulled out his phone and rang Mack.

Mack picked up on the first ring.

"Don't tell me: you want a ride? I'm not a flipping taxi service, Jim."

Usually, James would have laughed, but the best he could say was, "Cancel those instructions I gave before about Inky. And yes, you can come and pick me up, bring a couple of beat boys with you too. There's no rush, be here in about 30 minutes, yeah?"

"Okay, whatever you say," Mack said, scepticism in his tone.

James took a minute, then slowly walked back to the front door.

"We're not finished, Steve," he called.

"Go away and leave me alone, you arse."

"No, I'm not going to do that. I'm coming in: we need to talk."

"Like hell, you're coming in. Piss off!"

"What are you going to do, Steve? Call the cops?"

James heard Steve thunder down the hall toward the front door.

"Bugger off, James," he yelled in James' face. "Fuck off. Go back to your precious career."

"No, that's not going to happen."

Steve lunged at James, trying to push him off the front step. After a short struggle, Steve lay face down on the concrete driveway, his hands cuffed behind his back. James' knee pressed onto the small of Steve's back, his palm compressing his head into the green concrete.

"Eat that grass, dickhead; I told you, you should go to the gym," James crowed.

"Let me go, you arse, let me go."

James pulled Steve up and dragged him inside.

"Tell me about the tattoos on your back, Steve. What the fuck are they about?"

"What?"

"You heard me: what are the tattoos about? Who are the people behind those names?"

"They're not people, you fucking arse: they're cyclones!"

"What?"

"They're the names of cyclones that have hit the south pacific over the last five years; just fucking google them if you don't believe me!"

"Why would you carve the names of storms into your back?"

"To remember Donna. You wouldn't understand, but I thought it was a fitting tribute to her. Did you know she died during cyclone Donna? It was special to her. I just sort of continued the tradition."

His head hurt. James needed to get out of the house. He turned and walked away.

"Take these cuffs off me, you arse," Steve called behind him.

James paid no heed; he just kept on walking.

Six Months Later

The flight to Auckland arrived on time. The forecasted storm hadn't hit yet—it was due tomorrow, but the first hints of it were now revealing themselves. The trees started waving their warning as the taxi raced into the city. Not wanting to be outdone, clouds began changing colour, grey being the new white. The passenger in the back smiled; cyclone James was about to land.

The driver looked back. "What brings you to Auckland, sir?"

"Oh, please call me Inky, and I've come to visit an old friend."

Clack, clack, clack, he thought to himself, *clack, clack, clack.*

Tidying Up
Marian McMahon Stanley

A good-looking young cop stood on Rita Jean Anderson's front porch. She could see him from her chair by the living room bay window. Burly with a ruddy complexion and rusty hair under his cap, he reminded her of someone she used to work with. But that was a long time ago.

He was patient too, ringing the doorbell only once. The neighbors must have told him how infirm she'd become with her arthritis. Rita Jean reached for her aluminum walker with two tennis balls on its back legs. Leaning heavily forward with bent back, she rose and made her way, with a slow deliberate shuffle, to the front door.

"Morning, ma'am. Officer Heaney from the Emerson Police Department." The young man leaned down to greet her, so that she didn't have to twist her neck to look up at him. A thoughtful gesture for such a young man. Oh yes, she remembered him now. He'd come to the senior center to talk about phone scams – like if someone called to say her nephew will in trouble in the Philippines and needed money immediately. Silly - she had no nephew.

"You've probably heard about Walter Hauser at the end of the street?"

"Oh yes, horrible, horrible," Rita Jean replied. "Murdered in a parking garage in Boston, was it? Hit on the head with something heavy. Awful. He had such a nice family."

"Yes, that's right, ma'am. We're canvassing the neighborhood now to see if anyone might know something that would give us a lead in the investigation."

"I thought it was a robbery. Those parking garages can be so dangerous, especially at night."

"No, his wallet was untouched." Officer Heaney shifted his feet. "So, we're looking at other possibilities."

"Oh dear. Well, of course, I'm happy to help out if I can. Come in, come in. I'm just about to have a cup of tea with a few ginger cookies before Eddie's Taxi picks me up for my flower-arranging class at the senior center. Would you care to join me for tea?"

"I'm good, Miss Anderson, but maybe we could talk while you have your tea?"

"Yes, yes. That would be fine. I need to have a little something every two hours. Keeps the blood sugar up, you know."

She noticed the small smile on Officer Heaney's face as she maneuvered her walker in a series of skillful lifts to point it in the direction of the kitchen. Then, she could hear his steps behind her and sense the restraint in his pace so as not to crowd her as she crept along.

"I'm a little slow. It's this arthritis. It's in the spine now."

"Sorry to hear that."

"Well, I still get around. You have to try, you know."

As they made their way toward the kitchen, Rita Jean heard Officer Heaney stop before a glass Stueben eagle sitting atop the hallway desk.

"Nice," he said, "*Rita Jean Anderson, For Outstanding Program Leadership,, Sigma Defense Industries*. That you?"

Over her shoulder, Rita Jean gave the young man a look. "That's my name, isn't it?" Then, continuing toward the kitchen, "You know we weren't all born old and decrepit. We had other lives." A short pause. "I was pretty good. Back in the day, you know."

"My apologies," the young man murmured. "I'm sure you were."

Rita Jean talked as she shuffled slowly around the kitchen. Holding her walker with one hand, she filled a red tea kettle and placed it on the burner of an old electric stove. "Of course, now I'm happy tending to my plants, as best I can, going to my book club and my flower arranging classes. There is a time for everything, as it says in Ecclesiastes."

She leaned her elbows on the counter and reached for a blue teapot beside a ceramic tea canister decorated with a row of white ducks. "Mr.

Hauser struck me as a pleasant man the few times I encountered him, though he didn't appear to be home very much – always working. I saw his wife more, out walking with the children and the little white dog. But I have to say that I didn't really know the family."

Rita Jean warmed the teapot with water from the whistling kettle before measuring in the tea and putting in the remainder of the hot water. Then, she moved the plastic prescription bottles on her kitchen table aside and, covering the teapot with a yellow-flowered tea cozy, she placed it on the table to steep next to a plate of ginger cookies. "I like my tea strong enough to declare itself," she said. "We'll give it time."

She settled in a maple captain's chair of uncertain vintage. "Anyway, you can imagine that this neighborhood isn't as close as it used to be, Officer. Developers have been buying up all the little Capes and ranch houses around here as tear-downs to build those awful McMansions. Well, they didn't buy Rita Jean Anderson's, that's for sure. I refused to sell. I'm just fine where I am, thank you very much. Where would I go, anyway?"

Officer Heaney nodded in sympathy. Everyone knew that town employees couldn't afford to live in Emerson these days with all the prices rising and oversized, overpriced houses going up where close neighborhoods of small houses used to be.

"Oh", Rita Jean touched Officer Heaney's arm for emphasis, "the families are friendly enough, but they always seem to be running this way and that in those giant SUV's. Always in a hurry. No time to talk. Kind of annoyed if you try to start a conversation with them like you'd make them late for something much more important. Do you know what I mean?"

He did indeed, he said.

"Are you sure you wouldn't like a little cup of tea and a cookie now?"

After some hesitation, Officer Heaney allowed that, yes, that would be very nice. He took off his hat and placed it on the table, reaching for a ginger cookie while Rita Jean poured his a cup of tea in a flowered china mug. She ran a dishcloth over the counter once or twice after she'd given Officer Heaney his cup of tea.

"I like to keep things tidy. You can only do that if you are always sort of tidying up as you go along. Don't you think so?"

Officer Heaney looked around the spotless kitchen. "I guess that's true, but, anyway, about the Hausers?" he prodded Rita Jean.

"Oh, yes." Rita Jean laughed, "Sorry. We tend to wander at my age, you know."

"Now", Rita Jean said, "Mrs. Hauser was the exception. She used to take her children and their dog out for walks and she'd stop if she saw me on the porch."

"Can you tell me what you talked about, Miss Anderson?"

"What did we talk about?" Rita Jean thought for a moment. "Oh, the weather, my lilacs, the children, the fox that ran through her back garden. You know, little things. "

Rita Jean saw that the policeman looked comfortable and relaxed sitting in her tiny kitchen that smelled of sweet tea and ginger cookies. *A pleasant young fellow.*

Did the Hausers have many visitors, Miss Anderson?"

"Let's see, mostly young mothers, Mrs. Hauser's friends, playdates for the children and all that. Mrs. Hauser's parents came one time from the Midwest. Ohio, I think. Very friendly people. They're much friendlier out there than we are here. Don't you think?"

"Probably so, Ms Anderson. Anyone else?"

Rita Jean looked up at the ceiling to think. "Well, it wasn't really a visitor, but there was a silver van that sat outside the house a couple of times. I could see it from my seat at the living room window."

Officer Heaney held his pen in mid-air. "When would that have been?"

"Oh, it was during the past several weeks. Yes, I noticed it there right after I got home from my chair yoga classes at the senior center. They still let me go to the class, you know, though it's hard for me to keep up now. They're so patient."

The policeman was tapping his pencil on his knee.

"Oh, sorry, officer, wandering again. Anyway, it stuck in my mind because this was a strange car with New York plates and no one ever got out of it, just sat there. Let me check my calendar. It was the beginning of the new chair yoga session." Rita Jean reached across the table for a laminated Hallmark purse calendar from the local card shop. She opened the small calendar and her arthritic fingers traced the days and weeks. "Let's see, I noticed the van the 9th and the 11th, just week before last."

He leaned forward, moving his chair closer to Rita Jean's. "This is important now. Could you describe the people in the van?"

Rita Jean closed her eyes. Officer Heaney was scribbling in his notebook. "Hmmm. Big men. The one that I could see from my window had a grey sweatshirt with a hood. Hoodies. Is that what they call them?"

Officer Heaney gave a quick, impatient nod.

"With a black vest on."

"Did you get a look at their faces?"

"Well, only the one on the side of the car I could see more clearly. He had a workingman's face, a little rough."

"Caucasian?"

"Yes, white. It looked to me as if he had a tattoo on his neck, but it was so far away, I couldn't be sure."

Officer Heaney was chewing his lower lip. "This is very helpful, very helpful."

"Well, so glad I can be useful, dear. Now, not to be rude, but Eddie's cab will be coming soon to pick me up. I don't want to be late for my flower-arranging class. What else can I do for you, or can we continue this later?"

"I'll have to ask you to come to the station in the morning so that you can make a formal statement for us."

"Oh, my goodness. Really? To the station? How exciting." Rita Jean replied. "Well, yes indeed, I'll come in the morning after Mass. Eddie picks me up at church."

"Thanks, Miss Anderson. We appreciate your help. So, I'll be seeing you in the morning." He closed his notebook and rose. "Around eight o'clock?"

"Yes, that's about right, Officer. Maybe even a little before. Father Fleming says a nice, quick Mass, finishes by seven-thirty sharp."

"Great." As Officer Heaney walked down the hall and opened the front door, he happened to look up. "Screw loose on the spring here, Miss Anderson." He took out a small tool on a key ring from his pocket and tightened the screw. As he turned back from fixing the top of the door, Rita Jean saw him glance up the stairs and hesitate, with a perplexed look on his face, before he faced her again.

"Uh. Well. Thanks again for your time. See you in the morning."

Rita Jean watched the young man walk down the front path. Eddie's cab was coming along the street. She smiled when she saw Eddie slow at the sight of the police cruiser in front of her house. She had no doubt that Officer Heaney would, after some thought, decide he should have a conversation with Eddie too.

Rita Jean gathered her coat and bag, leaving the door open for Eddie. He came in just as she opened the top drawer of the hall desk and pulled out a blue folder. She removed a single sheet of paper with a list of names written in black magic marker.

Humming a nameless tune, Rita Jean ran her forefinger down the list. The tick of the regulator clock above the desk was the only sound in the front hall aside from Eddie's entering and his breathing as he leaned again the wall, watching her. Some of the names on the list were crossed off. She knew people in town would remember these names, and not with affection. There was the owner of the pizza shop by the depot that delivered drugs as well as pepperoni specials to his high school customers. A man who abused his dogs regularly and left them outside without food or shelter in the worst of the winter. And her favorite, the nephew across town who'd drained his frail, demented aunt's bank accounts and neglected her until she passed away

They had all met different ends. A fall from the roof of the apartment building above the pizza parlor, a recently purchased BMW sports car driven into a concrete highway barrier late at night or, in the case of the errant dog owner, hypothermia after being bludgeoned and left in the state forest during a long winter blizzard.

When he recently fell victim to an unknown assailant in a Boston parking garage, Mr. Hauser's name too had been crossed off.

Rita Jean put the list down and turned to Eddie. "They're probably going to call you about a silver van with New York plates that's been around the neighborhood. I'll fill you in."

"Don't like talking to cops."

"Oh, I know, honey, but I'll tell you everything you need to know. Don't worry." Rita Jean stretched and straightened her back, breathing a great sigh of relief as she did so.

"Well, I crossed Mr. Hauser's name off the list. He won't be knocking his poor wife and children around anymore. Good riddance to him."

She looked in the mirror over the desk and patted her hair into place. "You should have taken the money from his wallet, you know. Then, the police wouldn't be around asking all these questions."

Eddie shrugged his broad shoulders under his brown leather jacket. "I forgot. Not perfect, you know."

"I know, sweetheart, I'm not either. That cop looked up the stairs. I think he saw my fluffy red mules on the top step. I don't think that'll be problem. He just looked confused." They both laughed.

"So, anyway, I checked my accounts, Eddie. I have funds to pay you for the next few jobs and then you'll have more than enough for that move to Arizona," she looked at him out of the corner of her eye as she touched her toes several times, "if you still want to, that is."

Eddie smiled, a broad grin changing the character of his grizzled face to that of the young man he'd been before the Gulf War. "I don't know anymore. But maybe you'd like to come with me. The warm weather would be good for your...your condition." They both laughed. "Anyway, this is kind of fun. I might stick around."

"And I think you might like me, Eddie,"

Rita Jean executed a few leg lunges and winked at Eddie as he started to rub the tattoo on his forearm, which he did when he was uneasy. "Maybe."

She hopped to a standing position and talked as she swung her arms to loosen them up. "Everyone should leave a legacy. Mine is tidying up as much as I can before I kick off."

Eddie was not given to contemplating the nuances of their work. "If you say so."

Rita Jean stretched to either side again and put on her coat. "So glad we got to talking that day when you picked me up at the dentist's. My god, you had the perfect background to help me in my project. We're a good team, aren't we, Eddie?" Rita Jean reached her hand to touch the side of his face.

"Yeah, I guess so," he said as he looked at Rita Jean for a long moment.

"Okay, let's get this show on the road, soldier." She let out a long breath. "I'll skip the flower-arranging thingamajig. Let's take a ride up to the shore, and go to the new sushi bar on the harbor. They make a good dry martini."

Rita Jean bent her back in an elderly hump, resumed position on her aluminum walker with the two tennis balls on the back legs and tottered down the brick walkway with Eddie holding her arm.

"Remember to take the money next time, Eddie."

"Yes, ma'am."

In the Mood
Gerald Elias

They don't let me put a chain on my door. Maybe you think it's paranoid to want a chain in an assisted living facility—you won't say that to my face, but I can tell—but I say, you don't lock your door, you're asking for trouble. Life's a coin flip, and sooner or later it comes up tails.

I'm interrupted by a knock at the door as I'm rinsing out my coffee cup and brushing the crumbs off the plate and into the trash. I look at the clock radio on my kitchen table. Remember when the clock radio was state-of-the-art? With hands that glowed in the dark? "When the sun goes down, the dial lights up."

It's still forty-three minutes to Bingo hour. Why is someone knocking? I don't have a clue who it could be. See what I'm saying? This is why you should have a chain.

I always do the dishes right after eating, otherwise they get crusty and pile up and attract roaches. I use Dawn. I once read an article about an oil spill on a freeway in Cincinnati that they were only able to clean up when they hosed Dawn all over it. So what that it's more expensive? I can't stand Palmolive. The smell reminds me of dirty diapers. Makes me gag. There used to be an ad with housewives dipping their hands in it to show how gentle it was.

Housewives! That's when society said women were *supposed* to be housewives, like my mother. But just the word, *housewife*. Think about it. What does that mean? Married to a house? If women *had* to get a job, a *respectable* job, they had four choices: secretary, librarian, stewardess, teacher.

What was I saying? Yes, the clock radio. Time. That reminds me of an article I once read somewhere about a so-called *primitive* tribe somewhere in South America, I think. Their sense of time and space was the reverse of what we in *modern* civilization believe. Their philosophy went something like this: You can see what's ahead of you with the same certainty that you know what has already happened. On the other hand, you can't see what's behind you in the same way that you don't know what the future has in store. Therefore, one looks forward to the past and one looks backward to the future. I'm not quite sure I get it, but it's interesting.

Remember Playtex Living Gloves? *Living* gloves. That's a good one. What's the opposite of *living* gloves? *Dying* gloves? They were supposed to be so flexible you could pick up a dime. Yeah, right. Kids don't even know what a dime is anymore. Paper money? What's that? By the time they get Harriet Tubman on the twenty-dollar bill there won't be a twenty-dollar bill. They're even getting rid of credit cards now. They say you just point your *device* (aka phone) at those black-and-white Rorschach designs, and you've paid? Not my cup of tea.

I do use them—rubber gloves—occasionally, but not so much for washing dishes. You have a problem with getting your hands wet? I keep a pair handy, under the sink. They keep fingerprints off furniture. (And other things.) Someone is still knocking at my chamber door. They'll just have to wait until I've finished the dishes.

First it was affluence, then the Sony Walkman, but what put the final nail in the coffin of our way of life was the opening up of the workplace for women. Wait! Before you jump down my throat for saying that, wait a minute and listen to what I mean. All I'm saying is this: Until the seventies we had millions of brilliant women who had few career options other than to teach. Ergo, our public schools were the best in the world. But the pay was crummy, and when the doors of the workplace were burst open, rightfully so, by women who demanded equal opportunity to make a living, the best and brightest left teaching for greener pastures. And who can blame them? You gotta fight tooth and nail sometimes. Now look at our schools. The proof is in the pudding.

I open the door a crack. It's Gloria, with her walker. She's been here longer than me and is due to go into hospice. She's paler than usual and a little shaky. Not Parkinson's. Judy's the one with Parkinson's. Gloria's the one with the drippy stuff in her eyes.

I'd had a quiet breakfast, finally, until then. Same routine every day, except this morning there was no racket coming through the wall from Belikan's apartment.

While the canola oil—just a few drops—heated up in the cast iron pan, medium high, I put the English muffin in the toaster oven. Thomas' claims it's fork split, but they never poke it enough. I have to jab all around the muffin using a fork with long tines to finish the job, because if you use a knife you might as well say sayonara to the nooks and crannies. The toaster is set on five-and-a-half, brown but not burn-baby-burn, timed so that the scrambled eggs are done at the same time that the toaster oven dings. Ding! End of the round.

I cracked open two eggs—Can you believe there's a YouTube video instructing you how to crack eggs without getting shells in the bowl? Does someone really need that? Is that what this country's coming to? – against the side of the bowl and scrambled them with the same fork I split the muffin with—one less fork to clean. Okay, one "fewer" fork—until the whites and yolks were fully blended. No one likes when there's a glob of whites.

My mother used to make excellent scrambled eggs. I couldn't eat eggs by themselves in those days. They'd make me want to throw up, especially fried eggs. Don't even think about soft-boiled. Poached? *Aaachhh!* So, my mother had to make me bacon and toast (or English muffins) to go with my eggs so that I could choke them down, otherwise I refused to eat them. Or, as my evil third grade teacher used to say about virtually anything I had a hard time with, "You would if you could, but you can't so you won't." Whatever that meant. Bitch.

I poured the eggs into the pan and let them sear so that they wouldn't stick when I scrambled them. Who wants to scrub a pan when there's egg residue stuck like glue? I scramble with a wooden spatula. I could go into detail the myriad reasons why wood is better than metal, and forget plastic, but it might bore you. And we wouldn't want that, would we? Sorry, am I wasting your time?

My father, who did breakfast on Sundays, his day off, occasionally made salami omelets. He'd slice rings of Hebrew National salami and arrange them in a circle in the pan. Salami was a snack mainstay as well, along with Triscuits and Kraft Cracker Barrel sharp cheese. We'd sit in front of the TV watching baseball games together—like father, like son—when baseball was still baseball: Before slo-mo instant replay, radar guns, pitch counts, play reviews, helmets, batting gloves, designated hitters, free agency, and blood-sucking agents. It was hit-and-run, sacrifice bunts, stolen bases, fastballs high and tight, metal cleats raised to take out the second baseman, and kicking dirt at the umpire. "Ya bum! What are ya, blind?"

Speaking of cast iron pans and my father, not necessarily in that order, he once spent half of his one day off scouring a cast iron pan with steel wool to get off the black stuff. For some reason he didn't grasp the concept of a seasoned pan and scrubbed and scrubbed like a maniac until it was shiny as a mirror. No one dared suggest that maybe it wasn't worth it or, just maybe, it was stupid. By day's end, he felt he'd achieved a great accomplishment.

I've got Triscuits on my shopping list.

With a pan at the right temperature, it takes no more than thirty seconds to scramble two eggs. I emptied them onto my plate, side by side with the English muffin, which I buttered with a fairly new product that's a blend of butter and olive oil so that it spreads easier. It's also cheaper than pure butter. Remember margarine? Oleo is probably the most often-used word in crossword puzzles. Parkay? "Tastes like butter!" (Not really.) That's a crock. Bad joke.

The blueberry jam in the fridge had some fuzzy grayish stuff on its surface. Dare I? No, I don't think so. Let someone else eat it and kill themselves. I should've gifted it to Belikan. Add it to the shopping list.

We used to have Welch's grape jelly. Nothing else. Maybe once in a while we'd have strawberry. But that was "jam" or "preserves." We stuck with jelly for the most part. Thanksgiving we had blood-red cranberry jelly. You cut off both ends of the can and pushed it out like a placenta. Once a year was enough.

Thanksgivings were strictly traditional. It was about the only time we ate in the dining room and not at the green Formica kitchen table. The only thing different about our particular Thanksgiving dinners was the appetizer my father made—his pièce de résistance—individual chopped-liver sculptures shaped like turkeys, with black olives slices for eyes and celery and carrot sticks for tail feathers.

My doctor says if I eat chopped liver or any other organ meats, for that matter, it could kill me. Cholesterol. But I'm tempted. That and pastrami, corned beef, and tongue. My mother had a hand-operated meat grinder that she'd dump fried chicken livers into and turn the crank. The liver came out of the holes like wormy spaghetti. *Sweeney Todd*-esque. There's a van that can take us to the deli after stopping at the market.

I hated tongue when I was little. Along with eggs, it was on the list of things that made me want to barf. It was how my father made it. (For some reason, my mother kept her distance from this one.) He'd lower an entire, gross cow's tongue into a big pot of boiling water. It looked like it was still throbbing. When he deemed it done, he'd slice it, taste buds and all, into thick slices. One day, he made me a tongue sandwich for lunch. I faked eating it, waited until he left the kitchen, wrapped it up in a napkin and hid it in the bottom of the trash can under the sink. Somehow, he smoked me out and unearthed it in two seconds flat. Foiled again. I had hell to pay for lying and for wasting food.

These days, wouldn't you know, I love tongue, especially when it's thinly sliced, on rye bread with deli mustard. If my father could only see me now. But he also liked Liederkranz cheese. It would sit in the fridge, heavily wrapped, for about two years, and if you unwrapped it and the wind was blowing toward you, you could pass out from the smell. We always thought Liederkranz was European because of the name and because it stank so much, but amazingly it was invented and produced in good old U.S.A. I could never forgive him for the Liederkranz.

With the jam being inedible, I found a slice of Swiss cheese in the fridge.

At least there's no more noise from next door. Couldn't stand when that bastard, Eddie Belikan, blasted his Big Band crap. Didn't he know they don't make walls like they used to? They used to be plaster. Now it's sheetrock, and even the two-by-fours aren't two-by-four anymore. How can you eat breakfast in peace when you've got that racket in your ears? It's worse than the Super Bowl halftime show. You remember the first Super Bowl? It wasn't even called the Super Bowl and halftime wasn't the noisy, degrading extravaganza they refer to as *music*.

But it's not the thin walls that ruined society. You know what it is, or *was*, I should say? As I mentioned, if you were listening, it was the Sony Walkman. Yes, the Walkman. Before then, people listened to music together. It was a communal experience. With the Walkman, everyone went off into their own universe. The social fabric was rent asunder. Hey, I'm just the messenger.

I poured myself a cup of coffee to go with my breakfast items. These damn paper filters nowadays fall apart and let all the grounds stream through like a dam opening its gates unless you fold them along the edge. You never had to do that before. And if you grind the beans too finely, the water just sits there like a Superfund Pond. Remember those old aluminum percolators? My parents boiled the crap out of coffee, but I liked watching the water pop up in the little glass thing at the top, like blood in a beating heart, little by little getting darker. Maxwell House was their favored brand. Remember their slogan, "Good till the last drop?" My father wrote to the company. He said, "What's wrong with the last drop?" Very funny. They sent him a coupon. His moment of triumph.

I'm out of coffee. *Et tu, Brute.* I put it on the shopping list.

I'm enjoying the quiet. No more Big Band. I mean, how much Glenn Miller should one be expected to tolerate at nine in the morning? "Moonlight Serenade," maybe, but not "In the Mood." Definitely not. *Da-de-Da-de-Da-de-Da-de-Da-de-de-DAH! Da-de-Da-de-Da-de-Da-de-Da-de-de-DAH! Da-de-Da-de-Da-de-Da-de-Da-de-de-DA! Da-de-Da-de-Da-de-Da-de-Da-de-de-DAH!* Over and over again. It could drive you insane. I complained about it to the office. They said, "Have you tried bringing this issue to Mr. Belikan's attention? Maybe you could work it out." I said, "That's not my job. That's *your* job. That's what I've paid my life savings for, so that I don't have to work out issues with Mr. Belikan." They said, "We're sorry, but as long as it's not during quiet hours, residents are permitted to play music. There's nothing we can do about it, but please inform us if there is a problem during quiet hours." And they gave me their smiley face. So, I worked it out with Mr. Belikan. And I didn't buy him a damn Walkman, either.

Eddie Belikan was a lawyer before he retired. Not the corporate kind with the fancy offices, or even a public defender, God bless them. He was one of those sleazy personal injury attorneys who'd show up at funerals, say "I'm so sorry for your loss," and hand out his business card. An ambulance chaser, that's what they're called, and with good reason. The worst of the worst. That's why he can't afford a better old folks home than this dump. And with the nerve to blast his so-called music. He's deserved everything that was coming to him.

My kids put me here, against my better judgment. "Dad, once you get used to it, you'll love it." Blah, blah, blah. Right. They didn't know about Belikan. I threatened to hire a lawyer – that's pretty ironic – but who has that kind of money?

Actually, the social fabric started to unwind long before the Walkman. The Walkman just accelerated it. The coup de grâce, as it were. As I said, it started with post–World War II affluence. No, I'm not kidding. You see, what happened was this: Until then, in the evening everyone sat out on their front porch or stoop.

Why was this important? Isn't it self-evident? When neighbors walked by—yes, people used to walk—and you were out front, they'd stop and you'd talk. It was called a community. It was a neighborhood. But then, people started making more money, and what did they do? They moved to a *nice home* in the suburbs *with a backyard*, and then they *built a fence*. Voilà! No more community. People became invisible. Insulated, isolated family units. The return of tribalism.

Okay, okay, there were weekend family barbecues. I don't deny it. My father would squirt a half gallon of lighter fluid on the charcoals. He didn't really get it that after the initial conflagration, the coals took another twenty minutes to heat up. We ate burnt, benzene-soaked hamburgers and hot dogs. One didn't complain.

These days, it's fancy-shmancy smokers and temperature-controlled gas grills. You want to spend a thousand dollars, more power to you, bud. If my father hadn't been a tightwad and had bought a gas grill, I could never have burned the house down and no one would have died. Accidents will happen.

Most people don't understand that when you grill a hamburger you don't want lean. They think lean is healthier. Well, maybe it is, but it's also drier, and it's the fat that adds flavor. You want eighty-five percent, no leaner. Sometimes he'd grill them with chopped up onion inside.

I add ground beef, what we used to call *chopped meat*, and onions to the shopping list.

Do you know what they get for yellow onions these days? A dollar-sixty-nine a pound! Plain old yellow onions. Come on! And now they try to sell you even more expensive ones: sweet onions and white onions and red onions and Spanish onions and Vidalia onions. Honey, let me let you in on a little secret. They all taste the same.

And don't get me started on salt.

I poured a tablespoon of half-and-half into my coffee.

You remember when milk came in glass bottles, with paper caps? No one worried about someone poisoning your milk. These days it takes pliers to get the top off an aspirin bottle. *Child proof.* More like *human* proof. The milkman delivered to your doorstep and put it into the milk box to keep fresh. (Remember those jokes about housewives and milkmen? You can't tell them anymore or you'll get a frowny face, but my father didn't think they were funny, even back then.) It was pasteurized but not homogenized so you had to shake it to mix the cream on top with the milk. When nonfat milk first came out, it looked blue and tasted like dishwater. *Skim milk*, it was called. *Nonfat* sounds more marketable. Now it's much better. Once in a while I see one of the old-timers still shaking a carton. Habits die slow, like the people here.

I still have half a container, so I don't need to put it on the list until next week.

Fortunately, the cheapest brand is also the most environmentally friendly. It doesn't have that twist-off plastic cap that just adds to the huge garbage dump in the Pacific. The Great Pacific Garbage Patch is what they call it, three times the size of France and two billion pieces of plastic. I use as little as I can, but what can you do? Everything has plastic in it. It's killing us all. Death is in the air, and in the water, too.

How many times did I have to bang on the wall to get Belikan to shut off his music? Take a look. You can see my fist marks. Good thing I didn't punch a hole in it, it's so flimsy. A lot of good it did, trying to work it out in a neighborly way. The only thing I got was bloody knuckles.

When I was a kid, they didn't have plastic. Toys were metal or wood, and they lasted. Lincoln Logs are now made of plastic. Can you believe that? Logs. Plastic. Logs. Plastic. No wonder kids are screwed up. They say metal and wood toys are dangerous, but look what's dangerous! The earth is drowning in plastic. That's what's dangerous.

But that's not all that's dangerous. Look at the violence today. When I was little, if a kid got kidnapped, it was front page news. For a child to be shot was unthinkable. Unthinkable! And all of us had cap guns. We played cowboys and Indians and shot each other. "I got ya. No, you missed me. No, I got ya. Okay, but it was only a flesh wound." Politically incorrect now, but no one took it seriously then. Years ago, I think I read that almost all homicides were between people who knew each other. Not that killing someone you know is necessarily a great idea, but just that there was a reason. Sometimes the reason could be compelling, like if a wife got beat up or someone acted so loony you just had to put an end to it. You could justify it, in a way. Sure, you'd have to have a good reason. But the idea of the random massacre of innocent bystanders was off the radar. It would never happen. Now, it's every day, almost. Innocent people dropping like flies. What's the statistic? Thirty-thousand homicide victims every year? The new normal. More like the new abnormal. Guns, guns, guns. "Guns don't kill people. People kill people." Excuse me, sir. The second sentence is true, but the first one is false, though I'd amend it to say, "Weapons kill people."

Gloria is standing in my doorway in her white fuzzy robe and seems to be looking at me in a strange way. Well, stranger than usual, anyway. How long has she been doing that?

"You're early," I say. "It's not Bingo time."

"It's not that," Gloria says. "Have you heard? Eddie is dead."

"What did you say?"

"I said, Eddie Belikan is dead."

"Strangled, huh?"

She nods.

I start to close the door. Gloria starts to shuffle away on her walker with the tennis balls at the bottom of its legs, but then she turns back and sticks a walker leg in the door so that I can't close it all the way. See? If I had a chain, she wouldn't've been able to do that.

"What?" I ask.

She cocks her head and looks at me like a curious poodle. All I can see through the crack in the door is her rheumy left eye, a tuft of her puffy white hair, and her smeary pink lipstick. It's almost comical. When I was a kid I had a dog. It lived till fifteen-and-a-half. It was a mongrel, what we now call a *mixed breed,* named—

"How did you know that?" she asked.

Senior Call-Up
Gregory Meece

These days, Mildred Welker was content to sit by her breakfast nook window, enjoying a cup of jasmine tea with her crossword puzzles and her best friend, Mr. Patches, always nearby. Her beloved tabby provided comfort, and she read that tea made from the fragrant buds of the jasmine blossom helps to reduce stress for elderly folks.

Not that Mildred considered herself to be particularly stressed. Or elderly, for that matter. Still, she knew from many chats with the other residents of Appleton Acres, her senior living cottage community, that worrying was a real thing among the geriatric set—justifiably so. *How will I get my groceries if I can no longer drive? What do falling red blood counts in my lab work mean? Is this early-onset dementia, or did I just forget where I left my reading glasses this morning?* Seniors can become consumed with so many troubling questions and concerns, any one of which might portend something serious. Psychologists say that health and safety make up the base levels of the Hierarchy of Needs model of human motivation. For the geriatric set, health and safety seem to comprise the entire pyramid.

Her family advised Mildred not to become isolated after her husband, Frank, died and she downsized her life to fit into her new living space, nestled in the rolling Green Mountain foothills. But it was for more than for her social well-being that she became close with her neighbors. For Mildred and her fellow seniors, getting to know one another was also a practical matter. Ironically, though their community was marketed as "independent living," the residents felt that they were rather dependent on their neighbors if something were to happen to them. Living alone, often with family members far away or consumed with their own lives, they looked out for one another.

From her vantage point, Mildred could view many of the tiny cottages tightly arrayed like dominoes along her curving street. It helped her to keep in touch with the comings and goings of her neighbors. It also made for conversation starters when she spoke to them on the phone.

"So, Gertie, I noticed a young man visiting you yesterday," said Mildred when her friend, Gertrude Milcroft, answered her phone. "Was that the son from Omaha you spoke about? The architect?"

"Oh no," replied Gertrude. "He's too busy these days to come to visit his old mother. What with the new buildings going up in his city—that one has his hands full."

"So, who was he?"

"Haven't you met Appleton Acres' new maintenance man? His name is Jerrold something. I have trouble remembering last names lately. I believe it is one of those forgettable names—'Jones,' maybe. Anyway, I was working on my stamp collection when I realized that my dishwasher was still running from this morning. I couldn't get it to shut off! I called and Jerrold came right over to take care of it for me. Such a nice young man."

"What happened to Mr. Franklin? Is he still working in the maintenance department?"

"He's planning to retire at the end of the month. The manager brought in this new fellow so Mr. Franklin can ensure a smooth transition—showing him the ropes, you know. Jerrold told me he is going to be introducing himself to all the neighbors."

"That's a good idea. He hasn't been over here yet, but Mr. Patches and I will keep our eyes open for him."

"And you know what, Millie? I was telling that nice young man about how I worry about falling. Why they put our laundry machines down in that little basement, I'll never understand. Don't they know how many seniors fall carrying a basket of clothes on the stairs? Everything else is on one floor. I'm thinking of getting one of those small stacking washer-dryer units they have now. I got the idea from my granddaughter who just started college. She says all the dorm rooms have them these days. Anyway, I thought it might fit in my kitchen. I asked Jerrold if he would be able to install it if I purchased one."

"I worry about the laundry, too," said Mildred. "That idea of yours is something to think about. So, what did this young fellow tell you?"

"He said he would check with management to see if it would be permitted in our resident's building agreement. But then he told me about this great new service the city provides for the elderly who are living alone. Suppose we fall and can't reach a phone. Or, even worse—what if we pass away in the middle of the night—who would even know? So, Jerrold told me they offer a free program called ... Let's see, I wrote it down here—'Senior Call-Up.' You give them your number, and one of their volunteers phones you each morning. If you don't answer, they call whoever you name as your contact person. That person agrees to go over to check on you. Usually, it's a family member. They have to have a key to your home, of course. If they can't get a hold of your contact person, then they immediately dial 911."

"That sounds like a fantastic idea," said Mildred. "Who says our city government doesn't do anything for us senior citizens?"

"That's right," replied Gertrude. "I told Jerrold I didn't have anyone living nearby, so he offered to be my contact person. Maybe he would consider doing the same thing for some of the other neighbors. After all, we're all in the same position."

"Hopefully, that position is upright most of the time," joked Mildred.

✶✶✶✶✶

The next day, Mildred was hard at work on her crossword puzzle. She found herself stuck on number seventeen-across—*Moonwalking superstar*. "It starts with a 'J' and has seven letters. Doesn't look like 'Armstrong' will fit. Any ideas Mr. Patches?" Mr. Patches continued to purr as he sat on Mildred's lap. His expression suggested what he might be thinking: *How about a three-letter word for 'to stroke affectionately?' Begins with a 'P.'*

The knock on the front door startled Mr. Patches. Always fearing stranger danger whenever a delivery person came to the door, he bolted off Mildred's lap. With just two long leaps, he shot down her basement stairs to hunker down in his safe place behind the dryer. Mildred always kept the basement door open to reassure him that an escape route would be available if needed.

Besides the laundry appliances and a utility closet, the only other item in the small basement was an old clawfoot bookcase, which held the bulk of Mildred's library of detective stories. An avid reader of mysteries, she just couldn't bear to discard her Agatha Christies, Dashiell Hammetts, and Raymond Chandlers when she downsized.

Mildred opened her front door and was greeted by a tall, slender fellow wearing khaki cargo pants and a hunter green polo shirt with the words "Appleton Acres Maintenance" embroidered on the pocket. He had a broad smile on his face.

"Hello, my name is Jerrold Jones," said the visitor. "I'm the new maintenance man for the community."

"Oh, yes, come on in Mr. Jones," said Mildred. "My neighbor, Gertie, told me all about you. Can I get you a cup of tea?"

"No thank you. Just wanted to introduce myself to all the residents. And you can call me Jerrold. If there's ever anything you need, don't hesitate to give me a ring. I'm on duty seven days a week, and even when I'm not on the premises here at Appleton Acres, I only live a few minutes away, so I can come for an emergency. Like if your heat won't come on in the middle of one of those freezing winter days we get up here in Vermont."

"That's very reassuring, Jerrold. Oh, and speaking of things that are reassuring, Millie told me about the Senior Call-Up. I signed up this morning."

"That's great. I assume you have someone in your family who lives nearby and can be your contact person?"

"I gave them the name of my grandson. He'll be graduating from the university this June and then moving back to his parents' house in New Hampshire. I'll need to designate a backup contact person for him one of these days."

"Well, if you need someone, feel free to list me. I've been offering that to your neighbors, and quite a few of them have already put me down as their contact."

"That's so nice of you. I'll make that call today."

"Just happy to help out. As Mr. Franklin reminded me before he left, 'We're here to serve.'"

*****

A couple of days later, Mildred was sitting in her usual spot after breakfast, drinking her tea and casually staring out the window as she pondered some of the blank squares that remained on her crossword puzzle. She noticed Jerrold entering the house next to Gertrude's. It was Arthur Johnson's home. Jerrold was holding a cardboard box by one of its flaps as he pushed open the door and walked in.

"That's strange," she said to Mr. Patches, who pretended to be a very good listener. "I don't think I saw Mr. Johnson let him in. I hope he's alright."

A few minutes later, she saw the young man exit her neighbor's house. He was still carrying the box, but this time he held both hands beneath it. He put the box into his car, but instead of getting in and driving away, he turned around and went back inside Mr. Johnson's cottage.

"Maybe he's helping Arthur move some of his junk out to make more room for those antique German figurines he's been collecting," Mildred muttered to Mr. Patches. "They must be worth a pretty penny." Mr. Patches responded by looking up at Mildred to show her that he was ready for a scratch under his chin. His expression suggested that he was entitled to it. Suddenly, the shrill sound of approaching sirens shattered his repose and caused him to bolt down the basement stairs. Mildred watched as the ambulance pulled up behind Jerrold's car. Soon, two paramedics were wheeling a stretcher into Mr. Johnson's house.

It was later that afternoon when Mildred learned from her friend Gertie that Mr. Johnson had died in his sleep. When Senior Call-Up couldn't reach him in the morning, they contacted Jerrold who told the volunteer on the phone that he would run right over.

*****

Mildred attended Arthur Johnson's funeral service. Unfortunately, the ritual had become far too frequent. Knowing that the average age of her neighbors had to be around 80, a high turnover rate could be expected, but many of these neighbors had become her friends. It wasn't so much that they were close or went to each other's homes for parties. There was an unspoken bond among the elderly residents. It came from sharing a past that they knew was gone forever—experiences that couldn't be appreciated unless you were there. It came from being constantly aware that one's future has an expiration date on it. Whenever one of her friends departed, it took a piece of Mildred's heart with it.

When the summer months arrived, Mildred and Gertrude often sat together beneath the climbing rose arbor that covered Gertrude's small front porch. "More iced tea, Millie?" offered Gertrude.

"Thanks, Gertie. I'll pass on the tea, but I would love to sample another of your famous homemade ladyfingers."

"Coming right up," said Gertrude as she reached for the platter of delicacies. "By the way, did you hear about Mrs. Farnsworth down by the cul-de-sac?" she asked.

"I don't get to meet many folks on that side of Appleton Acres," replied Mildred.

"That explains why I didn't see you at her viewing the other day."

"Oh my! So, was she in poor health?"

"No. But it's what I keep saying. It was those darn stairs. Mrs. Farnsworth was carrying a large load of bed sheets down to the washer in her basement and she took a bad tumble. I heard they found her the next day with a broken neck and the basket of sheets on top of her."

"Just terrible! If only the sheets were under her, it might have broken her fall," said Mildred. Thinking that it might have sounded glib, she added, "Poor woman."

"Well, anyway, that was enough for me. I'm done with doing laundry downstairs. I found a very nice laundromat a couple miles up the road. It's not like I have that much else to do. So, now I just sit with a magazine and wait for my things to come out of the dryer. I plop them in my trunk and put them away when I get home. No stairs."

"I take it you never installed one of those dormitory appliances in your kitchen?"

"Jerrold checked on it and said it would overload the breakers or something like that. Did I forget to mention it? Jerrold is the one who found Mrs. Farnworth lying there at the bottom of the steps. He was responding to one of those Senior Call-Ups, and he headed right over. He's the one who called for an ambulance, but it was already too late. She might have fallen the evening before."

The two ladies sat quietly after that. It was a shame how worrying about such things could spoil ladyfingers and sweetened iced tea on a summer afternoon.

*****

During the next few months, two more residents of the Appleton Acres community passed away. Mrs. Greenblatt suffered a heart attack while loading a fruit cake into her car for the church's bake sale. A neighbor made the call to 911. But for Mrs. Strohmeyer, it was another fall down the stairs that caused her death. The police concluded that she must have gone to the basement at night to check her heater. It was the first cold day of fall, and her thermostat was turned up, but the heater in the basement had been turned off. It was Jerrold who found her and reported the accident.

Mildred was having an especially hard time with her crossword puzzle. Her mind kept returning to the friends and neighbors she lost during the past year. Their deaths were constant reminders of the fragility of life. "Well, Mr. Patches, I know you don't like to hear about it, but there may come a day when you will need to find a new lap to sit on," she told her cat as he burrowed his head into Mildred's flannel nightgown. "Do you think Gertie would agree to adopt you if I should pass before she does? Maybe I'll pop over to her place tomorrow and we can chat about it. One must always be prepared."

The next morning, someone else had been to Gertrude's house before Mildred had a chance to pop over. As Mildred was finishing spreading her toast with strawberry jam, something in the window caught her eye. A maroon Subaru Forester pulled up in front of her friend's house—Jerrold's car. Mildred couldn't explain why, but she had an odd feeling about his early morning appearance. Her view of her friend's front door was partially hidden because of the shade from Gertrude's arbor, but it appeared that he entered the front door rather quickly. Normally, she would expect there to be a waiting period. If he rang her doorbell, Mildred would have to check her phone first to see who was standing in front of her doorbell camera. Knowing Gertrude as she did, she figured that her friend would want to inspect herself in the mirror before opening the door. And, like Mildred, she did not move around as quickly as she once did. The whole process of inviting Jerrold to come in should have taken at least a minute or two. It appeared that Jerrold was inside her house in a matter of a few seconds.

Mildred decided to investigate. After settling Mr. Patches on a warm patch of sunlight that streamed onto the floor, she went into her bedroom to change out of her nightgown and put on a pair of shoes. She remembered to put her keys in her pocket, so she didn't get locked out of her own house and headed down her front walkway to the street. She started to cross, but quickly stopped in her tracks as she sensed something speeding toward her. An ambulance stopped in front of her house. "Oh, no," cried Mildred, as if exhaling the words.

Jerrold was already standing by his car as he introduced himself to the paramedics.

"Is the door unlocked?" the woman who drove the ambulance asked.

"Yes. I left it unlocked as soon as I called you guys," Mildred heard

Jerrold reply. "Her name is Gertrude Milcroft. I'm her contact person for the Seniors Call-Up program."

Mildred followed them as they went into Gertrude's home. "Are you a family member?" asked one of the paramedics.

"No. I'm Gertie's best friend and neighbor," Mildred explained as she pointed across the street to her home. "Do you mind if I come in? I want to be helpful."

"Is she in the bedroom?" the paramedic asked Jerrold.

"No. The basement floor."

Mildred's hands covered her face. She began to sob so hard that her body shook as she stood in a bent position beneath Gertrude's arbor, alone.

*****

Mildred watched the man carry boxes out of her friend's home. It had been a week since the funeral, and Kenny Milcroft had returned to remove some of the personal belongings from his mother's home. A truck would be coming soon to haul away everything else.

"So, you're the architect," she said.

"That's right. I'm Kenny. I think we met briefly at the viewing, but we didn't get a chance to talk. My mom spoke of you often."

"Gertie and I had a wonderful friendship. We both moved to Appleton Acres only a couple years ago, but we hit it off right away. I can't tell you how much I miss your mother."

"Thank you. I miss her very much too."

"Is there anything I can do to help? I can't lift heavy boxes, but I might be able to answer any questions you might have about her things. You know, the things that meant a lot to her, like those family pictures you're holding."

"That's very kind of you. There may be one thing you can help me with. Do you know if my mother gave away some of her things—maybe donated them?"

"I don't think so. Are you looking for something in particular?"

"I can't seem to locate her stamp collection. She often told me she started it when she was a little girl. I don't know if she added anything to her albums in recent years, but she saved them for so long. She said they would keep going up in value. I know she was proud of owning some very rare ones in her collection."

"I do remember her showing me her stamp albums. She kept them in the cabinet next to her television set."

"I checked there. Nothing."

"I can't imagine Gertie giving them to anyone besides her own son. And it's not the type of thing you would donate to Goodwill. I don't believe money was a problem. She wouldn't need to sell them. Do you think they were worth a lot?"

"From what I remember, she said they were worth a few thousand dollars—and that was more than 15 years ago. I suppose they could fetch quite a nice sum today if they were advertised on the right online sites. There are even online auction companies that will sell collectibles on consignment. But I'm not interested in their monetary value. I just think mom would have wanted to keep them in the family."

An idea popped into Mildred's head. She wrote down Kenny's phone number. If she learned anything new about his mother's stamp collection, she would let him know. In the meantime, she asked if he would give her access to his mother's front doorbell video footage. As he had no use for it himself, he turned over his mother's papers with the access information.

*****

Detective Emily Biederman sat at her desk sorting through the day's police reports when she looked up and saw Mildred standing outside her door. She was wearing a grey heather tweed overcoat, a paisley scarf, and a wool cloche hat. Mildred removed her gloves and stuffed them into her oversized handbag. The detective's first impression of Mildred reminded her of her grandmother, who also dressed that way as soon as the temperature dipped into the forties. She waved Mildred into her office and removed a pile of papers from one of the wooden chairs.

"Sorry, it's a little messy in here," said the detective.

"Thank you so much for agreeing to meet with me, Detective Biederman," said Mildred.

"The message you left on my phone was a little unclear. It said something about residents in your independent living community passing away lately?"

"That's correct. At least four that I know of. All neighbors. The last one to leave us was my dear friend, Gertie Milcroft."

Detective Biederman paused before she spoke. She wanted to be careful to not sound disrespectful when she asked her next question.

"And where you live—this is a retirement community? I mean, most of your neighbors are elderly?"

"Oh, we're a bunch of old-timers, alright. I believe Mr. Franklin was in his mid-nineties. But I don't think it was old age that caused their deaths."

"Mrs. Welker, may I ask what you *do* think caused their deaths?"

"I'm not certain. That's why I came to see you. I can only tell you that they all have a few things in common."

"Aside from being elderly and your neighbors?"

"They all died alone. They all signed up for Senior Call-Up. And they all named Jerrold Jones as their contact person. In each case, it was he who discovered their bodies and phoned for an ambulance."

"I'm familiar with how the Call-Up program works. Why would all these folks share the same contact person?

"Well, he is a very nice young man. He's also available every day because he works as our cottage community's maintenance man, and he lives very close. Everyone knew him as a friendly, reliable fellow. Many of us don't have family living in the area. And, to tell you the truth, once word gets around in our community, we tend to copy one another. Like when Mrs. Arbuckle put one of those dried flower wreaths on her front door with the ...."

"Let me stop you, Mrs. Welker," interrupted Detective Biederman. "I think I have enough information for now. But to be honest, ma'am, there's been no determination of foul play in any deaths that occurred at Appleton Acres since I've been working in this department, which is going on five years. And given the ages of the deceased, well, what I'm trying to tell you is that the department can't just launch a sweeping investigation of multiple deaths without any evidence of a crime having been committed. Please take these forms home with you and write down as much as you can—names, dates, contact information—that sort of thing. Bring back your report when you're ready and we'll see if there's enough to follow up. Stay warm out there."

Mildred huffed as she walked back to the parking lot. Once inside her car, she said to herself, *If she won't take this matter seriously, then I might just have to do some detective work on my own. I must ask myself, 'What would Miss Marple do?'*

*****

"Grammy, it's so nice to hear from you," said Mildred's grandson, Fred Welker, as he spoke into his car's Bluetooth microphone.

"What's all that noise I hear in the background?" asked Mildred. "Is that a train I hear?"

"I'm in my car, Grammy. Parked while the train passes."

"Oh, well, I don't want you to talk to me while you're driving."

"How about if I pull over after this train goes by? We can have a nice chat."

After she was sure her grandson was safely parked, she said, "I could use some of your help with another technology issue. I was wondering if you might come for a visit one day. If you have the time, there are a few things I'd like you to look into for me."

"Anything for you, Grammy." Fred made arrangements to return to The Green Mountain State to visit his grandmother on Saturday. Since he graduated from college, he had been enjoying his entry-level accounting position in New Hampshire, but he missed his Grammy Welker and was happy to help. She often relied on him when she couldn't get her computer to print or when her "smart" TV wasn't acting so intelligently.

After fixing Fred's favorite spaghetti and meatballs, Mildred and her grandson sat at her table where they shared a pot of tea and some of Mildred's homemade chocolate chip cookies.

"So, Fred, I told you about poor Mrs. Milcroft across the street," said Mildred.

"Yes. I know you two were very close. I'm sure you miss her a lot," said Fred.

"I think of Gertie every day. I ran into her son. A nice boy, like you. You'd like Kenny. I asked him if he would give me access to her doorbell thingy. She had one of those built-in cameras put in so she could see who was at her door before she opened it."

"Smart woman," said Fred.

"And it also records." She handed him a manila folder that Gertrude used to store the paperwork that came with her doorbell camera. This included a piece of stationery containing her password and username. On it, Mildred wrote a date. "When you get back home, I want you to see if there's anything recorded on this date. It's the day Gertie passed away."

"Shouldn't be a problem, Grammy. That is, as long as it's still in the system's memory. Sometimes, these things start erasing data automatically to save space after a certain amount of time goes by."

"Well, you'll let me know. Also, you have a way of looking up things on the internet, right?"

"Of course, Grammy. Anyone can do a Google search—even you."

"I'm referring to those online sites where people buy and sell things."

"Oh, you mean, like Craigslist and eBay. Yes, there are different sites people use depending on what they're looking to buy."

"Or to sell. Yes. I was wondering if you could see if anyone was trying to sell a stamp collection in this area. Also, some rare antique figurines. They were from Germany, I believe."

"Sure thing. I can search using those keywords for starters and filter the data for zip codes found in this general area. What range of dates are you looking for?"

Mildred wrote down the date Mr. Franklin died up to the current date.

*****

Fred called his grandmother to let her know what he found during his internet search. "The stamp collection was an easy one," he told her. "I checked a couple of the leading sites that specialize in collectibles, like coins, art—even baseball cards."

"Did you find anyone selling stamps?" Mildred asked. "Anyone who might list an address in my area?"

"Since you said to look for stamp collections, I didn't bother with anyone selling a single rare stamp. In your zip code, I found two listings. One was someone selling a set of duck stamps. But you mentioned the stamps were from all over the world. From what I read in the description; these were only U.S. stamps from the 1930s on up—all with ducks on them."

"How about the other one?"

"The other one appeared to be a single binder of rare international stamps."

"Who was the seller?"

"No name—just an email to contact for more information. I have it right here." Fred read the address to his grandmother who wrote it down on a piece of notepaper.

The expression on Mildred's face showed that something in the email address looked familiar. "Hmmm. I believe that could be it," she said. "And did you find anyone selling antique figurines?"

"Sure did. I used 'vintage figurines' and "German figurines' in my searches. I found something on one of the online auction sites. Since it was an auction company that was selling the items, I didn't see any seller information. I imagine the company handles the whole transaction and sends the seller the proceeds. After subtracting their commission, of course."

"So, that one looks like a dead end."

"Not exactly."

"What do you mean?"

"Well, I called the company and pretended to be a big collector who wanted to put in a bid. I asked if I could contact the seller first, to see if I could check out the figurines in person. I hope I didn't get the woman I spoke with in trouble, but she gave me the seller's email address."

"The same as the other one?"

"Yep. Same person. By the way, I also got into Mrs. Milcroft's doorbell cam."

"Oh, that's wonderful. You amaze me, Fred. Did it show anything for the day Gertie died?"

"It did. First, there was a man who entered her house. Took out his key and went in. Shortly after he left, two paramedics arrived with a stretcher. They went into the house with the first man."

"You say the first man went in with his own key. He didn't even ring the bell or knock first?"

"That's right. I assumed he was staying there. He was a younger guy. Mrs. Milcroft's son, I'm guessing?"

"Not her son, I'm afraid. Fred, thank you so much for all your help. I'll make you a delicious supper of spaghetti and meatballs next time I see you."

"With chocolate chip cookies, too, I hope. I'm getting hungry already!"

*****

Mildred put aside her crossword puzzle for the day so she could concentrate on filling out the forms that Detective Biederman had given her. The information she received from her grandson confirmed her suspicion that Jerrold Jones had been using his contact person status in the Senior Call-Up program to enter her neighbors' homes and steal their valuables. To Mildred, the real crime wasn't just taking items like Mr. Franklin's antique figurines or Gertrude Milcroft's stamp collection. What was truly evil was that Jerrold took advantage of her elderly friends. They were vulnerable. They were afraid of falling and being unable to call for help. Tormented by the fear of dying alone, with nobody knowing, they trusted him with keys to their homes. He coldly waited for them to die so he could rob them, stash the stolen items in his car, and then play the role of good-deed doer by calling 911. Mildred shivered when she thought of her best friend lying at the bottom of the stairs while this man violated her home and took something from her that was so dear to her that she saved it her entire long life.

Just as she was finishing the report, her doorbell rang. As usual, Mr. Patches sprang from the place where he was napping and flew down the basement stairs with his paws barely touching the treads. Still trying to sort out her thoughts, Mildred walked to her front door and opened it. There before her was a grinning Jerrold Jones. Perhaps she hadn't noticed it before—how the lower half of his face presented a kindly smile, while his eyes stared blankly. As when someone is faking their feelings.

"Hello, Mrs. Welker. Do you mind if I come in and check your heater? I've been changing the filters for a few of your neighbors. Maybe I should check yours. It'll only take a minute."

Mildred was without words. She wished this were not happening. Not now. Not before she had the opportunity to present Detective Biederman with her new information.

"Oh, Jerrold ... no, I believe my heater is in good working order," she said, trying not to let her nervousness show. "Thank you for asking."

"I have the filters in my car. It will only take a minute. You know what they say—an ounce of prevention."

Mildred was at a loss for what to do. She couldn't think quickly enough to come up with a good reply. She was afraid that something she might say could give Jerrold a reason to suspect that she was on to him. Maybe the best thing was to just let him check the filters. She would head to the police station the moment he was gone.

"Well, okay. You know where the basement is," she said as Jerrold stepped inside her home. On the way to the basement, he passed the breakfast nook where Mildred's papers were still spread on the table. Jerrold's eye caught a glimpse of the police department logo at the top of the pages. He discreetly tilted his head closer—close enough to spot his name written on the top sheet. Mildred gasped as he grabbed the papers and started reading.

"I see you must be getting a little senile, Mrs. Welker," said Jerrold while still staring at the forms. "I don't know where you came up with this garbage, but I'm afraid that's where it belongs." He tore the papers into pieces, as small as he could make them. Then he stuffed the scraps into his pocket. "Listen, granny, I think it's time you took a little trip down to the basement. Just like I did with your bestie, Gertie."

Mildred tried to absorb what she was hearing. Jerrold not only robbed her friend—had he murdered her too? Now, he was going to kill her. And when she failed to respond to her Senior Call-Up contact in the morning, he would head right over. Maybe strew some dirty clothes on the basement steps and toss the laundry basket on top of her. Then, pick up the phone and report that another old person had an unfortunate accident.

He moved toward Mildred—his arms grabbing for her shoulders. Mildred backed away, bringing her body in line with the open basement door. As he reached around her to flick on the light switch just inside the wall, a flash of brown, black, and beige fur shot across his feet. The startling flurry beneath him instinctively caused Jerrold to jump. His momentum was already carrying him forward. At that precise moment, Mildred used all her strength to thrust her hands into his back. He tumbled down the stairs, landing with a distinct crack on the concrete floor. Mildred quickly closed the basement door and pushed in the lock.

"Hey! Open that door, you old bat! I think my hip is broken. I can't move!"

Breathing hard, Mildred felt her heart racing. She thought she might faint. She needed to collapse into one of the breakfast nook chairs to catch her breath. First, she had to call the police emergency number.

After only a few minutes, Mildred heard sirens in the distance. Mr. Patches leaped onto her lap, all the while keeping his wary eyes glued to the basement door. "Oh, don't you worry about the nasty man at the bottom of our stairs," Mildred reassured him. "He can't hurt us in his condition. He's learning how it feels to be vulnerable and left all alone."

Detective Biederman watched as the ambulance pulled away with Jerrold Jones handcuffed inside. "I should have listened to you, Mrs. Welker," she said. "You would make a good detective. By the way, that's some collection of whodunits you have downstairs."

"I may have read them all before, but I am re-reading them," replied Mildred. "At my age, I can't remember how the mysteries were solved, so it's like reading a brand-new novel each time."

After she watched the lights from the detective's car fade into the evening as it turned past the curve of her street, Mildred returned to her seat by the breakfast nook window. Mr. Patches jumped into her lap and nuzzled her affectionately.

"Do you know that you are my hero?" Mildred whispered. Her cat responded with a purr suggesting that the feeling was mutual.

"Now, let's finish our crossword puzzle. Shall we, Mr. Patches?"

Introducing Agamemnon McPhee in
The Begging Machine
Neil K. Henderson

Some people seem not to have existed for most of their lives, then suddenly to be brought into being by the accident of getting noticed by a person who becomes *interested*. Such is the case of Agamemnon McPhee, whose unobtrusive activities in the backwaters of life only came to light when an abstract ripple in the continuum of credibility sent one hitherto unconnected individual on a 'fated' odyssey of collision.

Donovan Dimbledocky, inventor of Dimbledocky's Patent Patience Enhancer, was that unsuspecting catalyst. How he stumbled into McPhee at all is an interesting, albeit *pedestrian*, saga. Having graduated in engineering (with cut-price doctorate) from a mail order college down south, he had spent the time since then in waiting for his ship to come in — partly because he had failed his nautical science module, but mainly because, the morning after graduation, he had received an important-looking letter from the vicinity of the School, advising him that if he followed a "perfectly legal" set of instructions he "need never work again". All he had to do was send a one pound coin (or note in Scotland) to each of the five addresses supplied. Then, having deleted the top name and added his own at the bottom, he was to send two hundred copies with covering letter to new addresses from a "recommended" broker. Then wait to become rich.

Donovan was thirty-one when he graduated. By the time he was forty-two and still penniless, he had invented the Dimbledocky Artificial Patience Enhancer (pat. pending) and several other boons to life.

The longer, and more patiently, he sat and waited for an investor to come and market his machines, the higher went the insurance on the prototypes. It was a lot to fork out from a dole cheque. He began having nightmares about failing to pay — and Stan, Stan, the Insurance Man with a container truck at the door for his belongings. With each passing fortnight, his money seemed to stretch a little less, till one day he hadn't the potatoes to see him to giro day. Much as he hated it, he was going to have to go on the scrounge.

It was one of those magic days in autumn when God was throwing handfuls of leaves and old men into the air. Yet between the gusts a mist was edging in, making the playful sun look bleary-eyed. Donovan ventured warily, his bristly pudding-bowl hair peek-a-booing from his duffle coat like a toy hedgehog pencil-sharpener he'd once loved. Its head used to pop in and out its fuzzy body as it was pushed along on tiny wheels. His interest in engineering had been awakened even in childhood — though he remained stubbornly ignorant of the true locomotive processes of small mammals.

As he bobbed along Great Western Road through the blustery dampness, pausing only to wipe his spectacles with his handkerchief, the Old English lettering of the pub sign loomed ahead: *CAVEAT EMPTOR (Proprietor Colin Thessaris)*. The black-painted entry and dim, penny-pinching lighting boded ill for our hero's quest for spud money. Yet all was not as it outwardly seemed — for, on entering the premises, the landlord himself lurched almost actively towards him.

"Did you get it too? A hundred and eleven, like the others?"

Colin Thessaris was a bulky, red-nosed man in his early forties. His plummy drawl was difficult to make sense of, even in less breathless circumstances.

"A hundred and eleven what?"

"Beer vouchers."

"Believe me, Colin, if I had a hundred and eleven pounds *sterling*, I wouldn't be here trying to tap the price of five pounds of *spuds...*"

"No need! No need! They're all getting it. All the regulars! Everyone who's been in here says they've won a hundred and eleven quid on the slot machines at the *Nouveau Riche*. It's a miracle! It's like manna from—"

Well, Donovan already knew where manna came from — so he didn't wait for Colin Thessaris to tell him, but headed double quick for the *Nouveau Riche Speculation Emporium* to try his hand himself. With £111, he would have enough to buy his potatoes *and* pay Stan the Man's insurance instalment. But it was too late. The gaudy facade leered unsympathetically through the loose-leaf mistiness of the afternoon. He was greeted at the door by Pimpey the Nickel Tosser, an American who frequented the premises.

"Yo wanna hunner eleven pounds? Yo shoulda bin here *last night*, already! Dat wiz some poity dey had in dere!"

With head downcast, Dimbledocky shuffled in and looked half-heartedly around. The rows of electronic fruit machines were deserted. The lights were on, but nary a buzzer or bleep was heard. As he knelt to readjust the flattened cigarette packet between his sock and the hole in his shoe, he consoled himself that Pimpey would at least be in a position to lend him the price of the potatoes.

"I'll toss ya for it," says the Yank, producing his legendary nickel.

Much to his amazement, Donovan actually won, and was soon hot-footing it to the grocer's in a slightly more optimistic frame. (He'd need another go on the Enhancer, though. His levels of forbearance were getting precariously low.) As it happened, it wouldn't have mattered if he'd lost the toss with Pimpey. When he bent to sort the fag packet in his shoe, he had surreptitiously pocketed a fallen pound note which he'd spotted on entering the arcade. *That* would come in handy for a rainy day — and when he returned to his seedy flat, he secreted the money somewhere safe.

The potatoes he'd purchased turned out almost precisely average for the time of year — admirably fulfilling his expectations. Well did they complement the tinned pilchards and processed peas which comprised his entire larder. And after partaking of a modest belly-tightener, the impoverished inventor was able to ponder the state of his affairs from a comparatively laid-back perspective.

Patience Enhancer or no, it had irked him that he'd missed another life-boat in his floundering career. But now, on well-fed reflection, it occurred to him there might be more where that dropped note had come from. "Toffs are careless," as his auntie used to say. If, according to Colin Thessaris, the *Nouveau Riche Emporium* winners had all gone into the *Caveat Emptor* with their takings, maybe a few more 'beer vouchers' could have been mislaid after the evening's revels. Having nothing to lose but time, Donovan went back into the vaporous October dusk and was soon busily scouring the windfall-littered pavements connecting the new gaming hall and the pub.

And this was where Fate was to prod its knobbly finger into the proceedings. Most people slog through their humdrum daily grinds in total unawareness of those little whirlpools of temporal, metaphysical and material uncertainty which lurk here and there in their midst, set to unexpectedly rearrange time and circumstance into strange new patterns in an instant. There is one such 'enigma pocket' at Kelvinbridge, in the West End of Glasgow. The worldly pedestrians who daily pass over and through that particular Great Western Road location — just west of the bridge and to the right of the Hillhead steps — never give the risk they are taking with their dimensional stability a second thought. One has to be 'tuned in' to its presence by an unusual emotional exertion, or extreme longing or stress of just the right wavelength, before one is affected by the pull of its centrifugal force. Either that, or already interdimensionally destabilised beyond conscious control. Donovan Dimbledocky certainly had been under stress — and his search for folding money in the dark, among all the soggy autumn detritus, soon caused enough frustration to seriously counteract the Patience Enhancer's effects. Agamemnon McPhee, on the other hand, was simply unstable.

It is pointless to conjecture what Donovan would have thought had he actually witnessed McPhee materialising in a single bound from the enigma pocket, since, at the crucial moment, his eyes were glued to the ground in his painstaking hunt for dropped loot. The first he knew of McPhee's presence was when his head collided with the object in the latter's outstretched hand, which appeared to be some sort of spiked park-keeper's litter stick — with three prongs.

As he jerked instinctively back, Dimbledocky's gaze came to rest upon the knotted string around the stranger's too-big Crimplene trousers (with permanent crease). Raising his eyes slowly up — past the stained and holey cardigan to the faded ginger goatee on the smooth-cheeked, rather pinched face — he descried a spare-built man of some mature years, taller than himself, with a tacitly overbearing aspect and aquiline nose. He looked down suddenly to avoid eye contact, and amusement mingled with relief when he spotted the scabby carpet slippers on the strange man's feet. Obviously not much of a threat as potential muggers go. Donovan lightened up considerably, and nodded toward the pronged implement.

"Is the toasting fork for chestnuts, or are you out for your Halloween?"

"Don't be bloody daft! It's Trefoil O'Leary!"

"Terribly sorry, Mister O'Leary! I... er..."

"Not me, dunderheid! *This* is Trefoil O'Leary!" He brandished his spiky stick. "*I* am Agamemnon McPhee, conceptual entrepreneur and independent lifestyle operative. And you—" he pointed the O'Leary at Dimbledocky and examined some sort of illuminated gauge in the handle "- are carrying absolutely no money whatsoever."

"Erm, no... I... thought I dropped some, actually. Round about here, somewhere."

"Oh yes?" There was a glint of suspicion in McPhee's eye. "How much?"

Before he could stop himself, Donovan had blurted out, "A hundred and eleven pounds."

"Aha!" The stranger's expression lit up. "Just the *one* hundred and eleven pounds?"

"Well, when I say *a hundred and eleven*, I mean *some*... That is..."

And so the impecunious engineer explained about his visit to the *Nouveau Riche*, and how he'd found the loose note, and what Colin Thessaris had said about the winners being in the pub...

"Colin Thessaris? It's not like him tae give out free information. Words may be cheap — but not in *his* boozer."

"You know him?"

"Know him?! He wis one of my earliest... er, *customers*..." McPhee consulted the gauge in his O'Leary contraption again, shaking his head ruefully. "Well, there's *nae* hundred and eleven pounds... or *any* pounds... round here, Mister—"

"Dimbledocky."

"Dimbledocky? Of Dimbledocky's Patent Patience Enhancer?!"

The inventor nodded pinkly.

"I've read your paper in the *New Boffin*... Listen, if ye're short o' cash, I might be able tae help ye oot. That apparatus o' yours has definite possibilities. Tell ye whit — meet me here at noon tomorrow, with the Enhancer, and maybe we can do business... Oh, and bring that loose pound note. It might be significant."

The sound of inebriated students noisily emerging from the *Caveat Emptor* made Donovan look round. When he turned back again, Agamemnon McPhee had vanished into thick air.

*****

At first, Donovan was apprehensive about entrusting his precious Patience Enhancer to a stranger, but having survived without recourse to its beneficial influence since the business of the £111 wins began, he wasn't in a mood to hang about. After all, he'd already spent most of his postgraduate existence waiting for his ship to come in — so why hesitate now to decide whether this pea-green jolly-boat had his name on it? Next morning, therefore, he bundled up his prototype and his troubles in an old cat basket, and fished out the lucky pound note he'd found from its hiding place. Curiously enough, it actually did have someone's name on it, only it wasn't his: ERIN SCRUTTON was printed in blue block capitals. It must have been on the other side when he'd picked it up. Maybe it meant something...

Due to bad planning, Dimbledocky arrived at the Hillhead steps nearly half an hour too early. His reserves of patience enhancement had completely run out, and he was starting to go into withdrawal. This involved a lot of agitated pacing up and down, with his hedgehog head bobbing back and forth more than usually rapidly, his arms rising and falling at his sides like a penguin in distress. Well, what with the strung-out state of his nerves, and the repetitive pavement-pounding, he all-unwittingly thrust himself into the gaping vortex of the enigma pocket. Without a second's warning, he found himself sucked into an interdimensional conundrum — and he didn't know whether he was coming or going.

At this point, the reader may be interested to note that Agamemnon McPhee does not reside in a conventional dwelling — even by Glaswegian standards. In fact, he lives on an intellectual island floating in the air above South Knightswood, and signs on the dole by telepathy. The postman sends up his giro once a fortnight on the end of a series of long bamboo poles. (That's McPhee's story, and he's sticking to it.)

The enigma pocket shifted Donovan Dimbledocky right up to McPhee's intellectual front door. One minute he was striding past the steps at Hillhead Street, the next he came to rest at the top of a stairwell in what had every appearance of an ordinary tenement building. There was a nameplate above the bell-push by the side of the door:

AGAMEMNON McPHEE

CONCEPTS BOUGHT, SOLD & EXCHANGED

ACUMEN FOR HIRE.

Donovan found himself automatically pressing the button before the full impact of his teleportation experience had time to hit him. He heard a muted voice within, cursing angrily. Then the door opened, and the tirade boomed forth unhindered.

"I thought I said meet me at Hillhead steps at noon? Whit's the meaning o' this premature intrusion?"

Here was a very different McPhee from the cardigan-and-slipper apparition of the previous evening. His erstwhile grey, balding head now sported an ill-fitting red wig, while his upper legs and torso were enveloped in a traditional Highland over-the-shoulder plaid. The slippers had been replaced, somewhat incongruously, by a pair of calf-length cowboy boots. Dimbledocky was so confused already, that he simply stood and stared.

"Ahem." McPhee calmed down when he saw the basket his visitor was carrying. "*Kipper a hat, chief!* I'm afraid I haven't had time to change out of my... relaxation wear. Come away in, and bring your invention. Did ye remember the pound note?"

The unintended intruder snapped out of his trance. He followed his host through what were either several doors in close proximity, or the same door several times over, until they came to a halt in a large, but cluttered, parlour. Donovan produced the pound.

"It's got a name written on it. I wish I'd been in the *Caveat* that night... Colin Thessaris said *everyone* that went in there was loaded."

"Was his nose throbbing?"

"Yes. And quite bright red."

"Aye... I feel a wee bit... responsible there. He came to me for advice about expanding his business. (He'd need tae expand or bust, after all — he'd never be able tae sell it on wi' a name like *Caveat Emptor*!) As it happened, I'd just been trying out a new acquisition, the Simpson Modulator, to... 'adapt'... this theory I'd found in an old copy of the *New Boffin*. Are ye familiar with Giblett's Theory of the Expansion of Alcohol? Well, put *very* simply, it states that people who get incredibly drunk become like rubber, therefore people who drink expanded rubber alcohol will... distend pub landlords' bank accounts indefinitely. He got his inspiration from a mediaeval despot who used to make his vassals wear rubber bands round their noses in winter to prevent them sneezing — thereby inventing possibly the earliest rubber based, self-regulating, internal expansion intensification mechanism. (Mind you, Giblett himself eventually died of spontaneous human brain explosion, so what does that tell you?) Anyway, I took the Vladsbastard-Giblett technique back to first principles, ran it through the Simpson Modulator, and tried it out on Thessaris — got him drunk, stuck double-strength elastic bands round his hooter, then told him subliminally that when he sobered up, he'd be fabulously wealthy..."

McPhee shook his head and sighed.

"That's why his nose throbs even to this day, whenever serious money is mentioned in his pub. My data must have been incomplete... *I have created a monster!* Er... can I see that pound note?"

Dimbledocky handed over the Scruttonised banknote, and the inscrutable theory-adaptor perused it for some time, his lower jaw making a peculiar sideways chewing motion as he did so.

"Yes... very crumpled, isn't it... Erin Scrutton, eh? That name rings a bell." He turned an eye on his guest. "You don't mind if I hang on to this for... research purposes?"

"I... er..." Dimbledocky stood gazing helplessly as his nest-egg disappeared into the concept collector's sporran. Well... maybe he should consider it an investment. With the potatoes secured and his larder stocked till payday, he wasn't going to go hungry — so what the hell.

"Now then!" McPhee clapped his hands together briskly. "Let's have a look at the Patent Patience Enhancer!"

Donovan lifted the cat basket off the floor, and cast about him for a raised surface of some sort. It was the first chance he'd had of looking over McPhee's apartment. The place was crammed with bookcases and shelves — some jutting into the room at right-angles to the walls. Everywhere, strange items of machinery and glassware stood on platform stands, workbenches, even orange boxes and banana crates. Here and there, ominous-looking fishtanks — with or without water — lurked among a profusion of robust houseplants. The lino-covered floor, interspersed with threadbare rugs, supported tatty second-hand furniture (surely that dilapidated suite could *never* have been new) and neatly arranged piles of papers and magazines. Abstract paintings and arcane charts and diagrams filled the available wall space, while the single window at the back exposed a breathtaking panorama of the north-west corner of Glasgow and the hills beyond. Not the sort of thing one expected to see from a tenement... Indeed, it only struck Donovan later just how incredibly high up they must have been, to be able to see so far — but he was interrupted before he could fully appreciate it at the time.

"You can put it here," said McPhee, lifting a large, oblong tortoise shell from a side-table and nodding to the space. The inventor unpacked his Patience Enhancer, prompting an ecstatic gasp from his host, who handed him the carapace in his eagerness to inspect the device. The Enhancer wasn't very big — smaller than a portable typewriter — and outwardly consisted of a keyboard and adjustable funnel.

"The keys determine the setting and strength," said Donovan. "You'll see little labels for variables like age, sex, temperament and so forth, which are used in conjunction with the numbers and letters for preciseness of dosage strengths. (I've programmed it to accept a preset code for my own personal treatments.) Once you've set the co-ordinates, you simply stick the funnel in front of your face, turn the handle, and go with the flow..."

"Brilliant! And can the mechanism be adapted for... other purposes?"

"I don't see why not. It's a standard Bismuth-Axiomaster assembly..."

"No problem. The Simpson Modulator and a modicum of swearing will take care of it."

McPhee went out of the room and came back with the three-pronged device of the previous evening.

"I used the Simpson Modulator to develop Trefoil O'Leary from a flounder fork, a pressure gauge, some electro-magnets, a dynamo and the insides of a cash register. A few reversed polarities and an assortment of curses, and *Hoy! Velocity!* There we have it."

"What does it do, if you don't mind my asking?"

"Not at all! We're practically *partners*, aren't we? No need to impale yourself upon the beanpole of uncertainty! Trefoil O'Leary is my hand-held cybernetic dosh detector — suitable for locating currency of all kinds (even credit cards) in any situation, under any conditions. No more fiddling about through piles of rubbish or wet leaves looking for lost change..."

"So you were looking for money as well, last night!"

"Not just *any* money. It's these miraculous batches of a hundred and eleven pounds people kept winning on the gambling machines. They have to be... redistributed... before a social catastrophe of global proportions takes place…"

"Is it laundered money?"

"No, no, it's *perfectly legal*. But it's undermining confidence in world begging."

A chill ran up Dimbledocky's spine and waggled his ears. Any threat to world begging was a threat to him.

"Wh… what can be done to prevent it?" he gasped.

"As it happens, I have been taking some steps tae counteract the unsolicited generosity of the gambling machines before a virus of prodigality confounds the livelihoods of honest freeloaders everywhere. I have sent out a chain beggar tae cover the vicinity around the *Nouveau Riche* and *Caveat Emptor* and most of Kelvinbridge and Hillhead…"

"Chain beggar?"

"A simple enough idea. One of our operatives appears at a selected front door at some inconvenient hour, asking for a handout. Even if he receives a small sum, he refuses tae go away until the householder gives him the name and address of at least one other likely local benefactor. Then he turns up at the new place and says, "Your friend So-and-so gave me this, and said you'd double it." It's amazing how ready people are tae play 'Pass the Beggar' — especially in the early hours of the morning. It's as if they resent being disturbed, and want tae make someone else suffer worse than them. Sometimes they give our beggar quite a lot, just so that whoever it is they don't like will have tae fork out twice as much. Jist as well Pimpey's got a touch o' the tinker in him — with all the experience he's had grinding other folks' axes…"

"Pimpey? Pimpey the Nickel Tosser?"

"Small world, eh? 'Nickel tosser' is American slang for 'chain beggar', you know… In fact, the whole concept is an American import like 'Trick or Treat'. That's his opening gambit. He turns up at the first door and flips his coin in the air, kind of suggestively. "All I got off that last dude," says he, "is this lousy nickel." Nowadays, we try tae encourage him tae use a ten pence piece… but he still uses the nickel for training new recruits, and the nickname seems tae have stuck with his 'students'. As a matter o' fact, it wis Pimpey who first told me about the *Nouveau Riche* handouts."

"So how did he get on this time?"

McPhee lowered his gaze. "Bad... very bad... It's a whole new ball game, when you always want the same specific amount..."

"A hundred and eleven pounds?"

"Precisely. That's the fiendish thing about it. The person behind all this obviously knew how difficult it would be tae reverse their despicable philanthropy... But why *a hundred and eleven*? Why not a straight hundred? What's the significance o' the amount?"

"It's certainly irreversible, all right."

"How d'ye mean?"

"A hundred and eleven — it's a numerical palindrome. One-one-one — the same forwards as backwards."

McPhee looked at Dimbledocky with surprise — then genuine respect.

"I think ye may have hit on something there, Doctor D. Perhaps all this is more than just a plot by the well-to-do tae destabilise the shiftless classes for their own ends... And I think that machine of yours may be the very key tae the problem."

"As a matter of fact," said Donovan absent-mindedly, "one-one-one is also my personal patience enhancement configuration. You know — '*me, myself, I*'."

"*Melon heid!* Why did ye no tell me that sooner?"

"I didn't connect my machine with the money till now..."

"Right! Well, you just leave the machine tae me and the Simpson Modulator, and we'll see whit happens once we've rearranged the patience patterns tae a suitable persistence level for begging. It should be easy enough to set it tae beg a hundred and eleven pounds, if it's already pre-programmed tae recognise the number. Aye! We'll not only recoup the anonymously patronising generosity of the *Nouveau Riche* for the benefit of upright scroungers of the old school, but maybe liberate a few extra batches that have been sent out by the ringleader! Tell me, Dimbledocky — did anyone else know about the Patience Enhancer?"

"Only Stan, the insurance man. But he wouldn't know any of the details…"

"Whit insurance company would that be?"

"The Ergonomical."

"Ah! That would explain a lot… Never fear. They may trick us, they may bribe us, they may even pay us handsomely… but *they cannot buy off an honest beggar!*"

On McPhee's suggestion, Donovan left his invention with the conceptual rag-and-bone man and made his way home. This proved easier than expected, since the tenement stairs leading down from the "CONCEPTS BOUGHT, SOLD & EXCHANGED" sign conveniently deposited him back at the Hillhead steps in Great Western Road.

*****

A week went by, during which Donovan felt strangely at peace with himself. It never occurred to him to question his odd transportation to McPhee's dwelling. His giro came on time, and he stopped having nightmares about the insurance man. After all, Agamemnon McPhee had the Patience Enhancer now, and maybe he wouldn't bother keeping up the cover on his other appliances… He was finding it surprisingly easy to just 'let go'.

Then, at the beginning of the second week, he noticed an unusual advertisement in the Personal column of the *Daily Spurt* — next to the vacancies for mail-order engineers:

"COME IN, NUMBER 111 — YOUR TIME IS UP. Would the party seeking to recover an item of lost property connected to the above, please meet finder at Kelvinbridge Underground Station at 2.30pm today, where they will hear something to their advantage."

This must surely refer to the Patience Enhancer and the mysterious gifts of money. Donovan Dimbledocky would most certainly meet finder at Kelvinbridge Underground — it had been a long time since he'd heard anything to his advantage.

As he reached Great Western Road, and was about to cross in the direction of the subway station, Donovan was distracted by the sight of workmen at the *Caveat Emptor*. They were taking down the name sign.

Maybe Colin Thessaris was yielding to the inevitable — giving the pub a new identity to make it easier to sell. Indeed, now he came to think of it, Colin hadn't been seen since he'd spilled the beans about the great £111 mass giveaway. For all Donovan knew, the chap might have succumbed to spontaneous human brain explosion, like that fellow Giblett in the *New Boffin*...

As the scuttling inventor approached Kelvinbridge Underground, across the seasonally swollen river, his bobbing head came to a stop in the 'out' position. There was the still tartan-clad figure of Agamemnon McPhee. (Relaxation wear? A likely story!) He was skulking menacingly round the entrance foyer, with what looked like an old-fashioned bus-conductor's ticket machine secured to his person by an accordion strap criss-crossed over the shoulder-plaid. He seemed to be waiting for someone in particular — his gaze darting periodically towards the station escalators.

An echoing noise — like the distant quack of a duck flying south for the winter — made Dimbledocky glance to the water below, before he realised it was laughter coming towards McPhee from the underground. Then a well-rounded woman in her mid-thirties of, it seemed to Donovan, enchanting personal presence (he'd had a sheltered life) set off to a tee by her power-suit jacket and leather mini-skirt, became visible approaching the curiously-equipped concept collector.

"Is that your share-price indicator, or are you just pleased to see me?"

"So! You took the bait!"

"Not just me, by the look of things."

They both stood looking at Dimbledocky, who had arrived at the foot of the steps leading down from the bridge.

"Well met by... duck light!" said McPhee. "Ahem. Doctor Donovan Dimbledocky, esquire, inventor of Dimbledocky's Patent Patience Enhancer, allow me to introduce Ms. Erin Scrutton, get-rich-quick witch, and high priestess of financial investment swindles..."

"Oh no! Not "You Need Never Work Again"?!"

"To name but one. She and her associates have been responsible for a whole range of outrageous plots to take honest begging off the streets, where it belongs, and replace it with faceless bureaucratic fiscal soliciting…"

"Get real, granddad!" Ms. Scrutton's composure suddenly cracked as she turned on McPhee with a snarl. "This is the threshold of the New Millennium — the age of comfort importuning has arrived. Your door-to-door chain beggars are last century's thing."

"Taking the livelihood away from hard-working chancers! You won't get away with it!" McPhee was seething beneath his loose red wig.

"Wanna bet, old yin? You're totally past it — and that philabeg get-up belongs in a museum!"

"How dare you! This begging regalia was handed down to me by Pan-Handle Henderson himself!"

So, thought Donovan, that's what McPhee had just returned from when he'd called prematurely that morning and caught him on the hop. Of course! *Philabeg* — from the classical Glasgow Gaelic, meaning "for the love of begging"! (Dimbledocky had had a special-offer crash course in etymology thrown in with the engineering, as a reward for applying within 14 days.) Too bad it was the wrong kind of kilt.

"How dare you insult the memory of a genius?!" continued the wearer. "You've asked for it now…"

"Go on, shock me!"

Without further ado, but a fair bit of foul language, McPhee aimed the funnel of the modified Patience Enhancer toward Erin Scrutton's face. Then, running his nimble digits over the keys, he began to turn the handle of what was now the Begging Machine.

"Lend us a fiver!" he yelled with merciless bravado.

A look of horrified amazement assailed the bonny but businesslike features of Ms. Scrutton.

"Sod off!" she shrieked. But even as she did so, she found herself involuntarily fumbling in her handbag. Next thing, a five pound note was ungraciously tossed in the direction of McPhee.

"Grab it!" he called to Dimbledocky — who lost no time in obeying.

Strange tune-like sounds could now be heard emerging from the contraption. Could it be... country dance music?

"So, I'm just a has-been, am I? Give us a tenner!"

Erin tried to stamp her foot defiantly, and found herself breaking into a disjointed rigadoon as she began digging out more money.

"Better make that twenty!"

The lady jumped up and down with rage, but McPhee had her where he wanted her. He kept turning the handle and increasing his demands, like a bingo-caller at a ceilidh, while she jigged and reeled uncontrollably in a demented strathspey. At the end, his defeated and humiliated victim seemed to give up all resistance. She shuddered to a halt and turned out her bag on the pavement in front of them. The paper money totalled £110 precisely.

"Well, well, well," sneered McPhee. "Fancy that. All except one — and all with your name on, Scrutton. There's many a good tune tae be got out of an old fiddle, eh? Heh! Heh! Heh! And there'll be a few more tidy sums like that doing the rounds, I'll bet..." He made a swift adjustment to the Begging Machine, muttered a couple of obscure obscenities, then turned the handle again. "Come on, then! Names and addresses."

The broken businesswoman took a computer printout from an inside pocket, handing it to McPhee, who stowed it in his capacious sporran.

"That'll save Pimpey a lot of needless trial-and-error."

As if released from bondage, Erin Scrutton let out a forlorn wail and scurried back inside the tube station, arms flailing above her head like a deranged imitation of the Highland fling. Donovan made to follow her, but McPhee held him back.

"Let her go, Dimbledocky. I don't think she'll be any danger tae us now. In fact, I reckon she wis already discredited when the puggies gave her partners' funds away in the *Nouveau Riche*. And now we've got her computer list of members' IDs, we can easily get tae the winnings before she does."

"But I wanted to ask her about my "You Need Never Work Again" dividends. It's been eleven years now—"

"Ferget it. Put it down tae a wee smudge on yer CV of experience... Anyway, you *haven't* worked again, *have* ye? So whit's the problem?"

And before the inventor could raise any more objections, McPhee puffed out his chest and made a stentorian throat-clearing noise, by way of preamble to an imminent exposition.

"As it happens, Doctor, *you* have been unknowingly involved in this whole mullarkey right from the beginning. Before that, in fact. Does the *Ezee Studee School of Economic Opportunity* mean anything to you, at all?"

"That's where I got my engineering degree!"

"Quite. I knew I'd seen the name on that pound note before, and when I looked up the *Bust Executive's Business Directory* in the library, I discovered that Erin Scrutton was the head of that very centre of learning — with its spin-off "never work again" letters. She was also the "senior financial consultant" to the *Nouveau Riche Speculation Emporium*, when it took over the old *Three Kings Casino* place in Great Western Road. And on top of that, she's the president of the Ergonomical Assurance Company, who—"

"Insured my Patience Enhancer!"

"I knew it was too much of a coincidence that the code for your personal patience dose was one-one-one. Tell me... had you been having funny dreams before the money came out the machines?"

"Yes! I kept dreaming about... Stan the Insurance Man!"

"Post-hypnotic effect. There's been a technological race going on between certain unscrupulous organisations, to develop a high street begging machine suitable for placing in shopping centres, amusement arcades, even inside supermarkets. The *Nouveau Riche* was a front for Scrutton's undercover research centre. When you registered your Patience Enhancer at the Patents' Office, her ladyship must have got wind of the machine's potential and sent this Stan round with his mesmeric charm, to persuade you to take out one of their Ergonomical Assurance policies. (No doubt he came "recommended", like a certain mailing list broker.) Then, bit by bit, when he returned to collect the premium instalments, he could get all the details out of you by hypnosis, to take back to Scrutton without you remembering anything later."

"Bastards! That cover cost me an arm and a leg!"

"Hence the expression 'one-armed bandit'. But what they hadn't reckoned on was your treble-one coding in the matrix. When they developed their models, they must have discovered that they could only beg sums of a hundred and eleven pounds — no easy feat, even for a machine. And with the reversible nature of the number (as you yourself pointed out) perhaps their machines would have a tendency tae give it away sometimes, instead of begging — like a vacuum cleaner blowing instead o' sucking. Hence the names on all the banknotes, tae make sure everyone got the right dough after a blow-out. If each member of the big new begging consortium had a batch of a hundred and eleven pounds for test purposes, it's likely they'd mark their own wad so it couldn't be secretly swapped for doctored notes, to lay a trail back tae their H.Q."

"They're not very trusting, these greed merchants..."

"But they've got enormous egos. It's thanks tae Erin Scrutton's big self-advertising block capitals that we got on tae her in the first place. If Pimpey is successful with the names and addresses on that printout sheet, we may find more subtle markings on the other batches. Hopefully, the Simpson Modulator can 'neutralise' them for redistribution."

"I thought it was all to do with identifying the migration routes of loose money—" said the inventor "—like putting a ring on a bird's leg."

"Naw — just keepin' tabs on their golden goose. But that night in the *Nouveau Riche*, something must have overloaded the system. Maybe a lot of hard-up students were giving off heavy financial embarrassment signals. Anyway, all at once, all the experimental begging modules disguised as gambling devices decided tae go generous — and out came all the dosh in one go. Scrutton must have pretended tae be one o' the winners, and grabbed as much as she could from her own outlet. But in the stampede, one pound note got overlooked — which you found next day. And that has proved the vital clue. Look how eagerly she came tae reclaim it. Of course, the incident set off the chain of events which led you tae me, enabling me tae beat them in the great Begging Machine development race. Whatever shady investors Scrutton was trying tae entice won't touch her temperamental models wi' a barge-pole — especially when they find I can out-beg them at every corner with *your* machine."

Donovan ventured a polite cough. "Does this mean you'll be keeping hold of the Patience Enhancer, then?"

"It's a Begging Machine now, Dimbledocky! There's no turning back. At least you'll be free of the pernicious and addictive effects of unnaturally enhanced patience."

It was true. Donovan had felt like a new man in the last week. "Er... what about my original Scruttonised pound note?"

"We'll consider it a fee, shall we?"

"If you insist."

✶✶✶✶✶

And that was the last Donovan saw of his Simpson Modulated invention for some time. Then, after a winter of mixed excitements and slush, he found himself in George Square in the early summer sunshine, his attention drawn by a group of Japanese tourists with cameras, clearly enjoying some sort of performance under the statue of Prince Albert. A man swathed in ancient Highland plaid, supporting what looked like a bus-conductor's ticket machine with a funnel, was delivering a spirited rendition of *Ye're No Awa' Tae Bide Awa'*, while simultaneously dancing a caper with one arm raised above his head, and turning the handle of the machine.

"Kipper a hat, chief!" he concluded, with a flourish.

Agamemnon McPhee had ensured the survival of street begging, at any rate. And Donovan was pleased to have played his own small part. Maybe one day their paths would cross again. He had a strong yen for further enterprise.

All the same, something told him this was not the time. He would have to wait to be invited into McPhee's intellectual habitation, whenever himself should feel inclined to lift the DO NOT DISTURB sign from his life. Until then, the whereabouts of his dwelling would remain as much a mystery as its unfathomable *whateverness*. As for Dimbledocky's share in any profits from his first commercial success, the Begging Machine — well, he'd just have to be *patient*, wouldn't he?

-o0o-   -o0o-

<u>*Author's Note:*</u>

puggies is a Scottish term for gambling machines.

Swan Song
A short story celebrating food
AP Warren

The flight from Dubai was delayed and didn't touch down at Heathrow till gone 10 pm. Vexed and fatigued, all Gwen wanted to do was check into her hotel and sleep. Before jumping into bed, she texted her father, assuring him she'd pay him a visit the following day. Normally, she went under as soon as her head touched the pillow, but tonight she couldn't help replaying the conversation from the previous weekend. Her father had called out of the blue, the first contact in the five years that had elapsed since her mother's death from ovarian cancer. Once a world-famous chef, he was a self-invented bon-vivant, raconteur, and alligator-wrestler; loud and brash, possibly coke-fuelled, he was a perpetual motion machine. But despite the distinctive plummy voice, the man who called her sounded like a stranger — defeated, full of self-loathing, and slurring his words.

She slept till noon, awoken by a staff member knocking her door. She located a delicatessen, purchased a brioche baguette, and caught the train to Cardiff, where she checked into another hotel. She spent the day pottering around. First, a visit to her mother's memorial stone in a village churchyard, then coffee with a couple of old friends, and a pleasant solitary stroll through Sophia Gardens and along a section of the Taff Trail. She thought of her father's bad behaviour and his attrition of her mother's joy of life. The only saving grace had been a peaceful death in her sleep. It was nearly midnight before she acknowledged to herself that she was prevaricating. She was nowhere near tired, so she grabbed her coat and headed for her father's new restaurant.

As she arrived at the door of *Essence de Saveur* in Cardiff Bay, a tall, slender black woman was exiting; the woman smiled broadly, as if bumping into an old friend.

"I realise you're about to close," Gwen said, "but I'm here to see the owner." She noted how she avoided using the familial relationship.

The woman touched her wrist briefly. "I know who you are, chef. Who doesn't? You're an inspiration, the reason I wanted to become a chef."

"Oh," Gwen said, flustered. "Thank you."

A series of crashes and the slamming of a door came from within, followed by incoherent cursing.

"I take it he's in, then…?"

"Youma."

"Youma. Nice to meet you."

Gwen followed the noises through to the kitchen and beyond to an office door. She pushed the door fully open. The scene that confronted her elicited a double take. Her father was stalking a black swan around the office, holding a black bin-liner open wide, trying to throw it over the bird's head. Paperwork flew around, adding to the chaos.

"Shut the bloody door, girl, before it escapes."

His voice was still slurred; for someone with his track record of drinking, he must have really been hitting the sauce. She complied and watched, unamused. None of her father's escapades fazed her. No doubt, it was nothing more than fodder for a good drinking yarn. He changed tack, dropping the bag and lunged for the bird, wrapping both arms around it. It flapped and honked madly, but he managed to soothe it into docility.

"Hand me the Damascus."

"Pardon?"

"The knife, girl."

Gwen eyed the fifteen-centimetre blade on his desk. She moved it well out of his reach.

"What are you doing, you damn fool? I need the Damascus."

"You plan to butcher a swan in your office? I think Buckingham Palace might have something to say about that."

"This is a *black* swan, an Aussie interloper, not a bird native to these isles, therefore none of her majesty's concern."

"*His* majesty," she corrected. "And I think you'll find it's classified as a wild animal and is therefore protected."

Thirty minutes later, having returned the swan to the wild, they were sitting front of house like civilised folk, each sipping a mineral water.

"I have a vision to create a legacy of uncommon delicacies," he said by way of apology. "Braised swan legs, swan cutlets, swan neck broth. The meat is so succulent, gamey, light on the palate. Superior to both duck and goose."

Gwen rolled her eyes. "It would be difficult to sell a signature dish using a meat that everyone knows is illegal. We'd be shut down within a week. What other ideas do you have?"

"I'm considering offering blowfish."

"Blowfish, hmm. I'm not sure of the demand here in South Wales. And we'd need to hire a fugu chef."

"I've run some figures; it's feasible. It would generate massive press."

"Aside from the treasonable and the lethal, what other ideas do you have, dad?"

Ignoring the question, he said. "*Dad*, eh? So, you've decided to join me in my final foray."

"I have?"

"You said 'we'."

She paused, realising that she had indeed. The strange phone call had acted as a catalyst. She'd done a three-year stint as chef de cuisine at one of Dubai's most prestigious hotel-restaurants, overseeing a menu of some thirty-five dishes and a staff of forty. It had been a wonderful, if exhausting, challenge but the glamour of the position and of the desert paradise itself had worn off. Truth be told, she'd already been looking for an excuse for a change.

"'We' is still just a possibility. There'd need to be an understanding.

And changes; big changes."

He feigned disinterest. "Such as?"

"Shall I list them alphabetically?"

"Such a comedienne."

She raised her hand as a shield and looked up at the lights. "If your goal is to create the atmosphere of a Gestapo interrogation room, then you're succeeding. We need to soften the lighting, find the sweet spot between retinal after-burn and murkiness."

He grunted. "What else?"

She glanced around the dining area. "I like the antique pine furniture, but I think for the high end that you're aiming for, you can't go wrong with a crisp white tablecloth and silver cutlery. Also, we should lose a table, reposition, and reorientate. Some tall pot plants strategically located should provide a feeling of privacy and separation."

"You don't want much, do you, girl? You do know I've been in this game since before you were born?"

"Gold star awarded to father for longevity. The dinosaurs went extinct because they couldn't adapt to change. You don't want to be a dinosaur, do you, dad?"

She stood up. "Right, let's take a look at the kitchen and then you can show me the menu and financials."

She was satisfied with the kitchen appliances, but not with the separation of stations and the partition walls. She intended to rebuild the kitchen based upon an island layout. The menu was too large and too disparate. She wanted to rationalise and redesign it around a theme, possibly based upon intriguing variations of traditional British dishes. Her father, however, insisted he retain creative control but would take her counsel seriously. The financials showed that the business was making a small profit; she could immediately see how to reduce costs and increase revenue, but that discussion could wait for another day.

It hadn't escaped her attention that he'd been unsteady on his legs. Maybe that and the slurred speech were not, after all, the result of the booze catching up with him. Had he suffered a minor stroke? Disinclined as she was to show concern, she decided she had to put the question to him.

"Motor neurone disease," he said, hanging his head.

This took her by surprise. "Oh, no. How long have you known?"

"I was diagnosed last month, but the symptoms started coming on four or five months ago and have been gradually getting worse despite this so-called medication I'm taking, Riluzole."

"And the prognosis?"

"How long is a piece of string? It'll be fatal, but maybe not for many years. And well before that, I'll have trouble swallowing, breathing, even fucking *thinking,* if I'm really unlucky. But I'm not going to let it get that far."

She recalled more than one occasion during her adolescence in which he'd espoused the virtues of voluntary euthanasia. "Why, what do you have planned?"

"I've lived as a chef, and I'll die as a chef. With my fuguhiki knife."

She frowned. "Fugu…? I see, as in blowfish."

He smiled grimly, placing a fingertip on the right side of his neck. "A single forceful push here, take out the carotid and jugular, and it'll be goodnight, Vienna."

"Sounds great, dad."

"You don't believe me, girl? I've rehearsed it. I'll need a Magic Marker, a mirror, and both hands. I'm only human, so no doubt I'll consume a sherbet or two, first."

The last thing she wanted was to get into a serious debate on the minutiae of suicide by knife, so she decided to out-sensationalise him. "Why don't we record it, upload it to YouTube? It'll be one way of drumming up interest in the restaurant. No such thing as bad publicity, et cetera."

They stared at one another in silence. Finally, Gwen said: "How do you see the power dynamic working in this business?"

"There's only room for one chef de cuisine, of course, which will be you. My days of manual dexterity are behind me. I'll be executive chef, overseeing operations, holding the creative and strategic reins. You'll be the general on the ground."

"That could work. With the proviso that we make the changes I've outlined."

He sneered. "I'm not made of money. Everything I have is already invested in this."

"I have some investment capital."

He perked up. "Oh, so you're in, then, girl? With both feet."

"Why not?" she heard herself say, checking her watch. "I'll start later this morning. You can introduce me to the staff. And in front of staff, you can address me as 'chef' and not 'girl'."

*****

The staff assembled in the kitchen at 9.30 a.m. Youma smiled warmly at her. The other chef de partie was a stocky, tattooed man in his late twenties called Darren Bowen. According to her father, both were hardworking, competitive, and highly skilled, but the similarities ended there; Youma was softly spoken and 'a little Asperger's', whereas Darren was loud and prone to emotional, often teary, outbursts. The commis chef, Gabriel Augustinha, was a Brazilian youth barely out of his teens, who liked to hum folk songs to himself, particularly one beautiful piece called *Gaiana*. There were also a handful of servers and casual staff.

Her father gave the keynote address with the swagger she recalled from twenty years before. He outlined his vision for the business, including succession, before introducing her. She kept her speech brief, outlining her approach to running a successful kitchen and what she expected from her team.

She concluded with a call to arms: "I want you to enjoy your work. I'm always open to suggestions for improvement, but I also expect commitment, cooperation, and utmost professionalism. Let's make this fine dining establishment a roaring success."

She paused, surveying their faces. "Any questions?"

"Yes, chef," Darren piped up. "We're missing a sous chef." His tone indicated that he was throwing his hat into the ring.

"I know, and we'll fill that position in due course, hopefully from within. Any more questions? No, OK, let's get to work, team."

When the last of the lunchtime customers had departed and she'd supervised the cleaning of the kitchen in preparation for that evening, she sought out her father. He was in his office, standing at a white board, apparently deep in thought. She noticed he was leaning on the desk to support himself, his arm trembling. He appeared even thinner and frailer than the day before. Maybe she cared about him more than she'd believed.

"What are you planning?"

His eyes lit up in his drawn face. "My swan song. My legacy to the culinary arts. Seven continents, seven dishes."

"I thought we'd settled this, dad. We're going to focus the menu, structure it around a theme, that theme being traditional British food."

"Yes, yes," he said dismissively, clearly bored by the idea. "This will be a side project, a series of experiments. We'll offer them via the specials board. And yes, there is a theme."

"Seven continents is a theme? More of a catch-all."

"No, girl. *I* am the theme. I've travelled to all seven continents and sampled the cuisines and cultures of each. This is my curated shortlist. Each is unique, full of character, unconventional, and iconic. *Just like me*, did I hear you say, girl? Yes, just like me."

"You forgot to say modest. OK, dad, you can have control of the specials board. But nothing illegal, OK? No black swan cutlets."

"You're a killjoy. All right, then, I promise that swan will not appear on my shortlist."

She glanced at the items on the whiteboard. "Take me through them."

Again, his eyes sparkled. It struck her how important this creative project was to him. She made a mental note to be lenient.

"In no particular order, from Asia, we have century eggs. Want me to describe the dish?"

"Please do."

"Eggs, in this case duck eggs, are preserved for one hundred days in ash, lime, salt, and tea. At the end of this period, the eggs are shelled, sliced, and served with pickled vegetables."

She Googled the dish. "Oh, the eggs turn black. Interesting. It's a lot of time and effort, dad. Can you really see a demand?"

"For heaven's sake, girl, this isn't a popularity contest, it's culinary art and unashamed extravagance. It's about making a bold statement and sticking two fingers up to convention."

"If it makes you happy."

"It does, and they are heavenly. You should try them. I certainly intend to."

"What's next?" She squinted to read his scrawl. "From Africa. Bunny chow?"

"A food of the South African people, street food, if you will. In essence, one hollows out a loaf of fresh bread and fills it with a zinging curry. I'll use beans, garden vegetables, and goat meat, for authenticity. It sounds downmarket, but done well, it's exquisite."

"From North America, bombe Alaska. That's just a flambéed variant of baked Alaska, right?"

"There's no 'just' about it. Baked Alaska is notoriously difficult to do well. And I intend to play with the flavours."

"OK, great. Three down, four to go."

"It's a work in progress. Now, be a good girl and bugger off, would you? Tortured genius at work."

*****

At the following morning's shift, Gwen prepared six dozen century eggs and stored them on a dark shelf to mature. She sounded out Youma and Darren about preparing the bunny chow and bombe Alaska to her father's handwritten instructions. Darren was especially keen and insisted on taking ownership of the latter, as he obviously deemed it to require the higher skill level.

When the commis chefs were done with the prototype of each dish, she fetched her father to evaluate them. The entire kitchen staff watched in fascination, as he held up each with trembling hands, examining the visual aspect from every angle. He ripped off a hunk of bunny chow, chewed, and swallowed, poker faced.

"You've committed the biggest sin, girl," he said to Youma. "It's bland. It doesn't excite me."

Youma looked disappointed but not particularly upset. Gwen supposed she was used to his ways.

Darren smugly trickled spiced rum over the bombe Alaska and flambéed it.

"Help yourself, please, chef."

The adjudicator took a sharp knife and cut a cross section through it. An impressive, layered array of colours radiated out: from the orange sorbet centre, through blackcurrant ripple ice-cream, through dark chocolate sauce, to the peaked meringue mantle.

He threw a gaze of contempt at Darren, who reddened and looked like he might burst into tears. "I shall not be trying it. The structure is not up to the required standard. The layers need to be of uniform thickness and curvature. And the ice-cream should not intrude into the sorbet."

He shook his head. "Fucking amateurs." And shuffled out of the kitchen.

The second attempt also met with rejection of both dishes. Gwen questioned her father in private.

"What is the issue, exactly? The presentation, the texture, the aroma, the taste, they all seem fine to me."

"I agree with you on the first two criteria. It's the taste and aroma that are lacking. I want your team to inject some kinaesthesia. I want to be able to taste the colours and smell the textures."

"You're not making sense, dad."

"I want contrasts that synergise. I want an orgy of flavours. Throw caution to the wind, yet follow my instructions to the letter."

Gwen closely supervised the third attempts. To the bunny chow, she suggested that Youma add sweet and sour fruitiness, in the vein of a dhansak. To the bombe Alaska, she suggested that Darren contrast the sweetness of the blackcurrant ice-cream with a hint of coffee; and to try a fifty-fifty mix of spiced rum and honey bourbon as the flambé. She was simply plucking ideas from her subconscious without applying too much thought. How do you please a madman? But please him, both dishes did, and a teary-eyed Darren added them to the specials board for that evening.

The culinary union of father and daughter celebrity chefs had generated a lot of interest. She had several newspaper and magazine interviews lined up. She took an interview with Radio Wales but declined national radio and all TV requests. She was aware that her father, the inveterate publicity whore, had in the last few weeks given in excess of twenty interviews across all media. He had arranged for on-premise television pieces with ITV Cymru Wales and with S4C, the latter to be conducted by him in the Welsh language. She'd reluctantly agreed to participate in both but drew the line there. She insisted that from thereon in, all publicity would be achieved solely via word of mouth and unsolicited reviews.

At work, she confined herself to the kitchen, while her father prowled front of house with his stick like a demented PT Barnum, feeding off the rapport with his customers, milking every last ounce of his renewed celebrity and reputation, making offhand references to the TV shows and bestselling cookbooks from the salad days of bygone decades. When she sensed he was outstaying his welcome, she'd send one of the serving staff to fetch him on the pretext of a kitchen crisis.

As the months passed, he noticeably deteriorated. He sometimes struggled to swallow and would get panic attacks, treating himself with alcohol, which fuelled his rage at the unfairness of the universe. As was the nature of the industry, they all worked long hours, but he seldom left the premises. He continued to work on his 'seven continents, seven dishes' project, but progress was painfully slow, and one day, she heard screams and crashes from his office. She found him hurling his whiteboard ineffectually at the window. After this episode, he went AWOL for an entire day. After work, she drove to his home, a converted farmhouse on ten acres in Cowbridge. The house was dark apart from the lounge, from which lamp glow was visible through closed curtains. She spent several minutes trying to get him to come to the door, but the house remained silent and his mobile phone unanswered. She banged the door and yelled his name, certain he must be inside, and eventually he opened the door to her.

He was as drunk as a skunk, his eyes unable to focus, and he had a long, deep gash on his forehead that gleamed pinkly with a blackened bloody crust. She winced, imagining the pain.

"What happened, dad?"

"Oh, this?" he asked, fingering the wound. "What do you think happened? Motor fucking neurone disease happened."

He swayed and she feared he might fall and cause himself further injury. She helped him back inside, unable to decide if the booze had been imbibed before or after the accident. Probably both.

"Let's get your shoes on, I'm taking you to A and E."

*****

Gwen insisted he take a week off work. In addition to putting himself at risk, an appearance might scare the staff and customers. Inevitably, he argued, yelled, and otherwise threw his toys out of the cot, but finally he agreed and made it sound like a respite was his idea; it would give him the time and the space to complete his project.

She called around near the end of this period. He answered the door wearing several thick layers of clothing, a beanie, and a scarf. He told her that since his mobility had declined, he wasn't generating any internal heat.

"Why don't you just turn the thermostat up?"

"A warm room makes me drowsy. I'll be sleeping the big sleep soon enough. While I'm still breathing, I'll remain wide awake, thank you."

"Don't you think you're being a bit melodramatic, dad?"

"I'd like to see how you'd cope with it, you fucking insensitive brat."

Her stoicism in the face of the insult seemed to shame him, and he began to weep. He grabbed his stick and shuffled out of the lounge, locked himself in the bathroom, and refused to come out.

Staff morale improved during his absence. Under Gwen, they had a calm, predictable leader with a clear vision. Business was booming; front of house was full every lunchtime and evening, and there was a three-month waiting list. Promoting Darren to sous chef for a probationary period, she had hired two more commis chefs and had plans to extend the restaurant. Wine & Dine magazine had printed a review describing *Essence de Saveur* as 'a transformative union of traditional meets modern, every dish simply wonderful'. Even the specials were doing a roaring trade, a phenomenon she had to see to believe; they would run out of century eggs in two days, and it would be another fifty-five days before the next, larger, batch was ready.

Despite having vowed she would not play to an audience, she felt that her father had turned his showmanship into an expectation that would disappoint if it were to cease. So, she had taken a deep breath each evening and circulated briefly among the clientele, exchanging pleasantries and delivering anecdotes. On the eighth day, her father returned unannounced like Lazarus. Gwen heard his booming, slurring, yet mellifluous voice from the kitchen, and had emerged to see him strutting centre stage, dressed as Charlie Chaplin's clown, twirling his stick, and milking his audience for every available iota of adoration.

He was in the midst of telling the story of his illness, how it had affected him, and the prognosis. Never one for understatement, he told them he was baring his soul to them as he looked death in the eye.

"But fear not, ladies and gentlemen. I shall not be sliding downhill into a slow and undignified end. No! As the bard said, I shall not go gentle into that good night. I shall end it abruptly and fittingly with decisiveness and panache."

He ripped off his wing collar, and proudly displayed the right side of his neck, complete with bold period drawn in black Magic Marker. Crossing the period were several shallow, scabbing hesitation cuts, presumably from one or more practice runs.

Gwen fetched Darren and Gabriel. "Help me get him back of house."

"Yes, ladies and gentlemen," her father continued. "I shall be providing a visual spectacular for your delectation and delight by doing the dirty deed on this very spot."

There was laughter and a ripple of applause; they didn't believe he was serious.

He whipped out the fuguhiki knife and held the point to his neck with both hands. The room fell into a nervous silence. He stared around, smiling strangely, feeding off the energy.

"And perhaps my daughter will concoct a wonderful new dish to allow you to partake of my flesh."

Then, he removed the knife. "But not this evening, folks."

There was relieved laughter. Gwen took the opportunity to step in with Darren and guide him towards the kitchen, while Gabriel, humming *Gaiana*, deftly relieved him of the knife.

In his office, she sat him down and asked him if he'd heard of Dignitas.

"Of course I have. I'm not a bloody imbecile. I've considered it but I have two objections. One, it's too passive; as already stated, I intend to go out with a bang. And two, I'd need a travelling companion, and said companion would risk prosecution for manslaughter."

"That's a risk I'd be willing to take."

"Well, I wouldn't. End of discussion."

*****

No longer able to walk, not even with a stick, he'd petulantly agreed to a full-time carer, giving Gwen the simple direction that she must be under the age of thirty-five and 'have a great arse'. He'd ceased taking Riluzole, as it was 'a fucking waste of time and money' and replaced it with medicinal vodka and tonic. He took a bite from a century egg and asked her to bring his whiteboard closer.

He'd completed his swan song, the design of the remaining four dishes and wished to hand them over to Gwen for implementation according to his strict instructions. Representing South America, Chile en nogada (poblano chillies stuffed with spiced minced meat, topped with a walnut sauce and pomegranate seeds). Representing Antarctica, pemmican (a low-water biscuit composed of jerky and fat); not strictly a native dish, granted (there is none), but widely consumed by Victorian explorers. Representing Oceania, poisson cru (a Tahitian specialty of raw tuna marinated in lime juice, served with diced vegetables and coconut milk).

"And from Europe?" she asked.

"Why, consommé, of course.

"Consommé? Isn't that a bit mundane after all the exotica?"

"I needed a starter. And there's still no better measure of a chef than the quality of his — or *her* — consommé."

And with that, he seemed content.

Drowsily, he said. "You've booked the tickets?"

"Yes, dad."

"Switzerland can be cold this time of year. When do we fly out?"

"One week from today. It's all arranged."

"Good, one more week of purgatory and then, blissful release."

*****

His carer let her in and told her he was in bed, where he'd spent most of the last week.

As Gwen entered his bedroom, his eyes flickered open. He looked tired but she could still see the intelligence and the understanding in his eyes. She placed a pack of century eggs on his bedside table.

"Ah, thank you, chef. My appetite is not what it was, but I shall partake. Care to join me?"

"Of course, chef."

She helped him sit up in bed. She shelled a couple of eggs and handed him one on a serviette. They each took a bite. He chewed but struggled to swallow and ended up having a choking fit. She took the black egg from him, wiped his mouth, and dried his tears. Then, she laid him back down in bed, tucking his arms inside the quilt.

"Sorry about that," he croaked. "You can't take me anywhere these days. How are my latest specials doing?"

"Well, so far, we've only operationalised the poisson cru and the pemmican. Both are surprising successes."

"Not surprising to me. Do you have the tickets? Your passport?"

She shook her head, her stomach filling with butterflies. "I seem to have mislaid them."

"Ah, not to worry, I'm not overly keen on Switzerland." He gripped her hand with surprising force. "I'd rather die in my sleep. That is one thing your mother and I agree upon."

She stared at him, her eyes stinging with tears. Only then, did he release her hand.

She took an unused pillow and placed it over his face, leaning into it. He struggled reflexively, but her elbows pinned his arms beneath the quilt. When he'd stilled, she kissed his cheek, feeling something akin to love.

Skinning the pillow and stuffing its cover into her bag, she called for his carer.

The Nun's Habit
Michele Bazan Reed

Sally Shaffer got a hall pass toward the end of third period, so she was the first one to come upon Sister Francine. The elderly nun was lying on her back at the foot of the stairs, her black veil askew and her wooden rosary flung over the last step. Sister's ever-watchful eyes stared up unseeing at the shocked freshman's face. Sally's screams drowned out the class-change bell.

Sister Regina, the principal, came rushing out of her office to the right of the ornate marble stairway. She automatically crossed herself when she saw Sister Francine, and blessed the body of her colleague as well, muttering a prayer. Then she quickly went into action, calling to her secretary, Mary McCarthy, to phone the police, and ordering Joe Tubbs, the janitor, to cordon off the area with some of the green and white bunting left over from the pep rally the day before.

The entire student body of St. Dominic's was in motion, heading to their fourth-period classes, and Sister Regina directed them back to their classrooms to await further instructions.

*****

"Of course, the coroner will have the official word, but it looks like a tragic accident to me." Officer James Sampson snapped his notebook closed. A 1963 graduate of the Police Academy, he hadn't seen many deaths in his first year, but this one seemed pretty clear-cut. "Those stairs are mighty steep, well-polished, and with that long skirt…"

"We call that a habit," said Sister Regina. "Sorry, force of … habit." He grinned at that and she gave him the frown principals reserve for troublemakers. Sampson found his shoes very interesting at that moment.

"Here's the thing, Officer," Sister Regina continued. "After a distinguished career as our languages teacher, Sister Francine was assigned as our hall monitor, and she was noted for being a strict disciplinarian. She was diligent in her duties and sent many students to my office for infractions. She … well, let's just say she wasn't the most popular faculty member because of it."

"So, she was good at her job. I don't see how that would cause a fall," the officer insisted.

"Yesterday, she was particularly harsh on a trio of girls, who had been running through the hall, singing at the top of their lungs." Now it was Sister Regina's turn to look at her shoes as her cheeks reddened, where they showed outside the confines of her starched wimple. "It's not *that* they were singing. It's *what* they were singing: that obscene song, 'Louie, Louie.' Sister Francine was right to send them in, and you can be sure I meted out some strict discipline."

Sampson winced, picturing rulers on knuckles, but the principal continued.

"Detention for a week and they are banned from Friday's dance. As you can well imagine, they were very angry with Sister Francine for turning them in. On their way out the door, I heard one of them say, 'Don't worry, we'll get even with her for this.'"

Sampson sighed, and commandeered the library for interviews. "Send them in," he told Sister Regina. "See that no one leaves the building. I'll want to talk to the girl who found the body, too, and the other nuns."

*****

The gleaming oak surfaces of the library tables reflected the late afternoon sun, and Sampson ran his finger under the crisply ironed collar of his uniform, wishing he hadn't picked the table closest to the mullioned windows. He had to admit to himself that his discomfort wasn't only due to the heat of the late-September day. He was a parochial-school boy himself, and just the sight of those nuns in their habits brought back memories of his days at Saints Cyril and

Methodius.

To his childish imagination, the black-robed specters had seemed to levitate like some otherworldly apparition. He was so afraid of them that in first grade, he ran away during recess. He was almost all the way to downtown, when his Aunt Freida spotted him as she was returning to work from her lunch break. She bundled him into her Studebaker and delivered him back to school, where the worried sisters were so relieved that he was safe, he escaped with light punishment of three days clapping the erasers. His cousin Tommy, in the grade above him and tasked by the family with watching out for James, got in more trouble than he did, once Aunt Freida got home.

Officer Sampson still had a grin on his face, remembering the incident, when Sister Regina appeared at the door of the library and fixed him with an icy stare. She had three girls in tow.

"Murder is hardly a laughing matter, Officer Sampson," Sister Regina said. She gestured to the teens. "Karen Murphy, Marcia Kozlowski and Bonnie Romano. Your suspects." She drew out the word "suspects," beginning and ending it with a sibilant hiss.

Sampson cringed. "We're just asking questions right now, Sister," he said with as much authority as he could muster in the face of the principal. "Nobody's a suspect."

"Yet," Sister Regina said, and turned on her heel to glide back out the library door.

Sampson took a good look at the girls before him. Dressed in Black Watch plaid skirts, Peter Pan collared blouses and navy blazers with the school crest on the pocket, they looked suitably prim and proper. But as soon as the nun was gone, Karen, on the right, pulled her long blonde pageboy into a high ponytail and rolled up the waist band of her uniform skirt to a more fashionable length. Marcia, in the middle, popped a stick of Juicyfruit in her mouth and started loudly snapping it. Bonnie pushed down her regulation knee socks to slouch around the tops of her saddle shoes. Sampson could see why the strict nun was displeased with them, but he thought they were acting like ordinary teenagers, not murderers.

What did they teach you in the Academy, Sampson? he reminded himself. *Everyone's a suspect until cleared.*

"What's this about you girls singing an obscene song in the hallway?" he asked, looking from one to the other. "'Louie, Louie,' wasn't it?"

"Not obscene," said Karen. "Or at least, not the way we sing it. We can't understand what they're singing, so we just make up our own words."

Sampson made a note on his pad. He had been following the news and knew that the FBI was investigating alleged obscenity in the song. Sampson figured some record company exec filed a complaint with the FBI as a marketing ploy to sell more records. Given the song's rank in the Top 10, it seemed to be working.

"The sisters think everything's obscene, but what do they know?" Marcia made a face. "They just don't want us to have any fun. You'd think it was 1864, not 1964."

It was all Sampson could do to hold back a smile, when suddenly Bonnie burst out with: "Oh c'mon, tell the man the truth!" She was immediately met with a shocked look from Marcia as Karen shook her head and mouthed "No!"

Sampson sat up straighter at that and fixed each girl in turn with his sternest policeman's look.

"Tell the man what, girls?" he said. He waited, turning from one to the other and tapping his pencil on his notebook. The interrogator's best tool – silence. They'd taught him that at the Academy, too. Sooner or later the subject would break and tell you what you need to know.

I guess they didn't count on the Code of Silence of the Teenage Girl, Sampson thought after an uncomfortably long pause yielded no result.

When the girls remained tight-lipped, he confronted them one by one.

"Karen?" Another headshake.

"Marcia?" She folded her arms across her chest and kept her lips zipped.

"Bonnie?" She looked at her friends and rocked from one slouch-socked foot to the other, clearly weighing her desire to come clean against her fear of risking her friendships.

Then she nodded decisively. "OK, you guys, this is serious. We're being accused of murder here. We could go to jail or … or worse." As Karen covered her eyes with one hand and Marcia turned aside, scowling, Bonnie looked Sampson in the eye and blurted out, "We were singing it because Karen has a crush on Louie Bianchi. We'd passed him in the hall and thought maybe he smiled at her. It was our way of celebrating."

"You mean, your way of teasing me," Karen shot back.

Turning to Sampson she said, "Yes, Officer, she's telling the truth. Louie is the dreamiest ever. But you can't tell anyone, promise? I'll just die."

Sampson put his head in his hands at that point. *Lord, spare me from teenage girls,* he thought. But he had to admit, he could picture his younger sister doing exactly what these girls did.

Marcia filled Sampson in on the reason for Karen's consternation. "Louie is the quarterback of the football team. He's one of the coolest of the cool kids. We, however, are not. Cool, that is."

"They're both right. We'd be laughingstocks of the school," said Bonnie. "Can't you just say you found us innocent and not give the reason why?" All three looked at Sampson with pleading eyes.

"Well, there is the little question of your threat to Sister Francine," the officer reminded them. "Sister Regina said you were heard to say you'd 'get even with her' for sending you to the principal's office."

A look passed among the girls. With a sigh, Karen stepped forward. "She caused us to get banned from the dance on Friday. With the big game on Saturday, all the football players will be there. Since Louie smiled at me, I figured it was my chance to get a dance with him, maybe he'd ask me to wear his ring," said Karen, her voice trailing away in a sad little sigh. "I was so upset."

"You've got to believe us, Officer," Bonnie said, "We'd never really hurt Sister Francine."

"Yeah, we thought we'd pull a prank on her," Marcia added. "You know, pin a sign that said 'Kick me' to the back of her habit, or put salt in her sugar bowl so when she had her afternoon tea, she'd spit it out all over her desk. Stuff like that."

Sampson thought the girls were telling the truth, but he couldn't say so. And he still had a possible murder to solve.

"OK, you girls can go back to your classrooms," he said. "But remember, I'm going to be investigating this case thoroughly, so if you lied …" He let the phrase hang in the air. "And if you think of anything that can help, you know where to find me."

Next to come in was one of the nuns, a Sister Beatrice. Despite the fact that her hair was covered by a veil and her body disguised by the long habit, Sampson could tell she was not much older than the girls who had just left the room. She wore a white veil, which he remembered from his Catholic school education denoted her as a novice, a sort of trainee nun.

"Everybody calls me Sister Bea," she said with a perky smile that lit up her face. Fluttering her fingers in the air, she made a buzzing sound. Sampson liked her immediately.

The notes Sister Regina had given him noted that Sister Bea was a friend of Sister Francine's, and that she was particularly popular with the girls in the school, especially Bonnie, Karen and Marcia.

"Did I just see Karen, Marcia and Bonnie coming out the library?" Sister Bea asked Sampson before he could get a question in. "You can't be suspecting them? They are the sweetest girls."

"Well, Sister Regina says they were overheard making a threat to Sister Francine."

"That's about that song, 'Louie, Louie,' isn't it? They told me they got sent to the principal's office for singing in the hall. What nonsense." The young nun shook her head. "They were just having fun."

"Well, apparently both Sister Francine and Sister Regina thought it's obscene."

"Bah. You can't even understand the words. You may as well say 'Dominique' is obscene. You can't understand the words to that, either."

Seeing Sampson's bewildered face, she pointed to a record album propped up on one of the library shelves. Its white jacket had a black and white illustration of a nun playing a guitar and the words The Singing Nun. "The song is in French! And it's about St. Dominic!" She started laughing out loud then, a joyous and uninhibited giggle, and Sampson started to join in. He caught himself in time, thinking about Sister Regina's admonishment about his earlier grin.

"It tells how St. Dominic preached about the Lord, despite the hardships he endured travelling by foot throughout the land. How he stood up to the king for what he knew was right. We need to be inspired by that, to seek justice … for Sister Francine."

"Are you saying that you don't think Sister Francine merely fell going down the stairs, tripped over her skirt or something?" Sampson asked.

Sister Bea became quiet and focused on the ceiling. Contemplating? Or looking for heavenly guidance? Sampson wondered. But it soon became clear to him that young nun was struggling with her emotions.

She sighed and continued. "No, I don't think that's what happened at all. Sister Francine was very concerned about safety. She always scolded students who horsed around near the stairs, or who tried going down with their noses buried in a book," she told him. "She would never walk down the stairs herself without a firm grip on the stair rail with one hand, and the other holding up the edges of her skirt."

Sister Bea paused as Officer Sampson jotted notes about her comments on his notepad.

"I suggest you look at who else Sister Francine had disciplined recently for breaking the rules. See if anyone else had a motive for murder." When Sampson raised an eyebrow at her remark, she explained. "Sorry, I'm a student of G. K. Chesterton."

He still looked puzzled, so she elaborated. "He's the author of series of mystery stories where the detective is a priest, Father Brown." She looked down at her hands, folded primly in her lap. "Sister Regina says it's a bad habit. She tells me I shouldn't let my enthusiasm for solving mysteries run away with me."

Then raising her eyes to meet his gaze, she said, "But it goes deeper than that with this case. You see, Sister Francine was my friend and mentor. She saw something in me back when I was a student here at St. Dominic's. She took me under her wing, you might say, and helped me see that I had a calling to serve in the church. She even helped me get into St. Rose College and wrote to me while I was away from home, to keep my spirits up. I try to pass on a little of her kindness to the girls who are here today. But I'll never match her goodness or generosity."

Gone was the meek little sister he had seen in front of him just a moment ago. Sister Bea sat up a bit straighter and there was a determined look in her eyes. "So that's why I can't let her death go unexplained. I—we—have to see that justice is done for Sister Francine."

✶✶✶✶✶

"Well, have you solved the mystery of Sister Francine's death, so we can get back to educating our students?" Sister Regina looked up from her paperwork and fixed Officer Sampson with a steely glare.

"I'm afraid police work is not all that cut and dried, Sister. In fact, our investigations sometimes provide more questions than answers." He tried to remind himself that he was a grown man and an officer of the law, but being in the principal's still made him feel like that first-grade boy who ran away from school.

He straightened up and asked in most authoritative voice, "Do you have a list of the students who were sent to you for discipline by Sister Francine? I need to see the last couple of weeks."

The principal rummaged around on her desk and handed Sampson a ledger-like book. "This is the log of all our detentions. But seriously, most of them are for some small infractions of the rules. And no one threatened the good sister the way those girls did."

Officer Sampson scrolled down the list of recent detentions. One name caught his eye: Louis Bianchi.

"How about this boy?" he asked, pointing to the name. "What's his story?"

"Typical football player stuff—he and his teammates were horsing around when they started teasing one of the freshmen, and it got a little out of hand. When the parents of the other boy complained, I had to take disciplinary action. I barred Louie from playing in the game on Friday."

"Wasn't he upset?" asked Sampson, snapping the book closed.

"Not as much as Mr. and Mrs. Bianchi, I can tell you that." The principal looked out the window at the campus grounds, goal posts rising in the distance. "They're big donors to the school, even bought new uniforms for The Hounds."

Seeing his quizzical look, she explained, "St. Dominic's followers are the Dominicans, and in Latin that is the same as *Domini canes,* which translates to the hounds of the Lord. They got that nickname because they were so dogged in hunting down heretics—people who disagreed with the official teachings of the church. So, our team here at St. Dominic's is The Hounds." Her face lit up, and Sampson began to see that while the nun put on a stern face for her students—and intruding policemen—she might have a bit of a playful side.

*****

As Sampson left the principal's office, he ran into Sister Bea in the hallway.

"Hi, Officer," she said. "How's the investigation going?"

"Well, I did as you suggested and asked for the detention list," he said. "Louie Bianchi was on it. He and his friends were teasing a younger student and Sister Francine sent them to the principal's office. Louie has to miss this Saturday's game as punishment and his parents were not pleased."

Hearing that, Sister Bea sucked in her breath.

"What is it?" asked Sampson. He could tell something was bothering the young nun, as she fidgeted and looked around nervously.

"Well, after we talked earlier, I was determined to see if I could reconstruct Sister Francine's last day. I wanted to see if there were any clues that might help me figure out what happened to her."

"Now Sister, you know that's a job for the police. This is real, not some short story with a priest—or a nun—detective." Sampson frowned.

She reddened at the rebuke, but continued. "I know, but I was assigned to cover study hall, since Sister Francine …" Sister Bea bit her lip and looked down at the class roster she had twisted beyond recognition. "Basically, monitoring study hall means sitting there for an hour, and making sure the students are quiet and in their seats. I got bored and started rummaging through Sister's desk drawer. And I found this!"

She reached into the folds of her habit, where apparently the nuns had voluminous pockets, because she pulled out a black leatherette notebook with the single word *Agenda* outlined in silver ink.

"It's Sister Francine's calendar, and I was just going to bring it to you, when we ran into each other."

Sampson took the book and started flipping through it. There was only one entry for today, 9:30 a.m., the start of third period. It read: Father White.

"Who is this Father White?" he asked Sister Bea.

"That hung me up for a while, too. I figured it must be some visiting priest. We often get them here: missionaries raising money, friars wanting to speak at a retreat or something. Father White—I guess I was thinking of the fictional Father Brown." She gave a little shrug. "But when you mentioned Louie Bianchi's parents being upset, it was easy to put two and two together!"

Sister Bea looked around and lowered her voice. "Being an old language teacher, Sister Francine loved to play with words. She'd often write cryptic notes to me, half in another language. It was our little game. It looks like she used the same type of codes in her agenda, to keep her plans hidden from prying eyes.”

Sampson looked puzzled. “I’m glad it makes sense to you, but I don’t see how this can help solve the mystery of her death.”

“Bianchi comes from the Italian word for ‘white.’ Sister must have been meeting with Louie’s father. He probably hoped to convince her to rescind the punishment so Louie could play in the big game.” Sister Bea shook her head. “He wouldn’t be the first parent to try and get their kid off the hook. But Sister Francine rarely relented.”

“He must have been the last person to see her alive. I’d better have a chat with Mr. Bianchi.” Officer Sampson waved his thanks to the nun and headed for the door.

*****

The next day, Sister Bea was called down to the principal’s office. Officer Sampson was there, sitting on the other side of Sister Regina’s simple oak desk. She motioned for Sister Bea to take the seat next to him. “Sit down, Sister. Officer Sampson has some news for us. And he asked that you be present.” She kept her face bland, but her eyes showed her concern.

“Sisters, I thought you would want to know that Louie Bianchi’s father was present at the time of Sister Francine’s death.”

Sister Regina gasped and quickly crossed herself. Her shocked expression turned to one of puzzlement, as she noticed that Sister Bea registered no such shock.

“Sister Bea was kind enough to assist me in puzzling together the clues, which included Sister Francine’s agenda. It was Sister Bea here who figured out that a calendar entry for one ‘Father White’ was written in a bilingual code. It was actually not a visiting priest but a meeting with Louie’s father.” The young nun blushed and looked down at her hands, nervously clutching the rosary which hung from her belt.

“Bianchi. White. Ingenious,” said Sr. Regina.

Sampson consulted his notebook. “When we brought Mr. Bianchi in for questioning, he broke down and told us the whole story. He and his wife were extremely upset that Louie was disciplined by making him miss the game on Friday. Several top college scouts were scheduled to be there, and they hoped their son would land a football scholarship at a prestigious school."

Sampson shook his head. "Mr. and Mrs. Bianchi felt that because they were generous supporters of the school, their son should get preferential treatment."

"Not from Sister Francine," Sister Bea put in. "She believed strongly that everyone was to be treated equally—equally strictly in most cases, but fair play was her rule."

Officer Sampson took up the narrative again. "That's what Sister Francine told Mr. Bianchi, but he wasn't willing to accept it. Sister made it clear that the interview was over; she wasn't changing her decision. As she was escorting him to the exit, Bianchi stopped at the top of the stairs to try one last plea to change her mind, appealing to Sister's affection for his wife, who was a favorite student of hers here at St. Dominic's decades ago. As he stepped toward her, lifting his arms and beseeching her to reconsider, Sister instinctively backed away. She caught the skirt of her habit under the heel of her shoe and fell to her death. Mr. Bianchi ran away out of fear and sorrow over Sister's fall."

There was a moment of silence and Sampson watched both nuns, moving their lips wordlessly, heads bowed.

"A prayer for Sister Francine?" he asked when they were finished.

"For her … but also for the Bianchi family. They will need the Lord's help now as well," Sister Bea explained.

"I owe you a big Thank You," the police officer told the younger nun. "If you hadn't solved the riddle of Sister Francine's play on words, we never would have known what happened that day."

Turning to Sister Regina he said, "I hope you'll let me call upon Sister Bea from time to time, when I'm stuck on a case. Maybe she could be a kind of 'consulting detective,' like Sherlock Holmes."

"Or Father Brown," the principal said with just the hint of a smile. "As long as you don't make a habit out of it."

Hoodwinked
Bonnar Spring

I was upside down in *adho mukha svanasana*, known in the English-speaking yoga world as "downward dog," when Evan burst into the parlor. "Police at the door, Mamie."

I released the posture and sat back on my haunches. Evan, now appearing right-side-up, was wide-eyed. "If they're selling raffle tickets or something, can't you just give them a donation?"

Evan grabbed his formal black jacket off the back of the Queen Anne armchair. "They asked for you. By name. They know you're home."

"O-*kay*. Stall them for five." A headache pulsed in my temple. This was a lousy start to the day after pulling off a successful con. "And see if Alice is still home. It might be better to have her with me."

Getting into character with a stiff bow, Evan backed out of the room. And I dashed upstairs to shed my workout clothes. Five minutes later, a soft knock at the parlor door indicated that the show was about to begin.

"Yes?"

Evan ushered two men into the room. "Detectives Finch and Adams, ma'am. From the Rockport Police. They wish to speak with you."

I'd changed into a pearl-gray twinset and curled my ponytail into a bun. Alice, seated next to me on the mauve Chesterfield settee, was in her smart uptown outfit, ready for a reconnaissance mission on Newbury Street. In front of us, a low table held a tray with a china teapot and a plate of scones. Thanks to Gina, our *chef de cuisine*—and knife-wielding kitchen ninja—we could've been snooty society ladies having a natter.

"Officers?" I tilted my head to indicate offhand curiosity. "What can

I do for you?"

"Mrs. Margaret Longwood?"

"It's 'Miss' Longwood." I angled my hand toward the facing couch. "Please, have a seat."

Finch, the older cop, took charge. Only after he nodded did he and his partner sit. In keeping with my public persona, I allowed the silence to build. One does not welcome total strangers into one's home with excessive *bonhomie*.

Finch cleared his throat. "Do you know a Mr. Charles Beaumont?"

Uh-oh. The drumming in my skull went double-time.

Like a good butler, Evan had left the room after making introductions, but he was probably watching on our closed circuit. I hoped to hell he was taping it, too. I might need to replay this for his expert body-language analysis.

"Why, yes. Charles—Mr. Beaumont—and I have been...keeping company." I let out a chuckle. "I guess you'd say 'dating,' Detective Finch."

"Were you 'dating' Mr. Beaumont last night, by any chance?"

Ooh, he was a sharp one—what other knives might he possess? This was not likely to be good news but, like everyone in my home, I had a role to play. I set down my teacup and folded my hands in my lap, favoring him with that matronly crinkled eyes and wrinkled forehead thing. A mute expression of *why exactly do you want to know*? "No, we didn't have plans last night, but we're going to dinner at the Gleason's on Saturday."

"I'm afraid you'll have to make other arrangements. Mr. Beaumont was found dead this morning."

Shit! Now what? Fortunately, that outburst was only in my mind. The *oh* that squeaked out was in character. I covered my mouth with my hand and looked down, thinking furiously.

Alice flew to my side—the stage lost an award-winning actress when she joined our merry band. "Mamie, you poor dear!" She tut-tutted and patted, blanketing me from their view until I had time to arrange my face into a mask of sorrow and concern.

I'm sure I'd paled with their news. *Had they found something that linked to us at Charles' house?* Hands pressed as though in prayer, I quavered, "Poor Charles. I hope it wasn't painful. Was it his heart?"

Of course I knew police didn't go around making polite conversation with the known associates of heart attack victims. But *they* didn't know I knew—wasn't I some out-of-touch rich spinster?

Finch barely restrained an eye-roll. "This was not a natural death, ma'am. Mr. Beaumont was found in his study. Strangled."

I fanned myself with flapping fingers; I whimpered. Alice, still sitting at my side on the settee, recommended tutting. She whispered, just loud enough to reach the detectives, "Do you need to lie down, dear?"

Finch raised his hand to form a stop sign—*damn.* "We have a few more questions."

My eyes went wide with not-so-feigned trauma. "Yes?"

"In Mr. Beaumont's study, we noticed quite a few photographs."

Really? Not what I most feared. Deep breath. I inclined my head. "Some of me, I assume."

"Yes, and in one, you are wearing a blue scarf with gold swirls. Would you please show it to us?"

I was getting a seriously weird vibe. Nothing for it but to punt. "Unfortunately, I've misplaced it."

"So, you can't produce the scarf?" The steeliness of Finch's question had me praying my instincts would steer the conversation in a safe direction.

"No, officers, it's been missing for...Alice, do you remember the last time you saw me in my van Gogh scarf?"

"Weeks." She shrugged. "Gosh, have you even worn it since the Tremont art auction? That time we got so wet?"

Also, the time we walked away with the stolen Mary Cassatt— though, of course, I didn't mention that.

Finch's associate—or whatever the proper word in police language— spoke for the first time. "What did you call your scarf?"

"Oh, the motif is from a painting by Vincent van Gogh. I bought it at MoMA a few years ago. Since the weather warmed, I haven't thought about wearing it."

"Moving on, then." Finch flipped open a small notebook. "When was the last time you were at Mr. Beaumont's residence?"

"I, um, stopped by a few days ago."

"Could you be more specific?"

I narrowed my eyes, hoping to convey a genteel impatience with his persistence. This spanner in the works—aka Charles Fucking Beaumont getting himself killed—called for an immediate huddle with the gang. "Tuesday evening."

"What was the occasion of your visit, if I may ask?"

"You may ask, of course, but it was...honestly, must I go into details?" My bashful-lady routine was rusty, but I gave it my best shot.

And Tuesday evening had been a very good night, the culmination of two exasperating months of skullduggery. Charles, the man, wasn't the problem. He was a courtly, old-fashioned...thief, I guess you'd say. But he wanted to wine and dine me. It took a lot of maneuvering to get him used to me wandering into his office.

Finch harrumphed, but continued. "And you've not been to his house since?"

"No." *I got everything we needed.* "Why?"

"Would it surprise you to know that a drawer in Mr. Beaumont's desk contained a folder with information about you?"

My instant intake of breath was not an act. "About me?" I turned to Alice, whose eyes reflected my visceral panic. *This is not good.*

"Yes, notes and photographs."

The way Finch left the last word dangling, my first thought was *salacious,* but that—considering my lack of actual intimacy with Charles—was impossible. "What do you mean?"

"Pictures of you. Taken on the street at various locations. From a distance, so we believe it was without your knowledge. Along with them were a few notes. It seems Mr. Beaumont was blackmailing you."

"What?" Panic ratcheted up to horror. *The bastard.* I didn't see *that* coming! "He was most assuredly *not* blackmailing me." My voice shook in what I hoped sounded like righteous indignation, not fear.

"The notes in the folder were in draft form," the detective said, "so perhaps he had not yet approached you." When he turned to his partner, his smirk said, *or perhaps he had.*

Every scenario I could imagine to account for those pictures scared the shit out of me. And now the police had them. I needed to know more. "If you'd show them to me, perhaps I could help you figure out what Charles was up to."

In other words: Where was I in those photos? What was I doing? What did Charles suspect?

"Appreciate the offer, Mrs. Longwood. Perhaps we'll take you up on it later. For now, though, we need to ascertain your whereabouts from last evening at six o'clock to this morning at nine."

"I'm a...suspect?"

"Mr. Beaumont was strangled with your van Gogh scarf."

And with that, I gave Detective Finch the alibi he'd have the most trouble breaking.

*****

The second Evan shut the door on Finch and his almost-silent partner, Gina rushed into the foyer, barking into her phone. "Vic, get down here. It's shit-hit-fan time."

We gathered in the parlor. In any other establishment, you'd call it the living room, but a Rockport mansion like ours called for more elegant terminology.

"Hey, hey, the gang's all here." Evan pulled up the Queen Anne armchair while Alice and I reprised our positions on the settee. Vic and Gina took the other couch. Alice, of course, had been present for the whole conversation, and Evan had monitored it from the office. Gina had been in the kitchen and Vic in his apartment over the garage, but Evan had alerted both via text about the police presence. We recapped the whole shebang for them.

Vic ran his fingers through his long, artfully-tousled curls. "I guess Beaumont isn't ever going to know we dipped into his accounts yesterday."

I stuck out my tongue. "Not a good time for jokes."

Vic smirked. Although a nerves-of-steel getaway driver, our chauffeur spends most of his time playing the guitar and smoking weed. "But with the police butting in, *someone* might notice those last money transfers. Where's the money right now?"

"Our client's money is back in her account where it should be," Evan said. "And our cut is in the Caymans. Good work, Mamie, ferreting out Charles' user-IDs and passwords and installing the backdoor software. The rest was a cinch." He leered at me. "That was cute with the cops, too, your oh-please-don't-make-me-say-sex line."

I glared at my partner, both in business and in, well, life. "Would you two please act like grownups for a minute? We have to keep the fucking police from looking too carefully at me as a murderer."

"And," said Alice, "out of Charles' business, or they could stumble onto our scam."

We've been doing this for three years now—and by "this" I mean taking jobs to return items to folks who'd been ripped off and lacked the money or standing to go through endless legal hoops. Or else they needed the return accomplished a lot sooner than an official judgment could be rendered.

That Tremont art auction job had been one of the hurry-up ones: The husband of a divorcing couple decamped with a Mary Cassatt painting that had been in the wife's family for generations and immediately put it up for auction. Once it sold, likely to the Saudi collector who'd been eyeing it, repatriating the painting would take years. Our eighty-year-old client didn't have *years*. She did have lots of money, though and we had lots of costumes.

The Beaumont job was less physical—except for my light romantic playacting. Charles was an estate lawyer who'd pilfered from a trust he managed. When the trustor died unexpectedly, his heir—our client,

Rhonda Wilson—noticed the discrepancy, but she wanted her money back without the embarrassment of her insular Rockport world knowing her grandfather had been fleeced. We only needed a bit of computer hacking—Evan's specialty. He'd developed "h00dW1nk," a stealth backdoor software that flew under the radar of commercial security programs and allowed us total remote access to his computer.

"Let's put the jewelry project on hold." That was our next job, the one Alice had taken the lead on once we approached payday with Charles. "It's too risky. Now that I've had time to think about it, Charles snapping pictures of me 'on the street' suggests he was following me while I visited the jewelry stores."

Gina grimaced. "So while *we* were swindling *him*, he was running a hustle on us?"

"Yeah, I don't know how I screwed up. Charles always came across as pleasant, boring. Unimaginative even. But he must've suspected something." I blew out a noisy puff of air. "Finch wants me to sign my official statement this afternoon. While I'm at the police station, I'll try to get a look at Charles' notes and stuff, see how much he knew," I said. "But the best way to take the pressure off us is to find out who really killed him."

"And possibly, why they wanted to implicate you?" I guessed Alice was thinking about the killer using my scarf. I'd left it at Charles' on purpose for an excuse to stop by his place Tuesday night—the night when he was always busy with an intense online chess match. Charles played cut-throat. I knew he'd grumble, tell me to go find it, disappear into his upstairs study, and forget about me. After the scouting I'd done, it took only a few minutes to sneak into his office and install Evan's software from a thumb drive. Unfortunately, in my excitement, I forgot to retrieve the damn scarf.

But I was also thinking about my scarf in a different way. "What does using a scarf to kill him suggest?"

"That the murderer was a woman—don't look at me like that." Evan stood. "A man wouldn't pick up a silk scarf. He'd use his fists. He'd squeeze. Harder and harder." Evan was demonstrating on Gina's neck.

She escaped his grasp with a lightning-quick ninja move. "Doesn't it also suggest the lack of premeditation? An argument that escalated out of control?"

"The scarf could be a red herring." I rolled my eyes. "If Charles intended to blackmail me, he could've had other targets. Others who saw a potential weapon at hand."

"So, who could've been at his house last night?" asked Alice.

"His ex-wife, you think?" Evan took the words right out of my mouth.

"She'd be at the top of *my* list." Vic was scrolling on his phone. "Wait'll you see the texts she sent about him." Since this caper didn't require his extreme driving skills, Vic had been pressed into service to woo the ex—and mine her knowledge of Charles' secrets.

Evan scratched his cheek. "You don't suppose our client killed him, do you?"

A hush greeted his question. Then the muttering and *oh-shit*s began.

Alice spoke first. "Beaumont *did* steal a cool two mil from Rhonda."

"And she was pissed," Gina said.

"But she agreed to leave it to us," I said.

"Maybe she got impatient—"

Evan cut Gina off. "—and went to see him and things escalated."

I shook my head so hard the stupid bun sprang loose. "I told Rhonda we were moving the money this week. She'd have no reason to go to his office. And—think about the detective's question: Where were you after six pm last night?"

Alice's eyes widened. "Right, sounds like he was alive when his secretary left for the evening."

Gina finished the thought. "And dead—still in his office—the next morning when she came to work."

"Then the secretary's the first person to eliminate as a suspect." Vic stood, ready to roll.

"What's the plan?" After Evan spoke, everyone looked at me.

"Let's handle this like we do all our jobs—each take one piece of the puzzle and reconvene to compare notes."

*****

Gina whipped up a quick lunch—one of her meal-in-a-bowl salads with iced tea and leftover scones for dessert.

We divvied up the assignments. Vic would offer sympathy to Charles' ex-wife. Since Gina brought Rhonda's problem to us—they played tennis in the same league—she'd check in with her friend. Evan would do a deeper dive into Charles' business accounts to see if he could identify others who'd been a) swindled and pissed or b) blackmailed— and pissed.

I'd met Charles' secretary a few times. Irene Connors was an efficient middle-aged woman. I thought I'd make her my responsibility, but the gang vetoed that.

"Because of the scarf, she's gonna know you're a suspect," Evan said. "Your sniffing around could freak her out." So, Alice got that assignment. And I was stuck with clearing up my mess with the police.

After we helped Gina clean the kitchen, I left for what was initially an aggravating afternoon at the police station.

The detectives had prepared a written statement for me to sign, but it had several errors. Correcting them, reprinting the document, doing it a second time, a third... After they finally reworded everything to my satisfaction, I got lucky because Adams, the younger cop, came to witness my signature. He hadn't yet learned to keep the impassive face of an experienced policeman, and it became obvious that he and Finch had introduced 'mistakes' into the statement to see if they could trip me up.

I'm a better actor than that! I never forget my lines *or* my cues.

I guess Adams was embarrassed about their deceit because he doled out an interesting tidbit, and when I again offered to help with Charles' spying on me, he produced photocopies. They were as Finch described: me, walking toward various establishments. If the police investigated the locations, they would show, as I'd suspected, me about to enter a series of high-end jewelry stores in Boston. Our client's jewelry had gone missing. Because she suspected her son, who had a gambling problem, she wanted the retrieval done quietly. I'd been pretending to have jewelry that lacked proper documentation, searching for a shopkeeper who might've looked the other way for a chance to make a huge profit.

I gasped when I saw the last picture.

A hand partially obscured the image as the photographer shaded the lens from strong directional light. A woman's hand—long crimson fingernails and a ring with a broad band.

Charles was working with a woman. *She* had followed me. What woman did Charles trust with his business dealings?

My money was on Irene Connors.

I texted Alice:

When you locate Irene, look at her left hand.

✶✶✶✶✶

Over dinner, we pooled our results.

Some were highly suspicious: Charles' ex-wife had left that morning for Montreal, a trip she called "a long-planned getaway"—but since she'd never spoken of it before, Vic would follow up.

Some suggested innocence: Rhonda had hugged Gina and thanked her for our help. She appeared shocked to hear that Charles was dead—also rather nervous, but Gina put that down to the fishy timing of his murder.

Some were frustrating: Evan, grousing that he wasn't a forensic accountant, said he was still plowing through Charles' accounts.

Since we didn't know how to contact Irene Connors now that her boss was dead, Alice Googled her. But although she knocked on Irene's door—in a purloined UPS uniform—no one answered.

I saved my news for last. "Update on Irene. Detective Adams told me they've learned Charles made and received phone calls the evening he died. The calls were with people in his chess club about setting up an in-person tournament. Irene isn't high on their list because she'd gone home by then."

"She could've come back." Evan was sticking to his the-woman-done-it scenario.

"Yeah, but wait 'til you hear the kicker—" And I explained about a woman's hand in the surveillance photo.

"They were *both* in on it?" Alice and Gina spoke in unison.

I threw out my arms—narrowly missing Vic's nose. "They'd worked together for ages. Charles called her—with no apparent irony over his sexism—'my right-hand man.'" I rolled my eyes. "Stands to reason he might need help. But first we need a visual on Irene's *left* hand."

We agreed to, in the immortal exhortation of Curtis Mayfield, *keep on keeping on*. The best thing about the gang was that, with each other, we could be our authentic selves: out-of-work actors playing rich and famous. The house really was mine, though. It was all I had left. After my dad died, a smooth-talking conman full of empty promises swindled my grieving mom out of everything else. I was determined to keep the house—but insurance and property taxes on an oceanfront estate run to a cool hundred thousand every year.

I'll get even with that swindler one day. For now, we're honing our skills on smaller, more manageable targets.

*****

Evan tossed and turned all night, keeping me awake. Dawn found the bedclothes twisted—and me with an idea.

Evan was right: he was a top-notch programmer and hacker but, while he understood numbers better than the rest of us, he wasn't an accountant. He needed more than lines and numbers to make sense of whatever Charles was doing.

And Charles was old-fashioned enough to prefer a paper trail. I'd seen his meticulous notes about legit tasks. I bet he also annotated his extra-curricular efforts—and that's what Evan needed.

I decided to go there after breakfast to see what I could find.

Charles ran his very exclusive law practice from a ground-floor office in his home. And I knew he left a spare key to the kitchen door inside a fake rock in the back garden. I wasn't sure what I expected to find.

I certainly didn't expect to see the coffeepot on and a half-eaten bagel on the kitchen counter. Someone humming. Footsteps in the hall. I ducked into the pantry and peeked out through the narrow opening. Irene, mug in one hand and a sheaf of papers in the other, came into view. She set the mug down and took another bite of bagel. Since her employer was dead, we assumed she was out of a job. But she was in her usual elegant attire, so Charles' heirs must've kept her on to organize his papers, settle accounts and stuff.

Irene took another bite, swallowed more coffee, and put the mug in the sink. She drummed her diamond-bedecked fingers on the counter.

Yes, that was Irene's hand in the photograph.

Her presence put my plan to search Charles' desk on hold. I'd skedaddle as soon as the coast was clear.

For the first time, I considered Irene, not as "the secretary" but as Charles' partner in crime. How much did she know? She could've been simply his loyal foot soldier: *"Follow Mamie and take pictures of where she goes."* Or she could've been his co-conspirator. Maybe it was even something I mentioned to Irene that prompted their curiosity.

My cell phone chirped with an incoming text. I froze, as though that would keep me from being spotted if Irene inspected the pantry.

Irene whirled around but mainly focused her attention on the window. The chirp had probably made her think of chattering birds. After a minute, she began riffling through the papers she'd brought.

Dodged that bullet.

I slipped my phone from my pocket. Evan' text:

Someone was just online in C's accts, moving money around.

Irene.

Chills ricocheted along my spine. Was there any way this could be innocent?

Looking at the files, even copying them—that would be within the scope of her job. But *moving money around?*

I didn't think so.

With Charles dead, she was either cleaning up his mess—or, more likely, taking over. I texted Evan:

It's Irene.

Irene dropped the paper and walked out of sight. The downstairs bathroom door creaked.

Time to get out of here.

I eased open the pantry door and glanced around the corner—all clear. I tiptoed toward the back door. Irene's papers were on the counter. In a black Sharpie on the top page, I read my name.

The toilet flushed. I stayed one second too long, trying to decipher her angular script—a bunch of dollar signs, what might've been "Evan," maybe "gemstones" followed by a question mark...*oh, shit!*

My hand was on the door when footsteps clattered behind me. I tugged the knob, but Irene yanked my ponytail and twisted it, toppling me to the floor. By the time I scrambled to my feet, Irene had moved between me and the door. I took off running toward the front of the house, figuring I'd be faster in sneakers than she would be in her heels and could get outside that way.

But no.

Two steps into the hall and I slipped on the polished wood floor. Something pounded my head.

*****

"I need some information." Irene sat at Charles' desk, sounding just like the efficient secretary I always imagined she was.

"First, let me go." I was trussed with several lengths of rope in a chair next to her.

"No, first, you're going to retrieve the two million dollars you stole."

I wrinkled my forehead quizzically, much the same as I'd done with the detectives twenty-four hours earlier.

It worked better with them.

Irene leaned over and slapped me. "I knew you weren't what you pretended to be. You were just using Charles to steal from me."

With my ringing head, it took an embarrassingly long time to parse her words. "From you?"

"You think he was smart enough to pull off this racket? He had all that *access* and he ignored the possibilities."

"So, you took advantage?"

Irene shrugged. "What would you do?"

I thought for a second. "I'd help those who needed it—and only take from people who could stand to lose."

Irene's smile was a death's-head grimace of bared teeth. "Rich people like you make me sick to my stomach."

That was almost funny. Still, I didn't think a heart-to-heart talk about my financial woes would be fruitful.

Anyhow, Irene was still talking. "And Charles—what a stuffed shirt—he didn't need all that money. And neither did his clients. When he discovered I'd been…appropriating some of their excesses, I told him I'd put it back, but he threatened to call the police. I couldn't have that. It was a shame that I had to do it because he was the perfect person to front the operation."

"So you…?" I wasn't sure how to finish the thought.

"Using your scarf was a fantastic idea. I had suspicions about you from the start. And now I've got you." Irene shoved back Charles' big office chair and clacked down the hall.

I strained my arms and legs but I was tied too tight to move. That text to Evan was my only chance for rescue—but would he understand that my writing "It's Irene" led to "and the reason I know that is I'm at Charles'"?

Rescue took on even greater importance when Irene returned, kitchen knife in hand. With all she'd admitted to me, how could she let me go?

"Now you're going to show me how you stole that money." She dragged my chair over to the computer. Light dawned: *Irene doesn't know about our remote access. She thinks I did it while I was here.*

"Move it back into my account." She brandished the knife. "I won't cut your hands—don't want blood on my keyboard. I think I'll start...here." She slashed downward, opening a gash in my jeans. Blood oozed.

My vision swam with black spots, and my breath sputtered.

Hemophobia is the medical term for an irrational fear of blood. Only my closest friends knew I suffered from it. Charles didn't; Irene's choice of weapon was a lucky guess.

"Do it." She swung the knife like a kid playing pin the tail on the donkey.

How long had it been since I sent Evan that text. Fifteen minutes? Could I fake it enough to sound like I knew what I was doing? Gobbledygook. Hoodwink. Improv!

"I have to get a code." That sounded legit.

She sliced through the cord binding my arms, pointed the knife at the keyboard, and nodded, "Go ahead."

Praying that Evan was still monitoring this computer, I opened the browser and typed http://SOS7354. Asking for help in the most discreet way I knew, adding the numbers of Charles' street address.

Irene moved the knife to the side of my neck. "You bitch."

"Wait!" I raised my hands in surrender. "That's—that's the URL for the program to, um—to Switch Our Strokes. You know, to override the permissions." I had no freaking clue whether any of that made sense.

But Irene lowered the knife. "Now what?"

I pressed more keys: auth-code.

"It's like waiting for credit card confirmation." Wow, how did *that* drift up from my subconscious? Maybe I could really pull off this improv game. "Once I get the code, I can make changes."

I don't know how I would've replied if she'd asked, "But aren't you already making changes?" She kept quiet, though, watching the screen.

I wished she'd go away. While half of me begged Evan to reply, the other half was frantic he'd type some question that would give the game away.

But he didn't. Letters appeared on the screen: b-r-o-w-n-m-a-n

Brown man? Huh.

Now what? If I hit <enter> the browser will complain that the website doesn't exist.

The doorbell jangled. Irene looked out the window. Moving into the hall, she called, "Just leave it by the door."

"Can't. Signature required."

Gina's voice.

I sagged with relief. Gina, in her brown UPS uniform.

Irene took a roll of duct tape and slapped a piece across my mouth. "No funny business." And she walked away.

The second Irene stepped outside, two uniformed men rushed from the back of the house. I couldn't see much from my chair, but Irene was trapped between a ninja and two policemen.

Evan followed the policemen. He pulled the tape from my mouth and kissed me.

"Knife." I jutted my chin to where Irene had left her weapon before going to the door.

Evan cut me loose, and we joined Gina, who stood smiling on the front porch. Vic and Alice came running from down the street.

We watched the police lead Irene to the back seat of the patrol car. As they pulled away, the five of us linked arms and took a bow.

Death on the Tile
Carol Goodman Kaufman

Kiki Coben entered the vast cruise ship check-in area and gasped. She stopped mid-stride, placed her hand on husband Tim's arm and gazed up at the high ceiling, at the rows of chairs lined up like soldiers, and at the queues of travelers waiting to be served. Echoing voices amplified the noise level in the massive hall.

"This must be what my great-grandparents felt like when they arrived at Ellis Island. This place is gigantic, Tim," she said.

"They do have to process a few thousand passengers," Jane Darcy said, dropping her carry-on bag to the floor with a thump.

"Are all these people here to play Mah Jong?" Kiki asked, eyes wide.

Phyllis Bacon laughed. "Oh no! There'll be no more than a couple of hundred people here for that."

"Let's find a seat and wait our turn," Dale Valenti said and headed toward a line of folding chairs. Kiki sat next to the woman occupying the lone seat in the row.

"Hi. I'm Kiki. Are you by any chance here for Mah Jong?"

"I am! I'm Fran. Nice to meet you."

"This is my first cruise, and I've never played the game outside my own group. I'm a little nervous."

Fran's eyes lit up. "No need! You'll be matched with people of your own ability. I've been playing for years and I'm really good, so we probably won't be at the same table. Not to brag, of course."

Kiki smiled. "Of course."

Fran's head jerked up and she dropped her voice to a whisper. "There she is, the Black Widow."

"Who?" Kiki asked.

"Right there," Fran said, pointing with her chin in the direction of a tall brunette pulling a small suitcase on wheels.

Dressed in a strapless floral sheath with a necklace of big white beads and retro cats-eye sunglasses, the woman looked as if she had stepped out of 1960s Miami Beach.

"That bag is probably filled with all her jewels. She won't let it out of her sight."

"Why do you call her the Black Widow?" Kiki asked.

A buzzing came from Fran's pocket. "Oops, gotta go. My friends are here. See you at the Meet and Greet tonight!" Fran called as she darted off.

A gold-digging heiress? That's gonna make this cruise more interesting.

*****

As Kiki watched Fran cross the hall toward her friends, she recalled the neighborhood barbecue the past summer when her friends, Phyllis, Dale, and Jane had convinced her to join them for a week-long Mah Jong-themed cruise in the Caribbean.

"We deserve a vacation after the trauma we've been through," Dale said.

"You are so right," Phyllis said, sipping an Arnold Palmer.

"Especially in winter," Dale said, a misty look in her eyes. "Wouldn't it be nice to see palm trees gently swaying in the breeze? And little paper umbrellas in colorful cocktails?"

"And the sun warming your bones while back home people are shoveling snow and slipping on the ice?" Jane said.

"Never in my life would I have dreamt that we'd have a murder in our neighborhood," Phyllis said.

Jane agreed. "Or that someone we actually knew would have murdered his wife."

"Poor Macy," Dale said. "I miss her. And not just because she was a great Mah Jong player."

"If not for Kiki, we never would've known the truth of how she died,"

Phyllis said.

Dale shivered. "And buried in your basement. How awful!"

Tim looked up from his post at the grill and waved a spatula at the smoke curling around his head. "And that will be the last time Kiki gets involved with a murder investigation."

"Speaking of murder, the smell from the barbecue is killing me," Dale said. "When do we eat?"

Changing the subject, Kiki said, "I've never been on a cruise, much less one dedicated to a game. Frankly, I'd rather go on vacation with Tim."

"But guys come, too!" Dale said, her chocolate brown eyes twinkling.

Jane tsked. "Of course. I wouldn't leave Conrad home for a whole week."

"She doesn't trust me not to burn the house down," Conrad mouthed behind her back.

"Won't they be bored if we're playing all day?" Kiki asked.

"We play for three hours in the morning and only when we're at sea," Phyllis said, "unless of course you can't get enough of the game. But I want to see the islands."

Dale's husband, Chuck, laughed. "Don't worry about us. We'll play poker and hang out at the pool."

"And the bar," added Jeff Bacon.

Jane pursed her lips. "The bar, Jeff? In the morning?"

"Well, maybe the buffet," Jeff said.

Phyllis laughed. "That sounds more like you, honey."

"Do we play together like at home?" Kiki asked.

"No! That's the beauty of it," Phyllis said. "We'll rotate and you'll get to meet all kinds of people. Islands and people. That's what it's all about. Expanding our horizons."

Spoken like a true educator, Phyllis.

Kiki frowned in concentration. "I'd have to get my columns to my editor before we leave."

"You do that," Jane said. "You simply must come with us."

*****

The friends gathered for dinner the first night out of port and were directed to their table on the far side of an enormous dining room. The aroma of herbs and spices, grilling meats, and caramelized sugar enveloped them.

"Ooh, my mouth is watering!" Dale said.

"Did you notice that everybody on the crew has a nametag that says where they're from?" Kiki asked.

"And they're from all over the world!" Dale said. "I love all the different accents."

At that moment, a tall young man appeared and introduced himself with a broad smile.

"I can't see your nametag from here," Jane said.

"Put your glasses on, Jane," Conrad whispered.

"I am from Haiti, madam," he said. "My name is Pierre and I will be very happy to be your waiter tonight. Would you like wine?"

At agreement all around, he circled the table, pouring wine into glasses. Conrad made a show of swirling the wine in his glass and sniffing it before taking a sip.

"So, how was the meet-and-greet cocktail party?" Jeff asked.

"Very educational," Dale said. "We learned all about the Black Widow."

"Did I miss something?" Chuck asked.

"Her name is Tandy Davis and she's on her third husband already," Dale said.

"They say she's a gold digger," Jane said. "Just look at the size of that rock on her finger. It must be five carats! And the Dior resort wear she parades around in."

"How do you know it's Dior?" Tim asked.

"I read all the fashion magazines in the nail salon," Jane said.

"So why is she on a cruise and not in prison?" Jeff asked.

"I heard they could never prove anything," Phyllis said.

"She must have inherited a lot to be able to dress like that," Kiki said.

"I wonder —"

Tim sighed. "Remember, Kiki, we're on vacation. Please don't even think about sticking your nose into her business."

✶✶✶✶✶

Kiki awoke with the sunrise and hopped out of bed.

"Huh," Tim mumbled.

"I need to get some exercise if I'm going to be sitting for three hours. You go back to sleep."

Tim mumbled something unintelligible and rolled over.

Kiki threw on her workout clothes, slid her room key into the lanyard around her neck, and exited the cabin, closing the door so gently that the lock barely clicked. She headed straight for the running track on Deck Five and when she opened the door, the smell of fresh salt air greeted her. She took a deep breath and began to stretch. She heard a woman's voice.

"Hi. I saw you at the reception last night. You're here for Mah Jong, right?"

Kiki looked up.

The Black Widow?

"Yes. I'm Kiki Coben."

"Tandy Davis."

Yes, I know. Everybody talks about you.

"Would you like to walk together? I just started."

"Sure. Why not?" *I could get some great info here.*

The two women headed out on the track, keeping to the right to allow runners to pass them.

"Have you been on one of these Mah Jong cruises before?" Kiki asked.

"This is my fourth."

"No kidding!"

"My sister-in-law introduced me to the game after I married her brother Paul and moved to Jacksonville. She taught me how to play and helped me find a regular game."

"Do you keep up with her?"

"I've tried, but Sandy was really shattered by Paul's death. He was her big brother and she adored him."

"How sad."

"It's a shame because we were really close when Paul and I were married. We were 'Sandy and Tandy, the Mah Jong twins.' We still exchange Christmas cards every year, and she remembers my birthday. But we haven't seen each other since I got remarried to Ed."

"That must have been really hard to lose the relationship," Kiki said. "Is she on this cruise?"

"She could be, but I haven't seen her. Or heard from her." Tandy shook her head as if trying to rid her mind of bad memories. "But the game has served me well wherever I've lived. I'm a fairly shy person and Mah Jong has helped me to make friends."

"You've moved a lot?"

Tandy winced. "Afraid so. I've been widowed twice."

A lump formed in Kiki's throat. *What would I do if Tim died?* "I'm so sorry."

"Y'know, we've just met. I shouldn't dump all this on you."

"Sometimes it's easier to talk to a stranger."

"Well then, you should know that I'm a jinx."

Huh? Is this a confession?

"That's a heavy burden to carry."

"But it's true. I've been seeing somebody really terrific for about a year and he wants to get married, but I'm afraid that if I agree, he'll die, too."

"Why would he die?"

"Jack's a firefighter."

"Wow. Small world. My husband Tim's a firefighter, too."

Tandy stopped mid-stride and turned to Kiki, her voice low, her eyes filling with tears. "So, you understand."

I sure do.

"Of course I worry, Tandy, but do I want to live my whole life in fear?

I know Tim loves what he does. That makes me happy."

Tandy bowed her head as if absorbing new information. Looking up again, she asked, "Is Tim here on the cruise with you?"

"All the husbands in our group came with us."

"Maybe we could introduce Tim to Jack?"

"We're all going into port tomorrow. Why don't you two to join us?"

"We'd love to!"

The two resumed their walk and amped up the pace. They passed other, slower, walkers and early birds heading to do laps in the empty pool.

"Tandy, I couldn't help noticing your clothes. When you boarded the ship, at the cocktail party. You look like you stepped out of the pages of Vogue or Elle. Are you a model?"

Tandy laughed. "No! I'm a seamstress."

Kiki's mouth dropped open. "You make your own clothes?"

"Of course! I couldn't afford to wear originals. I just copy what I see in fashion magazines, or I make my own designs."

"You don't make your own jewelry, too, do you?"

Tandy laughed. "No. I find that in consignment shops or yard sales."

"No kidding. You are amazing."

"I have to be creative." Tandy blushed as she added, "Luckily, I am."

After fifteen laps around the deck, Kiki checked the clock over the pool.

"I think I'm done here. Time to get ready to play." *But there's so much more I need to ask.*

"See you tomorrow, same time?"

"Sure. We'll have plenty of time to work out before we dock."

Tandy raised one eyebrow. "Meet me in my cabin, Deck 12, Cabin 1273? I can show you some of my designs."

"That would be fabulous!"

On her way back to her cabin, Kiki mulled over her conversation with Tandy. She wondered why anybody would ever start such nasty rumors about such a seemingly good person. She began to strategize how to get more information.

*****

The bell dinged as the elevator door to Deck Three opened. Kiki followed the signs to the conference room, although she only really needed to follow the aroma of coffee to its source. She showed her ID card at the door and entered a large room packed with card tables, each one equipped with a game set and a little metal stand that held a number. Players, mostly women, gathered around the buffet table filling their coffee cups and examining the snacks on display.

Didn't we just have breakfast?

"Can I help you?" asked a smiling woman seated at the registration desk.

Yes, please. I'm new," Kiki said.

"Well, then, welcome to the family! Just tell me your name and I'll tell you which table you'll sit at this morning. You'll need to check in every morning to get that day's table number."

"There are so many people here," Kiki said.

"This is the biggest crowd we've ever had. A little over three hundred people, so we've had to use additional rooms to accommodate everybody. But don't worry. Every room is on this deck."

Kiki thanked the woman and scanned the crowd for the number matching the one in her hand. She headed toward her assigned table, where she was happy to find a group of smiling women. They introduced themselves and sat down to play. Within minutes the chatter ceased and the room filled with the soothing music of clicking tiles.

Three hours later, Kiki got up from the table, pleased to have won one game. She searched the room to find her friends from Sherwood. When they had all gathered, she told them she'd join them in the dining room before taking off for the Internet café.

Given the time of day, there were plenty of empty stations, so she pulled up a chair and started a search for information about her new friend. Tandy's website popped up immediately, and Kiki gasped.

Tandy's a very modest woman. This stuff is spectacular.

*****

Early the next morning Kiki made her way to Tandy's cabin on Deck Twelve, where she found her new friend lacing up her running shoes. Tandy stood up and opened the door to the closet, where a dozen colorful outfits hung.

Kiki examined each one before sliding its hanger to the side. "These are gorgeous, Tandy!" she exclaimed.

"Thank you. I'm really fortunate to have found something I love doing."

"Let's get moving. Between all the sitting, eating, and drinking on this cruise, I'm in serious need of calorie burning,"

"Me, too. But first, I have to apologize. When we talked yesterday, I never asked you what you do," Tandy said as the two headed out the cabin door.

"No need to apologize. We were talking about important things. I write about food for our local newspaper."

"Yum."

"Very yum. It's not exactly the journalism career I had planned on, but I hope my editor will promote me at some point to something better."

"Like what?"

"Investigative journalism would be fabulous."

"Is your town a hotbed of crime?"

Kiki laughed. "Not quite, but there's always a corrupt official or businessperson lurking in the shadows of little Sherwood."

Although we did have a murder last year that did require investigation.

"It's gotta be hard to deal with all kinds of goodies on a daily basis and not indulge."

"I sample everything. That's why I work out."

"Then we need to pick up the pace! There are so many different restaurants on this ship and I want to try every single one."

"Let's go!" Kiki said.

*****

"That was fantastic," Kiki said as she kicked off her sandals before collapsing onto the bed.

"St. Thomas is beautiful," Tim agreed.

"What did you think of Tandy and Jack?" she asked.

"They're great. I'm glad you invited them. They both seem so down to earth."

"You can tell Jack's totally smitten, but Tandy's terrified to marry him. She thinks she's a jinx."

Tim raised his eyebrows. "You mean because two previous husbands have died on her?"

Kiki swatted at his arm. "She's really nice. I don't know why people talk such trash about her."

"Probably jealous, hon. Look, she's gorgeous, she dresses like a model, she's built like a—"

Kiki rolled her eyes. "Okay. I get the message. But why the nasty talk? I can understand jealousy, but who accuses a woman of killing not one, but two husbands?"

Tim raised an eyebrow and moaned. "Kiki, what are you thinking?"

"Thinking?"

"We're on vacation. No snooping."

"Aw, c'mon, Tim. I'll just do a little research. I am a trained journalist, you know."

"I know you are, babe. But prying into other people's business can get dangerous. Remember what happened last time? I don't want any more murderous psychopaths cornering you in the kitchen. Put away the deerstalker."

Kiki thought about a retort but decided it would take too much effort. Instead, she put her head on the pillow and fell asleep.

*****

On Wednesday morning, Kiki found herself at a table with Jane Darcy.

"I thought we wouldn't be put together," Kiki said.

"They don't know that we're in the same group at home. It's just random that we were put together."

Kiki looked over her tiles and wondered if she had the courage to go for a closed hand. She had half of one in the first tiles she had drawn, but would she be able to make Mah Jong without drawing from the center of the table?

This is a game, Kiki, not life or death. Go for it.

Loud and urgent voices snapped her out of her musings. She looked up to see three women at the registration table waving their arms.

"What's going on?" Kiki asked.

"How would I know?" Jane replied. "Don't go snooping. We're in the middle of a game here. Stop talking."

Leave it to Jane to play director.

Kiki had trouble concentrating, wondering what had caused the ruckus at the registration table. When she discarded a much-needed flower, she groaned.

"Damn. I can't believe I just did that," she said.

"Language, Kiki. And pay attention," Jane snapped.

Yes, mother. If I roll my eyes, will you ground me?

Dale suddenly appeared at their table. Kiki noted that her normally sparkling eyes were a muddy brown, and a frown creased her forehead.

"What's the matter, Dale?" she asked.

"Did you drip coffee onto your tiles?" Jane asked.

Jane, just once can you keep your judgmental comments to yourself?

"Tandy Davis is supposed to be at our table, but she hasn't shown up."

"Maybe she's hung over," Jane said. "The woman does love her Cosmos."

"What should we do? We can't play without her," Dale said.

Kiki stood up. "Let's go find Jack. Maybe he'll know what's going on. He should be with the guys."

"Kiki, we haven't finished the game!" Jane cried.

One of the other women at the table turned to Dale. "Go. We'll combine the two tables and play together."

"Perfect. Thanks so much," Kiki said.

"Go find your friend. That's more important than a game," the woman said.

"I guess I'll come, too," Jane muttered.

Behind Jane's back, Kiki mouthed the words "thank you" to the women at the table. As she turned to leave, she ran smack into another player whose hobo bag banged her hip.

"Oh, I'm so sorry," she said. "I shouldn't have been in such a hurry."

"Uh, no problem."

"Are you okay?"

"Yeah, I'm fine."

Kiki rubbed her aching side. *What did she have in that bag? Rocks? I'm going to have a big black-and-blue mark.*

*****

Jack unlocked the door to the cabin and led the way inside. The first thing Kiki noticed was the odor of rusty iron assaulting her nostrils. She went straight to the bathroom, thinking that Tandy might have fallen ill. Halfway there, she heard Jack groan. She turned around.

Tandy Davis lay prone on the floor behind the bed, her arms extended. Dark red blood formed a pool around her head. A wooden Mah Jong case was open next to her, tiles and racks scattered across the rug. Kiki spied more blood on one corner of the case.

Jack blanched and his knees buckled. Tim went into first responder mode and caught him, setting him down in a chair. He pressed his head down between his legs.

"Call the emergency number, Jeff," Tim said. "And everybody, stay away from the body."

Just when I was going to take a look.

The ship's doctor arrived within moments of Jeff's call. He immediately went down on one knee and felt for a pulse. He shook his head and looked up at the security officer who had accompanied him.

"She's gone. This happened not too long ago. She's still warm."

"I only left the room an hour ago," Jack said.

The officer looked at Jack and stood up.

"And you are?"

"I'm her fiancé. Jack Canfield."

Kiki swallowed. *Fiancé? When did that happen?*

"You must leave the cabin," the security officer said, interrupting her thoughts.

Kiki checked his nametag. Rafi Oron, from Israel. *I guess he should probably know a thing or two about security.*

"We'll find for you another cabin, Mr. Canfield."

As Oron escorted the friends out of the cabin, Kiki fell to the back of the group, trying to get a glimpse of the body on the floor. Something white flashed in the corner of her eye. She squinted and saw that Tandy's right hand was clutching something.

"Officer Oron, there's something in her hand."

Oron knelt down and pried Tandy's fingers open to reveal a Mah Jong tile. South.

Kiki sucked in her breath.

Poor Tandy must have been desperate, clawing for something she could use to defend herself. A tile wouldn't have been much help. She was probably trying to reach the hard case.

Oron looked up. "Madam, you must to leave this cabin and, please, do not touch a thing. There will be a guard on the door until the FBI is to meet us in Charlotte Amalie. And please leave the investigation to the professionals."

Kiki pulled a face. *How did he know what I was planning?*

"The FBI?" Dale asked, eyes wide.

"Yes. The crime took place in U.S. waters. The local police will probably also join them. They will want to interview you."

"Will this delay our departure?" Jane asked.

"We'll probably stay docked in Charlotte Amalie until they finish their investigation," Oron said. "And until they do complete it, I'm afraid we will have to ask you to stay onboard the ship."

"This is horrible," Jane said.

"Not as horrible for us as it is for Tandy," Kiki said.

"Well, at least they have good duty-free shops here," Jane said.

Oh, Jane, you have such empathy.

Once out of the room, Kiki pulled Jack aside in the hallway and said, "Jack, you know they're going to ask you where you were."

Jack ran his hands through his sandy hair. His face still showed some pallor. "I know. The first suspect is always the intimate partner, right? Isn't that what the cops always say?"

"So where were you?"

"You know I was playing poker with the guys."

"When did you last see Tandy?"

"She was putting on her makeup when I left."

"Did you hear or see anything?" Kiki asked.

"Like what?"

"Just think."

Jack closed his eyes as if trying to envision the scene. His eyes popped open.

"Yeah, actually I did. While I was waiting for the elevator, I heard a knock on a door from somewhere in the passageway. Then I heard Tandy's voice. She said something like 'What a surprise. It's been so long.'"

Kiki probed further. "When did you get engaged?"

"Last night. We were having drinks out on the balcony, watching the sunset. Tandy said it was something you told her, Kiki, that made her change her mind."

Kiki's mind churned, trying to remember what she had said that could have convinced her new friend to agree to marry Jack.

Do you want to live your whole life in fear?

"We even went to the captain to ask him to marry us onboard the ship."

That's easy enough to check.

"Did you go back to see who it was?"

"I peeked around the corner, but the person had already gone into the room. And then the door closed. But Tandy sounded really happy."

Kiki frowned. *She sounded really happy.*

"Could you tell if it was a male or female voice?" Kiki asked.

"Definitely female," Jack said. "Tandy wouldn't cheat on me."

"That's not what I meant, Jack."

"You're right. I guess I'm in shock. I just can't believe Tandy's dead. We were so happy. We had such plans."

At that moment, Oron called Jack over, leaving Kiki to ponder the conversation.

Is he telling the truth or is this a good act?

She pulled Phyllis aside and shared her thoughts.

"Do you think they were really engaged?" she asked.

"Jeff and the guys are taking a tour of the bridge this afternoon. The Captain will be there. They can ask him."

"I'd forgotten that, Phyllis. Good work!"

Phyllis paused for a moment, then dropped her voice. "Do you think Jack might have killed Tandy for the insurance money? A bit of 'turnabout is fair play?' Not that I think Tandy killed two husbands, but he may have gotten the idea from all the rumors."

Kiki shrugged. "If it's true, they just got engaged last night. How would Tandy have had the time to change the beneficiary? If she even had life insurance. With no kids, no parents, and no siblings, why bother? Who'd benefit?"

"Isn't that the question they always ask on *Law & Order*? Who benefits?"

*****

Kiki swirled the martini in its glass, then pulled an olive off the cocktail pick with her teeth. She chewed slowly, enjoying its salty tang as much as the knowledge that Tandy and Jack had indeed spoken with the Captain about marrying onboard.

"Something's bothering me," she said. "Two things, actually."

"Uh oh," said Dale. "I think I recognize that look in Kiki's eyes."

"Why would Tandy have had a Mah Jong set in her cabin? Didn't you tell me that the program provides the sets?"

"That's true," Jane said. "Some people just can't get enough of the game and play outside the tournament."

"What's the second thing bothering you?" Phyllis asked.

"Everybody's been saying such nasty things about her," Kiki said.

"Like what?" Conrad asked.

"Like she inherited a lot of money," Dale said.

"Why is that nasty?" asked Chuck.

"If you'd heard the tone of voice, you'd know," Kiki said. "Like they really believe she killed her husbands for the insurance money. But she wasn't rich."

Jane tsked. "Well, just take a look at the way she dressed. If that doesn't tell you something— "

"She was so talented. She could look at fashion magazines and copy things she liked."

"You mean she had them made," Jane said.

"She was a seamstress, Jane."

"That could just be something she told you so that people wouldn't turn around and rob her," Jane said.

"I saw the outfits in her closet. Not a single label in anything other than her underwear."

Jane frowned. "She could have ripped out the labels."

Phyllis and Dale were quiet.

"And I looked up her website. She's the real deal. And 'seamstress' is a very modest term for what she does. Or did."

"D'ya think we might have been a little judgmental?" Dale asked.

"Where did we hear all those bad things about her, anyway?" Phyllis asked.

"I'm not sure. I remember hearing the rumors the very first day at the meet-and-greet cocktail party," Dale said.

"And even before that," Kiki said. "Remember that woman Fran who called her 'The Black Widow'"?

"And we swallowed every nasty bit," Phyllis said. "We should be ashamed of ourselves. And I more than most. As a teacher, I always stress doing one's research and checking it twice."

Jane persisted. "Unless, of course, the rumors are true, and she did kill her husbands. Just because she made her own clothes — or said she did — doesn't mean she didn't want the insurance money. And what seamstress do you know who can afford a cruise?"

Kiki pushed back. "It's a Caribbean cruise, not so expensive, Jane. And, since she and Jack live in Miami, they didn't have to fly to the port like we did."

"Yeah," Tim said. "They have no kids. They work hard. Why not take a cruise?"

Kiki blew out air. "We're all getting off track here. Designer clothes or handmade, it doesn't matter. The woman is dead. We have to find out what happened."

"Kiki," Tim said, "you have to stay out of this. Let the FBI investigate."

"I won't get in their way. I promise."

Tim groaned. "Just promise me you'll be careful."

*****

After a full morning of Mah Jong, Kiki pulled Phyllis aside. "Come with me after lunch," she said.

"Fine with me. I really need to get some exercise after all that sitting."

"We'll go to the pool afterwards, but first we're going to sit some more. We have some research to do."

"Uh oh. Nancy Drew-ing are we?"

Kiki just smiled.

*****

Kiki led the way to the Internet cafe and sat down in front of one of the desktop computers.

"Isn't Internet service expensive onboard?"

"My boss at the paper is paying for it. I promised to do a couple of articles about cruise food and the islands."

"Why do you need me?"

"Two heads are always better than one. And you have a good one for research."

Phyllis snorted. "Flattery will always get you what you want."

Kiki logged in and sat back to strategize.

"Okay, we know her second husband's name is Ed Davis, right? Unless, of course, Tandy went back to her maiden name."

"We have to start somewhere, so let's go with husband number two," Phyllis said.

Kiki nodded in agreement. She hunched over the keyboard and tapped in keywords in her search for information. Ed. Edward. Davis. Florida. Wife Tandy.

Within seconds the obituary for Edward Davis of Orlando popped up. After stating that the man had died of lung cancer, it listed survivors that included one sister and two brothers. It also requested that donations in his memory be made to two cancer-related charities. Kiki then searched for any other information she could find, but came up empty.

"Why don't we look for her first husband next? What was his name?" Phyllis asked.

"Um, I think she said it was Paul. But I don't know the last name."

Sandy and Tandy. The Mah Jong twins.

"Oh! But I do know that Tandy had a sister-in-law named Sandy," Kiki said and immediately typed in "leaves wife Tandy, sister Sandra, Jacksonville." And up popped Paul Redlin. The obituary didn't list a cause of death, but in lieu of flowers, the family had asked that people send donations in the man's memory to one of two cancer-related organizations. One was for research into the disease, the other for service to families of children suffering from cancer.

"Neither of these sound like the obituaries of somebody who was murdered. They must have died of cancer," Phyllis said.

"But most likely neither man wrote his own obit," Kiki said. "A killer could have written it to look as if he had died of cancer."

"True."

"Or, he might have had cancer, but somebody could have put a pillow over his head."

"You mean like a mercy killing?" Phyllis asked.

"If he was in so much pain and was expected to die anyway, it might have been an act of love." Kiki hesitated. "Or for the insurance."

"I don't know, Kiki. This sounds a little too far-fetched for me."

Kiki sighed. "For me, too. I really think Tandy was genuine. And Jack really seemed to be in love with her."

Neither seems like a killer. But then again, neither did Matt Stannard.

"Is there a possibility that there might have been an autopsy?" Phyllis asked.

"I doubt it since he would most definitely have been under a doctor's care. On the other hand, if he died unexpectedly, I suppose there might have been an autopsy."

Kiki went back to typing. "Phyllis, you're a genius! I can tell you that Paul Redlin did indeed die of cancer. Unlike in Massachusetts, once an investigation is complete, Florida Medical Examiner records become public and are available for review by anybody. Here's a link to the record."

"But why would a cancer death get an autopsy?" Phyllis asked.

"Apparently somebody requested one."

Maybe that's where the rumors started.

✶✶✶✶✶

"They're letting us off the ship today, so we have five hours on St. Maarten. What do you want to do?" Phyllis asked at breakfast.

"Let's take a tour of the island," Dale said.

"That sounds good," Jane said. "I think we need something quiet and calm after everything that's happened."

"True," Tim said, "but after that, Kiki and I are going to shop for her birthday gift."

"Lucky you!" Dale said. "St. Maarten is supposed to be a great place to get buys on jewelry.”

“Tim is just trying to make me feel better since the FBI guy told me to keep my distance,” Kiki said.

✶✶✶✶✶

Kiki perused the display cases containing rows upon rows of bracelets, rings, pendants, and watches.

“I’d like something I can wear every day,” she said, “so bracelets are out. They’re always clinking against the keyboard.”

“How about a ring?” Tim asked.

“Nope. I like my wedding and engagement rings.”

“Maybe a pair of earrings?”

Raised voices on the far side of the shop drew their attention. A woman wagged a finger at the salesclerk, her voice shrill.

She looks familiar. Where do I know her from?

“Don’t you dare try to cheat me! I’ll have your business shut down!” she shouted. Heaving her hobo bag over her shoulder, she stormed out of the shop.

The salesclerk shrugged her shoulders and heaved a sigh.

“Are you all right?” Tim asked.

“I’m fine, thanks.”

“What was that all about?” Kiki asked. “The woman seemed really upset.”

“Sometimes people come in after they’ve gambled away their money. They want to sell their jewelry—especially if their spouse doesn’t know they blew it all at the poker table or the slot machine.”

“So, you don’t buy jewelry?” Tim asked.

“Oh, we do, but she was under the impression that her stuff was worth a lot of money. I told her that she had some great pieces of costume jewelry, but none of it was made of precious, or even semi-precious stones. She didn’t believe me. She was sure it was expensive and even accused me of trying to swindle her.”

“We heard that loud and clear,” Kiki said.

“Whoever gave it to her is probably going to get an earful tonight,”

Tim said.

"Unless they broke up," Kiki said, "and she wanted to be entirely rid of the memory."

"And now her memory will be even more bitter," Tim said.

*****

Kiki swam lap after lap, churning through the water as she tried to put evidence into an order she could understand.

She reviewed every conversation she had had with Tandy on their morning walks.

Jinx. Jack. Seamstress. Firefighter. Sandy and Tandy, the Mah Jong twins.

She stopped swimming to let a woman cross in front of her, then kicked off the end of the pool to start another lap.

South. Why was she was holding the South tile? What am I missing?

Kiki's arms sliced through the water, faster and faster.

Sandy and Tandy, the Mah Jong twins. Yes!

Kiki jumped out of the pool, dried off, threw on a cover-up, and dashed off to the Internet cafe. Every desktop was in use. She plopped herself into an upholstered chair to wait. Her heart pounded in her chest and her fingers tapped in sync. Within seconds she felt the cushion underneath her becoming wet. Embarrassed, she hopped up and ran to her cabin, taking the stairs rather than waiting for the elevator. She prayed that a computer would be available when she returned.

But none were free. Kiki began to pace the room, willing somebody—anybody—to get up and leave the room. Finally, after four circuits of the room, a man rose from behind the computer he had been using. She gave him a grateful smile and grabbed the chair. She immediately pulled up Paul Redlin's obituary and ran her finger down the lengthy narrative describing his early life, education, career, and volunteer activities. Then she came to the list of survivors.

His wife of six years, Tandy, his brother, Alan Redlin (wife Jennifer) of Denver, and his sister Sandra Stoddard of Miami. Sandra.

Sandy. S. South.

Could Sandra Stoddard be onboard? Could she have been the surprise visitor to Tandy's cabin?

Kiki leapt up from her seat and raced toward the stairway. Again too impatient to wait for the elevator, she headed down to Deck Five.

*****

Kiki spied the sign for Guest Services, only to find four people standing ahead of her in line and only one woman, Elena from Spain, staffing the desk. She took her place in the queue.

How could they have only one person here?

Her heart pounding, Kiki closed her eyes and began prana breathing. After about ten minutes, during which she was sure her head would explode, it was her turn. She hustled to the counter and leaned forward.

"I need to find a guest. Can you give me her cabin number?"

"We do not give those out, Ma'am. For obvious security reasons."

"Of course. What was I thinking? Can you tell me if she's on the ship?"

"Of course. Please to give me her name."

"Sandra Stoddard."

Elena tapped some keys on her computer and nodded.

"Yes. She is here."

"May I have her phone number?"

"I can connect you."

Kiki pressed her lips together. *Security.* "Okay. Let's do that."

Elena dialed the phone number and handed the receiver to Kiki. Ring. Ring. Ring. Ring. Kiki was about to hang up when she heard a voice.

"Hello?"

"Is this Sandy?"

"Yes. Who's this?"

Kiki hung up and pondered her next move. She decided on the Mah Jong room. If Sandy was such an avid player, somebody was bound to know her and would be able to point her out. As she turned to hand the phone back, she noted the frown on Elena's face.

I'm trying to solve a crime, lady. Don't judge me.

But it was already past five o'clock. The conference room would be empty as all players would be getting ready for cocktails and dinner. She'd have to wait until tomorrow.

*****

Having slept only fitfully the night before, Kiki ran at a hard pace the next morning, trying to get a handle on her nerves. After she had finished ten laps around the deck, she showered and dressed in a hurry so that she could get to the conference room before it became too busy.

"Good morning! You're here bright and early," the woman at the desk said. Her nametag said Barb. "Can't get enough of the game, right?"

"Actually, I'm wondering if you know Sandy Stoddard and can point her out to me."

"Of course I know her. Everybody does. She's a regular on our cruises."

"If it's okay with you, I'll hang around here," Kiki said. "But first, can I get you some coffee and danish?"

"Thanks so much. Coffee with cream and two sugars. And maybe one of those lemon tarts. I can't seem to get enough of 'em."

Kiki headed over to the coffee urn and filled a cup, then placed some pastry on a plate. As she walked back to the registration desk, she saw Barb signaling to her.

"You just missed her!" she said. "That's Sandy over there, with the blue and white striped shirt."

Kiki lifted her head and squinted her eyes, trying to get a fix on her quarry. And then, her jaw dropped. The woman in stripes was the woman in the jewelry store.

"Blond hair? About five six?" she asked.

"Yep. That's her."

*****

Kiki turned on her heel and ran to find Tim. He wasn't in the cabin, so she ran to the gym. No luck. Then she tried the poker table the guys had favored. Again nothing. Finally, she tried the cafeteria. He and the Mah Jong husbands were wolfing down omelets and hash browns. She hurried over to their table.

"What have you been up to, Kiki?" Jeff asked. "You're out of breath."

"I know who killed Tandy. Or I think I do."

Jack, who had been slumped in his chair, straightened up. "What? Who?"

"But first, I need to know, Jack. Is any of Tandy's jewelry missing?"

"She kept it in the room safe. I haven't been in it since …" His voice trailed off.

"Let's go look now," Kiki said.

The whole group stood as one and started to head out.

"Wait a minute. We need to call the security officer. Remember, they moved me to another stateroom after, uh, you know. I don't have a key to the old room."

*****

Jack headed straight for the high shelf in the cabin's closet, where the safe stood.

"Don't touch anything," Oron said. He pulled on nitrile gloves and went to open the safe door, but there was no need for a code. The door was closed but not locked.

He pulled it open. Empty.

"Could the cabin attendant have taken it?" Jack asked.

"No. The cabin has been sealed since the murder. It's still a crime scene," Oron said.

The hobo bag! Kiki put her hand to her hip and touched the bruise. It still smarted.

"Then it's what I thought. The killer is Tandy's former sister-in-law, Sandy Stoddard. She's here on the ship."

"How do you know?"

"She's the one we saw in St. Maarten trying to sell costume jewelry. I'll bet if you search her cabin you'll find Tandy's things."

"I'll call Reese, the FBI agent in charge," Oron said.

*****

Sandy was playing Blackjack in the casino, where the dealer had just given her a card that gave her twenty-one. With a grin, Sandy looked up.

"Ms. Stoddard, please come with me," Reese said, taking her arm. He led her through the ship to a chair at the table in the center of the command center.

Sandy plopped into the chair and folded her arms in a gesture of defiance. "What do you want?"

"You know why you're here. What have you got to say for yourself?" he asked.

"The bitch deserved to die. She always got things her way. She won at everything."

"Like what?" Reese asked.

"She got Paul. He adored her and he treated her like a queen. I got stuck with a cheating, gambling, boozer husband. I hated her guts."

"She lost two husbands to cancer. How can you be jealous of that?" Kiki asked.

"Look at the way she dresses! Look at the jewelry! Don't you think she got really lucky with life insurance?"

"Their medical bills were huge. She worked as a seamstress," Kiki said.

"Insurance!"

"But the jewelry was all costume," Kiki said. "We know you tried to sell it at the jewelry store in St. Maarten. We saw you there."

"She must have left the good stuff at home."

"So, you killed Tandy out of sheer jealousy," Kiki said.

"You bet I killed her. And I'd do it again."

*****

The ship departed Charlotte Amalie that afternoon and the friends gathered around the pool, subdued and thoughtful.

"How did Sandy get Tandy's jewelry?" Phyllis asked.

Kiki explained. "Remember, it was morning. Jack said that Tandy was getting dressed, so the room safe was probably open when Sandy surprised her. After killing her, Sandy took everything in it."

"She must have figured that only expensive stuff would be stored in the safe," Phyllis said.

"And then she tried to sell it all," Tim said.

"Was it Sandy who started the rumors?" Dale asked.

"Yes," Kiki said. "Tandy told me that Sandy took her brother's death really hard."

"She must have had some sort of breakdown to go the route of a killer," Phyllis said.

"Such a shame. The two had been really close at one time," Kiki said.

"Both husbands really did die of cancer," Jack said. "Even though Tandy had nothing to do with either death, she always blamed herself. She believed she was a jinx. She didn't want to marry again for fear of losing me, too. But Kiki said the magic words to her and …"

"She did love you, Jack. Of that I'm absolutely sure," Kiki said.

"And she managed to find new friendship and happiness while playing the game she loved."

All That Kissy Stuff
An Old Stuff Mystery
Kathleen Marple Kalb

I expected good Italian food, a little Renaissance poetry, and a lot of spiraling about the goodnight kiss when Joe Poli and I went on our first real date. I didn't expect to help catch a killer.

But I suppose it kept me from overthinking the kiss, so maybe it worked out in the end.

Overthinking is pretty much my job, as a trained historian, duly accredited expert on old stuff—as in 18th and 19th century personal goods—and current director of the Unity, Connecticut, Historical Society. None of which was going to help me that night.

So I thought.

"I'm not sure about these shoes, Garrett," I told one of my babysitters as I walked into the living room.

"For God's sake, Christian," he said. "This is the third change. Stop this."

"Shoes?" Ed, his husband, asked, looking up from the Sorry game board, where my eight-year-old son Henry was giving them both a beating.

"Yeah," I said. "I don't know about kitten heels…maybe flats would be…"

Ed, a former state trooper with zero patience for trivia, just looked at me. "You've got shoes on. That's enough. Guy's not gonna be looking at your feet anyhow."

"What he said," Garrett agreed. "You're just nervous."

"Ma's worried about all that kissy stuff!" Henry piped up.

"Henry!"

"Well, you told Uncle Garrett you were worried about your lipstick." My cherub beamed. "Isn't that why?"

"Kid's right," Garrett said through a laugh. "You did go through three different ones."

"Because I wasn't sure if I needed the extra-stay kind for dinner."

"Like I would know." Garrett, a semi-retired Lincoln scholar, threw his hands up in despair. Fair to say he and Ed do not hew to gay stereotypes.

The doorbell rang.

Everyone froze, except our big, fluffy tuxedo cat, Cookie. He gave us all a disgusted look and swaggered out to the kitchen for his treat bowl. Stupid humans.

"Okay." I took a deep breath and smoothed the long skirt of my summer dress, a coral rose print number that (I hoped) was attractive without being salacious. Or at least made me look like something better than a giant redheaded tomboy.

I opened the door.

Joe stood on my step, tall and dapper in a light-gray tropical wool suit, with a blue oxford and deeper blue tie that set off his Northern Italian blond hair and deep brown eyes. Oh, my.

"'If ever any beauty I did see, which I desired, and got, 'twas but a dream of thee.'"

Double Oh My.

I knew Joe liked his John Donne; he'd sprinkled in a quote here and there once we discovered a shared fondness for the Renaissance poets.

But it was still quite the opener.

"Hi, Joe." I motioned him into the living room.

"Here." Joe handed me a blue box with gold lettering. "Thought good coffee might be better than flowers."

"Perfect." I looked at the label. "Italian."

"There is other coffee?" A grin.

"None better."

"Much more appropriate than a floral tribute for this one," Garrett said, holding out a hand. "Nice to see you."

"Same here, Professor." He shook and called to Ed. "You, too, Ed."

"Yep." Ed didn't move from the game board and gave Joe a hard look. "Have a good night, now."

Ed wasn't entirely convinced it was a good idea for me, a widow of two years with a young child, to be dating a prosecutor, even one he considered a standup guy. Because he knew what a law-enforcement career could do to a marriage, he didn't want to encourage Joe.

Still, as Joe kept coming around, dropping by my office at the Historical Society for coffee, and sometimes joining me to walk Henry to school beforehand, Ed was slowly thawing.

Very slowly.

"Doing my best to show the lady a good time," Joe said, as if it were perfectly normal to explain himself to the parents of a fortyish mother. "We have a reservation at Due Fiori."

"Very nice." Garrett, at least, gave him an approving nod.

"Hey, AlysDad!" Henry popped up from behind the couch. He knew Joe's daughter from school, and had no trouble accepting Joe as a friend of mine. There was no question of replacing his dad; even as young as he was, Henry was very aware of himself as his father's son.

"Hey, buddy." Joe shook Henry's hand with the same polite gravity he'd given Garrett. "Maybe next time we go play mini golf."

"Yeah." Henry smiled. "Way more fun than that kissy stuff."

Joe's eyes widened, and he laughed. "Well, each thing in its own time."

"Have a wonderful night," Garrett said, nodding to the door.

"Remember to check his numbers before-" I started.

"He'll be fine." Ed patted Henry's back with a reassuring smile. "Get out of here."

From Ed, that was practically an endorsement.

Joe nodded to Henry, and then me.

Out on the walk, Joe took my hand. "First time leaving him since…"

"Yeah. He was diagnosed a year after Frank died." I took a deep breath. Henry's Type-1 Diabetes doesn't rule his life, but it's always there.

"He couldn't be safer."

I nodded. "Did you know they both took the Red Cross CPR course with me?"

"I'm not surprised. Standup guys."

One of the many things I like about Joe is that he just accepts Garrett and Ed as my family. Originally, Garrett was my mentor at Shoreline State University. When Ed married Garrett, he just added me to the three children from his long-ago first marriage to a woman, and Henry became the adored youngest grandbaby.

"Your chariot, Madame," Joe said, a teasing gleam in his eyes as he opened the door of his car. It was a silver sedan, foreign and very high-end, but not new, a relic from his days as a partner at one of the top firms in New Haven. The tag, though, was an announcement of his new status: TRUBILL, as in an indictment.

"Thank you, good sir."

It was just a short drive. In New Haven County, you're never far from two or three Italian restaurants, and each one occupies a particular space: the pizza takeout spot, the informal red-sauce place for family and friends, and the special romantic one.

Due Fiori, with candles, flowers, and intimate little tables, was the romantic one. I'd never been. Frank and I had kept promising ourselves we'd get there the next milestone anniversary…and it never came.

"What do you think?" Joe asked, as he held the door. I'd be surprised if he hadn't confirmed with Garrett that Frank never brought me here.

"Lovely," I said. I'd forgotten how much I enjoyed the old-school courtesies. Joe, like Frank, believed such small courtly gestures were a sign of respect, not sexism. "You can hold doors for me anytime."

"I hold chairs, too." He grinned. "I am a full-service date."

"Nice."

A wicked little shared laugh, not missing the subtext.

"Well, now that I know you're not going to slug me…" he said.

"Highly unlikely."

Joe talked to the hostess and stepped back to let me go first while she showed us to our table, resting his hand lightly on my back as we walked. Not possessive, just a little physical acknowledgement of presence. And connection.

I'd missed that too.

Most of the couples were too busy gazing at each other in the candlelight to notice us as we walked in and settled at the table near the French doors, but an older man, sitting corners with a well-dressed woman about his age, looked up and smiled when he saw Joe.

"I'm sorry. I have to go say hello," Joe whispered. "An old mentor of mine. You don't have to come with me if you don't want to."

"Do you want me to?"

"Of course."

"Then I'm coming."

"Joe Poli," the guy pronounced when we got there. "The traitor himself."

It was said with affection, but a tiny edge. Joe had been a high-end hired gun until a drunk driver almost killed his brother and got off because of a junior prosecutor's bad lawyering. A bit of edge in his reply, too: "And you, still going to the highest bidder."

"The wages of sin are good, my friend," he said as they shook. "Who's this?"

Despite the low light, I could tell Joe was blushing. "Wendell Lionetti, I'd like you to meet Dr. Christian Shaw."

"Delighted to meet such a pretty – and smart – lady." His round face was friendly, and the grin genuine.

I shook his hand and made sure to smile at the woman, whose shiny-glossed mouth had tightened visibly. "Please. I'm an historian, not a neurosurgeon."

"Well," she said, with a definite edge in her voice, "I *am* a physician. G.P., but you get the idea. Marni Lionetti. Nice to meet you, Professor."

As we shook hands, I noticed a huge ring on her first finger. Old,

Victorian-gothic style, with a great big dark topaz stone in a heavy frame. A mourning ring, I thought.

Must be a family heirloom. And I'm an idiot to be noticing it when I should be putting on a good social face for my new guy.

Though my new guy would probably appreciate my powers of observation.

"Special night out for you two?" asked Wendell. It would have sounded dirty from a lot of people, but from him, it sounded cute.

Marni glared at him. "They don't need to tell you their business."

"Well," Joe said with a Jimmy Stewart shrug. "Been drinking a lot of Dr. Shaw's coffee lately, and figured I owed her a nice dinner."

Wendell caught the downplay and smiled. Marni's mouth tightened enough that her lip gloss oozed a bit at the corner of her mouth. Annoyed.

"Well, you've got the right place for it," Wendell said. "Have a wonderful night."

He meant it. The polite agreement his wife murmured wasn't nearly as sincere.

Not that I really cared. Joe put his hand on my back as we returned to our table and held the chair for me. We were sitting corners too.

"Clerked for Wendell years ago, and stayed close," Joe said. "Good guy. And I'm glad to see he and Marni are back together."

"Oh?"

"Yeah. I don't remember the details – I was right in the middle of leaving Magen and Renzulli for the State's Attorney when it happened – but they broke up for a while." An uncomfortable shrug. "Looked like they were headed for a really nasty divorce, and then they didn't."

"Nice when people can work it out," I said carefully. Since Joe's ex had bugged out for a CFO when he stopped bringing home a partner's share, this was a rather fraught topic.

"I tend to think people who are meant to be together find a way to be together." Joe took my hand.

"That works."

Shared smile.

We were well into a lovely meal (gnocchi pesto for me, ziti Bolognese for him), when we noticed the Lionettis leaving. Wendell held his wife's chair as Marni stood, and she leaned back, holding his gaze, then hesitating just a second before giving him a very serious kiss.

"Wow," Joe whispered.

"Yeah."

For a moment, our eyes locked. Clearly, I wasn't the only one who'd been devoting a lot of thought to that first kiss.

Then, he took a breath. Grinned. So infectiously my nerves evaporated.

"You're even prettier when you smile, *Dottore*." He uses the Italian for my title as an endearment.

"So are you."

Shared chuckle.

"'We gave each other a smile with a future in it,'" Joe said.

"Donne, of course." Smart Girl 101: when awkward, stay academic.

"Who else?"

We had just laced fingers when the crash came from the door.

Neither of us hesitated; between my first-aid training and his experience as a prosecutor, we were both programmed to run and help. It wasn't clear there was much we could do, though. Wendell Lionetti was on the ground, not breathing.

The hostess had started chest compressions.

Marni was standing there wringing her hands. "Call an ambulance!"

"Already called!" an older man, probably the owner, assured her.

"What happened?" Joe asked Marni.

"He collapsed!" She wrung her hands some more, bringing attention to that big ring.

Oh, holy hell. I sure didn't like what I was thinking.

Joe shot me a little glance. He was picking up something, too.

"I'm so sorry," I said, reaching for her hands as innocently as I could.

She didn't realize what I was doing until I flipped open the ring.

I'd recognized the design.

Sometimes those big, high-framed rings held a picture or a lock of hair in the little receptacle under the stone.

Sometimes they didn't.

You've probably seen a witchy character dosing her unfortunate victim with a poison ring in a movie. It happened in real life, too.

I would not have thought of it, except that it struck me as very wrong for a doctor to be standing around flapping her hands while a restaurant hostess worked on her husband.

And speaking of very wrong…

The ring held a sepia-toned picture of a woman in mid-Victorian clothes.

For an instant, I was speechless. Then: "Oh, I'm so sorry…"

Marni Lionetti stared at me. "How dare you?"

"I'm-" I started.

The rescue crew saved me, bursting in the door right then.

*****

Less than ten minutes later, Wendell Lionetti was in the ambulance, and Joe and I were in the car.

"I'm sorry," I said as he pulled out of the parking lot. "I don't know how I got it so wrong."

"I don't think you did."

"What?"

"She was acting guilty as hell. A doctor isn't trying to revive her husband? Plus, the way she went for you over the ring."

"But it wasn't a poison ring, even if it looked like one," I reminded him.

"No, but why did she take it as an accusation?" Joe shook his head. "Sure, people act weird at stressful moments…"

"It doesn't add up."

"No." He patted my hand. "I'm sure she did something. I just don't know what, or how."

"I don't either," I said. "The ring was all I had. That and your comment about the divorce that wasn't."

"And it was good math. I've been divorced. Once you start that train, it's extremely hard to stop. Even with a strong emotional incentive. Never mind a financial one."

"Would there have been a financial one?"

"Oh, sure. Wendell's a partner in a white-shoe firm. And a G. P. doesn't make nearly as much as you think in the Yale New Haven system." He shrugged. "Old pal practices there."

"So you don't think I'm rude – or crazy?"

"I think you're right on point. And pretty slick, honestly." A trace of that wonderful smile. "If you hadn't opened the ring, she wouldn't have given herself away. So I'm going to make sure there's an autopsy."

"If it comes to that."

We were at a streetlight, and he turned to me, his eyes now bottomless and sad. "We both know it will."

"Yeah."

He took my hand. No need to say anything, the only sound the purr of the spiffy sedan's engine as Joe turned down my leafy street.

It was still insanely early, just barely dark. The night lights on the brick path to my little house gleamed. Garrett and Ed were probably watching a planet documentary with Henry.

Joe parked the car.

Turned to me.

Despite everything, we were two healthy adults in close quarters on a summer night.

He leaned in a little closer.

Oh, yes.

I caught my breath.

My breath.

I had a sudden flash of that big kiss Marni had given Wendell as they left the table. And the shiny lip gloss she'd been wearing.

"Oh, hell," I said. "I know how she did it."

Joe pulled back, confused for a second, then snapped right back to canny prosecutor. "How?"

"It was on her lips. If he has a peanut or seafood allergy, she could get enough to cause anaphylaxis in the gloss…"

"Damn." He ran a hand through his hair. Took a breath. "Okay. Back to work for a bit."

He pulled the phone out of his pocket.

"I'll be outside," I said. It was as much about getting a little air as respecting his space.

"Thanks."

I leaned against the car, enjoying the warm night and the scent of the roses and lilacs on the breeze. I was out of sight lines from my bay window, but I could see that the TV was on and all seemed to be well inside.

All was well outside, too.

Joe got out of the car and leaned on the roof with a wry little smile playing at the corners of his mouth. "You're awfully good, *Dottore*."

"Am I?"

"Yep. Yale-New Haven says he was pronounced when he got there, and it looked like anaphylaxis. I called my friend in homicide and he's heading over to take a look. I'm probably going to have an arraignment Monday."

I smiled. "Good."

"But that's Monday." He walked over to me, stood close again.

"Yeah?"

"Right now, I'm more interested in tonight. Well, if all of this hasn't ruined everything for you."

"Kind of comes with the job, doesn't it?" I shrugged. "Remember, I was married to a reporter."

"Yeah." He smiled. "Nice that you get it."

"I do." I took a breath. Frank had died in a stupid car crash on the way to a story. And here I was, two years later, trying to rebuild. Not forgetting what had been but finding a way to live in the world I had now. "Life's uncertain. You have to take happiness when it comes. John

Donne probably said it better somewhere."

"I like yours just fine." Joe put his hands on my arms. Didn't quite pull me in, just waited. "And I agree."

I looked up at him. I did like having to look up. I think I might have had more trouble with all of this if he'd been more like Frank. "Where were we?"

Now Joe pulled me close, slowly and carefully. Not scared or awkward careful. Careful like he wanted to enjoy every second and make sure I did too. "Right about here, I think."

"That's the spot." I leaned in, making the final move myself because I knew it mattered.

I'd thought I'd had my last first kiss and I was more than okay with that. Done with trying to figure out where the noses go, how much to respond without giving someone the wrong idea, why so many men use awful-tasting lip balm.

None of the above with Joe.

Hot but still comfortable, entirely different than Frank. Not in a bad or scary way.

Just good.

Sooner than I wanted him to, he pulled back, and smiled.

"'What miracles we harmless lovers wrought.'"

"Ah, the good Reverend Donne."

"I'm saving the more—colorful—stuff for some other night." He pushed a stray curl back from my face, traced my cheekbones, finally resting his thumb on my lower lip.

"Some night soon," I said.

Not One Word
John M. Floyd

"Boys?"

Three ninth-graders in T-shirts, gym shorts, and sneakers turned to look as a bald and red-faced Father O'Neal hurried toward them down the empty hallway. Twenty feet away, through the open door of the teachers' lounge, a tall, burly man in a sweatsuit was talking into a wall-mounted telephone and holding two basketballs under his other arm. Nine or ten more balls were scattered about the room, and a desk drawer in the corner was standing open.

"You the boys who caught the snake?" O'Neal asked. He was blowing and puffing like a draft horse.

Two of the youngsters pointed to the third. "There's your hero," one said. "Jungle Jimmy Todd."

O'Neal's eyes narrowed. "Ah yes," he said. "James and I are acquainted."

"Hello, Father," Jimmy murmured.

The priest—and head of the school—studied him a moment. "What happened, exactly?"

Jimmy drew a long breath. "Coach Steen said somebody's been stealing sports stuff from the storeroom, so he asked us to help him move a dozen basketballs from there to a spare room in the gym." He pointed through the door of the lounge to the balls lying there on the floor like giant orange marbles. "We each, Coach and us, took three balls and were on our way to the gym with 'em when it crawled right up to us."

"The snake, you mean? Here in the hall?"

"Right over there," Jimmy said.

"What happened then?"

"It bit him," one of the other boys, Eddie Hendon, said.

Father O'Neal blinked, still breathing hard. "Bit you?"

"Bit my sock," Jimmy said, "not me." He reached down to touch his ankle. "Then it wrapped itself around my leg."

"Heaven help us," O'Neal said. Jimmy could almost read his mind: Thieves in the school, pranks in the classroom, and now snakes in the hallway.

"It was a python," Eddie observed, looking pleased. "They're not poisonous. There was a thing about 'em on the Discovery Channel last week."

"A python?!"

Chuck Thomas was squinting at Eddie. "You watch the Discovery Channel?"

"Or a boa constrictor," Eddie continued. "We ain't sure which."

"Aren't," Father O'Neal corrected.

"It was a small one," Jimmy said. "A baby, probably."

"How small?"

"Four or five feet long, I guess. But it was strong. I grabbed it behind the head, like this, and Chuck and Eddie helped me uncoil it."

"Good *grief*. What was it doing here, anyone know?"

All three boys shrugged. "Somebody's pet, maybe," Chuck said.

The priest looked around, frowning. Coach Steen was still on the phone in the teachers' lounge.

"Where's the snake now?" O'Neal asked.

"The broom closet," Jimmy said, and pointed. "Just down the hall."

"How'd you get it in there?"

"Really fast," Chuck said. All the boys grinned.

"Eddie opened the door and Chuck and me threw it in and slammed the door shut," Jimmy explained.

"Chuck and *I*," Father O'Neal said. He seemed to think all this over, rubbing his forehead, then asked, "What's the deal with the teacher's lounge?"

"Coach told us to put the balls in there till this gets worked out."

"No, I mean what's Coach Steen doing in there now?"

"He was looking for a key to the broom closet's door. To lock the snake in."

O'Neal nodded, then regarded the group in solemn silence for a long moment. "That was excellent work you did, boys. Excellent work." To Jimmy he added, "It appears you have redeemed yourself, James."

Jimmy looked uncomfortable. "You mean that thing last month?"

"I think you know what I mean."

Jimmy swallowed. "It was just butyric acid, Father. A few drops, in a wastebasket in the chemistry lab. Nobody got hurt—"

"No, what everybody got," O'Neal said, "was a free day at home, because it stunk up the whole school."

"Stinked," Chuck corrected.

"In my opinion," Eddie said helpfully, "the evacuation was very well organized."

The priest gave him a stern look, but didn't press the issue. "And I still haven't found out who switched the nameplates on the doors of the boys' and girls' restrooms last week."

"A terrible thing," Eddie agreed.

"Parents are still calling me about that," O'Neal said. "What a mess. Nobody knew for sure which was which. I can still hear the screams. Half the boys were in the girls' and half the girls in the boys'—"

"Sounded like an outside job to me," Chuck said, deadpan. "Somebody from St. Richards', probably."

For a moment Father O'Neal actually looked amused. "Regardless of that," he said, serious again, "you boys did a good thing today. If you hadn't been here, or if this had happened between classes, with students packing the halls..." He shook his head as if picturing that. "Anyhow, I think this calls for an afternoon off. I'll speak to your teachers."

Well, *that* was unexpected. The boys all beamed. At that instant Coach Steen emerged from the lounge, looking flustered. He seemed to realize he was still holding two basketballs, so he went back inside and added them to the others, for the time being. When he came back again he said, "Mornin', Father. Boys, I couldn't find a key for the broom closet. It was supposed to be in that desk in there—"

"Doesn't matter," O'Neal said. "The boys filled me in. That closet's hardly ever used, nobody'll go in there." O'Neal nodded toward the still-open door to the lounge. "I hope you were calling the fire department, or the zoo, or whoever can come take this thing off our hands."

"I was talking to the folks who run the carnival," Steen answered. They all knew the tri-county fair was in town, at the fairgrounds on the far side of a wooded area that bordered the school property. "I heard on the news this morning some animals had got loose. Sure enough, the carnival guys said it sounded like one of theirs. They're sending somebody over."

The priest nodded, said "Good," and frowned. "Where were *you* during all this, by the way?"

Steen's face reddened. "I was, ah, on top of the lockers over there, holding onto my balls."

"Excuse me?"

"My basketballs," he said. "I'm scared to death of snakes."

"I am too. I'd probably have been up there with you," O'Neal said. "Better get outside, Coach, and watch for the cavalry." As Steen hurried off, O'Neal turned to the three boys. "I meant what I said, men. Outstanding work. Don't any of you bother coming in after lunch."

"Aye aye, sir," Chuck said. Jimmy and Eddie were grinning from ear to ear.

"But not one word about this to Sister Agnes." The priest stared gravely into Jimmy's eyes. "Especially you, James," he said, pointing a long finger. "Not *one word*."

Jimmy nodded. All of them had a healthy fear of the school's Second in Command. Sister Agnes was a bitter, ruthless woman who disliked the schoolchildren only slightly less than she disliked Father O'Neal. This fact—though not very nunlike—was common knowledge. The only good thing about her was that she usually stayed in the batcave, which was the way most of the students referred to her office.

But this was, alas, no usual day. Ten seconds after Father O'Neal disappeared around the corner of the hallway, Sister Agnes appeared at the other end, striding along like an executioner on the way to the gallows.

When she saw the boys she stopped dead, her already scowling face darkening further. She stomped up to them, planted both hands on her hips, and thrust her chin forward.

"What are you hoodlums doing in the hall?"

All three stared at her, petrified. An enraged python was nothing compared to this woman.

"You heard me," she said. "Why aren't you in class?"

"We're on an errand with Coach Steen," Eddie croaked. He pointed through the open door of the lounge to the load of basketballs, as if they explained everything.

She followed his pointing finger, then gave him a laser stare. "Coach Steen is in the gym. And you're supposed to be, too."

"No ma'am, he's outside," Eddie said. All three boys cast a hopeful look at the sunlit doors at the east exit, but there was no sign of Coach Steen's wide body.

"I thought you said you were helping him."

Jimmy started to answer, then hesitated.

Not one word, Father O'Neal had said...

"All of you stay right where you are," she snapped. She turned, charged through the door of the lounge, and stood there a moment. Then she stormed out again.

"What were you doing in the teachers' lounge?" she asked.

"We weren't in the teachers' lounge," Chuck said.

"There's a bunch of basketballs in there."

"It's just temporary," Eddie said.

"We were told to put 'em there," Chuck said.

She seemed to be growing taller by the second. "By whom?"

"Coach Steen."

"Why would he tell you that?"

Eddie looked ill. Since any answer would probably let the cat out of the bag, no one replied.

"Why don't you just tell me," she said, glaring at them, "where it is."

Chuck blinked. "Where what is?"

"You know what. My cell phone."

"Your cell phone?!"

She nodded toward the teachers' lounge. "I left it in there on that desk, half an hour ago. Now it's gone. Plus, the door's wide open, everyone else is in class, you're in gym clothes, the desk in there looks ransacked, and the room's full of basketballs. Add it up."

Eddie Hendon swallowed. "We didn't steal your phone, Sister Ag—"

"You stole it, you little hooligans," she hissed, through clenched teeth. "There's been a rash of thefts at this school lately, and by all that's right and holy, I do believe I have found the robbers."

All of them stood and looked at her, wide-eyed.

Then she focused on Jimmy. "I know you, James Todd," she said, her eyes as black and still as a lizard's. "You're the leader of this band of misfits. So tell me, where is my cell phone?"

Silence.

"WHERE," she roared, "*IS* IT?"

Jimmy took a deep breath and let it out.

"The broom closet," he said.

It was suddenly very quiet in the hall. She gave them all another withering stare, then turned on her heel and marched away toward the closet.

The boys wasted no time. All three headed for the outside door, and fast. On the way there, Jimmy looked at Chuck and Eddie, who were gaping at him as if to say *What have you done?*

"I did what he told me to," Jimmy explained. "That was *three* words."

His two friends nodded. That made sense.

Besides, her socks were at least as thick as his...

Where is the Truth?
Dave Dempster

A fine autumn Sunday morning in 2019. Enjoyable after so much rain on the Friday night. Fine for a family walk in the woods. Horsford Woods, just up the road. Beautiful trees, invigorating exercise. The joys of life. Sam and Jane had to make sure the kids were wearing their gear, despite the usual protests. Dogs, or what they leave behind, can be a nuisance but nothing could prepare them for what was to come.

Hide and seek was a favourite, especially for Jamie. At 8 he left sister Amy, three years his junior, far behind. Even dad Sam with his Scout Leader experience found it difficult to keep up.

After nearly ten minutes Sam was concerned. He'd told Jamie until he was blue in the face not to go too far from the trail. It was not funny anymore.

He called out.

No response. He moved further into the density of the trees, emerging in a clearing. Shouted again. An unusually pale face rounded a bush. A mixture of relief and anger.

"Why do you not do what you're told? You must stay near the path. How often have I told you?"

But Jamie looked frightened. Then Sam realised something was up. "What is it?"

Jamie just pointed. He couldn't speak. A few metres to his left was a felled tree. But that wasn't all.

Sam didn't see it at first. Then, slowly, as if in the seconds before a car collision, he saw. A hand protruding from the soil.

＊＊＊＊＊

Not another bloody one. He hated them. Talks. Talks about talks. He was a doer. Not a talker. He regretted promotion to inspector. Inspector Robinson. How grand it had sounded. The pressure of a neglected mortgage following the trauma of divorce (thank God there were no children) had made a step up irresistible but there was a price to pay. Sergeants do the *real* investigative police work. He knew that well from thirty years on the Force. It was what he liked and what he was good at. The two so often go hand in hand. Any rank above sergeant deals with recruitment, public relations, administration, gender and equality issues, strengthening ties with local officials, and the list goes on. He truly missed the challenges of *real* police work. So, how could he escape a one hour gathering to discuss such compelling issues as 'Morale in today's Police Force' and 'How to deal with the media?'.

"I did knock, sir," woke him from his daydream. "A body's been found in Horsford Woods."

Hallelujah, he almost shouted. Saved, at least for now. Here was an opportunity. A challenge. "Okay, I'm on my way."

By now Ryan had come to the door. "Found by a family out walking, Frank." DS Ryan Jenkins was everything that DI Frank Robinson was not. Sensible and sociable. He had only been in Norwich for two years. *A highflyer. Assistant Chief Constable, at least,* thought Frank. And yet they seemed to work well together.

*****

In the short drive ahead, Forensics had been summonsed as well as counselling for the unlucky family. They had to act quickly. In no time the press would be getting in the way.

Ryan could deal with them, a skill beyond Frank.

As they edged closer the sheer beauty of the spot was clear. Leaves were not yet ready to fall and there was a thick canopy. The trees towered above. If only they could talk.

"That storm on Friday night hasn't helped us," concluded Ryan.

"That's for sure," agreed Frank. A small forearm could be made out. "We'd better get the pathologist here to try to make sense of this."

"He's already on his way." When Frank looked puzzled, Ryan

explained that he got in a call to the morgue before leaving the office. *Yeah, a highflyer indeed*, thought Frank. Both men knew of course that an unnatural burial like this meant murder, but the first question was identification of the victim. The pathologist was the best start.

"Hope I'm going to be thanked for this. I'm missing a golf match," complained Dr Thornton. Ryan was sympathetic, beating Frank to the draw. "Peter, that's good of you."

For his part Frank was relieved that Dr Thornton had drawn the short straw. His colleague Dr Norris did not see eye to eye with Frank at all. In fact, most of those around Frank saw Frank as introspective and unsociable. And that's how Frank was. More than reluctant to express himself. Difficult to understand at the best of times. Without true friends. At least mildly autistic, shades of Asperger's, as a psychiatrist would have it.

The good doctor did not wait for more and bent down. "Sorry, all I can tell you at this stage is that this was a young girl, aged about 14 to 16, who died some weeks ago. Can't say anything about the cause of death at this point but all will be revealed at the post-mortem. You'll have to be very careful about removing the body but I'm sure I don't need to tell you that. Dr Norris is the expert in this sort of case, and he should do the post-mortem."

Frank sighed openly. Ryan understood. Frank couldn't get over the Sugden trial. Norris was shredded in the witness box. Reasonable doubt is always a small step away and when the Crown pathologist under cross-examination by a sharp silk could not be sure about the cause of death, the accused walked. All the hard work by Frank's team went down the drain.

Thornton continued "Norris was involved in a similar case when he was in Suffolk and has given well-received lectures about that."

"Thanks again" said Ryan, intervening abruptly before Frank could complain. Thornton walked away. "I'll assist at the post-mortem if that helps," Ryan added diplomatically.

Another sigh from Frank, this time of resignation, accompanied by a nod and a request.

"Can you ask Scotty—a reference to DC Donald McAllister, an experienced team member—to sus out all available CCTV nearby?"

*****

Frank did not have a great sleep. He was preoccupied with his less excited outlook now that the investigation was underway. Probably a lack of confidence. He often felt uncomfortable. He didn't see the world as others did, but he couldn't change that. A breakfast on the move seemed to restore his faith in his abilities and spurred his drive to the office.

"Morning, sir. The preliminary forensic report is on your desk and DS Jenkins would like a word."

"Yes, ask him to come in."

Ryan's uniform was neat and carefully kept, a reminder of Frank's unruly appearance. "I'll go down to the mortuary at 11," Ryan announced.

"Fine, we'll catch up when you get back. I'd like to hold a team meeting for say 2pm so we can try to work out a game plan."

"Great, I'll set that up," Ryan replied enthusiastically.

When Ryan left, Frank looked again, this time in detail, at the preliminary report. The body had been wrapped in tarpaulin. Items of clothing, vaginal and anal swabs, hair and nail samples, the usual stuff. *A blank canvas but the post-mortem will get the show on the road*, he assured himself.

Frank felt he was ready to speak to the team.

A photo of what was once quite a pretty girl had been added to the whiteboard. And a hushed solemnity had come over the gathering. Even seasoned detectives find it hard to contain their emotions. Frank was the exception. He was so business-like his colleagues found his detachment hard to understand. No-one there could call Frank a friend in the ordinary sense.

He began with a summary of the initial post-mortem findings. "Pending toxicology, forensics and intimate swabs, we know that this young female, aged around 15 years, was strangled with a ligature of some kind. Minor bruising to the legs. There was nothing on the body or at the scene to identify her but a forensic odontologist has been contacted to give us a check against dental records."

He paused in case anyone had any questions, then, "Some of the first questions—was she killed there, or somewhere else? Had she been reported missing? John, can you go through recent missing persons files to see if there's a match?"

John Richmond had begun as a detective constable with Frank's team only months earlier. He was attentive, keen to learn on the job and a little bemused by his rather odd superior. "Will do, boss," he replied quickly.

"I'd like you, Tom, to man the fort." DS Tom Benjamin was next in seniority and more than capable. He would probably retire with the same rank, left far behind by Ryan, but that didn't reduce his dependability. "Everyone else to search the wider scene for evidence. We'll take Phoebe." Phoebe, an Alsatian, would be borrowed from the Dog Unit and Frank had already arranged that with Phoebe's handler.

*****

On the way back to the scene Ryan asked about the forensic odontologist. "Faye something?" Frank was a little hesitant, keeping his eye on the road.

"Not Dunaway, unfortunately!" quipped Ryan.

"Turner," Frank continued, ignoring Ryan's comical slight.

Truly, Faye Turner was hardly an oil painting, but Frank couldn't care less. If Faye did her job that was all that mattered. Her looks were secondary.

The area surrounding the newly erected police tent would surely tell them a helpful story, even if the recent storm had put paid to meaningful tyre tracks. The team was dedicated. Missing something could be catastrophic. Tough going but after what seemed longer than half an hour a shout came. DC Gareth Thompson, who had been in the team for a year or more, excitedly pointed to what looked like footprints within the gorse.

The others rushed up.

Here was something! Great. "We'll get Forensics out."

On the return journey Ryan wondered openly "I'm hoping Beth gets this one." Frank managed a tiny wry smile but would not be drawn. Bethany Williams was the nicest looking forensic officer by a country mile.

*****

DC John Richmond could not contain his enthusiasm. "Melissa Watson, reported missing on Sunday 28th July, is a match!"

"Right, can I have the file?" came Frank's clinical response.

"Oh, yes." The young detective came back down to earth swiftly, picked up a nearby folder and handed over.

"Now for the awful part. Can you ask Mary to do the notification, Ryan?" Mary O'Reilly, now well into her fifties, was the Family Liaison Officer. She had unrivalled skill in dealing with bereaved people. Empathy and patience in spades. She's had to deal with all manner of reactions, some surprising, some violent, over the years. Apparently, she lost her mother early in life and the experience fortified her. Frank and Ryan would travel with her, not merely because they were leading the investigation but to ensure Mary's safety. Reactions are unpredictable.

*****

The Watson residence was in Newmarket Street, an affluent side of Norwich city. As the police cars left the broad tree-lined street, they turned into a long driveway bordered by walled garden with manicured bushes. Money talks.

When the front door had opened, and before a word could be uttered by the three police officers, Susan Watson asked anxiously, "Have you found her?"

When the three heads bowed slightly in silence she burst into tears. A boy aged around eleven or twelve in a school uniform came up to the door, curious to learn what was going on.

"Can we come inside?" Mary O'Reilly ushered Mrs Watson, who had recovered her composure slightly, into what appeared to be her living room. Polished oak flooring and framed pictures, a well-furnished and cared for home.

Absently, Susan Watson said, "Simon, can you please go upstairs?" The schoolboy scowled before leaving.

After introductions Mary took over, consoling the girl's mother as best she could.

Just then, a car could be heard on the gravel driveway. Ryan looked carefully out of the window. "It's a silver Bentley."

Susan Watson smiled weakly. "That'll be David, my husband."

"We'll wait until he comes in," Mary interjected.

A man with the beginnings of greying hair and dressed in an expensive looking suit must have come through a side door but soon emerged. Introductions were repeated. Mr Watson sat on a large sofa a good distance from his wife who was still visibly upset. An observation not lost on the police.

Susan Watson through tears said "We dreaded this day. We thought it would all just be a bad dream." She was in a poor way, but her husband maintained his unfeeling distance.

Ryan stressed that they had to be sure and gently proposed that either dad or mum could accompany Mary to identify the body. There were more tears from poor Susan before David finally volunteered. "Can I have your contact number and I'll arrange to take you there at a convenient time?' asked Mary.

"Was she, you know...."

Ryan answered Watson's unfinished but readily understood question. "We don't know yet. We're waiting on test results. I'm afraid we'll have a lot of questions, but we'll come back later when it's better for you."

On the gravel outside, before Mary stepped away to her car, she told Frank she would try to speak to the boy alone. "The boy may tell us what his parents don't know or don't want us to know."

Frank waited until he and Ryan were inside their car, well out of earshot.

"He's a cold fish, that one."

"Maybe just grief," suggested Ryan.

Frank made a mental note.

*****

Back at the office Frank had a chance to look at the missing person file. Dismay. Zilch. His anger began to rise. "What's the point, Ryan. Look at who authored this tiny gem." The two men looked at each other for a moment before Frank exploded. "What a fucking waste of time."

They knew that complaining officially would get nowhere. The author, newly promoted DCI James Ritchie, was hardly respected. Feared was more like it. Lower ranked officers might have a justified grievance, but they knew too well that Ritchie would use his superiority against them, sooner or later. It just wasn't worth it. Then Ryan passed on a message.

"The Super would like a word with you, Frank."

*****

"Look Frank, I remember the mess you made of that press release in the Nelson case. David Watson is well connected. I've just heard from the Chief Constable's personal secretary. We are being watched. For God's sake keep a muzzle on the media. The Watsons value their privacy."

Frank grinned and bore it. Sounding off about the leads which the blank missing person enquiry might have missed, for all time, wouldn't have helped. "We'll be discreet, sir."

Supt Jones hardly looked convinced, but it was left there.

Down the corridor Mary was waiting for him. "ID confirmed, sir."

"That was quick. Anything arising?"

"I'm not sure. Susan Watson's a real mess. Seems troubled by a lot of things but she's not yet able to share."

Frank said "I'd like you to come along tomorrow when Ryan and I speak to her. I don't expect her husband the businessman to be there, but you may get the chance to speak to the boy. Can you set up a meeting at Newmarket Street tomorrow morning to suit the three of us?"

"Will do, sir."

✳✳✳✳✳

It was raining heavily the next morning as the same two police cars pulled into the Watson driveway. *Fitting weather, really*, Frank thought, in keeping with their depressing task.

"We're sorry to have to ask all these questions," Frank began, "but it's vital that we find out as much as we can, as soon as we can, to try to track down who is responsible." He thought better of apologising for the preceding lack of interest in the hope of saving face but it was not to be.

"Shame you couldn't be bothered when Melissa went missing months ago."

Frank almost took a step back. This was a quite different Susan Watson. Less than 24 hours on, she was angry, very angry. Frank couldn't blame her. The police had let her down badly. They would never know if something had been missed those months ago, when the trail was fresh. He tried promising to do his best, but Susan wasn't finished.

"If you had been out looking for her she might have been saved!" She descended into a tearful collapse and had to be assisted into a red leather chair. What could they say? Mary stepped in to do what she did best and helped to comfort. There was a necessary pause. When he thought he might get a response, Ryan asked in a soft voice:

"Could we please have a look at Melissa's room?"

The group moved upstairs by way of wide carpeted steps below crystal chandeliers. Turning right at the top they soon came to a room with a 'Melissa' decorative door sign. What lay inside looked like what was to be expected.

"She had just turned 16 when she went out that Saturday night." Susan Watson's anger had abated. Ryan spotted a photograph on the dressing table. Susan's face turned sour. "Gabriel Johnson. Not the best of boyfriends. I thought she had disposed of that."

She leant forward. Frank put out a hand. "Please…" Susan sighed and turned her head away.

"Do you know of anyone who might have wished Melissa harm?"

"I didn't like her boyfriend."

"Gabriel Johnson?"

"No, the one after him, Alan something or other. Just didn't like the look of him. Only saw him once. Hanging around outside school one day."

"Which school is that?'

"Honestly, you know NOTHING." She was starting to well up again.

Mary took the lead. "Norwich High School for Girls?"

"Yes" came the reply. *Private school fees would certainly be no problem for this family*, thought Frank.

"We'll leave you in peace soon," promised Frank, playing for time. "I understand that Melissa went out that last night about 8pm. Did Melissa have internet access?"

"Yes, but we were strict about that. We were concerned about the dangers. Melissa and her brother could only use the home computer in the downstairs study, it's the only one we have, between 6 and 7pm."

"Could we see that computer?"

"I'll have to ask David about that."

Ryan picked up a framed photograph. "Is this a recent photo?"

"That's from a school trip last May, I think," Susan explained.

"Could we have that? It would really help, and you'll get it back." Susan nodded her assent. "And the last one, did Melissa say where she was going that night?"

"Oh, really. I told you all this months ago. She wouldn't say but she had to be back by 10pm. That was the last…" Susan became tearful again, and the group thought the best course was to call it a day.

*****

Back at home base Frank cancelled the forensic odontologist, remembering that Luke would be pleased. He saw a report on his desk but then it hit him. He turned his head sharply at his open office door. The clock on the far wall confirmed the worst. 3.15pm! Frank hurried inside and picked up the phone, knowing he was in deep trouble. Ryan's outline appeared suddenly at the door.

"Not now, Ryan." Ryan closed Frank's door behind him. Frank's door was usually open, but Ryan didn't need to be asked twice.

Frantically Frank searched for the number. *Fuck.* There it was. Where it should have been after all. Hurriedly he phoned the course organiser at Police HQ at Wymondham, fully ten miles south of Norwich.

"Really sorry. I've been tied up in an urgent murder investigation here in Norwich."

When the course organiser, who was a sergeant Frank didn't know from Adam, suggested that Frank's 3pm talk in Wymondham could start late when he arrived, to avoid disappointing two dozen recruits there, Frank forgot himself and retorted "Seriously? To hear about Information Management?" The cat was out of the bag. Frank apologised and put the phone down.

He knew this wouldn't go unnoticed. It wasn't the first time he had let the side down. Had he dropped everything and turned up late, it would have been so much worse because he hadn't just overlooked the date and time, he hadn't prepared at all for the talk. He would have ended up entertaining the recruits with anecdotes about detective work which might have amused, even inspired, some of the newcomers but would have infuriated the bosses at HQ.

These talks were scheduled weeks ahead. An essential part of the work of an inspector. Only death or insanity could excuse, provided there was a supporting certificate!

Shrugging his shoulders, as if to brush off the episode, Frank returned to the report. Here was more positive news. He noticed that the report had been signed by the attractive Bethany Williams. That would get Ryan's full attention. Frank called Ryan in.

"Forensics have worked fast. They've identified the footprints at the scene. Class characteristics but nothing individual, unfortunately. They suggest drag marks in the surrounding area."

Ryan asked for a look and Frank handed over the report. *Incorrigible*, thought Frank, as Ryan's eyes immediately went to the foot of the report.

Ryan looked up. "This is significant. I'd like to verify exactly what this means down at Wymondham."

"Yes, I agree you should *verify* it with Bethany!" laughed Frank. Such moments keep detectives going. Male detectives, that is.

Time for an impromptu team update.

Standing in front of the whiteboard, alongside the new photo of Melissa, which had replaced the post-mortem version, Frank wrote 'Gabriel Johnson' and 'Alan__'.

"Gabriel is an ex-boyfriend and Alan, surname unknown, is Melissa's boyfriend at the time she disappeared. We're still waiting on the intimate swab results, but CSI have identified the type of footwear at the scene. Likely to be a trainer. They also suggest that there are drag marks there, so she may well have been killed elsewhere before being dumped in Horsford Woods. Ryan will check that out with the lovely Bethany as to how far we can rely on that, so we don't unravel in Court. So, James. I think this is one for you. Find out what you can about the shoe: sales, suppliers etc. locally. You know the drill."

"Yes, sir." James sounded enthusiastic. He had been in Frank's team long enough to appreciate the value of tedious and time-consuming tasks and long enough to hide his natural impatience at the allocation.

"This is probably our best lead so far, so thanks in advance," Frank added by way of encouragement. "Also, the tarpaulin wrapping the body seems common or garden but can you check that out too? I'm sure we can learn much more from the family. Ryan and I will continue with that."

Frank paused for a moment, then added, "One very important thing," he waited for young John Richmond to turn back around. "This really is important." Frank picked up a file from the nearby table. "This missing person report is just useless." He threw the file forcibly on the ground.

That got everyone's attention. "We are going to have to start from scratch. The family are angry with us. The Chief Constable has been contacted already. All Hell will descend on us if we make more mistakes. We must keep everything close to our chests. Don't for goodness' sake even hint at anything. The media must be kept at a long distance. Understood?"

There was a general murmur of agreement.

"We need to find out everything about this poor girl. Her friends, enemies, habits, everything." Frank ended by dishing out specific tasks. Contact with the school; a background check on Gabriel Johnson; tracking down the boyfriend Alan; door knocking neighbours and so on.

*****

Early that evening the full post-mortem report landed on Frank's desk. Strangulation by ligature. Bruising to lower limbs. Otherwise, the victim was in very good health. The nail samples analysis had not yet been completed. Some hairs had been extracted from the lower clothing and sent for analysis. Frank was about to curse the lack of lab results when a figure appeared at the door.

"Inspector Robinson?"

The name was on his door but admin staff seemed to come and go with increasing speed. She stepped forward gingerly and handed over a couple of sheets.

Intimate samples analysis at last.

And a surprise. This 16-year-old was not *virgo intacta* but she had not been raped or, more exactly, there was no sign of forceful sexual assault. Burial had made analysis difficult, so the findings were consequently tentative. The whole team, Frank included, had assumed that a sexual predator was at large.

Who else would want to kill a 16-year-old girl? Frank quickly corrected himself. A sexual predator may have met resistance, or panicked, and overdid the stranglehold. Nonetheless it was puzzling.

Forensic services must have overheard Frank's grumbling because only half an hour later the remaining forensic report appeared. The hairs attached to the clothing turned out to be dog hairs. Oh dear. *Alsatian* dog hairs. We don't need to wait for a defence silk to ask if Phoebe came too close. That's going nowhere then. Simply nothing from beneath the nails. Frank was convinced now that she knew her attacker but had been taken by surprise.

Then he realised that toxicology had not come back yet.

Frank looked around. "Lorraine, can you chase up toxicology on the Melissa Watson murder, please, it's urgent."

"Will do, sir." Lorraine was one of the two women in the team, which cannot have made her work life particularly easy. Unlike Frank, who had followed the traditional uniform first route, Lorraine had arrived courtesy of the newer accelerated entry graduate scheme. More importantly for Frank, she had a 2.1 from Nottingham Trent University in Forensic Psychology. Understanding criminal behaviour is a *sine qua non* for detectives.

Just then DS Luke walked in, looking uncharacteristically glum.

"'What's up?" asked Frank. Luke moved into the privacy of Frank's office.

"I'm just back from CSI. She's engaged to some lucky bastard" moaned Luke, who clearly needed time to recover.

"That's a shame. Can we catch up in ten? More reports are in and we'll have to see the pathologist."

"Okay, I need a very strong coffee." Ryan faded away to lick his romantic wounds. Minutes later, after he'd recovered, it turned out that the otherwise engaged Bethany was confident about her findings. She had taken measurements and produced impressive photographic slides demonstrating a pathway in the undergrowth consistent with dragging the body to its final resting place.

Frank remarked "Not just a pretty face, then. It's a distance from the nearest road to the burial scene. The drag marks only run about 10 metres. How heavy was Melissa?" Frank and Ryan went sharply to the post-mortem. 51 kilos. "Could be carried by one, I suppose, who found the last stretch awkward. Could you set up a meeting with Dr Norris? Might be faster coming from you, Ryan."

*****

Next morning dramatic word came from reception. A man had just walked in and wanted to confess.

"I'll be right down."

Frank opened the interview room door to reveal a slight man in his thirties wearing a jacket which had seen better days.

"Are you the officer in charge? I want to confess to killing that girl in Horsford Woods."

Frank's heart sank. "Just hang on a minute." DC Jennifer Smith came in and closed the door behind her.

The interview recorder was activated. "Present Detective Inspector Robinson and Detective Constable Smith. Time is 10.15am on Wednesday 9th October 2019." Frank let five seconds roll by so he could compose himself, then: "Can you state your full name and address, please?"

"Mickey Martin Taylor"

"Address?"

"I don't stay in one place."

"No fixed abode," added Frank. "Date of birth?"

"Where's the camera?" The suspect kept looking around.

"Don't worry about that. Date of birth?"

"Ah, is that the camera up there?"

"What's your date of birth?" Frank's voice was raised in exasperation.

"Second April"

"And the year?"

"Mm, not sure. 1988, I think."

"What can you tell me…"

Frank was cut off. "I killed her."

"Who did you kill?"

"That girl in Horsford Woods"

"Do you know her name?"

"No."

"How did you kill her?"

"I hit her with a hammer."

"Why did you do that?"

"She stole my wallet. I had 500 quid in it."

Frank could take no more. "Just wait here, please. Interview suspended at 10.18am. Inspector Robinson and Detective Smith leave the room."

Just outside, Frank exclaimed "What a waste of time. Can you arrange a section 136 assessment urgently? My guess is attention-seeking but it's clearly a false confession."

Taken aback at the shortness of the interview, DC Smith enquired "That's section 136 of the Mental Health Act?"

"Yes, Jenny," snapped Frank in frustration, heading back to his office.

As soon as he reached his door Frank found the Super sitting in his chair. Frank closed the door and took a deep breath.

Before Frank could say anything, Supt Jones waded in with, "What are you playing at? I warned you about this. You can't go on behaving like this. Just not turning up to a scheduled talk which is an important part of the recruitment and training programme. The bosses at HQ are furious. I managed to make excuses for you, but there will not be another time. Do you want to be demoted? Because that's where this is heading. You may not like parts of the job but if you keep this up you won't have the job. Do you understand me? I can't protect you again. Don't let yourself, and everyone else here, down, Frank."

"Sorry, sir."

Frank had returned to his seat. There was a plus side amidst the gloom. He could continue with this murder investigation. It was becoming an obsession.

*****

"Best if you do most of the talking," Frank suggested as they approached the mortuary. Ryan understood at once. Frank simply couldn't forget the painful role Dr Norris had played in the Sugden trial.

Down in the cold room, Ryan opened with "What can you tell us about the time of death?"

Norris forever seemed annoyed. "At least two months ago, perhaps a bit earlier than that."

"Dr Thornton thought it was more likely weeks, but he told us you were the expert for this type of case," Ryan added diplomatically.

Norris continued, "Insect activity is really the best indicator, although weather conditions and the degree of exposure are factors too. I'm confident that we are talking about at least two months."

"And strangulation, so the hyoid bone was broken?" asked Ryan.

Warming to Ryan's interest, Norris said, "No, that's a common misconception. This young woman had only just turned 16. The hyoid doesn't usually form fully until the late 20s. In any case the hyoid is only broken in about a third of strangulations. A clever defence counsel might well suggest suicide by hanging as the cause of death."

Frank bit his tongue and let Norris continue.

"The lack of hyoid fracture does not tend to support that theory, even if most strangulations do not have hyoid bone fractures. But the complete answer here is the neck findings. The subcutaneous bruising is entirely consistent with ligature strangulation, applied from behind."

"Can you say what sort of ligature was used?" Ryan continued.

"Not sharp, more like cord or rope. What is remarkable is the absence of external injury. No sign of trauma. No real indication that there was a struggle of any kind. The internal organs were healthy. This was a fit teenager. The bruising to the lower legs was not extensive. It's to both legs, so bumping into furniture, for example, would not explain that. I was able to exclude internal trauma, so whatever caused the bruising was external to the body. There's more on the thighs where there is loose tissue."

"If the body was dragged, could that cause the bruising?" asked Ryan.

"Yes, that's possible."

"Can you say if the bruising was before or after death?"

"Very difficult to answer. Pathologists have problems aging bruising in a scenario like this. Opinions differ. Sorry about that."

Up to this point things had been going well but the next long ten minutes descended into a narcissistic account of highlights to date in the career of Dr Norris.

When he could take no more, Frank finally intervened. "Goodness, is that the time? Sorry we have to go." To Frank's surprise Ryan had been lapping it up and came across as reluctant to leave. Norris' ego was soothed suitably before the detectives left.

*****

"He knows his stuff," Ryan commented, no doubt impressed by the scholarly rebuttal of his knowledge of the hyoid bone. Frank had to admit that he found the distinction, between suicide by hanging and strangulation by ligature, informative.

Frank changed the subject. "I wonder if Scotty got anywhere with the door knock?"

"A dead end, I'm afraid," Scotty began. "Only a few small businesses nearby and only one with CCTV. They had just wiped the old tapes, leaving nothing before September. On top of that no-one saw anything suspicious in the last couple of months. Hopeless, I'm sorry to say."

Ryan sighed. "More bad news, boss. The shoe size is given as eight and a half to nine and a half. Nine is the most common male shoe size, for half the population."

Frank summed up. "Locard's 'every contact leaves a trace', that's what we were all taught, but we have next to nothing from this crime scene. There are a lot of secrets hiding out there, somewhere, so on we go."

Then the toxicology report landed and changed everything. The deceased had a low level of cocaine in her system shortly before death.

The chemist had reached that conclusion by working out the redistribution levels in the internal organs from the post-mortem tissue samples.

When Frank learned that other team members had made progress, it was time the team got together.

"Gabriel Johnson, the ex-boyfriend, is a real piece of work. He's done juvenile detention for actual bodily harm. He's currently on probation for drug possession."

"Thanks, Lorraine. Why would a girl from a well to do family take up with someone like that and have cocaine in her system? This lad has earned a visit."

"That might be a problem, sir. His probation officer has lost contact, but I have his mother's address in Lakenham."

"So, Luke, Scotty and you Lorraine to go there first thing tomorrow."

Next Jenny Smith spoke up. "Mickey Martin Taylor"

"The fruitcake from yesterday?" Frank was irritated that there was even a second mention.

"He's been detained."

"I should hope so."

"Okay, sir. Now the girl's school had quite a bit to say," she paused, then got a nod from Frank and carried on.

"Melissa was a bright student with a promising future. She achieved A grades in just about everything until she fell apart during the summer term of this year. She went AWOL often and her grades suffered badly. One of the teachers close to her put it down to boy trouble. I think she had quite a sheltered upbringing. Her boyfriend at the time of her disappearance, Alan Littlejohn, told me that she was unhappy at home. I didn't have time to take a full statement. I think he has more to say. I'll have to go back. And there's a male teacher there who was noticed showing unusual interest in Melissa around the time she got into trouble. A Martin Haywood. I've ordered a background check".

"Excellent, Jenny. You and Ryan can come with me to the Watson home hopefully tomorrow. Which reminds me, John, did you get their computer?"

"Mr Watson is refusing to hand it over. Says it has his business on it."

"Really? We'll see about that too then." Frank's voice had gone up a notch.

*****

The following day the contrast between affluent Newmarket Street, home to the Watsons, and Lakenham, the erstwhile home of the wayward Gabriel Johnson, could not have been starker. They parked an intelligent distance from the Lakenham address. An almost forgotten suburb. Rundown and neglected. Emphasised by the constant city traffic flow.

Scotty took the rear. No-one gets past Scotty—not even an athletic 17-year-old with local knowhow.

The front door wasn't answered. When Ryan knocked for the third time, with Lorraine by his side, the welcome came.

"What the fuck do *you* want?"

"Police. We're looking for your son, Gabriel."

"He's not here, so fuck off." As the door was closing a loud noise rang out from the rear of the tenement building. Gabriel's mother was quicker with the door than Ryan was with his foot, and had it closed before he could jam it open. It was still a dubious move, mainly as they had no warrant.

In a flash they ran down a side lane to see Scotty clambering over a fence. They caught up. A few minutes later Scotty came back over the fence, nursing a hand.

"The bastard bit me."

"Better have that seen to—the bugger might have rabies, or worse. We'll get him, don't worry."

Sure enough, within the hour, with generous help from the uniformed ranks, they had their young man.

*****

Gabriel wasn't the sharpest tool in the shed. He hadn't asked for a lawyer, at least not yet. In the interview room he appeared to be petulant and antagonistic.

Ryan opened the questioning. "Why did you run away from us?"

Arms crossed, looking down at the table. "Yous are always after me. You never give me a chance."

Ryan became more direct. "When did you last see Melissa Watson?"

"That stuck up bitch. Dunno."

Frank asked quietly: "Why don't you like her?"

"She tried to dob me in, didn't she?"

"So what did you do about that?'

"She didn't get any more."

Gabriel really wasn't that bright at all.

Frank continued in a moderate tone. "No. You were angry with her. Right? So what did you do?"

"I didn't fucking kill her. Fuck no. You're not fitting me up for that."

Ryan came back into the conversation. "Gabriel, it's not looking good for you, is it?"

Then the penny finally dropped. "I want a fucking lawyer. I know my rights. Now fuck off."

Outside the interview room, Ryan leaned against the corridor wall. "He's a real charmer, but I doubt he has the wit to carry out something like this."

Frank half smiled. "I agree."

As they spoke Ryan received an urgent text message. Lorraine had gone through the Incident Logs, and had found that Police had been called out at 7.56pm on Saturday July 27th to reports of a brawl in the city centre. It had left some poor sod with a broken jaw. Gabriel Johnson was one of the suspects detained but later released without charge at 11.07pm.

Ryan grimaced. "There we are. He'll be charged with aggravated assault for biting Scotty but that's all."

*****

The next lead came three days later.

Around 6pm DS Tom Benjamin had reason to be excited. "When Scotty and I were door knocking on Newmarket Street yesterday, I found the gardeners next door to the Watsons. They had just come from a week's work at the Watsons. I saw one of the gardeners and I knew his face. It really bugged me. Later it hit me. He was a dead ringer for Simon Wheeler."

There were gasps. Not all, but some, remembered the name.

More than a decade earlier Simon Wheeler had eventually been convicted of several counts of sexual assault, preying on young women. He had operated in neighbouring Suffolk, but the attacks had gained him notoriety and had made it from the local to the national news.

"So I asked the gardening firm. They had never heard of Simon Wheeler, but when I showed the boss a photo they said they knew him by another name. They eventually gave me an address, so hopefully that's not false as well."

"Great work, Tom." Frank paused, then asked, "Where's Scotty?"

"He wasn't feeling well, so I dropped him off home."

"Okay, we'll aim to go first thing. 7am. A wake-up call for this guy."

Before he could leave the building Frank's buoyant mood crashed when his phone rang. An invitation from the Super.

"Have you seen this?" Supt Jones threw the evening edition into a nearby chair. Frank saw the headline *Police release suspect in Horsford Woods murder*. The story also mentioned that police had released someone who had confessed.

"If I catch who let this out." Frank hated the media with a vengeance. In his experience they mostly got in the way, and what they didn't know they either surmised, or made up.

The Super looked exasperated. "That's not the point, Frank. Why didn't you keep these beggars in for further questioning? Can you see how it looks? Public confidence is vital. We're going to have to organise a press conference to try to dampen things down. I've already heard from the top but this time from the Chief in person. This guy Watson is a pain in the neck but he has friends in high places. You have a good track record, but the pressure is piling up."

Frank tried to stem the tide. "Ryan and I are as one about this case. We're making progress and expect an arrest tomorrow, sir."

"God, I hope so, Frank."

*****

Another broken sleep for Frank. It was all beginning to get to him. But his spirits revived when he met Tom and Ryan at the address at 7am on the dot.

It was a big, old Edwardian mid-terrace, that had been split into as many bed-sits as the landlord could get away with without impinging on health and safety regulations for an HMO.

"Police" was announced at the front door intercom, and eventually a woman in her 70s emerged on the tenement ground floor.

"We're looking for Simon Wheeler."

"Can't you leave him alone?"

"What do you mean?"

"There was terrible shouting last night when that other policeman went up to him. He left Mr Wheeler distressed and shaking like a leaf."

Frank sounded bewildered. "What did this policeman look like?"

"He was big, with a beard and a Scottish accent. I was frightened, too. The poor man is in the top flat."

As they climbed the stairs, Frank muttered, "What the Hell is Scotty playing at?"

There was no answer at the top. Tom bent down to the keyhole. He turned pale. "Christ! I can see feet off the ground." He took a few paces back and charged the old wooden door, and it gave way easily.

Inside, the three were horrified, and it was a moment before Ryan ran forward to support the lifeless body hanging from a rope attached to a metal loft hatch surround. Frank and Tom rushed to assist but it was hopeless. His skin was cold, and his face was badly bruised.

With the body on the floor, Frank said, "Someone call an ambulance, then let HQ know we're going to need a full forensics team out here."

With Tom on the calls, Ryan looked around.

There were signs of a struggle—the floor of the modest bedsit-cum-flat was strewn with unconnected items. Everything would obviously have to be left in situ, but a pink mobile phone was sticking out from under a bedsheet, looking out of place.

Ryan used his mobile phone to take photographs, then pulled out an evidence bag from his trouser pocket and dropped the pink phone into it.

"I'll make sure this goes to the IT guys at Wymondham."

*****

With the scene secured, once the ambulance and Scene of Crime Team were in place, the three of them headed out to try and find Scotty.

Perhaps there was some innocent explanation but none of them could imagine one.

Finding him hadn't been hard, but when Scotty's initial denial didn't work, he came out with the truth.

"That filthy bastard raped and killed my niece!"

Frank was furious. "Why didn't you tell us, you idiot? You can't have anything more to do with this case. You'll have to face the inquest on your own, but the team's still going to get caught in the backsplash."

"At least the bastard did the decent thing," Scotty retorted.

At that, Frank left. He would have to report everything to the Super, who would have a field day over it. What a headache. *How could someone as experienced as Scotty lose control like that?* He shook his head, admonishing himself: *Just didn't see it coming.*

*****

When the experts analysed the pink phone there was no doubt. It was Melissa's. The last phone record was a missed call from her boyfriend, Alan Littlejohn, on the morning of her disappearance.

At least the Super had been initially appeased. "You had me worried for a while there, Frank, but you got the result in the end. We can lay this to rest now. There's a press release at 2pm. Well done."

But Frank wasn't happy. "Something doesn't ring right—it doesn't quite gel."

"What? For Christ's sake, man. He's a known sex offender who has a record of attacking girls her age, so that's motive. He had opportunity where he was working at her home, so he could easily target the child. His shoe size was nine. And he also had her mobile phone. He realised we were onto him and decided to kill himself. What more do you want?"

Supt Jones glared at him, but Frank remained adamant. "I just get a feeling that we haven't looked deeply enough."

"That's the trouble with you, Frank. Forever overthinking, and getting side tracked."

It was a cheap dig at Frank's missed lecture appearance, but he let it go by.

When he remained silent, Jones said, "That's an end of it. We don't need to agonise over niceties. The Watson family have closure and we're moving on. Pass on my congratulations to the team."

Frank thought further protest pointless. It was obvious that careers hung in the balance, and not just his own. He could hardly halt the organisational machine, but something about it all just didn't feel right. His 'copper's nose' bothered him.

Ryan, however, took the party line. "You must be pragmatic, Frank."

Frank reminded himself that Ryan seemed destined to go far. Pragmatism gets you there. That was why Frank was on his own.

*****

"Just for the record, Jenny," Frank lied by omission, "did anything come of the background check on that teacher, Martin?"

"Straight as a die."

"What about…" Frank half snapped his fingers trying to remember. "What was the name of the boyfriend again?"

"Alan Littlejohn."

"Ah, yes. Didn't he live quite close to the Watsons?" Frank tried not to make it obvious he was fishing.

"No, he's somewhere in Eaton. The Super asked for all the paperwork to be sent up, otherwise I'd get you the file."

"Well thanks, Jenny." Frank had to be careful. He was willing to lay even money on the probability that the Super was now watching him like a hawk.

Later that night Frank sat at home and mulled the whole mess over.

He'd found Alan Littlejohn's address easily enough from a basic search of the Electoral Roll. He'd done it through Google rather than using the Police databases—so as not to leave any digital footprint to show he was still chasing after the closure. If the Super caught him asking more questions of Melissa's boyfriend, when added to his recent indiscretions, it would probably lead to a disciplinary, and no doubt to a suspension or a demotion.

After his third whisky his judgment didn't improve. This thing would just not let go. He had to explore every possible angle, and Saturday morning was his best shot at going incognito.

✶✶✶✶✶

Luckily, as Frank approached the semi-detached, a lad of around the right age wearing casual clothes exited the front door. He had a heavy bag of golf clubs over his shoulder.

Frank waited until the pavement had been reached, aka public ground, then called out, "Alan?"

The lad turned to face him.

Showing his warrant card Frank introduced himself. "It's about Melissa. Don't worry, you're not in any trouble."

"I thought you got the bastard."

"Yes. I'm just looking to wrap up a few loose ends."

Alan dug out his phone and checked the time, then put it back in his pocket. "I'm due to tee off soon."

"Can I walk with you and then I'll leave you alone?"

"Okay." And they set off.

It was a good ten-minute walk to Eaton Golf Club, so again Frank was in luck. "It must have been a shock. You were close to Melissa." No reply, but Frank could see that the young man was affected. He pushed on with the questioning. "We know Melissa was a clever girl who went downhill towards the end."

Alan stopped, obviously angry. "That creep, Gabriel Johnson, got her onto drugs. She was so unhappy."

"How did you first meet her?'

"One Saturday night in the city centre, I heard her screaming. A guy was close to her but she just kept screaming and shouting at him not to touch her. She was pulling a bit of a crowd, and I guess someone called it in, as not long after that the Police came. As soon as they turned up the crowd started to scatter. The guy didn't run away though. She calmed down eventually, and I thought nothing more about it."

He started walking again. "Then I bumped into her on Newmarket Street about a week later. She was just sitting on a wall, looking sad. I didn't want to get close but we talked and got on. Mel told me she wanted to run away."

"Had enough of school?"

"No, home. She was terrified of her father."

The words spoke volumes to Frank. "Do you know why?"

"She didn't say." They could see the golf course ahead.

"You've been very helpful, Alan. One last thing. I think you saw Mel on the day she disappeared?"

"Yeah. We'd arranged to meet but she turned up late. She'd lost her mobile. Couldn't find it."

"The pink one?"

"Yeah. We only talked for a few minutes. She had to be home for lunch. Her family's very strict. She just said something or other about having a plan."

He dug the phone out again, and Frank wondered why he didn't just get a watch.

"Sorry, got to rush."

Frank nodded. "Hope you get an eagle on the first hole."

Alan grinned. "Not likely. It's a par 5!"

*****

At last, a revelation! Melissa had supposedly lost her mobile phone, but had been seen alive afterwards, so Simon Wheeler could *not* have been the killer.

What evidence was there against anyone else?

Not even a whisper.

Frank's personal theory—that the respectable David Watson had sexually abused and then murdered his own daughter—was nothing more than a hunch. How do you prove sexual abuse when the victim is long dead? It was going nowhere, and Frank felt as if he were on his own again.

The police had missed their man. No, they had happily missed their man and had closed the case down. All very neat and tidy.

But if Frank had it all wrong, then he could kiss goodbye to Norfolk Constabulary. Full stop.

*****

Frank had reached a crossroads. It felt as if he had been brought to this point, not just by his career in the Police, but by his whole life.

Would he do the *right* thing and tell the Super about what Alan Littlejohn had said? Obviously, there would be consequences. Detention, if not dismissal, loomed large.

But far worse was the absolute certainty that Frank could have no further part in the investigation.

It would doubtless turn from cold to icy case overnight. Frank knew that he alone could pursue this, whatever the outcome and whatever the cost.

*****

Weeks went by. Then months. And then years.

It was early in 2022—the COVID pandemic was beginning to grip the nation, Ryan had progressed to Chief Inspector in Traffic—*Tedious Traffic*, thought Frank, *but then that's how you get on, isn't it?*—and everyone had long since forgotten and moved on, except Frank. How could he find the evidence?

Time passing has two opposing effects, Frank reasoned. *Detection was more difficult, but the criminal mind became over-confident and careless.*

Frank had discovered that in 2015 David Watson had bought a parcel of about three hectares of land around twenty miles northeast of Norwich. Apart from an ancient farm shed there was nothing there. The ground was reasonably flat, as befitted Norfolk, and it was initially assumed that Watson had bought the land as an investment.

He had tracked Watson there. Watson and his Dobermann. From a safe distance Frank had observed a complex padlock arrangement, supported by security cameras. The overdone security was promisingly suspicious. Later surveillance led to the discovery of a security weak point in the form of several blind spots in their coverage.

Leaving his car parked to enable a quick escape, Frank had approached from the rear, using a blind spot, and through the only window he had seen a small table with drawers, some garden tools and a roll of tarpaulin.

One of the drawers stood out—it was also padlocked. Frank had then withdrawn, hoping that he had not been spotted.

*****

From the safety of his home, Frank pondered. Was the shed potentially a second crime scene?

He went over everything, again and again. Above all, what secret did the padlock on that small drawer protect?

He also considered, yet again, the two obvious options open to him.

He could take the easy road. Switch off and drift into peaceful retirement. That would certainly please his superiors.

Or he could have the courage of his convictions and risk everything on his gut feelings. Not merely his career—dismissal would be inevitable, and the least of his worries—but a possible jail term for burglary, coupled with what the lawyers would call victim harassment.

And if he was right, but interrupted, it would become a question of survival, especially if Watson had killed before.

Decision made, Frank planned meticulously.

He bought power assisted bolt cutters, so as to snap the locks quickly as no doubt a remote alarm would be activated as soon as the first cut was made. Watson's home was at least 25 minutes away, even ignoring speed limits. But if the alarm went directly to Watson's smartphone then he could be anywhere.

Daylight would be better as torches not only attracted attention from a distance, but he'd known some fail pretty spectacularly. So the less Frank had to carry with him the better. He'd also need a personal police radio with video and an emergency alarm, just in case anything untoward happened to him. Add to that a taser, if not for Watson, then as security against being attacked by his Dobermann. He could sign that out for 24 hours—maybe 48 if he told the armourer he was doing a talk and needed a live one for a demonstration. He'd probably be charged with breaching regulations, but only if he discharged it without taking down his attacker.

He photocopied the notes he'd originally taken after talking to Alan Littlejohn, for safety's sake, before sealing the original notes in an envelope addressed to the Super. He planned to leave the envelope on his front passenger seat before he set off on foot.

*****

Everything had been ready and in place by the following Wednesday. That morning he'd signed out the taser and the vest with the recording equipment. Putting both in the boot of his car, he'd been thankful that the weather was holding. Clear, with no chance of rain.

He'd parked up a short distance from the shed, put the protective vest on, and strapped the taser around his waist. He picked up the sports bag with the bolt cutters—though God knew why he was trying to be discrete—and several minutes later he was outside the shed door, looking at the length of chain held in place by a large Chubb padlock.

There had been a moment's hesitation as he'd rounded the side of the shed and had seen the motion detector switch from a small green, to a small angry red light.

The alarm had gone off somewhere and the race against time had begun. Then there was a problem. It was proving difficult to get a grip on the chain link with the bolt cutter jaws. He kept trying from slightly altered angles, but the cutters whined, and then slipped. *These are supposed to be heavy duty, for fuck's sake!*

Another whine, and finally the chain gave way and he was inside.

Switching from video to still, he immediately took half a dozen high resolution images *in situ*, then back to video again.

It was obvious that the tarpaulin had been cut at one end. In the corner lay a length of loosely coiled rope. More photos were taken before Frank concentrated on the padlocked drawer. The bolt cutters whined and sliced the lock off cleanly.

Unconsciously holding his breath, Frank pulled the drawer open.

And there it was. A little A5 hard bound diary, and by the fourth or fifth page it was clear that it was Melissa's. Frank flipped through to the last entries, which spoke volumes. Melissa had decided that she was going to call Childline. She was going to let the world know about her father's abuse.

Frank had only a moment of elation before it was back to business with his final photos. At least he'd been proven right.

He was about to put the diary in an evidence bag when he heard another car coming to a sharp stop, rapidly followed by the sound of car doors opening, and the barking of a dog. Reflexively he pressed his radio alarm as he stuffed the bagged diary into one of the pockets in his vest. Photographic evidence was one thing, but being able to present the original was something else.

As he reached down for the bolt cutters, a figure stood in the doorway. Then the Dobermann.

The dog didn't need an instruction. It ran at Frank as he reached frantically for the taser. It launched into the air with bared teeth, leaving Frank with no choice but to fire at the last moment. The hound yelped and ran away, but the force of the attack had pushed Frank away from the table.

From the doorway, David Watson shouted, "You! I know the Chief Constable and you're finished!"

"I know you killed her because she was going to tell about the abuse!"

"Rubbish. You can't prove anything."

Watson glanced at the open drawer, stepped forward and picked up the bolt cutters. The motor whined as Watson grasped the handle and squeezed on the trigger.

Frank saw his chance and dodged forward, grappling with Watson for control of the weapon, before being swung round and losing his grip on the makeshift weapon.

Timing was everything. As Watson's right arm came down, Frank's left blocked the blow, allowing Frank to punch Watson in the stomach. With Watson doubled over, Frank took his chance and made for the door. He was running for his life.

Out of the shed, he saw the Dobermann off to one side, backing away from him, and in seconds he'd managed to reach his car. Getting in, his right hand automatically went for the ignition button. He remembered the engine catching and starting, then an almighty crash and sudden blackness.

*****

Frank felt confused, disorientated, and a touch lightheaded. Looking around, he slowly realised that he was in a hospital bed. He looked along the cables attached to various parts of his body, until he found the machine they were attached to. It made regular 'beeps', which he found comforting. He closed his eyes and went back to sleep.

*****

He tried to lick his lips, but his mouth was dry. He reached over to the side cabinet and fumbled with the half full water bottle. From off to his left, a nurse said: "Let me do that."

Tongue now back in action, Frank asked, "How long have I been in here?"

She smiled at him. "Just over two weeks. You had some serious injuries to the side of your head. You were quite a while in surgery, and then they put you into an induced coma for several weeks."

"I…It's all a fuzzy blank."

"I'll get Dr Singh to have a word with you." She left him, and Frank tried not to fall asleep again.

When the nurse returned with Dr Singh, Frank learned what had happened. Watson had pulled open Frank's car door and had used the electric bolt cutters to beat him around the head several times before the patrol cars had finally arrived on the scene.

"You were in surgery for a good 17 hours. We did what we could to sort out your skull damage, but the soft tissue is going to be a bit of a mess until you're ready to undergo reconstructive procedures."

"And there's no brain damage?" Frank closed his eyes, fearing the worst.

"Not that we can find. We've been taking regular progress scans since we put you under—checking for any subsidiary bleeding—but nothing untoward. You were lucky, there wasn't much room to take a real swing at you."

"I'll remember that the next time."

Singh just *Hmm*'d, checked the display above Frank's head, then said: "And the answer to your next question is, around two to three weeks, provided you continue to make a good recovery."

Later that evening Supt Jones paid Frank a visit.

After he'd settled in a chair next to the bed, there was an embarrassed silence. Then Jones said quietly, "Watson's in custody, charged with murdering his daughter and attempting to murder you. His solicitor's not even contesting—the judge agreed Watson was a flight risk, so no chance of any bail."

Frank stayed silent, unsure how he felt emotionally.

Jones carried on, "The evidence recovered at the scene is overwhelming. The graphic diary, the matching tarpaulin and rope. And a formal statement from the boyfriend, of course…"

"But—" Frank was cut off.

"Your alarm was picked up by a nearby traffic patrol. Watson ran when they pulled up but he didn't get away."

"I'll thank them when I get out of here." Frank didn't know what else to say.

Jones took a deep breath. "DC McAllister is in the process of receiving an official reprimand for his attack on Wheeler. I'm going to ask for his transfer once that is over. You could argue that he pushed Wheeler into taking his own life, but that's something for the IOPC to deal with."

Jones pursed his lips slightly. It must have been hard for him to say the words: "Frank, I'm sorry I doubted you. I'll work with you, and not against you, in future. You are a true hero. When you come back, as I hope you will, the Chief Constable wants to present you with the Queen's Police Medal."

All Frank could say was, "Thank you very much, sir. But if you don't mind, I'd like to get some more sleep." He let his head settle deeper into his pillow, and he closed his eyes.

The praise was certainly appreciated. But what really counted, for Frank, had nothing to do with the others.

He had done his job and, in the end, had uncovered the truth.

There was no greater satisfaction.

The Usual Unusual Suspects

Richard Zaric has lived in various cities in North America before settling back in his hometown of Winnipeg, Manitoba, Canada. *Hiding Scars*, his first book, is a historical fiction novel. He is presently pitching a young adult novel called *Stealing Amazing Fantasy #15*. His short stories have appeared in several anthologies. He is just as likely to read the latest hot literary novel as he is to flip through an old comic book. His website is zarko543.wixsite.com/richardzaric. He can be reached through Facebook (**richard.zaric**) or Instagram (**@richardzaric**).

Daniel Marshall Wood leads a double life as proprietor of Edgefield B&B in Sharon Springs, NY and in NYC as editor of corporate investigation reports — as well as an identical twin. He is a member of Mystery Writers of America, with a number of mystery short stories published online and in print magazines.

S. B. Watson lives in Keizer, Oregon. When he's not spending time with his family, practicing historic English quarterstaff techniques, or playing Bluegrass guitar, he can be found in his library, constructing mystery novels and writing peculiar pieces of short fiction. Learn more at www.SBWatson.com.

Ron Bruguiere writes while viewing the isle of Manhattan and has told stories from his life in *COLLISION when reality and illusion collide.*

Aimee Kluck writes about bold female crime busters: homicide inspectors, gangster's girlfriends, nosy neighbors, and wise elders who avenge crimes against other women. Her work appears in *Murder Most International*, *Shotgun Honey*, *Punk Noir*, and *Inkd Publishing Noncorporeal*. She has completed a murder mystery novel, *The Last Cut*, which takes place in San Francisco during the cocaine crazed 1980's. She is a member of MWA, SinC, WFWA & SFMS. Formerly from New England and S.F., she lives in southern California. Catch her dancing in the streets or on her website, Facebook and Instagram.

Alexander Frew—known locally as "Alec" (that's how they do it in Kilmarnock)—has been writing for as long as he can remember. He has produced an eclectic mix of books, short stories, and poems and makes a point of writing every day. Now retired, Alec has worked in around twenty different jobs, with the word "career" never really coming into play. Over the years, he's been a factory worker, engineer, call centre agent, care worker, and more, gathering enough life experience to enrich his writing—and even get some of it published. He's also a big fan of Crimeucopia, by the way.

Roly Andrews lives in Nelson, NZ. In his spare time, he enjoys tramping and cracking jokes. After many years of practicing, Roly is still learning to play the trombone, dreaming of playing in a ska band one day. A champion for everyone, he has previously mentored rough sleepers in London and supported people affected by suicide. He is a strong advocate for the rights of people living with disabilities.

Marian McMahon Stanley enjoyed a long international corporate career and, more recently, a senior position at a large urban university. She is the author of a number of short stories and essays and has two published mystery novels. *The Immaculate*, a story about the murder of an elderly nun, and *Buried Troubles*, a murder set in the context of Irish-American support for the IRA during the Troubles. She is a dual citizen of the US and Ireland. Marian lives and writes in a small New England town with the help of a faithful Westie named Archie. For more information and news, go to marianmcmahonstanley.com

Gerald Elias leads a double life. He is the author of the critically acclaimed Daniel Jacobus mystery series that takes place in the dark corners of the classical music world, other novels, and many short stories and essays.

Elias is also an internationally recognized musician who has been a violinist with the Boston Symphony and music director of the Vivaldi by Candlelight concert series in Salt Lake City since 2004. He divides his time between the shores of Puget Sound in Washington and the Berkshire Hills of western Massachusetts, where he continues to expand his literary and musical horizons. Visit him at: https://www.mysteriesandmusic.com/

Gregory Meece's education career covered every grade from kindergarten through college, including 20 years as head of school. He earned degrees in English, communications, and education from the University of Delaware. His short fiction appears in various anthologies—*Malice Domestic's Mystery Most Traditional* and *Mystery Most Humorous, Larceny & Last Chances*, and *Love Letters to Poe*—as well as magazines like *Ellery Queen Mystery Magazine, Thriller Magazine, Black Cat Weekly, Bristol Noir, Yellow Mama,* and *Flash Fiction Magazine.* He lives in Pennsylvania, where he moonlights as an Amish taxi driver and woodcarver. Visit him at *MeeceTales.com.*

Neil K. Henderson stubbornly resists categorisation by curling into a ball and begging to be left alone. If further pressed, he has been known to beg for spare change, £5 notes or a free lunch. Sometimes he will even do the pressing himself, in order to save time. Left to his own devices, Neil enjoys scampering through the hinterland of contemporary social unreality, dispersing thoughts through the holes in his butterfly net. Thus he has a fun time going nowhere, which he prefers, rather than arriving at serious conclusions. Sometimes he tries to pretend he's an adult—but, so far, he hasn't fooled anybody.

He is the author of an anthology published by Atlantean, starring his consultant defective, um detective, Sherry Hormones: Hormones A-Go-Go and authored an edition of Xmas Bards, *Smells Like Plastic Santas.*

He has also been submitting his own brand of idiosyncratically humorous and bizarre works of imaginative self-expression for publication since 1987. Many of his stories, poems and oddities have appeared in magazines of all descriptions in the UK, USA, Canada and Australia.

Alan Warren is a software engineer by day and aspiring author by night. He lives in the UK's rain capital of Swansea, South Wales, but has previously lived in the drier climes of Australia and New Zealand. He has had fiction published in NZ print magazines and in online publications, and in the distant past sold a screenplay that, sadly, was never produced. His current interests lie in short fiction, particularly in crime noir, and he's working on a collection of noirish short stories set in Wales, each with a female protagonist.

Michele Bazan Reed's stories have appeared in *Woman's World* magazine and several anthologies, most recently *Mayhem on the Cheddar Express* in the Sisters in Crime NY/TriState Chapter anthology, *New York State of Crime: Murder New York Style 6*. A member of SinC's Guppies, Private Eye Writers of America, and Short Mystery Fiction Society, she lives on the shore of Lake Ontario in New York State. Like her fictional Officer Sampson, she's always had a healthy fear of the principal's office.

Bonnar Spring is a Derringer award-winning author whose work has appeared in many anthologies. She made the switch to short fiction from international thrillers to satisfy her urge to write morally ambiguous characters. Bonnar also hosts Crime Wave (https://bonnarspring.com/index.php/category/crimewave/), the top-rated podcast on the Authors on the Air Radio Network. She lives in a tiny house perched at the edge of a New Hampshire salt marsh and, when not concocting nefarious plots, she loves to cook meals with difficult-to-pronounce names.

Carol Goodman Kaufman, in a prior life, was a psychologist and criminologist who reached her limit on writing about abuse and violent extremism. She now writes about happier subjects, from food history to children's picture books, but when she decided to take the plunge into fiction, she chose to write mysteries, quite often of the murder variety. Ironic, huh? But not totally out of character. Since her first encounters with *The Happy Hollisters* and *Nancy Drew*, her guilty pleasure has been curling up with a good whodunit. Her first novel, *The First Murder*, came out in 2024, and her collection of cozy shorts, *Crak, Bam, Dead*, in 2025.

Kathleen Marple Kalb describes herself as an Author/Anchor/Mom… but not necessarily in that order. An award-winning weekend anchor at New York's 1010 WINS Radio, she writes short stories and novels including the Old Stuff, and (as Nikki Knight) Vermont Radio Mysteries. Her stories have been in Crimeucopias, *Alfred Hitchcock's Mystery Magazine*, other major publications, and short-listed for Derringer and Black Orchid Novella Awards. She, her husband, and son live in a Connecticut house owned by their cat.

John M. Floyd is the author of more than a thousand short stories in publications like *AHMM, EQMM, Strand Magazine, The Saturday Evening Post, Best American Mystery Stories*, and *Best Mystery Stories of the Year*. A former Air Force captain and IBM systems engineer, John is also an Edgar nominee, a Shamus Award winner, a six-time Derringer Award winner, and a past recipient of the Edward D. Hoch Memorial Golden Derringer for lifetime achievement.

Dave Dempster is a retired lawyer and aspiring writer, who was an enthusiastic chessplayer in a previous life. His *Thank God for the Nineteenth Hole* appears in *Crimeucopia — A Load Of Balls*. His work can also be seen online in *Jonah, CafeLit* and *East of the Web*.

Don't You Never Look Inside the Mojo Bag…

…'Cos it got the juju! An' that is hot stuff…

However, it's true to say that all the wordsmiths contained within the covers of this Crimeucopia, have been looking inside all sorts of Mojo bags, and are more than willing to recount what it is they've seen.

So sit back, relax, and let:

Anthony Kane Evans, Carlos Ramet, Tristan J. Deehan, Christopher Deliso, Tucker Struyk, Ed Teja, Gene Kendall, Hal Dygert, Ian Blackwell, L.C. Adams, Patrick Ambrose, Kamal Mouhoune, Rand Gaynor, Rob Loughran,
and *Edward St. Boniface*

take you on guided tours around their worlds—going from Cosy Country to Noir Central, and back again, provided you booked a return ticket that is.

Because we hope that, whenever and wherever these authors take you, you'll find something that you immediately like, as well as something that takes you out of your GPS and Timezone monitored comfort zones—and puts you into a completely new one.

Because, in the Random Shuffle sprit of our Murderous Ink Press motto:

You never know what you like until you read it.

Paperback ISBN: 9781909498648 — eBook ISBN: 9781909498655

It would be hard to pinpoint exactly when Crimeucopia moved from being a 'scratch project title' and became a masthead—but it seemed to match our idea of presenting as wide a spectrum of Crime fiction genres as we could.

From there it was probably *Fate* which brought together the Aly Fell base artwork, and the 16 contributors who went on to become the initial Countesses of Crime, and appeared in Crimeucopia—The Lady Thrillers.

4 years down the proverbial publishing line, we felt it was time to celebrate the anniversary with another all-women anthology—and let these 19 Countesses of Crime tell it like it is, was, or could have been....

Because, in the eclectic, off-centred spirit of our Murderous Ink Press motto: You never know what you like until you read it.

Paperback Edition ISBN: 9781909498662 — eBook Edition ISBN: 9781909498679

I Remember the Dame Well...

Mainly as she had a laugh that reminded me of two cheese graters energetically fornicating in an iron bathtub. I looked out the open window at the Johnson Memorial, standing upright and resolute in the persistent rain. The clock on it said it was 3:15 in the a.m. and I figured, what-the-Hell, it was time to review the 14 case files scattered across my desk.

I glanced back out across the skyline and wondered: *Why is it* always *raining in Noir City?* I got up and moved over to the chess board. I hadn't see the cat in several hours, so I rearranged the pieces a little to give myself a bit of an advantage...

As with all of these anthologies, we hope you'll detect something that you immediately like, as well as something that takes you out of your investigative comfort zone — and puts you into a completely new one.

Because, in the spirit of our Murderous Ink Press motto:

You never know what you like until you discover it.

Paperback ISBN: 9781909498624 eBook ISBN: 9781909498631

Investigators and investigations are the mainstay of most Crime fiction sub-genres. Everything from the original *Golden Age* of country houses and the amateur sleuth, through to the high tech ultra-modern 21st Century – a place where the cyber investigators sometimes appear to be baffled by old-fashioned motivations of power and greed, and human foibles such as love and revenge.

So is there any real difference between the Private and the Public Sector investigators? Not much, if writers are to be believed, and the two can often be found straddling both sides of the 'what's legal procedure?' fence.

Of the twelve authors contained within, eleven are voices new to the world of Crimeucopia - and although the theme is *Investigators*, the material ranges from Cosy, through to not too Hardboiled - and most are touched with a vein of humour, be it light or dark. Rather like a box of chocolates...

Paperback ISBN: 9781909498327   eBook ISBN: 9781909498334

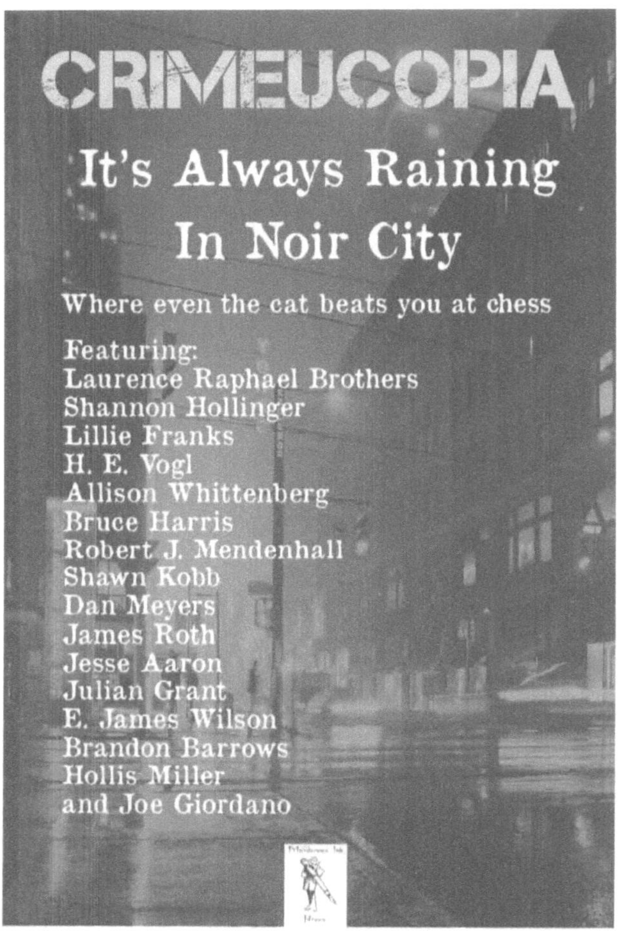

Is the Noir Crime sub-genre always dark and downbeat? Is there a time when Bad has a change of conscience, flips sides and takes on the Good role?

Noir is almost always a dish served up raw and bloody - Fiction bleu if you will. So maybe this is a chance to see if Noir can be served sunny side up - with the aid of these fifteen short order authors.

All fifteen give us dark tales from the stormy side of life - which is probably why it's *always* raining in Noir City....

Paperback Edition ISBN: 9781909498341
eBook Edition ISBN: 9781909498358

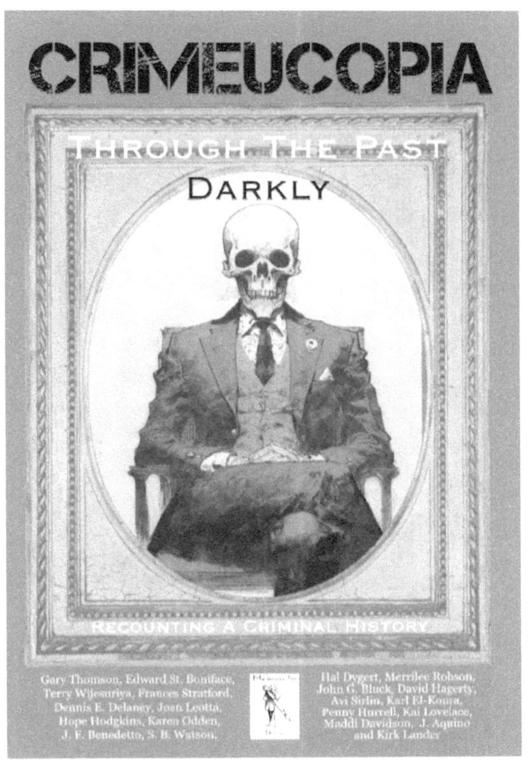

It Was In The Year Of....

Historical/Period Crime short fiction ranging from Cosy. Noir, PIs, Narrative Crime, and a whole spectrum of Crime sub-genres in between

21 authors — Gary Thomson, Edward St. Boniface, Terry Wijesuriya, Frances Stratford, Dennis E. Delaney, Joan Leotta, Hope Hodgkins, Karen Odden, J. F. Benedetto, S. B. Watson, Hal Dygert, Merrilee Robson, John G. Bluck, David Hagerty, Avi Sirlin, Karl El-Koura, Penny Hurrell, Kai Lovelace, Maddi Davidson, J. Aquino and Kirk Landers — take you from 420 BC through to AD 1969, and give you a criminal history, laid out in a case by case Crimeline.

Paperback 9781909498587 eBook 9781909498594

This is the first of several 'Free 4 All' collections that was supposed to be themeless. However, with the number of submissions that came in, it seems that this could be called an *Angels & Devils* collection, mixing PI & Police alongside tales from the Devil's dining table. Mind you, that's not to say that all the PIs & Police are on the side of the Angels....

Also this time around has not only seen a move to a larger paperback format size, but also in regard to the length of the fiction as well. Followers of the somewhat bent and twisted Crimeucopia path will know that although we don't deal with Flash fiction as a rule, it is a rule that we have sometimes broken. And let's face it, if you cannot break your own rules now and again, whose rules can you break?

Oh, wait, isn't breaking the rules the foundation of the crime fiction genre?

Oh dear....

Paperback ISBN: 9781909498426 eBook ISBN: 9781909498433

CRIMEUCOPIA

Let Me Tell You About...

If Looks Could Kill, She Would Have Been An Uzi...

...Or more likely a shotgun. I mean, Lawd knows what those two ever saw in each other in the first place, and that's a fact. Don't believe me? Well, let me tell you about the time when.... But that's how it usually starts, doesn't it? Someone says something, which reminds someone else about.... And so the anecdotal avalanche begins.

This time there's 19 storytellers: **Vinnie Hansen, V.S. Kemanis, David Krugler, Robert Jeschonek, Beverle Graves Myers, Kirk Landers, James Lee Proctor, Victor Kreuiter, K. Arlington Andrews, Michael Bracken, Kevin R. Tipple, William Flores, Robert Sumner, Jim Guigli, James Roth, Michael Zimecki, Sebastian Corbascio, Martin Zeigler, and John Bertram Fawet III**

All gathered around the front counter of the Crimeucopia *Shots to Hell* Bar & Grill — and more than willing to tell you about how it is, or was, or even will be....

So, over the background sounds from an old jukebox loaded with worn out 45s (vinyl rather than the likes of a Px4 Storm), settle back and take in their individual stories – and we guarantee there's going to be Crimesapleanty indeed...

Paperback Edition ISBN: 9781909498600 — eBook Edition ISBN: 9781909498617
Amazon Paperback Edition ISBN: 9798337923338

With 16 vibrant authors, a wraparound paperback cover, and pages full of crime fiction in some of its many guises, what's not to like?
So if you enjoy tales spun by
Anthony Diesso, Brandon Barrows, E. James Wilson, James Roth,
Jesse Aaron, Jim Guigli, John M. Floyd, Kevin R. Tipple, Maddi Davidson,
Michael Grimala, Robert Petyo, Shannon Hollinger, Tom Sheehan,
Wil A. Emerson, Peter Trelay, and Philip Pak
then you'd better get
CRIMEUCOPIA - Strictly Off The record
by the sound of it!
Paperback ISBN: 9781909498464 eBook ISBN: 9781909498471